Bonds of Cupidity

Raven Kennedy is a California girl born and raised, whose love for books pushed her into creating her own worlds. The Plated Prisoner Series, a dark fantasy romance, has already sold in over a dozen countries and is a #1 international bestseller with over 1 million copies sold to date. It was inspired by the myth of King Midas and a woman's journey with finding her own strength. Her debut series was a romcom fantasy about a cupid looking for love of her own. She has since gone on to write in a range of genres. Whether she makes you laugh or cry, or whether the series is about a cupid or a gold-touched woman living in King Midas's gilded castle, she hopes to create characters that readers can root for. The Plated Prisoner series is being adapted for series by Peter Guber's Mandalay Television.

BONDS OF CUPIDITY

HEART HASSLE BOOK TWO

RAVEN KENNEDY

PENGUIN BOOKS

PENGUIN BOOKS

UK | USA | Canada | Ireland | Australia
India | New Zealand | South Africa

Penguin Books is part of the Penguin Random House group of companies
whose addresses can be found at global.penguinrandomhouse.com

First published in the United States of America by Raven Kennedy 2018
First published in Great Britain by Penguin Books 2023
001

Copyright © Raven Kennedy, 2018

The moral right of the author has been asserted

Printed and bound in Great Britain by Clays Ltd, Elcograf S.p.A.

The authorized representative in the EEA is Penguin Random House Ireland,
Morrison Chambers, 32 Nassau Street, Dublin D02 YH68

A CIP catalogue record for this book is available from the British Library

ISBN: 978–1–405–96078–6

www.greenpenguin.co.uk

MIX
Paper | Supporting
responsible forestry
FSC® C018179

Penguin Random House is committed to a
sustainable future for our business, our readers
and our planet. This book is made from Forest
Stewardship Council® certified paper.

To all the people whose cupids keep getting it wrong... And for those whose actually got it right.

CHAPTER 1

*E*veryone is staring at me.

But not in like an *oh, they're checking me out because I look hot as hell* kind of way. Not even in a curious *I wonder if she's fun to hang out with* kind of way.

For the record, I *am* fun to hang out with. Ask anyone.

Or, I mean, actually, just ask the only three people that I know—the three very hot genfins currently being held prisoner.

Okay, fine. Ask two out of three of them. Ronak probably wouldn't classify me as fun. Mostly because he wouldn't know fun if it put on lipstick and kissed him on the ass.

But Evert and Sylred for sure think I'm fun. Usually. Most of the time. Like, at least half the time.

Anyway, back to the dozens of fae currently staring at me. I try to ignore them as I walk down the town square with my head up high. My pink hair trails down to my waist, but it was definitely a mistake to tuck it behind my ears. My very non-pointed, non-fae ears.

Not only do I not have pastel-colored skin like the high fae, but I'm also too short. The fae don't really know what to make of me. I don't really look like any one type of fae.

One of them, hell if I know what kind, steps forward to block my way. He (or she?) towers over me like a tree, even taller than the high fae. He has shiny skin that looks like copper, fur all over his arms and legs, and teeth like iron spikes. Super attractive.

"What *are* you?"

Psh. Like he's one to talk.

"Emelle, nice to meet you," I say, holding out a hand.

I sort of have to hold my hand up like I'm ready to give him a high five, because that's how tall he is. He doesn't make hand contact, though. I have to drop it back down like a loser.

Awkward.

"An Emelle?" he asks, his coppery skin pulling in a crinkly frown. "I have never heard of this Emelle fae. Are you a mutt?"

"Hey, who are you calling a mutt? You're the one with fur, buddy."

I hear someone gasp. Looking over, I realize that I have spectators gathered around us. Apparently, the entire crowd has stopped to watch our exchange. They're all interested to see what my answer will be.

Which honestly is a little offensive. I don't look nearly as weird as some of them. That guy over there has a nose that looks like a sponge. Those nostrils are just way too porous to be hygienic.

Copper fur man looks angry at being called a dog. He straightens up to full height and crosses his arms in front of him. And he has four of them.

My irritation immediately deflates as I take in his limbs. "Gosh, four arms!" I exclaim. "That must make things super helpful. I'd love to have four arms. Sometimes, I'll be carrying something, and then this itch will crop up," I say, pointing to a spot on my right arm.

That spot is where my original itch lasted for over fifty

years, and I had no way to scratch it while I was incorporeal. Can you imagine having an itch for fifty years? Yeah, it was torture.

"Anyway, I'll be carrying something, right? So both my hands are full, and I don't have any way to scratch this spot. It makes things really inconvenient. But four arms—that's just plain handy. Pun intended. I'll bet you carry stuff and scratch things simultaneously all the time, am I right? That must really be something. Seriously, congratulations."

He stares at me and blinks.

I get that reaction a lot. I kind of have this condition where my mouth just spews word vomit. It's chronic.

I sidestep around him. "Okay then, you and your arms have a good day."

Before I can take two steps, another fae steps in front of me, and this one looks like he's half octopus because he has *eight* arms. Seriously, they're just rubbing it in now.

"What kind of fae are you?" he asks.

I've been trying to avoid this question, but I know it's inevitable. They know I look different from any other fae they've seen, and that's because I'm not really a fae. I don't belong in this realm at all. I'm a cupid. All that attention I wanted? Yeah, I'm getting it right about now.

My wings are currently hidden from view, and thank the gods, because if I were to let them out, the jig would really be up. My wings are completely unlike the wings of any other fae. They're bright red and feathered and downright lovely if I do say so myself.

But I can't wear them here. Not when Prince Elphar is looking for me and there's a bounty on my head. Someone would recognize me with my wings for sure. If I keep drawing unwanted attention, I'll surely have the palace guards come down on me even without my wings. I need to give the crowd some sort of an answer, so I lie.

I clear my throat nervously, looking around at the staring

crowd. "Umm, I'm half high fae," I say, indicating my pastel pink hair that could certainly pass for one of their traits.

"Half high fae?" he asks dubiously. "I've never known a high fae to have mutts. They're too good for us other fae," he says with disdain, looking around at the crowd as they nod and make noises in agreement. "What's the other half?"

I cough a little and answer at the same time, "Human," as I try to dart around him. Of course, the crowd doesn't let me pass, so I get trapped by a wall of nosy fae.

"What did she say?"

"Did she say half goblin?"

"I think she said Huaca."

"Can't be Huaca. Her skin's not made of stone."

The crowd keeps tossing around commentary until I finally clap my hands to get their attention.

"I'm half human, okay?" I shout.

The dozens of fae shut up immediately to balk at me. Yeah, humans aren't very common here. Or popular, apparently, based on their sneers.

I take advantage of their shock and bend down to sneak between the arms of two fae, managing to break through the circle. I definitely don't want to know what their reaction would be if they found out what I really am. That would be a disaster.

I don't need any more attention, but my handmade fur outfit isn't helping me blend in at all. Most of the people who live here on the kingdom island are really wealthy, and they wear expensive fabrics and always dress to the nines. Beast fur that smells like a wet dog is not exactly on trend.

I loose my hair to cover my non-pointed ears and try not to make eye contact with anyone. When I look down, I remember my feet are bare, too. Yeah, I probably should have planned this better.

I hoist up the quiver that's strapped to my back, hearing the comforting sound of arrows shaking around. It's not my cupid set, but it's still nice to have some kind of weapon at my disposal. I lost my set when the fae prince blasted me with magic at the palace. Who knows what the jerk did with it. I'd love to shoot him with some non-Love Arrows this time around.

And yeah, I'm a badass with a bow and arrow. I am a cupid, after all. It's kind of my thing.

When the guys were taken from the banishment island and escorted here, I followed them, flying at a safe distance away. I can't be too far away from them, or I'll start getting sick and go invisible again.

They're my anchors to the physical world—although they don't know that. They have enough on their plates already with facing the trials of the royal culling. I can't let them face that with the extra burden that my life depends on theirs, too.

I'll just have to find another way to anchor myself before something bad happens. Somehow.

I watched my guys get taken over the stone wall surrounding the castle and then escorted toward the prisoner's towers. I can see the towers from here. They're not far away.

I just need to find a way to get past the wall or at least keep watch so I know where they'll be taken next. But I can't stealthily find my guys if fae are constantly stopping me.

I don't make it very far through the crowd before the shouts and hollers follow me, and I'm surrounded by meddlesome fae again.

I let out a frustrated sigh and look around. They're all talking about me, staring at me with way too many eyes and voices. I don't like feeling cornered. I also don't like being stared at like I'm about to have tomatoes thrown at me.

Note to self: I've been invisible way too long to deal with this crap. And, being a somewhat unprofessional cupid, there's only one way I know how to work a crowd. A smile curves my lips.

"You wanna make a scene? Then let's make a scene."

I take a deep breath, filling my lungs as full as they'll go, and then I blow out a huge trail of pink Lust-Breath into the crowd's faces.

It takes me a few breaths to get them all, but when I'm done, their eyes are glazed over with burning desire, and they're looking around in search of a favorable partner.

A couple of them take an interest in me, but I redirect their amorous attentions to someone else. The shift in the crowd is almost laughable. Now that the crowd isn't focused solely on me, I walk around, trailing my finger along some of the people that seem to need an extra push, and hit them with some Flirt-Touches to really seal the deal.

That seems to do it. By the time I circle back around, everyone has forgotten about me. Ladies are giggling, men are putting on the moves, tongues are tangling, hands are petting, and several groups have wasted no time and seem to be getting down to business right in the middle of the street.

Huh.

Orgies are *way* easier to start in the fae realm than they were with humans.

I nearly trip over a couple on the ground, where a female is straddling a guy. She rips his shirt down the middle and starts attacking him with her boobs. I smile to myself and dust off my hands. Now this is what I call crowd control.

I weave through couplings until I get past the chaos. Hopefully, they'll be distracted for a while and won't remember me once the lust-haze lifts. I reach the market stalls, where people are too busy buying and selling to pay me much attention.

I keep going until the lust scene I ignited is far behind me. I may have redirected the crowd's attention for now, but it won't last forever, and I can't just keep using my cupid powers to create street orgies. The fae may be sexually open, but even they'd catch on that something was off. I need to blend in better.

I search the stalls until I find the perfect combination. A man selling clothes. I slip inside the tent and take a look around. There's fancy fabric and shoes everywhere, as well as several full-length mirrors.

"Good day."

I whirl around to look at the fae man who greeted me. He's wearing a silk tunic and hat and has bright blue wings. Pixie.

He's thin and only slightly taller than me, with pointy ears, chin, and nose, but he's not one of the scary-looking fae, and for that, I'm grateful. If my plan is going to work, I need to be able to seduce him. Let's hope he's attracted to me. Time to turn on the charm.

"Hi there," I smile coyly at him. "Ooh, I love this color shirt on you," I say, carefully trailing my finger down his chest, letting my Flirt-Touch sink into his skin.

It comes out in a silvery wisp. He doesn't notice a thing; he's too busy staring at me.

He blushes and clears his throat, and when he looks down at my finger, I take the opportunity to quickly blow out a burst of Lust. The pink color quickly dissipates before he can see it, and he breathes in slowly before raising his large eyes. When he looks at my face again, his gaze is hooded with desire. Bingo.

I remove my finger from his chest and instead use it to twirl my pink hair. "I so love these silks you have," I say, looking around his tent. "Do you think any of these colors would look nice on me?"

I turn around in a full circle, letting him look my curves up and down. There's not much that this fur outfit leaves to the imagination. My midriff is showing, my boobs are pushed up, and my skirt is fairly short. He notices.

He clears his throat and smiles. "You would look good in any of these colors, I assure you. Allow me to dress you, and you can see for yourself."

I put a hand on my chest to draw his eye down to my cleavage again. "Oh, I couldn't possibly. I'm just visiting today, you see, and my mother won't allow me to buy anything. She says I don't deserve to wear such lovely things," I say with a sad sigh as I look longingly at a dress.

The man frowns. "Nonsense. A unique flower such as yourself deserves for her clothes to match her beauty."

"If I bought anything, my mother would surely punish me."

He takes a step forward and puts his hand on my bare shoulder. "Then it will be a gift from me to you."

I flutter my lashes and smile up at him shyly. "A gift? You're too kind. I really shouldn't."

"I won't take no for an answer."

I smile. These cupid powers are awesome. Good thing he isn't into only guys or a specific type of fae, because this could've gone very differently. The people I use my magic on have to at least be willing for my powers to give them the push they need.

"Well, if you insist…"

"I do," he says quickly, turning around. "And I'm the best. So I already know your size. Go behind that curtain there, and I'll pass you garments."

"This is the most fun I've had in ages!" I say, skipping to the dressing room.

I carefully set my quiver and bow aside and then strip out of my fur. I pull on the clothes he passes over. A corset that laces up in the front is first, along with matching silk panties.

They're both a soft pink color that matches my hair. Next is a pale purple dress that fits like a glove and flares out at the hips, letting the soft fabric trail slightly at the floor.

I step out of the room and turn around for the Pixie to

inspect. He eyes me up and down like he can see the under-garments he chose for me. "Beautiful."

"You really are the best," I purr.

It's all about using a mix of my powers with a side of ego stroking. I can feel the pulse of his desire, and I can smell it, too. It nearly makes me sneeze.

"Is there something I can put my old things in?" I ask, motioning toward the pile of furs and my bow and arrow on the floor. This dress wouldn't exactly go with it.

"Hmm, I have just the thing." He comes back holding a box in one hand and a shoulder bag in the other. "You can put your things in this," he says, handing me the bag.

I stuff my quiver and bow inside and then pick up my old clothes to add them to the bag as well. I can't just leave them behind. Sentimental reasons and all. I pull the strap over my shoulder and let the bag rest on my other side. It fits comfortably, and it's not too awkward considering what's inside.

"Here," he says, handing me the box he's still holding. I open it and find a pair of lovely silk silver slippers. "May I?" he asks.

I nod, and then he kneels down and puts the shoes on my feet with tenderness like I'm Cinder*freaking*ella. I almost feel bad for using my powers on him, because he seems like a real sweetheart. When I have some money of my own, I'll have to come back here and pay him properly.

"There," he says, straightening up. "Now you're perfect."

I beam at him as I look in the mirror. I look much more fae now. As long as no one looks too closely at my subtle differences, I should be able to walk down the street without sticking out so much. My fur clothing was what made them first look, and then the rest of my appearance was what made them keep looking. I won't make the mistake of showing my ears again.

"Thank you!" I exclaim, planting a kiss on his cheek. He

nearly turns beet red. "Oh! That's my mother calling me," I say, pretending to hear something.

His face grows worried. "Can I see you again?"

"I don't know," I say, hurrying to the exit. "My mother is very strict. But if I can slip out, I'll try to look for you tonight before you close!" I feel a stab of guilt when his eyes light up. Poor guy. I hope he doesn't wait for me too long. "Thank you again!" I say with a wave before stepping out of the tent.

I make my way out onto the street again and soon get lost in the crowd. No one even bothers looking my way this time, and I'm able to breathe a little easier. Whew. Now all I have to do is get to the tower where my genfin guys are without any of the palace guards seeing me.

Somehow.

CHAPTER 2

The tower sits inside the castle walls of the keep, and the walls are manned by intimidating fae soldiers in full armor. I've been really close to the tower this whole time, but that damn wall might as well separate us by leagues.

I stand in the shadows at the base of the stone wall, watching the guards make their rounds on the wall above. They all rest their hands on their sword hilts like they're ready to take someone's head off at any moment.

Night fell hours ago, but I'm still stuck in this spot, trying to figure out the best way to get into the keep. The only people permitted to pass through the gate are searched and cleared first, which just isn't an option for me.

I *might* be able to seduce someone, but with the guards looking so serious and alert, it's highly doubtful that their minds and bodies would be open to desire while they're so vigilant in their duties, and I'm not brave enough to try it right now.

I close my eyes and focus on the wings that are hidden inside of me. With a forceful push, I make them come out. The pain steals my breath for a moment before fading away.

With my wings out again, I ruffle my feathers and stretch them out to work out the kinks. I rub at the edges, glad to have them back out, even if they are really heavy and somewhat cumbersome. I just feel more like me with them.

Timing it as perfectly as I can, I wait until the two guards above me walk to the other end of the wall. With a leap, I shoot into the air.

My wings are nearly silent as I flap, and I gain as much height as possible. I have to get far above the wall so the guards don't spot me. I don't know how well high fae can see in the dark, and I don't want to get caught.

I spot the silhouettes of the prisoner's towers ahead. There are four of them, all the same height with intimidating spikes on the rooftops and more spikes propped up on the ground in case someone were to try to scale the wall. There are bones littered on the ground between the deadly spikes, showing the success rate of that endeavor.

Not a good visual.

There are no windows in the prison towers, and when I fly around them, I realize that there are no doors either.

"Well, that's just freaking great," I mutter.

I scan my surroundings before flying over to the second tower. I know this is the tower where my guys are being held. I can feel it. Now that I'm closer, whatever inside of me that anchors me to them pulls me in their direction with a tug in my gut.

I fly around the tower, trying to find a point of entry, a weakness, even a spot to land, but there's nothing, and the spikes are too sharp for me to try anything. There will be guards walking past the wall on this side soon, so I need to move.

Grudgingly, I fly back over the wall and crouch down on the ground. I can't stay inside the keep's walls and risk getting caught. I pull my wings back inside my body and lean against the wall. Biting my lip, I try to think of what to do next.

Problem is I have no idea. Either the door to the tower is concealed by magic or the entry point is underground, neither of which I'll be able to breach. "Shit," I whisper to myself.

"State your business."

A squeal escapes me as I spin around. I have no idea how the fae guard snuck up on me, but he's scowling down at me with a suspicious sneer.

I try to smile but it comes across as more of a grimace. "Umm, nice night."

"What?"

"What?" I echo.

The guard's scowl deepens. "There is no loitering at the palace walls. Move along, or I'll move you myself."

I nod emphatically. "Yeah, sure. No problem mister guard sir." I start to back away.

Before I can turn around, his eyes narrow. "Wait."

My feet freeze and I try not to show how much I'm freaking out, but I'm not sure I'm successful.

Play it cool, Emelle. Just freaking play it cool.

My hands start to shake as he walks toward me, and I notice that I'm breathing weird. Dammit. I really need to work on my playing it cool technique.

"How can I help you?" I ask in what I hope is a sweetly innocent voice.

His eerie fae eyes look me up and down. "What type of fae breed are you?"

"Oh, you know, a little bit of this, a little bit of that. I'm a mutt, really. My father was a mutt, my mother was a mutt, heck, even my grandparents were mutts. Maternal *and* paternal. We're just a big ol' group of mixed up. You should see our family reunions. It's pretty wild. No one looks like anyone else. Makes it kind of understandable that some of

13

them became kissing cousins, if you know what I mean. They didn't know they were cousins, you know? Can't really blame them there. The family tree is a real mess."

His brows stay furrowed.

I smile again as I watch my meaningless chatter slowly filter through his brain.

It takes a while.

Not the smartest guard, this one.

"Anyway, me and you are probably third cousins once removed or some crazy thing like that. Makes me real apprehensive to do any kissing of my own, you know? I've tried telling Granny and Gramps that they should just start branding us all so we can recognize each other on sight. I think it's a good idea, but cousin Brue is being a real dick about it. Course, he would be, since he married our second cousin. He's real sore about it, too. Can't get rid of her."

I can see that the guard's patience has run out. My hope is that all this talk will make him so frustrated with me that he—

"Go away."

I smile and nod. "Yes, sir. You have a nice night guarding. I'll be sure to look for you at the next reunion!"

Whew. That was close.

I turn and all but run away back toward the town square. It's mostly quiet and empty now, with only a few street lamps to light the way. A deep pain in my stomach begins to grow with every step I take further away from my guys.

When I'm far enough away from the wall to pose no threat, I take a careful glance behind me and see the guard returning to his post by the gate doors. I sigh in relief and then sit down against the back of a shop, staying as close as I dare.

I clamp my arms around my middle, trying to staunch the pain, but it does little good. The only remedy is my guys, and since they're currently imprisoned and I have no way of getting to them, there's really no way of getting rid of it anytime soon.

I don't know how it's possible that I fall asleep, but the next thing I know, I'm jarred awake by someone yelling over me.

"Wha..."

"Oh, she wakes! The little vagrant mutt wakes!" I look up blearily at the scowling fae woman standing over me with her hands on her hips. She's high fae with pale orange skin and cat-like eyes.

When I look up at her, the crick in my neck sends a painful pinch down my spine. Ouch. That's what I get for sleeping upright against a hard stone building all night.

"Don't just sit there with the drool on your chin," she snaps. "Get off of my building!"

I stumble to my feet ungracefully, my bag flopping against my back. My limbs tingle as the blood circulation slowly returns.

"Sorry," I mumble.

"Sorry? *Sorry?*"

Her voice is getting really high-pitched now. I wonder what she'd sound like if she pinched her nostrils together. She notices me staring at her nose and self-consciously wipes at it. I hold back a smile.

"This is a highly respectable business. I serve the most influential and respected fae here. There is absolutely no place for tramps to hang around. I don't know where you're from," she says, looking me up and down with disdain, "but here on the kingdom island, fae are respectable. There are certainly no fae lying around on the street like rodents."

Geez, lady. She acts as if I hocked a loogie on her front window. Can't a girl take a nap? I open my mouth to answer when a small entourage rounds the corner.

The moment I see the two palace guards in tow, my heart starts racing. Then my eyes settle on the person leading

15

them, and it nearly stops and drops right through my feet. *Uh-oh.*

"Gunkope? I thought I heard your voice."

I can't help it. I snicker. Her name is Gunkope. No wonder she's so ornery. Gunkope twirls around and plasters on the fakest smile I've ever seen in my life. She curtsies so low she might as well kiss the ground.

"Your Highness! I beg your pardon. I was just coming to open the shop for you. Take no notice of this vagabond. I've made sure she knows not to loiter any longer."

If I weren't shitting bricks, I'd roll my eyes.

Princess Soora looks right at me. Her periwinkle hair is coiffed with ribbons, and her dress looks like it's softer than silk. But I've seen those fae eyes filled with tears as she cried herself to sleep over a broken heart, and that's all I can see now as I look at her behind her proprietary mask. "I see."

Does she? I sincerely hope not. She may have let me past when I was fleeing from Prince Elphar, but who knows what she thinks of me now.

Please don't recognize me.

Another moment of intense studying happens, but Gunkope unwittingly comes to my rescue. "Your Highness, why don't you come inside now, and I'll show you all the newest fragrances I have. There is a moonflower-infused perfume I think you will really like."

The princess's eyes flicker back to the shop owner. "That sounds lovely, Gunkope."

Without another word or backward glance, the group moves away from the back of the building and leaves me behind.

Thank the gods.

I sag against the wall in relief and try to slow my racing heart when a periwinkle hand clamps down on my arm. The princess's face is suddenly there in front of me, our faces inches apart.

16

"I remember you."

My mouth goes dry, but I don't dare move or speak.

A guard's voice calls behind her. "Princess?"

"I just realized I dropped my handkerchief," she calls back.

"I will search for it, Highness."

She straightens up, still not releasing my arm, and looks behind the corner at the guard. "No need, I think I've spotted it, it's just blown over here."

She tugs me away from the wall and to the other side of the building to stay out of view.

"I don't know why you've come back here, but it isn't safe. You must leave," she says in a rush.

My shock must show on my face because she sighs. "I am no enemy of yours, but the prince is. You do *not* want him to find you. Leave."

"I can't."

"Princess?" the guard calls again.

"Coming, I've found it!" she says, digging a handkerchief from her pocket and balling it up in her fist. She looks back at me and her voice drops to a whisper. "If you can't leave, then you must hide. You're much too close to the palace."

"I can't leave," I say adamantly.

I hear the guard's steps coming closer, and Princess Soora looks at me frantically. "Midnight. Wait at the castle's west wall."

Without another word, she whirls around and leaves. "So silly. I'm always dropping this," I hear her say to the guard as their footsteps recede.

Filling my cheeks up with air, I blow out a long breath. I'm not really sure what to make of Princess Soora. Can I trust her?

My gut says yes, but my gut also thought it would be a good idea to drink my weight in Evert's homemade alcohol. Might not be the best judge.

$\mathcal{I}$ have until midnight to decide if I'll show up like she told me to. In the meantime, I definitely can't hang around Madame Gunky's shop, or she'll probably try to throw me out with the garbage.

I walk slowly away, heading in the general direction of the castle walls to try to get closer without actually looking like I'm loitering. I don't want another guard to spot me hanging around there again. But I can't go very far, either, because if I go full on invisible again, I'm not sure I'll be able to come back from it.

I do *not* want to get stuck as an invisible cupid in the Veil again. Just the thought makes my insides tense with anxious loneliness.

I walk past more shops, keeping the castle walls in my peripheral vision. There are just as many guards during the day as there were at night. My dress is a little wrinkled from sleeping in it, and I frown at the dirt smudges now staining it. I'm certainly not dressed for living on the street.

I walk parallel to the wall, passing the town square and the marketplace, and then I find myself in a residential area. The houses are all mansions with gates and elaborate lawns.

Finding a bench on the sidewalk, I take a seat to rest my aching feet. The trail of my dress is pretty much toast. The end is frayed and the color is more brown than purple. My slippers haven't fared any better.

I stay here all day watching people pass by. Most of them don't pay me any attention. By the time night falls, hunger pangs are tormenting me.

I haven't eaten since I left the banishment island with my guys, and after not eating food for over fifty years as an incorporeal cupid, I do not like to skip meals.

Under the cover of night, I slowly make my way to the west side of the walls surrounding the castle. By the scent of manure and hay in the air, I'm fairly certain that the palace stables are on the other side.

The wall is off the beaten path on this side, with only a small forested area behind me. The only guards I have to worry about are the ones passing by on the top of the wall, so I time it perfectly so that I sidle up next to the wall without them seeing me.

I sit on the grass and wait. And wait. And wait some more. I'm hungry, my anchor pains are hurting, and all I can think about is everything that can go wrong. Finally, when the moon is bright and huge in the sky, I hear a noise that makes me jump to my feet.

Ahead of me by about thirty feet, a part of the wall pops out and a secret door creaks open. My fingers fist my dress in case I need to hoist it up and make a run for it. But a figure holding a lantern is none other than Princess Soora.

"Hurry."

Looking around to make sure no one sees, I quickly follow her into the lion's den. Once I'm through the door, I see an older fae woman. I can tell she's a hearth hob right away based on her tight brown ringlets in a pouf on her head. Even her eyebrows are curly.

She's tiny, too, only about four feet tall, and has the telltale working calluses on her hands from hours spent cleaning. Her kind gets power from it somehow. She quickly closes the stone door behind us and takes the lantern from the princess to lead the way ahead.

I follow behind them as we pass through a narrow cellar filled with dusty crates. After pulling open a trap door at the top, we climb a short ladder and end up inside the palace stables. Passing by dozens of sleeping horses, we make our way out of the stables, past a track, and into a small side door of the castle.

When we enter a kitchen, my stomach immediately clenches with hunger. There's no food cooking or anyone inside, but I can smell the remnants of what they'd probably served for dinner. I look around for a scrap to take with me, but there's nothing. Dammit.

After leaving the kitchen, the women, still silent, lead me up a servant's stairway, down a plain corridor, and into a small room. It's plain, with a bare wooden floor and stone walls, but it's clean and there's a tidy bed and desk inside.

The hearth hob closes the door behind us, and it seems all three of us take a collective breath of relief for getting this far without being caught. "I suppose we need to make proper introductions. I'm Princess Soora, and this is my hand-maiden, Duru."

"I'm Emelle."

"It's nice to officially meet you, Emelle."

I notice that Duru does not seem to share that sentiment. In fact, she's staring at me like she'd have no problem plucking out my eyes.

"Duru, it's alright," the princess says, noticing our stare-off.

"She could be an enemy, princess. You shouldn't have brought her here. What if she's playing you? What if she's using you for some grand scheme?"

"I would *never* hurt or betray you," I say, letting the

20

conviction of my honesty fill my tone. "You don't know me, but I swear I wouldn't do anything to intentionally hurt you."

The princess just nods once. "You'll stay here for now. This room is for servants, and you'll find a uniform in the drawers under the bed. I've made you a lady's maid, so you'll be waiting on me. Don't worry, I've made it so that you won't be around many people, especially not the prince. You'll strictly be in charge of keeping my room tidy, but you'll have Duru here to help you," she says, gesturing to the hearth hob. "Now, if you'll allow me to glamour you, I can make you look more high fae."

"Umm…"

I know from experience that glamouring doesn't work on me, but I say nothing as she comes forward and touches my skin. I can feel her magic pooling around me, but then it just fizzles out.

She frowns. "That's strange. Glamour doesn't work on you?"

I shrug.

"Hmm. Well, that is a complication."

The hearth hob tilts her head in thought. "Her pink hair looks high fae. Her skin doesn't, but we can dye it, princess. She'll have to be careful not to get wet, but I'm sure I can fix her up. She'll also need to wear heels to give her extra height. Her ears will need to stay hidden, too," she says, circling around me. "If she's going to stay here, she'll need to blend in. I won't have her presence coming back to hurt you, princess."

She gives the hearth hob a kind smile. "Thank you, Duru. Those changes should be enough, as long as she keeps to herself." The princess gives me an assessing look with a tilting head. "I remember you with red wings."

"Yeah, that's right. They're just hidden right now."

"So you can hide them like high fae? Good."

I just look at her, completely baffled. "Why are you helping me?"

She considers the question before answering. "Perhaps I'm wrong, but when you attacked the prince, it felt like you were doing it for me."

"Oh, well...I was."

"Why?"

I shrug. "He's a cheating ass."

Princess Soora's lip twitches slightly. "What are you? You must be very powerful to have broken through the castle's magical barriers and stayed hidden. No entity is able to stay invisible inside these walls. Not to mention that magic the prince hit you with. You should have been killed."

She looks at me thoughtfully, and I fidget under her intense scrutiny. "What are you?"

"You wouldn't believe me even if I told you."

She lets that reply go. "Tell me, why is it you can't leave? Are you looking for something?"

I don't know if I should tell her, but I already didn't admit that I'm a cupid from the Veil, so I have to give her something. She's stuck her neck out for me by bringing me here. The least I can do is repay her with some truths.

"I'm waiting to see the prisoners who are being taken to face the royal culling trials."

Surprise flashes across her face. "And you know these prisoners? The ones that will be facing the culling trials?"

I look from her to the hearth hob and back again.

"You can trust Duru, and you can trust me," the princess assures me. "Duru is not from here. She was my nursemaid back on my home island. Her loyalty is with me, not the prince."

At the mention of the prince, Duru snorts. "I'd rather be loyal to a viper. Be less likely to get bit."

I like her.

"The three genfin males that were brought there

yesterday from their banishment island. I'm here for them. I can't leave them."

Princess Soora nods. "Well, I don't know anything about the prisoners, but I'll try to see if I can discreetly get some information. I do know that the culling will take place in one week's time."

One week. I have to hide out here in the palace, under the same roof as the prince, for one whole week.

My dismay must show on my face, because the princess smiles softly. "As long as you follow my instructions, you will be safe. Duru? Could you gather what we'll need? Perhaps some food for her as well."

Duru hesitates, as if she doesn't want to leave me alone with her, but then she nods and slips from the room.

Princess Soora and I study each other in silence for a moment. She really is beautiful, but her eyes hold a sadness, too. After a moment, that sadness turns into something else. Determination.

"I'm afraid I haven't led you here for purely altruistic purposes."

Well, I don't love the sound of that.

CHAPTER 4

"**O**h yeah? What's the other purpose for you helping me?" I ask the princess warily.

She taps a long finger against her arm in thought. "There is a movement against the current monarchy," she says, throwing me off.

"What?"

"Fae all over the realm are unhappy with how things are currently done. A rebellion has been formed. And I am one of them."

She couldn't have surprised me more if she'd gone down on all fours and started licking the ground. Whoa. Weird visual.

"Umm, maybe you haven't noticed, but you're kind of part of that monarchy now."

"I am. I had hoped I could bring forth some changes within once I became queen. It is clear now that that plan is fruitless with the way Prince Elphar does things."

"Where do I come in with all of this?"

"That depends. Tell me why were you spying on the prince."

How can I explain that I wasn't spying but doing my job?

She might have taken me in off the streets, but I can't just admit to being an entity that belonged in the Veil.

"I wasn't spying for any sort of political reason."

"Hired by an assassin then? I admit, you don't look the part, but that may be part of your disguise."

The thought of being a badass assassin makes me snort. I might be a pro at the bow and arrow, but as far as any other physical skill, I'm less than impressive.

Or average.

Okay, I pretty much suck.

"Yeah, no. Not an assassin."

"So…" She looks at me questioningly.

"Look, this is probably going to sound creepy, but I was mainly here for you."

Her purple brows shoot up. "Me?"

"I wanted to see that you and the prince had a happy marriage."

She doesn't believe me. I can see it in her face. Heck, *I* barely believe me, and I know I'm telling the truth. Still, she's a princess through and through, because she doesn't blatantly call me out on it. She's careful to be diplomatic.

"I see. Well, in that case, I am sorry to disappoint you."

"We both know it wasn't your fault. The prince is a giant jerkwad."

"Indeed," she says with a glint of humor in her eyes.

"So what do you want me for?"

"You have the ability to turn invisible and resist harmful magic. I want you to spy for me."

That takes me aback. "I can't. I mean, that invisible stuff was…" I sigh in frustration at my lousy explanations. "Okay, look. You're probably gonna think I'm insane, but I'm just going to lay it all out there. I'm a cupid."

She stares at me and blinks her huge eyes twice. "I'm not familiar with that type of fae. Is it a mixed breed?"

"I'm not a fae at all. I don't even belong here, to be honest.

I'm meant to live in the Veil—the dimension that separates me from your physical world. Cupids use their powers to spread love and desire. We're basically glorified match-makers."

She frowns fiercely, her eyes growing a darker shade of violet that makes her seem suddenly scary. "So it's *your* fault that the prince—"

I interrupt her. "No! Gods, no. He's a dog all on his own. I was trying to fix it, I swear. I was trying to make him loyal to you. I tried everything," I say, my bitter frustration dripping from my tone. "Nothing would stick. That guy is slipperier than lube on a toy."

She blinks at me like she can't believe this is her life. I guess the lube bit was too much for a royal princess? But the furious color of her eyes has faded, so that's good.

"So that's why you were invisible? Because you are a Veil entity? Not because you have any great power?"

I bristle a little. "Hey, I might not be some awesome assassin, but it's not like I'm a slouch. A cupid has some impressive powers, if I do say so myself."

"Like?"

"Like I can start an orgy faster than you can say 'slam-o-rama.'"

Okay, that didn't sound as impressive out loud as it did in my head. But still.

"...Alright. So you're a cupid. We will just have to work with your unique...strengths."

I won't embarrass myself and say I don't have many strengths except good hair and a winning personality. "Okay."

"Nothing to worry about for now."

"There's something I'm confused about," I admit.

"What's that?"

"I sort of...well, I liked to check on you, you know?

Follow you around, make sure you were alright." Did "checking on" her sound less creepy than stalking her? Here's hoping. "I watched you at night. You cried. A lot."

Her eyes harden. "What's the question?"

"It's only been a couple of months. How did you go from crying over the prince not loving you every night to heading the rebellion and wanting his head on a spike?"

She lets out a humorless laugh. "You think I was crying over *him*?"

I frown. "Well, yeah. I could feel your heartbreak."

"My heart was breaking. But not for him."

"Oh." Then, "*Ohhh*. You loved someone else? Before you married the prince?"

She doesn't reply, but I can see the truth in her eyes.

"I didn't know. I'm sorry. So why'd you marry Prince Prick, then?"

"For the fae who want change. So I could be in a position of power."

"You've been planning this for a while, then."

She nods her head.

"The one you love, where is he or she?"

She swallows hard. "Gone."

"Did the prince..." I let my question trail off. If the prince killed the fae she loved, that just makes me hate him even more.

"That is not a topic up for discussion."

I put my hands up in surrender. "Sorry. Cupid tendency. Needing to unbreak a broken heart is like needing a drink of water when you're super thirsty," I say, running my tongue over my teeth. Who knew dry mouth was a side effect of heartbreak? "I always just assumed your broken heart was because of the prince," I admit. "But if there's anything I can do to help fix your heart, I'm here."

I tilt my head in thought. "Or even if you just wanna get

back at him. I could so get down with that. You wanna catch a 'hay ride' with his favorite guard or something? That would probably piss him off. Or I could try to make him fall in lust with one of those gross goblin chicks. That would be hilarious."

The corner of her mouth tips up slightly. "I think I'll pass for now, but thank you."

"Anytime."

"So, Emelle, when I think of something you can do for the rebellion, can I count on you?"

"I mean, yeah, but what exactly is your goal here?"

She looks me dead in the eye and says, "Overthrowing the king and prince, of course."

I blanch. "You can't be serious."

"Indeed I am."

"But he'll kill you."

Suddenly, the demure lady is gone and a fiery princess stands in her place. "Not if I kill him first."

I whistle under my breath. "Wow. You're, like, super scary right now."

My words surprise a laugh out of the princess, and the sound is so contagious that I laugh, too. It feels good to laugh, but then I remember my guys being locked away in the tower, and the smile falls from my face.

"I'll help you, but can you help my genfins?"

After a moment of thought, she nods her head. "I won't lie to you. I can't do much while they're awaiting the culling, or even while they're competing in it. But I will do what I can."

"Thank you."

The hurt in my stomach lurches suddenly, making me hiss in pain.

Princess Soora frowns. "Are you ill?"

"Not exactly."

How in the realm am I supposed to explain it? I didn't want to admit that I'd go invisible again in case she wanted to use me that way. I couldn't risk going full invisible and not being able to turn back. No, I have to keep this to myself for now.

"If I go too far away from the genfins, the ones in the prison, then I sort of start to feel...not well."

"I see. I'm afraid I don't have the power to undo any kind of spells."

"Oh, that's okay. Don't worry about it. I can handle it."

"There isn't any sort of herb or tonic I can get for you?"

"No, I just need to see them."

"I don't think that will be possible. You may have to wait until after the culling."

I wince. I don't know if I have that long. It seems it's not just a distance thing, but a time apart thing, too.

"Now, the story is that you were my handmaiden at my home island and I've requested you here. No one will question it, but don't expect any sort of welcome here, because you'll get none except with Duru. Under no circumstance should you trust anyone inside these walls. Loyalty is just a seven letter word here."

Since I lived here for a few weeks during my last cupid stint, I know that all too well. This place is filled with more backstabbing pettiness than a human prep school.

"Got it."

Duru pops her head back in the room. "I have everything ready for her, princess."

"Very good, thank you, Duru." Turning back to me she says, "I have to go now, but Duru will take you to the baths and get you sorted. No one will be there now. She will dye your skin so you look more high fae and get you anything else you need."

"Thank you," I say, pulling off my bag and leaving it on the bed.

"And I don't have to stress to you the importance of secrecy for this, do I?"

"Nah. I got it." At her arched brow, I go on, "I mean, no ma'am. Royal Highness. Princess. Top secret rebellion equals Emelle shutting up."

Her lips tilt up at my staggering eloquence. I don't blame her. Then she sweeps out of the room.

CHAPTER 5

I'm left to follow Duru to the servant bathhouse. The room is rather large and has several inlaid baths in a stone floor.

"All servants bathe here," Duru says, still carrying a bag with her. "Get in and pull that chain there. The water will come. It'll be cold, so be warned."

I groan. Cold baths. The bane of my existence.

I quickly strip off my soiled and very wrinkled dress and step into the stone bath.

Pulling the chain on the wall beside the tub, a plug is yanked out of the wall and cold water gushes out. When I have enough to bathe in, I quickly fit the plug back into the hole.

Duru wastes no time. She tosses me a bar of sweet smelling soap, and I quickly wash my hair and body. I wish I could let my wings out and wash those, too, but I don't want to risk someone coming in and seeing them.

Once I'm done cleaning, she pulls a bottle from her bag and starts pouring red liquid into the bathwater. When she empties the entire contents of the bottle, she nods at the bright pink water.

"Good enough. Dip under and let yourself soak for as long as you can."

Taking a deep breath, I submerge myself in the water. I stay under until my lungs start complaining and then sputter up to the surface.

"Again," Duru orders.

I do it again and again and again until Duru is satisfied that my skin looks pink enough to pass for high fae.

"Good enough," she says again.

Looking at my arms, I see that my skin is no longer ivory but fuchsia-colored.

"Your hair turned a bit darker, too," Duru says. "Get on out, but you'll have to let yourself air dry. Wiping yourself off with a towel would only take off some of the color."

I haul myself out of the tub and then stand here like an awkward rain cloud as I make puddles on the floor. I can't help the shivers and goose bumps that rule my body.

"Is there a fire somewhere? I'm cold."

I hate being cold.

Duru puts her fists on her wide hips. "Oh, sure. Let me just bring you up to the princess's private rooms so you can warm yourself by the fire like a proper lady. Maybe you'd like a foot rub, too?"

I grin at her sarcastic tone. "That'd be great, thanks."

She rolls her eyes at me. "You're dry enough. Put this on, but be careful not to wipe the dye off. It will settle into your skin as it dries, but we might need to have you soak again in a few days."

She tosses me a nightgown that fits over me like a burlap sack. It clings to my still-damp skin, but it's better than being naked.

"What, no silk?"

She wants to smile, I can tell. I can also tell that the puddle of water left behind on the floor is killing her a little bit inside. As a hearth hob, her instinct is to keep everything meticulously clean.

"Come on," she says, casting a longing look at the puddle. "We'd better get you back to your room. The guards do a sweep down here every couple of hours."

She leads me back to my room and then empties the rest of the contents in the bag she's been carrying. A smile immediately lights up my fuchsia-colored face.

"Duru, you really do like me," I say, hurrying over. I scoop up the food she's pilfered for me and start shoveling bread and cheese into my mouth.

Duru shakes her head at me. "Good goddess, you're eating like a wild boar. I'm surprised you're not grunting."

With cheeks full of food, I look up at her. "If you're trying to make me not like you, it's not going to work. You fed me and insulted the prince. We're practically best friends now."

Duru rolls her eyes at me again, but it doesn't fool me. "You like me, admit it."

"Stop talking with your mouth full," she reprimands. "Now, go to sleep. You'll hear the servant's bell in the morning to wake you. Get dressed in your uniform. You'll find a pair of heels in the bag I brought you. It's the best I could find in such short notice, and they may not fit exactly right, but you'll have to make do. You'll need them to make yourself appear taller. You're much too short for a high fae. You have ten minutes to get ready once the first bell sounds. Then, you'll have another fifteen to get to the servant's dining area and eat. I'll find you there, and I'll escort you to the princess's rooms for cleaning. You'll be under my supervision."

I give her a two-finger salute. "Yes, ma'am."

"Don't be late," she says, pointing a finger in my face.

"Wouldn't dream of it."

"Good. Get some rest. The bell will be ringing in only a few short hours."

Duru opens the door to leave when I stop her. "Hey," I say, swallowing down a huge bite of bread. "Thanks, Duru."

She levels a look at me that seems to weigh me down. "Don't get caught, and don't you dare betray my princess, or I will kill you myself. Understood?"

Wow. She'd probably smother me with some cleaning supplies.

"Umm, yeah."

"Good. See you in the morning."

She shuts the door after her, and I quickly eat the rest of the bread before crawling under the covers and collapsing on the bed on my belly. This is much better than sleeping outside against a hard building.

I release my wings and stretch them out with a sigh. That's better.

I'm clean, I'm fed, and I'm pink. I close my eyes and fall asleep wondering how in the heck I got in the middle of a fae rebellion when all I want to do is protect my genfins, find a new way to anchor myself, fall in love, and have some epic sex.

I fall asleep still imagining the sex bit.

Right when things are getting good, there's an annoying ringing sound going off that jars me from my dreams.

I grab the pillow and pull it over my head, trying to stifle the noise. I keep trying to shift back into that blissful state of sleep, but the ringing noise keeps forcing me awake.

Damn bell. Who rings bells, anyway?

My memory comes surging back to me, and I sit up with a start. "Shit!"

I have no idea when the servant's bell started ringing or if this is the first one. I scramble to my feet and rip off my nightdress. I'd inadvertently ripped it last night when I let my wings out, but oh well.

I suck my wings back into my body and leave the torn nightdress in a heap on the floor.

Digging for the drawer under the bed, I quickly pull on the servant's uniform I need to wear. The bells have stopped ringing, but I don't know if that's a good or a bad thing. I really need a clock.

The dress is made of thick, coarse material in a drab gray color. Fabric pools at my feet. I grab the pair of lace-up black boots that Duru left me and pull them on, noticing that the heels are at least four inches tall.

Ugh.

I get to my feet, but it's a struggle not to fall flat on my pink face. I pull my hair back so that the sides sit snugly over my ears and then tie it in place.

I don't have a mirror, so I have no idea how silly I look, but I'm already at risk of being late, so I quickly go to the door and yank it open, only to almost collide with an exasperated Duru.

She steps away from my stumbling halt and scowls at me. "You're late! You've missed breakfast."

"Sorry! I'm not so good with bells. Or having to wake up."

Duru throws her hands up in frustration and whirls around. "Follow me and be quick about it."

I scramble after her, trying to keep up, but let's face it, I'm not even balanced when I'm walking barefoot.

My poor, newly corporeal body simply isn't ready to run in four-inch heels.

My ankle twists, and I nearly topple down a set of stairs, only managing to stay upright by clutching onto the banister.

Duru shoots me an exasperated look over her shoulder. "Stop playing around and come on!"

"Duru, if this is playing to you, you really need to get out more," I pant. Damn, for a short thing, she sure does move fast.

Once we get out of the servant's corridors and into the main part of the palace, I see other people for the first time.

Guards and servants are busily working inside the

grandeur of the palace. I get more than a few curious looks and even some outright sneers.

I rub my pink arm self-consciously, but it helps that I recognize most of them. They can't exactly intimidate me when I've watched their secret lover's trysts inside broom closets.

Okay, yeah, I caused those trysts. I got up to twenty-six in one day. It was a busy day for the broom closets.

I'm panting by the time Duru stops in front of a door and leads me inside a closet stuffed full of linens. She starts sorting through everything and then piles fabric in my arms. She doesn't stop until the pile is taller than my head.

"Come on," she says.

I nearly drop the pile as she pushes past me, and I can't see over it, so I have to constantly move my head around to try to get a peek at her to make sure I'm still following her.

When I trip over my heels again, the whole pile of laundry nearly falls with me, but luckily, or unluckily depending on perspective, I run into Duru's back, stopping my fall.

"Good goddess above, you're as unsteady as a newborn calf," she hisses. "Don't you dare drop those."

I get a handle on them and straighten up again. "Nope, got it. Totally not gonna drop them."

I hear her huff and then open a door, so I follow her inside. "Put those on the chaise."

As soon as I do, I'm able to take a look around. Princess Soora's rooms haven't changed. Her receiving room has a warm fire going, bookshelves, and a small desk with embroidery setting on it. Through the doors is her closet, her bedroom, and her bathroom. The windows are open, letting in the fresh air, and I can see a nice balcony filled with potted plants.

"Her rooms are my favorite," I say.

Duru pauses from gathering some sheets from the pile,

and narrows her eyes at me. "Seen a lot of rooms in the palace, have you?"

Yep. All of them. "Ummm, what? No. I mean, not really. I might've seen one or…sixty. This seems like the best, though, don't you think? Very nicely decorated. Princess Soora has good taste, am I right?"

"Did you spy on my princess when you were invisible?" she asks me bluntly.

"Spying is such an ugly word. I prefer to think of it as observing."

Duru scoffs and starts muttering under her breath about pink-haired tricksters.

A pair of servants come through the door and stop dead in their tracks when they get a look at me. They're both hearth hobs, too, but unlike Duru, who wears a dark purple servant's dress, they're both wearing white.

One is a male and the other a female, barely past their teens. The tight curls that stick out all over their heads help their short height. It gives them another six inches at least.

"Who's she?" the girl asks with a curled lip.

"This is Emelle," Duru says without looking up from sorting the linens. "I won't be needing you in here today. You two can take the halls. Be sure to get the carpets, too. I saw a speck on my way up."

The boy tries to draw himself up higher. "I cleaned the carpets myself two days ago, and there wasn't a single speck."

Duru levels him with a stare. "There was a speck."

The boy's cheeks redden slightly, but he keeps his mouth shut.

Whoa. Specks are a serious business.

The girl crosses her arms. "What's a high fae doing cleaning? They aren't any good at it."

Oh, gods. Hearth hob cleaning politics. "Hey, high fae can clean just fine," I say defensively. I don't even know why. I just can't help myself.

She scoffs like it's the most ridiculous thing she's ever heard.

"Enough. You're wasting time," Duru says. "Go."

The two hearth hobs turn and leave but not before shooting me another look filled with disdain. When we're alone again, I laugh. "Geez, I didn't know I'd be getting into a hearth hob cleaning territory dispute."

"Don't mind them. They're just put out. They get more of a power boost when they clean in here than they do in the hall. There are less shiny surfaces out there."

Huh. Who knew?

"Well? Don't just stand there. Strip the princess's bedding. We have a long day ahead of us," she says with an excited glint in her eye. Wow, hearth hobs really do love cleaning.

She wasn't kidding about us having a long day. We changed the linens in the bedroom and bathroom, scrubbed the floors and walls, dusted the shelves, washed the windows, and watered the plants, and there were a lot.

By the time the servant's bells ring again, my arms are so sore they're shaking and my feet are swollen and painful from being stuffed in uncomfortable heels all day.

Duru tuts at my disheveled and exhausted appearance. I look like something the cat dragged in. It doesn't help that her hearth hob magic has made Duru look more energized than ever. I swear, she's shed ten years. She practically glowed when she scrubbed the toilet.

She holds up my arm and shakes her head at my bicep. "Weak arms. No calluses on your hands, either," she says, looking at my blistered hands with derision.

"Cleaning's hard," I whine.

She rolls her eyes at me. "You'd better get used to it and not look so obvious about your inexperience. Servants have been punished for less. Come, let's eat."

"Now you're speaking my language."

I follow behind Duru as we make our way to the servant's

38

dining room to eat. Gods, my feet hurt. If it weren't for the promise of food up ahead, I'd pop a squat right here in the hallway and call it a day.

Or maybe I can blow a bit of Lust in some guard's face and get him to carry me the rest of the way?

Before I can find any guards and put my plan into action, we get to the servant's dining hall.

There are over a hundred servants inside eating and visiting. There are several long tables with benches set up, including a long table filled with buffet food.

After grabbing a plate, I follow Duru and load up as much food as I can fit on it. Since I missed breakfast, I'm starving, and the separation pain in my stomach isn't helping, either.

Duru and I sit down alone, and I notice that even though we get a lot of looks, no one seems keen to approach us. Duru glares at anyone who stares for too long.

"I guess we won't be getting an invite to the popular table anytime soon."

Duru sips at her soup before answering. "They don't like outsiders, and you're an outsider, same as me. At least you look high fae, though. You have that going for you."

"Hearth hobs are just as important as high fae."

She snorts into her bowl. The steam has made her already curly hair even frizzier. "No other high fae will share your sentiment, so if you don't want to blow your cover, I suggest you not say that again where people can hear you."

I lower my voice and lean a little closer. "What do you know about the culling?"

She shrugs. "Nothing. I've never been here for them before."

I sit back a bit with disappointment. If I can get some insider information to take to my guys, maybe they'll get the upper hand.

"What about the prison towers? Is there any way inside?"

She narrows her eyes at me. "Don't even think about it."

"I need to see them."

She shakes her head. "You'll be caught. No one gets into those towers. The king himself set up the enchantments centuries ago."

"But someone must go in there. To take the prisoners in and out. To bring them food and water."

She pats her springy hair with her hand in thought. "Yes, I believe someone from the kitchen brings their meals."

That was my way in. See? I'm gonna be an awesome spy.

Duru must see the gleam in my eyes, because she shakes her head. "If you get caught…"

"I know, I know. I better not implicate your princess. Believe me, I won't. I'm too scared you'll drown me in the toilet bowl."

She gets this look in her eye like she's imagining doing just that. Dammit. Why did I have to go and give her ideas?

She looks around the dining room and then motions with her head for me to look. "The earth sprite, there. See her?"

I squint. "The girl with the sunflowers growing out of her head?"

"That's the one. I've heard her talk of going to the cells before."

So I just need to get in with flower power over there, and hopefully she can get me into the towers to see my guys. I can totally do that. Probably. Like, there's a thirty percent chance of succeeding.

Once we finish eating, Duru takes me back to my room so that I don't get lost on my way. When I'm alone, I fall asleep almost immediately after slinging off my heels and pushing out my wings.

Being a servant sucks soapy balls.

CHAPTER 6

Two more days go by much like my first day. I have more blisters on my hands from cleaning than I do on my feet from the uncomfortable heels.

I also have to soak again in the bath to re-pink myself, but no one questions what type of fae I am, so my disguise must be working.

Unfortunately, the pain in my gut grows worse, and I go to sleep at night feeling a tingling start to spread up my arms and legs.

When the servant's bells wake me up on the fourth day, panic grips me.

"Crap!"

I jump out of bed and try to rub my hands together, but it's no use.

My right hand is gone. Invisible. Completely translucent.

"Oh, shit."

I'm no further away from the guys than I was before unless they've been moved. Either they've been moved away from me, or it's a matter of having gone too long without their presence.

Either way, I need my anchors to get a hold on this

physical world, and fast. But I certainly can't walk around with an invisible hand. Not only is it just invisible, but I can no longer touch physical things with it, either. This is bad. If my other hand goes, too, I won't be able to grip or touch anything.

I quickly dress, which, by the way, is *way* harder to do with only one hand.

When I finally manage to get buttoned up, I see that the sleeve isn't nearly long enough to hide the fact that my hand is missing.

Biting my lip in thought, I look around the room for some inspiration, and then a light bulb goes off.

I grab a stack of clothes and balance it on my forearm so that it looks like my hand is just beneath the fabric.

There. That should be good enough for now. I think. How often do you really notice someone's hands, right? Or is that saying about shoes? Oh well. Close enough.

I rush out of the servant's quarters and head for the kitchens. It's time to find myself an earth sprite.

This early in the morning, the large kitchen is a hubbub of frantic activity. Cooks are barking orders, pots and pans are steaming and spitting, and servants are rushing around each other as if they're competing in a race.

I hover near the door, getting shoved aside and stepped on more than once.

"What are you doing here?" one of the other servants asks me. "You're the princess's personal maid. What are you doing in the kitchens?"

"I'm, umm…"

Wow, Emelle. Way to be prepared.

"I'm not feeling well," I blurt out. "I was told that the earth sprite who works here has an herb I could ask for."

The fae quirks a brow. "You mean Mossie?"

"If she's the one with the big yellow flowers growing out of her scalp, then yes."

"She's out in the gardens in the morning, picking what's needed. Go that way," she says, pointing toward a door at the back of the kitchen.

"Thanks."

I swerve through the bodies and then escape out the door. Outside is a lush garden filled with vegetables, fruits, herbs, and flowers. I see several different earth sprites scattered around, growing plants and collecting them for today's menu.

When I see a bouquet of giant yellow flowers bobbing around the fruit trees, I make a beeline for her.

"Mossie?"

The girl straightens up and turns, her bright green eyes taking me in. "Yes?"

I look around to make sure no one else is close enough to overhear. I probably should've planned what to say before I came over to her. I really need to brush up on my super awesome spy skills.

She dusts off soil from her palms as she waits for me to answer, keeping hold of her basket filled with fruit.

I shuffle on my feet, but I'm careful not to jostle the stack of clothes I'm still balancing on my arm. I know it looks ridiculous based on the way her eyes keep darting to it.

Hmm…what to say…

Fuck it. Might as well just go all in. "I heard you sometimes bring food up to the prisoner's towers?"

Her green brows go up in surprise. "Yes…"

"I was hoping you'd let me come with."

Her mouth opens in surprise. "You, the princess's personal maid, want to come with me to deliver prisoner's food?"

"Yep."

Her expression turns suspicious, and the sunflowers on her head all shift to look at me accusingly. Whoa. Sunflower stare down. It's scarier than it sounds.

43

"Why?"

Why, why, why. I study her for a second. What do I know about earth sprites besides the obvious plant-growing stuff? Not much, but sprites are still fae, and fae are always guaranteed to like four things: power, parties, sex, and games. They're also usually up for a bribe.

But in Mossie's case, I think I know just the way to play this. Because I can hear her heart beating to the tune of unrequited love.

"Well, there's a guard…" I begin suggestively.

I watch her suspicious expression turn to anger. Bingo.

"Which guard? It better not be Blix," she says in a rush.

The petals on her sunflowers close slightly. It looks like they're squinting at me all aggressive-like.

"No, nope. Definitely not Blix. It's another guard. A totally different one."

And, just to give her a boost, I add, "Blix is way out of my league, anyway. I heard he likes earth sprites."

Not subtle, but I'm in a hurry.

She lifts her chin, her anger dissipating as she reaches up to pet one of her flowers. The sunflowers relax and go back to looking up at the sun.

"Yes, well. Good luck with that," she says bitterly. "Nothing catches those guards' eyes when they're on duty. I grew my best flowers, and Blix barely even glanced at them."

I scoff on her behalf. "What? That's just rude. Your flowers are the best I've ever seen."

"I know, right?"

"Well, if you let me come along, I guarantee we can get him to notice you this time."

I can see the spark of promise in her eyes even though she tries to keep it in check. "Oh? Well, maybe I'm not interested in him anymore," she says, tossing some vines behind her shoulder.

"Of course. I mean, a sprite like you should be chased.

Wooed. Doted on. Blix would be lucky to have you. But there's no harm in making him want what he can't have, am I right? Show him what he's missing, girl."

She smiles for the first time, revealing her small green-tinged teeth. "Meet me in the kitchens after last bell."

My lips curl into a smile. "I'll be there."

CHAPTER 7

I fake being sick when Duru comes to my room to fetch me. I can't exactly clean with only one hand without her noticing, anyway.

When the last bell rings for the night, bringing the servant's dinner to an end, I leave my room and head for the kitchens to meet Mossie.

It's obvious that she's prettied herself up more than usual. She's wearing a clean dress free of soil stains, and her flowers are newly pruned.

"You look super nice."

Her sunflowers practically preen. "Thanks. You too."

I didn't do anything except re-braid my hair, but I smile anyway.

She picks up a basket of food and hands me a stack of wooden trays. "You can take these. Ready?"

"Totally."

Instead of leading me outside, she takes me down a dark corridor off the kitchen and leads us into a cellar.

"Where are we going?"

She casts a look over her shoulder. "To the prison tower's entrance of course."

"So, it is underground," I say more to myself than to her.

"Of course."

When we get to the cellar, she pulls open a door in the floor, and we descend a narrow set of stairs. Underneath the palace, the corridors are dark, damp, and musty.

I sneeze repeatedly before Mossie tells me to please stop, like I'm doing it just to annoy her. At least she's polite about it.

After a while of going along the same narrow corridor, we come to a room where three guards are sitting around playing cards.

One is a fire fae, with smoke for hair and skin that glows like embers.

"Whoa," I say before I can stop myself. "Smoke hair. That's awesome. You don't even have to brush it, huh? I hate brushing my hair," I confess, pulling my braid forward. "It takes forever. Plus, I have a sensitive scalp. It gets very tender up there, you know? I'd love to have smoke hair, though. Talk about volume! But what about when you go to sleep? Doesn't your pillow combust? Ooh, I bet hats are real tricky, too."

All three guards stare at me.

The fire fae makes a face at me and then turns to Mossie. "What the fuck?"

Mossie waves a hand and laughs, although it comes out a bit hysterically. "Oh, don't mind her. She's new here. Hasn't seen many other fae except her own kind."

She shoots me a wide-eyed look over her shoulder that says, "Shut up and stop being an idiot."

I clear my throat. "Sorry, I guess I'm just a little bit nervous," I say, going closer to their table.

The fire fae shakes his head and goes back to his card game. "Get on with it."

Mossie hurries forward, motioning for me to do the same. She sets up the basket of food on a long table beside the door, and I help her divvy up portions on the trays I carry.

It's not that easy to do with one hand. She hasn't noticed yet, so there is that at least. I hold my arm awkwardly under my apron, trying to make it look like my hand is simply in my pocket.

As we serve up the small trays of food, my stomach clenches. Every tray only gets a tiny hunk of hard bread alongside the worst looking soup I've ever seen. Besides the grossness factor, it's not even enough food to sustain a child.

"What is this?" I hiss.

"It's the prisoner's food," she replies as if I'm an idiot.

"This is disgusting. And not enough."

"They're *prisoners*. You think the royals really care? We feed them what we're ordered to feed them."

I'm furious. So much so that I'm seeing red, but I swallow it down.

"Which one is Blix?"

The guards are talking amongst themselves, totally immersed in their cards, but Mossie points out the object of her desire. He has deep blue skin and eyes that look like the ocean.

"A water sprite?" I ask.

She nods. "Yeah, and my flowers could use a little watering, if you catch my drift."

I snort out a laugh. The third guard looks like a cross between a goblin and a giant. He's all bulbous and clunky. Not a looker, that one.

"Let's get Blix to notice you then, shall we?" I whisper, making her grin in response.

She adjusts her boobs in her dress and the flowers on her head to her satisfaction. And because I'm a cupid of my word, I approach the table where Blix is sitting, pulling Mossie with me.

I pretend to trip, bringing her down with me, and practi-

48

cally shove her into Blix's arms. I immediately blow a hit of Lust into his face and then straighten up.

I watch as the Lust hits his system, and he stares down at the girl in his arms like he's seeing her for the first time.

One second they're staring at each other, and the next, the sprites are making out like they're trying to suck each other's faces off. It's awesome.

The other two guards stare in shock for a moment before clunky guy starts laughing. Fire dude reaches over and smacks the water sprite on the back of the head. "Blix. Knock it off and put her tongue back in her own mouth."

Blix rears back, panting slightly. He looks at Mossie and then to his comrade sheepishly.

"Sorry," he grumbles.

"You can be the one to serve the prisoners," the fire fae sneers at him, making Blix groan in response.

"Sorry, gotta go," he tells Mossie, lifting her out of his lap and setting her on her feet. "Duty calls."

Mossie still looks dazed from the kiss, but she manages to give him a nod.

Crap. I thought when Mossie said she served the prisoners, she really meant served them, not just brought up the food. I have to get in there.

"I could help you," I blurt out a little too loudly.

All four fae look over at me. "I mean, it was my fault, I tripped and shoved Mossie into you. I could help you serve the prisoners if you'd like."

My heart pounds in my chest. I really need to see my guys. I'm close. So close.

Blix opens his mouth to answer, but fire fae beats him to it. "No. Only guards are permissible in the towers. Run along now," he says condescendingly. "I'm sure you have a stone to polish or a rug to beat somewhere."

I glare at him. "First of all, you don't polish stone, you scrub it. And second, beating rugs is harder than you think.

So if you're one of those assholes who don't wipe their feet before they walk inside on the carpet, I hope a kelpie kidnaps you the next time you take a bath."

He scowls at me and his fiery skin glows a deeper red. His hands erupt into flames. Whoa. Guess I pissed him off.

"She's kidding!" Mossie says quickly with a nervous laugh, coming up beside me. "We'll be going now."

"Yeah, we'll let you get back to your super hard job of playing poker," I taunt. I don't even know why I do it. My brain certainly isn't happy with my behavior. It keeps yelling at me to shut the hell up.

Fire fae guy glares at me some more, and yeah, with his flame hands he looks pretty scary, but clunky guy breaks the tension when he rasps, "What's poker?"

Right. Human card games aren't exactly common knowledge around here. Mossie doesn't let me answer. She simply gives Blix a wave and pulls me out of the room.

She doesn't let go of my arm until we get all the way back to the cellar, and then she whirls on me. "What the hell was that?"

"Sorry, I know. That fire guy just really irritated me."

She rolls her eyes. "Ferno irritates everyone. But he's powerful, and you don't want to get on his bad side, trust me."

"Noted."

"But Blix..." She sighs and her eyes go all sparkly as she gazes off to the side. "He was a wonderful kisser. He tasted like a lake."

I scrunch my nose. I'm not sure I'd think a kiss was wonderful if it tasted like pond water, but who am I to judge?

"Thanks for your help. Good idea with that push."

"Anytime. Matchmaking is my thing."

When we make it to the kitchens and go our separate ways, I can't help the disappointment clawing at me. This endeavor was a total bust. If the guards are the only ones allowed inside the towers, how am I going to get to my guys? Will I wake up in the morning with more of my body missing? It's not a good thought. What if my lips disappear? Or my boobs? I need those.

When I open the door to my room, I nearly jump out of my skin to find that I'm not alone. "Holy balls of hellfire, you scared me."

Princess Soora turns around from the window to face me. "I'm sorry. I didn't mean to startle you."

I quickly close the door behind me and stand before her, keeping my missing hand hidden from view. "What are you doing here?" I cringe at how that sounds. I probably should be more eloquent when I'm talking to the freaking princess of the realm. "Sorry, I mean, how can I help you, Your Highness?"

She clasps her hands in front of her all regal-like. She's super good at being regal. I wonder if she ever doesn't look regal? Maybe when she gets the stomach flu? It's gotta be hard to look regal when you're puking your guts out. Although, if anyone could do it, it would be her. She's even a regal crier. She was all cute sniffles and pretty purple cheeks.

"How have you adjusted here?" she asks. "Any trouble?"

"Everything's been fine," I tell her.

I wonder if she knows about my trip to the towers? But how could she have found out so quickly? Maybe I'm in trouble. The thought doesn't sit well. I need at least one royal on my side.

"You told me that you were here for the genfin prisoners."

Shit. She does know. "Yeah. I mean yes, Your Highness."

"I made some inquiries after you told me that, and I discovered that there are only three genfins that we have in the towers right now. The noble house of Covey Fircrown."

"Yes."

She starts walking around my small space, but her

movement just makes me nervous. Is she going to throw me out? Maybe put me in a cell, too?

Ugh. I'm just not made for jail. I'm pink, for crying out loud.

"Unless you knew the covey from many years ago, which I think is not the case since you've only just become corporeal, that means that you met them just recently. Which means you somehow breached the barrier over their banishment island."

Oh. So this is what she's here for. Still, I don't know what she's getting at.

"Yeah, I did. It's like the glamour. Some magic doesn't work with me."

"But some magic does?"

"The guys, I mean, when the genfins used magic on me, it worked." I'm not going to mention the potion Arachno had me drink.

"Hmm. Well, regardless, it seems our most powerful barriers have no effect on you. You can simply pass through them."

"I guess so."

She stops walking and faces me again. "I want you to fly to an island, pass through the barrier, and gather information for me."

"What island? And what kind of information?"

"One of my informants gave me information on an island that the prince is using in secret. We don't know what he's using it for, but there have been whispers of him building some kind of weapon. I need to know what's on that island, and you're the only one who can access it without raising alarms by lowering the barrier."

"But if it's that secret, it's probably protected with more than just a barrier," I point out.

"That's true. Which is why I'll lend you one of my personal guards to take with you in case they have a protection perimeter set up around the barrier. He'll also act as your guide. He has the rough coordinates of where this island is supposed to be located."

Crap. This all sounds way above my pay grade. Wait, do rebels get paid? Something tells me no.

"I want to help you, Princess Soora, but I'm not sure I'm cut out for this kind of thing."

She comes forward and takes my hand. Thankfully, it's the one that's still there. That would have been awkward.

"I need you to do this, Emelle. If the prince is building some sort of weapon, I need to know what it is and what his plans are for it. There have been talks of him using it to take out entire islands of the fae who have been most vocal about dissension and calling for change. If he succeeds, he'll not only be killing thousands, but he'll squash the rebellion as well. Many good fae will die."

I blow out a breath. I know I have to help her. Not just because I owe her, but because I don't want the prince to get away with this, either. There's just one problem...

"Umm, okay, I want to help you, but there's a little bit of a problem."

She looks at me curiously, and I raise my other arm and hold it out to her. She looks down in confusion for a moment before she realizes what's missing. A gasp escapes her purple lips. "Your hand! What happened?"

"I'm sort of...turning invisible again."

Her eyes meet mine. "You can't control it?"

I shake my head and come clean. "It has to do with the genfins. Apparently, because they were the first fae to make skin-to-skin contact with me, they also became my anchors to this world. Whatever magic Prince Elphar smacked me with wasn't permanent, but the magic leeched onto the guys and made it so that I can stay as long as I keep close to them. If I'm apart from them for too long, or too far away, well..." I motion to my hand to show what happens.

"Can you come back?"

"Right now, I'd get my arm back if I touch all of them. If I turn all the way invisible…I don't know. I don't think so," I bite my lip.

"This is very troubling, Emelle."

I snort. "Yeah, understatement of the century. Believe me, I'm not in any rush to go back to the Veil where no one can see me. And even worse, once the genfins take a mate, the magic binding me to them will most likely dissolve, and I'll be screwed. And not in the good way."

She frowns and starts walking again. "This is problematic."

"I know. I tried to sneak into the towers tonight to see them, but it didn't go as planned."

"No one can get in there except for the guards. Not even me," she admits.

I make a disappointed sound. "More of me will disappear the longer I'm away from them. And if I travel to that island, I'll be gone for sure. It's too far away. I don't know if I can come back from turning totally incorporeal, even if I get back to the guys."

Princess Soora sighs and rubs her eyes. "This changes things. I need to think. It will be no use sending you if you cannot relay the information back to me."

"Plus, you know, I'd really like to stay alive in this realm and all."

She smiles slightly. "Indeed. Do they know? The genfins?"

I shake my head, and her smile turns sad. "Someone did tell me there may be a way to anchor myself to something or someone else. If you can find me a way to do that, then I'll help you and fly to the weapon island."

"Do you know how this can be done?"

I shake my head. "No clue."

"The culling trials start soon," Princess Soora points out.

"Yeah, and I need to be there with them."

She nods once. "Alright. Let me think on this, and I'll contact you again tomorrow. Will you be okay until then?"

No idea. "Yep. Totally."

"Okay. I will leave you now. Rest and stay in your room tomorrow. I'll come for you as soon as I can."

"Sure."

When I'm alone in my room again, I undress and pop out my wings before lying on the bed. Maybe with the princess's help, I can find a new anchor. Let's just hope I don't disappear before then.

CHAPTER 8

'm sleeping peacefully when a sudden knock jars me awake. I jump to my feet and stagger to the door, throwing it open with bleary eyes and a barely-aware brain.

In front of me is one of Princess Soora's personal guards. I can tell, because he's wearing her house colors that remind me of a peacock and has a sigil of a violet on his breastplate.

He's not high fae—that much is obvious. High fae are sinewy in their lean gracefulness. This man is not lean. Or graceful. He's built like a bear, and although they look nothing alike, his massive size makes me think of Ronak with a pang of longing.

But while Ronak is big with perfectly chiseled muscles, this fae is bulkier and wider with equally impressive muscles. He has a thick, longhaired mohawk down the center of his scalp, and his hair is as bright red as a stop sign.

He also has a golden ring pierced through his septum. "Gods, that had to have hurt," I say, pointing to his nose piercing. "Did it hurt? Never mind, you don't even have to answer that. I would cry if I got a piercing like that. This one time, I was watching this tattoo parlor all day, because I kind of have a thing for guys with tattoos, so it was like, the perfect place to watch, you know?"

He doesn't say he knows, so I just shrug and keep going. "Well, anyway, then this girl got her nipples pierced. Her nipples! And as if that wasn't bad enough, then she got a piercing *down there*," I say in a mock whisper as I point to my crotch. "I didn't even know they did that at the time. Now *that's* gotta be worse than the nose, don't you think?"

He still doesn't answer me, so I soldier on. "She didn't cry, but I'm pretty sure she was high on something. She kept giggling and talking about boiled eggs. That can't be normal. But if I ever get a piercing, I'll just be sure to get hooked up with some drugs first. Did you take drugs when you got pierced? Wait...what kind of drugs do fae have? I bet fae drugs are awesome."

I look up at him expectantly, but I can see from his expression that I've rendered him speechless.

When I finally drag my eyes away from his nose piercing, I notice that his face is rather handsome and that he has a circle of red around his irises that matches his hair. I also notice that those eyes are locked onto my chest.

I look down and notice that my gaping nightdress with the rip in the back has slid down at some point, and the top half of my boobs are out for display. I quickly pull up my shirt, but his eyes just flick to the red wings behind me instead. I cringe.

Crap. I really should think before opening the door to strangers.

"I'm hoping the princess sent you?" I ask. When he nods, I breathe out a sigh of relief. "Good. Come in, then."

I turn so that he can pass by me. The second he takes a step inside my room and gets closer to me, he freezes. His entire bulky body tenses, and he snaps his head in my direction.

Without preamble, he brings his nose to the crook of my neck and *sniffs* me.

Yeah. Sniffs.

I freeze in place at the hot air of his breath that travels down my skin.

"Umm, what's happening right now?"

As covertly as I can, I bring my nose to my armpit and take a whiff, just in case. Hmm, I'm not picking up anything stinky. After another sniff from him, he pulls back with great reluctance, and I notice that the red circles around his irises are much larger, and they're sort of...pulsing.

"Your eyes are doing some weird shit. Are you, like, losing it? Are you gonna have a psychotic episode? Do I smell bad to you? Because seriously, I bathed. Stop making this weird."

His nostrils flare and he closes his eyes as he breathes in again. When he opens them and looks at me, the red in his eyes seems to have calmed down. In a super low, gravelly voice, he says, "You do not smell bad. Your smell is..." He trails off, unable to find the right words. "You are my mate."

My eyebrows shoot up, and I open my mouth in surprise, but before I can say anything, his hand has snaked around the back of my neck, and he's crashing his lips against mine.

Whoa.

The kiss isn't soft or polite or even tenacious. His kiss is meant to make me feel one thing—claimed.

And yeah, I let him claim the hell out of me, because he's a super good kisser. Face-turning, hair-yanking, tongue-sucking kind of a good kisser.

Plus, every time he inhales, it's like he's trying to drink me in through his sense of smell.

It takes several hot and heavy seconds for me to open my eyes and have enough wherewithal to push him away. He doesn't budge.

He's way too big for my pathetic little shove to make any impact whatsoever. And let's face it, I wasn't really trying.

Of course, that's when I realize that not only is my right hand still missing, but now the invisibility has spread all the way up to the shoulder. I squeak inside his mouth, and at my sound of distress, he opens his eyes and pulls away.

I stare down at my arm in shock. "Oh no, oh no, *oh no*."

He holds my shoulder, seeing the gaping space where my arm should be and frowns. "Princess Soora warned me of this," he says in that low voice of his. "It was the reason she sent me to you. I am to guard you and watch, in case you leave completely."

Hearing that I might totally poof-out of the physical world makes me freak, and I feel my eyes fill with tears. He forces me to look at him with a gentle hand that comes up to cup my cheek.

His hand is so big that he basically paws the entire half of my face, making me smile through a sob. "I'm fine," I say. I wipe my eyes and step back, his hand dropping away.

I can feel that my lips are swollen from his very intimate greeting. "So...you're not gonna hear me complaining about that kiss because we both know I enjoyed it, but umm, who are you?"

He cringes. "I apologize if I scared you. I am not usually that way. I am an honorable fae, I swear it. The mate scent just took me by surprise," he says earnestly.

The way his eyes plead with me to forgive his presumptuous greeting makes me melt.

"I am Okot, my beloved."

My brows hit my hairline.

"Your beloved?"

He nods.

"Yes. I am a lamassu. When we smell our mate, we know it immediately. Your smell. It is intoxicating. I want to kiss you again."

I grin. "It was that good, huh?"

"Of course," he says seriously. He flicks his eyes just past my head. "Your wings are red."

I look over my shoulder. "Yep. Just like your hair. And your eyes. We match."

Now it's his turn to grin. "Yes."

Looking out the gray window, I realize it's still early. First bell hasn't even rung yet. My room seems tiny with him in it. His bulk takes up so much space that he looks almost comical.

"So, Okot. What does Princess Soora want us to do? As you can see, I'm getting worse," I say, lifting my vanishing shoulder.

"I will not let you disappear," he declares earnestly.

Aww.

"That's sweet, but I'm not sure this can be stopped."

"We will find a way."

Gods, we just met, and he's already become my champion.

I knew it. I'm totally lovable. My first impression with the genfins was a one-off. Or a three-off, whatever. Point is, this dude is a fan of me, and I'm pretty psyched about it. Too bad the guys aren't here to see this.

"I wish I'd met you years ago. Too bad I was in a different realm. And a different physical plane. I would've jumped on this whole mate thing before."

He frowns. "Before?"

"Yeah," I sigh in disappointment, and I sit back on my bed to undo the messy braid from my hair with one hand.

When my hair gets tangled and I make a noise of frustration, I feel the bed dip as Okot sits behind me and takes over. The gentleness with which he slowly loosens my hair is so dissimilar to his lumbering look that it makes me smile.

"Why just before?" he asks quietly, the tension evident in his tone.

I hesitate. "Princess Soora told you what I am?"

"She did. But she swore me to secrecy, so you need not worry. She told me you are a cupid, although I admit I do not know exactly what that is. She also told me that powerful magic from the prince caused you to manifest here, and that your magic is fading because you are being kept away from your anchors. She has only entrusted me with this information. I have served the princess and her family for many years. You can trust me."

I nod. "Well, aside from the fact that I don't belong in this realm, and that I'm probably going to fade completely in a few days' time unless I can get to my anchors...there's also another thing you should probably know."

"What's that?" he asks, his thick fingers kneading at my scalp, giving me delicious chills. I guess I'll just come clean. I don't like beating around the bush. What did the bush ever do to be knocked around like that, anyway? Nothing, that's what.

"Well, see, there's this covey of genfins..."

CHAPTER 9

"**A**nd these genfins have become important to me. Like, *super* important, if you catch what I'm throwing," I explain.

Okot's fingers go still on my head. I turn around to look at him to gauge his expression. He looks like I just took the last cookie out of the jar and stomped on it.

"Oh, don't look like that. I'm sorry. I didn't know about the mate smelly thing. Maybe it's just a coincidence? Maybe you just *think* I'm your mate because cupids smell differently?"

He shakes his head. "No." He leans in and inhales me from the tip of my head to the edge of my shoulder. "No. This smell. It's calling to me. You are my mate."

I clear my throat because this sniffing thing is really getting to me. Like, in a good, sexy way. It doesn't seem like sniffing would be intimate, but somehow, with him, it is.

I want to lie down in a pile of pillows while he runs his stubbly jaw all over my skin and let his nose go to town.

He clears his throat. "These genfins...they are the ones in the prison?"

"Yeah."

The last thing I want to do is hurt him. Goddess knows how long I've waited for someone to declare his heart to me. But it wouldn't be fair to him if I didn't tell him the truth. He's too endearing and completely unaffected, unlike any other fae in this whole damn palace. There are no pretenses with him, and I like that. He wears his heart on his sleeve and says what he means, just like me.

And the fact that he looks at me like he wants to keep me forever makes me want to keep him, too. Questioning insta-love? Psh. I invented that shit. I once made two people fall in love in only four minutes. At a gas station. While they were eating chili dogs. Yeah. I'm badass like that.

"I'm sorry," I tell him. "But I don't know how this can work if—"

My words cut off as Okot leans in so his face is in the crook of my neck, and he inhales deeply again. Big guy just can't get enough.

When he leans back to look at me, his voice is even raspier than before. "Now you."

My heart is going about a million beats a minute. "What?"

When did my voice get so breathy?

He cocks his head to the side and bares his neck to me. "Now you."

I suddenly feel shy, but the look on his heated face draws me in anyway, and before I know it, I'm inhaling his scent.

And...holy mother of mate sniffs. Did I just moan?

"You smell...you smell..." I can't even get the words out before I'm sniffing him again. "You smell warm. Like sunshine on trees. Or a fire in wintertime. Spicy. But like the sweetest spice ever. *Ohmygods*."

I feel his huge paw of a hand cup the back of my head again, and then we're both inhaling each other at the same time.

63

"I thought about it," he says, nuzzling his nose against my cheek.

I can feel the cold metal of his piercing against my flushed skin. "Hmm?" My voice is husky and my nose is still buried in his neck like I'm a horny vampire. "Thought about what?"

"About me leaving you to your genfins."

My eyes snap open, and I pull back. Disappointment floods me. Yeah, I just met him. So what? I want to keep him, dammit.

"Oh."

"I thought about it, and I decided that it's not going to happen."

Hope flares. "Which part?"

"Me leaving. You're my mate. I'm yours. If your heart has love for others, I will accept them," he says all romantic-like. "Unless they hurt you. If they hurt you, I will end them." He says this last part with such macho-intensity that I know it's not just an idle threat. And by his sheer size, I know even Ronak would have a hard time going head-to-head with him. I pat him on his huge bicep just to drive the thought home.

I'm grinning again. I can't help it. This burly, handsome teddy bear fae guy just declared me as his mate. He smells super yummy, and he played with my hair. Plus, he kisses like a god.

Like I'm going to fight this? *Puhlease.*

"Well, alright then. Sounds good to me."

He seems surprised at my acceptance. "Sounds good?"

"Yep. We're mates. Is there, like, a special mate thing we're supposed to do?"

"Our mating will be confirmed when we are intimate."

Well, mating sex sounds great. Except, we really did just meet, and… "Could we possibly, like, table that?"

His face falls. "You don't wish to be my mate? You are rejecting the mate match?"

At his disappointed look, I rush to explain. "No! I mean, yes. I mean...gods." I huff out a frustrated breath.

Stellar vocabulary skills, Emelle. Really top notch stuff I'm spewing.

"What I'm trying to say is that I'd love for us to get to know each other. I'm not rejecting the mate match. Not at all. Anyone who rejected you would be the biggest idiot in every realm that ever existed. And I'm not just saying that because you're superhot, either. Although, if I'm honest, it's a real plus. The mohawk and piercing is doing it for me."

He grins.

"And based on your kissing skills, I'm sure sex with you would be awesome. Believe me, I have spent decades wanting some awesome sex. But besides the fact that we just met fifteen minutes ago, I'm sort of going invisible right now, and my genfins are facing the culling, and I just—"

He stops me with a hand around my neck. His thumb caresses my throat gently. The touch is possessive yet sweet, and I find my anxiety draining out of me. "You do not need to explain more. I have waited for you for a long time. I will cherish our time together. When you are ready, then we will confirm our mate match. There is no rush. As long as you are not rejecting me, I am happy. Okay?"

I breathe out a sigh of relief. "Okay. Thanks for understanding."

"Can I kiss you again?" he asks.

I thought he'd never ask.

I crash my lips against his. Before I know it, I'm on my back on the bed, my hand is tangled in his red mohawk, and both of his hands are holding the sides of my face. Gods, this guy. He may look intimidating, but he is seriously a sweetheart.

Before things can go any further, another knock sounds on my door, and then Duru is suddenly storming in and frowning down at us.

She leans over and smacks Okot on the back of the head, making him grunt and stand up. Even though he's a good three feet taller than her, he looks thoroughly chastised under her glare.

Hands on hips, she looks at us as we smooth out our clothes and hair like we're a couple of horny teenagers she just caught behind the bleachers. "Just what do you think you're doing?"

"Sorry, Lady Duru, but Emelle Cupid is my mate."

He said cupid like it's my last name, and he claimed me as his mate like it's the end-all to any question she could possibly ask. I like his style.

Duru sighs in exasperation and then starts picking up the dirty clothes that are on my floor. She can't help herself from tidying up. "Mate or not, Princess Soora did not send you here so you could have your way with Miss Emelle."

Okot straightens. "Yes, Lady."

I stand up and try to cross my arms but end up just flopping my left arm against my stomach awkwardly. Ugh. Having one arm sucks. "Hey, don't yell at him. Maybe it was *me* who was having my way with *him*."

Duru snorts at my pathetic display of protectiveness of a guy I just met. She moves on to dusting my windowsill using the corner of her apron. "No matter who the irresponsible party is, we don't have time for those shenanigans. The princess just sent me with news."

"What news?"

"The culling. They're starting today."

My heart gets stuck in my throat. "Today?"

She gets down on all fours and starts scrubbing at a spot on the floor that I'm pretty sure is just part of the stone. She frowns at it when it doesn't come off. "Yes. Get dressed and hide your wings. Okot and I can take you to the portal. The prisoners will be leaving within the hour."

Crap. We need to time this just right, or I'm a goner.

Okot must see my panic, because he forces me to look at him with a hand on my cheek. "What's wrong?"

"I can't be that far away from them. If I do, it's bye-bye, Emelle. They can't pass through the portal without me."

A line appears between his thick red brows as he frowns. "I will not allow you to disappear."

He turns to Duru, who's still scrubbing at that spot on the floor. "We need to know precisely how and when they're being transported."

Duru gets back to her feet, but she's still glowering at the floor like she can't believe that spot is defying her. "All the prisoners competing in the culling are being transported through a portal near the towers."

"When?"

"Like I said, within the hour."

"Not good enough," he says. "We need to know exact timing."

"Do I look like a prison guard to you?" she snaps.

They glare at each other, and I carefully step between them. "Alrighty, you two. Let's just focus on the problem at hand." I look down at my invisible limb. "Or the problem at *arm*."

No one laughs at my terrible joke. I shoot a look at Okot. Some mate he is. He tries to smile, but we both know it's too late.

"Is there any way I could go through the prisoner's portal with them?" I ask hopefully.

Duru shakes her head and rubs her curly eyebrows. I really want to poke them to see how fast they spring back up. "No, definitely not. You'd be caught immediately for going anywhere near there."

"Okay…then can we somehow time it so that I'm going through my portal at the same time as the guys through theirs?"

Duru and Okot both go quiet in thought.

After a moment, Duru snaps her fingers and blurts, "Twiddlefairies."

"Bless you."

She shoots me a frown. "What?"

"Nothing."

She sighs at me. "We can use twiddlefairies. They can communicate with each other no matter the distance. We can have one go where the prisoners are and one with us."

"They won't be seen?"

"No. They're very small, no bigger than a butterfly."

"Okay, perfect. How can we get them?"

She licks the corner of her apron and uses it to start polishing my doorknob.

And I mean that literally. Not in a weird, sexual innuendo kind of way.

"They like brussels sprouts," she muses.

Behind me, Okot scoffs, "Impossible. Nobody likes brussels sprouts."

Duru shrugs. "It's what I've heard."

I've never tasted brussels sprouts or seen a twiddlefairy, so who the heck am I to have an opinion on the matter?

"Okay…can we get some of these gross sprout thingies to try to lure the twiddles with?"

Duru nods and drops her hands. My knob is practically gleaming now. My *door*knob. Geez.

"Emelle, get ready to leave. Wear something to hide your…disappearing predisposition."

That's a fancy way of putting it.

"And no trading tongues while I'm gone," she says, pointing between Okot and me.

"Yes, ma'am," I tell her.

She huffs and leaves. The second the door shuts after her, Okot grabs my face and starts kissing me again.

I pull away and give him a pointed look. "If you're my mate, you have to laugh at all my jokes," I admonish.

His face sobers, and he nods seriously. "Of course, my beloved. I won't fail you again."

I smile. This mate stuff is fun.

CHAPTER 10

The portal is like a vertical whirlpool suspended in the air. It's set up in the palace courtyard, and there's a line of fae passing through every minute or so after being cleared by the guards maintaining it. I'm standing in the front with Okot and Duru, but with every shake of Duru's head, I let a fae pass me to go through first.

The guards overseeing the portal transportation keep shooting me curious gazes, but because Okot is with me, they don't challenge my hesitation to cross through.

I look over and up at Okot's unyielding face. If I were those guards, I wouldn't say shit to him either. I see Duru tilt her head slightly as she listens to the tiny twiddlefairy that's hidden in her poufy hair. No one else is any the wiser about the fairy's presence.

When she shakes her head again, I sigh and turn to the group of three servants behind me. "After you."

The fae give me curious looks but pass by to approach the guards and go through the portal. I think part of their looks have to do with my clothing. I'm hotter than a pepper's armpit in this getup.

The cloak I'm wearing is meant for wintertime, but it was

the only thing that concealed my missing arm. Every minute feels like an hour as I stand here under the sweltering sun, and my sore feet are once again stuffed into heels. It makes my ass look great, though.

I feel myself lean more and more into Okot until he finally snakes an arm around my waist and all but holds me up. Gods, he's helpful.

I'd jump onto his back and make him carry me if all of these damn nosy fae weren't around. I have a feeling he'd let me do it regardless.

He doesn't talk much, but I've learned that Okot is a man of few words. Unlike me. And everyone else in line, apparently. Everyone is talking excitedly about the culling, which only adds to my nervousness. Already, I can hear bets being placed and speculation about which prisoners will come out victoriously. Apparently, there are over two dozen "contestants." I don't know these other prisoners or how they stack up against my guys, but I especially don't like the buzz around someone called The Dragon. By the sounds of it, he's a vicious motherfucker. I don't want him anywhere near my guys.

I let four more groups pass by before Duru cocks her head again and starts nodding to whatever she's hearing from the twiddle.

"They're next in line," Duru whispers. "Get ready, but you'll need to stall a bit."

I nod and step up to the guards. "Finally ready?" one of them asks.

I laugh nervously. "Oh, yeah. I'm just nervous, you know? It's my first portal and all. I guess you could say you'll be popping my portal cherry."

The guard starts to cough like his spit went down the wrong tube. His wide eyes look me up and down, and his green cheeks turn dark with a blush.

Okot points at his face with a glare. "No."

The guard blanches and then quickly looks away from me, as if trying to rid every lust-filled thought that swarmed his mind so that Okot doesn't deck him. "Right, um, this... umm...I just need names and titles."

"Officer Okot. Personal guard to Princess Soora, assigned to accompany Duru and Emelle, personal handmaidens to Princess Soora," Okot answers, still glaring.

The second guard starts writing it all down while the first nods timidly, looking anywhere but at me.

Duru clutches my hand and squeezes. "They're going through now!" she whisper-yells.

I frantically look at the guards, but they're still writing and checking out our names. Shit. I am *not* going to turn invisible because of fricking paperwork.

Before the guards can stop me, I push past them to the portal and jump.

Portals are weird. I feel wet. Like I jumped into a pool of slime. And yet my skin feels powdery? Then there's this spinning feeling. Except it's like the world is spinning while I'm stuck still. Then there's the falling. I'm definitely falling. *Or am I rising?*

The portal spits me out, and I land hard on my feet. Unfortunately for me (and my feet), I'm still wearing heels, which means both my ankles turn at the sudden crash, and I fall to the ground face-first.

The wind gets knocked out of me, but before I can even contemplate trying to stand up on my own, I feel strong arms come around me as he helps me to my feet.

I wince at my sore ankles, making him frown. "You're hurt."

"Heels suck."

Duru enters right behind us, and then there's a bored guard shooing us on. "Move it along."

I take one pained step before Okot scoops me up and carries me. I practically melt in his arms and bury my face into his chest to breathe him in. "This mate scent stuff is seriously amazing."

I feel a rumble of approval in his chest as he sniffs my hair.

"Would you two knock it off?" Duru snaps.

I look around at the new island. We're on the top of a hillside. Far below, I can see a huge amphitheater. The thing is massive.

"Is that where the culling competition is being held?"

"Yes," Duru answers, looking down at it with displeasure. "Just an elaborate execution block if you ask me. Don't be fooled by the pomp. The prince doesn't want any of those banished fae to live. He designs these culling games so that few of them will make it out alive."

I clench my jaw in determination even as my stomach drops with worry. "My guys will make it."

Okot turns us and starts walking away. On the other side of the hill, I see hundreds of square wooden buildings erected.

"What are those?"

"Those are all of the cabins for everyone to stay in for the week until the culling ends."

"Huh. Even the prince and princess are staying in one of those?"

Duru gives me a look that says, "No, idiot," and then points to a spot behind us. "The royals will be staying there."

It's a castle.

Of *course* it's a castle. Not as big as the palace back in Highvale on the kingdom island, but it's not anything to sneeze at, either.

"Yeah, that makes more sense," I say.

The gray stone castle sits alone on the grass, a single dirt road connecting it to the wooden cabins and then the amphitheater further away.

"Since your condition is deteriorating, you'll be staying in one of the cabins with Okot," Duru explains. "My place is with the princess, so I won't see you much while we're here unless the princess wishes to bring you a message."

"Okay."

Duru looks between us. "Behave. Stay out of sight, and here," she says, shoving a bag toward Okot. "You'll find some more dye in case you need a refresher, and some new clothes. When you go to watch the culling, you'll need to be dressed like a lesser noble, not a servant, or you won't be able to watch. Okot can try to find out where your genfins are being held. But don't get caught."

"I knew you liked me."

Duru scoffs, but I see a smile trying to emerge. "You still owe my princess a favor, and you can't fulfill that if you're dead."

I grin. "You're a real softie."

"And if you *are* caught, I will deny ever knowing you."

"Stop it, your loyalty is making me blush."

She rolls her eyes and starts walking down the hill toward the castle. "And don't sniff each other in public so much. It's indecent," she says over her shoulder.

"So fae can have sweaty revelry sex in the middle of a party, but if mates smell each other, it's indecent?" I ask, looking up at Okot.

He just shrugs. The fae are weird.

"Hey, what did you say you were, again?"

"I am a lamassu."

"Oh...right. Lamassu. Duh. Of course."

He levels me with a look. "You have no idea what that is, do you?"

"Not even an inkling."

He grins, showing his nice big teeth. "I'll show you. Can you stand?"

I nod, and he gently sets me down on my feet. There's a

slight twinge in my ankles, but nothing I can't handle. I'm tough like that.

Okot takes a few steps back and then hunches over. One blink, he's standing in front of me, and the next, a gigantic winged bull is in his place.

A. Giant. Flying. Bull.

"Wow. Holy cow," I exclaim.

Then I snicker at my own unintentional joke, because I'm hilarious.

Just like in his human form, he still has his bright red mohawk and the gold ring through his nose. He's huge. His hooves are as big as my face.

Aside from the long hair on his mohawk, the rest of him is jet black. He paws the ground when I step closer. I draw my hand up to pet him, but when I hesitate, he leans his head down and nuzzles my hand with his nose, making me laugh.

"You're adorable."

He grunts in displeasure.

"Oh, right. I mean...you're very strong. Ferocious. Fierce. Intimidating. Big. And, umm..." I breathe out through my nose, at a loss for words. "Is that enough manly descriptors? I've run out."

He grunts again, so I think I'm in the clear. Without warning, he shifts back into his fae form.

"Impressive. You're the best looking flying bull I've ever seen."

He tilts his head to look at me. "It pleases me that you are satisfied with my lamassu form."

I look him up and down. That's not the only form that pleases me.

"Will you fly me one day?"

He nods. "Of course, my beloved."

Beloved. Gah. Gets me every time.

Finally, this cupid is getting some lovin' of her own.

"Come, let us find your cabin so you may rest."

I could really get used to this whole taking care of me stuff.

"I need to see them," I say, stopping him with a touch on his arm.

He sighs, as if he were afraid I was going to say that. After a moment of studying my determined expression, he nods. "I will make it so."

CHAPTER 11

Okot is true to his word. Soon after claiming a cabin, he leaves to go see if there's any way we can get to the guys.

Meanwhile, I switch out of my servant's uniform for the finer gown and heels that Duru packed for me. My skin is still dark pink enough to pass for high fae, so at least I don't have to worry about that, but I do need to tidy myself up a bit if I'm going to pass for a noble. Even lesser nobles don't walk around with frizzy braids and naked faces.

Okot doesn't come back to the cabin until nightfall. I'm pacing around the small wooden space when he walks in, and I nearly jump out of my skin. "Where have you been? I was worried! I thought you got caught or something."

He tilts his head at me like my freak-out confuses him. "I apologize, my beloved. I did not mean to cause you distress."

"What happened? You were gone for hours."

"Come," he says, holding out his hand for me.

Giving him a curious look, I place my small hand in his, and he leads me outside.

There are still fae arriving from the portal on the hill, so the rows of cabins are busy with fae coming and going as they claim their spaces. Word is that the culling will start first thing in the morning, although I have no idea what time or what to expect.

Okot leads me past the cabins, all the way to the amphitheater. At night, it looks ominous. Its sheer size is intimidating. A guard stands at one of the entrances, but all he does is nod to Okot as we pass him by.

Inside, he leads me down a curving passageway until we get to what can only be the backstage area. But instead of a green room, there are prison cells. Another guard stands watch here, and his steady gaze meets Okot's.

"Ten minutes. That's it."

Okot nods and pulls me forward toward the passageway where the cells are. The guard closes the door behind us, making it even darker than before. A lone lantern hangs on the wall, but it casts more shadows than light.

The further down the passageway we go, I notice that the constant pain in my gut lessens significantly. My body is tingling, too, and with more than just anticipation. I can feel the magic of my anchors trying to grab hold of me. My missing arm buzzes.

As we pass by the cells, I notice they're all slightly different from the others. Some are visible through bars, some are completely enclosed in stone or wood, and one is made entirely of iron. Some of the contestants eye us as we walk by, but none of them say anything.

At the very end of the hallway, I find them. I run up to their cell, my hand gripping the bars, and I'm unable to stop the sob that escapes me. At the sound, the three figures lying on the hard floor stir slightly.

"Okot, can you bring over that lantern?" I whisper.

He turns to go get it while I continue to stare inside the cell. When he gets back, he hangs the lantern beside their cell so I can get a better look. What I see makes my jaw clench.

My guys are curled up on the hard stone ground. They're

dirty, and I can only imagine how uncomfortable and hungry they must be. They weren't given a pallet bed or even a blanket. There's a single bucket in the corner that I'm sure isn't filled with water.

"Guys?" I call out, my voice shaky.

At my voice, three heads pop up on high alert, their sleep immediately ended. Evert gets up so quickly that I can't even track his movements. He's just suddenly in front of me, his tired face taking me in like he was afraid he'd never see me again.

"Fucking hell, Scratch. I've been worried."

I can't help the tears that start to trickle from my eyes. "Me too," I say, my voice cracking. "I missed you guys so much."

I try to memorize his face, his thick black beard, his bright blue eyes. The dimples are hiding, but I know they're there. I look over at Sylred and Ronak as they come over to join Evert by the bars. With all three of them in front of me again, all I want to do is squeeze into the cell with them.

"Don't cry," Sylred says quietly.

"Yeah, it fucking kills me when you cry," Evert chimes in.

I raise my hands to wipe away my tears, but I stop awkwardly. Duh, Emelle, you're still missing a freaking arm. Could I be any more obvious about it?

Ronak's eyes zero in on my empty sleeve. "What happened?"

His strong hands grip the bars until his knuckles turn white. Ronak's intense gaze makes my heart stutter a little. She gets excited when he goes all alpha-mode.

"Nothing," I say, quickly shifting away.

I'm not quick enough. Ronak's hand snaps out from between the bars and grips the empty fabric where my arm should be, yanking me forward.

Okot suddenly steps up behind me, grabbing my other

arm gently but firmly. I feel like I'm about to be the rope in a tug-of-war match.

"Do not manhandle her," Okot growls.

It's like my three genfins suddenly notice his presence, and crackling tension fills the air.

Evert's gaze flicks from me to Okot and then back again. "Who the fuck is this, Scratch?"

Hmm. How to introduce them... I open my mouth to answer when I feel Okot step closer, his chest pressing against my back. I can't help but relax against him, and the movement is not lost on anyone.

Did I just see flashes of jealousy cross their faces? I perk up a bit. I shouldn't love making them jealous, but...yep. I love it.

"Are you okay?" Okot asks me, ignoring the others' glares.

"I'm fine." Okot relaxes slightly and even releases his hold on my arm, but not before he leans down and inhales the scent of my hair.

"What the fuck? Don't smell her," Evert snaps.

"It's okay. We sniff. It's our thing," I explain.

The genfins just frown more.

"Right. Introductions. Okot, Evert is the one who says 'fuck' a lot. Sylred is the nice one. And that muscly one who always frowns is Ronak. Guys, this is Okot. I'm his mate," I say, wagging my brows.

All three genfins stare at me incredulously. Evert pinches the bridge of his nose and closes his eyes as if he just can't deal with me. I'm pretty sure I can hear him counting under his breath.

He looks up at Sylred. "She's been gone for a week. A. Fucking. Week. And she has a *mate*?"

"I'm right here—you can talk to me."

He shakes his head, still looking at Sylred. "No, I can't. Because if I look at you, then I'll have to look at him, and if I look at him, then I'll want to punch him in the fucking

80

throat. And based on the fucking size of your so-called fucking *mate*, that probably wouldn't end well for me."

I can't help but snicker. "You should see his bull form."

Evert tilts his head back and sighs. "Great. A fucking lamassu."

Sylred holds his hand out through the bars to shake Okot's hand. "I'm Sylred. Nice to meet you."

See? Always the nice one.

Evert rounds on Ronak. "This is your fault."

Ronak frowns. "My fault? How is this my fault?"

"You were a dick, and now she has a fucking mate!"

Ronak clenches his jaw. "Fuck you."

"No, I wanted to fuck *her*, but you put some covey guilt bullshit on me so I couldn't. I told you assholes this is what would happen. I told you she'd leave. And I told you, I'm fucking done with this covey if that happens. You want to go chase some female genfin's tail? Go for it. I'm done."

Evert is pissed. Like *really* freaking pissed. The way he's glaring at Ronak makes my stomach hurt, and I'm almost positive they're about to flip to beast mode and go at each other. I don't want them to get hurt.

Even more than that, I don't want them to destroy the tentative peace they've rebuilt over the last couple of weeks. I know the friendship is there, and I won't let them ruin it. Not over me. I'm supposed to be the glue. I'm the cupid that's supposed to heal their hearts. Not rip them further apart.

"Wait a minute," I interrupt. "Let's back up here. First of all, who said anything about me leaving? I didn't leave. I've been trying to see you this whole time. You're a hard covey to get to, you know? And I don't want you three to break up. I told you that already, remember? You aren't leaving your covey, Evert."

He levels a glare at me. "I can do whatever the fuck I want."

81

Gods, he's infuriating. Also really hot when he glares like that.

I narrow my eyes on him. "Stop. You three need each other. You have to get through this culling, and to do that, you need to have each other's backs. But even after that, you three belong together. I'm not going to leave, but if you dissolve the covey, I won't speak to any of you ever again."

The three of them stare back at me in varying frowns. "Is that clear?" I prompt.

Evert clenches his jaw but nods tersely.

"Good."

"What about you?" Evert snaps.

"What about me?"

"Scratch. You can't have a mate," he says through clenched teeth.

"Uh, he's right here, so obviously I can."

"I don't give a flying fuck about him. I care about you. I've been going crazy in here worrying about you. You're supposed to stick with us. You landed on our island, remember?"

"How could I forget when Not-First shot me down with an arrow?"

"Never gonna let that go," Ronak mutters under his breath.

"So you're really sticking with this mate shit?" Evert asks, glaring at Okot.

"Yeah. He sniffs me and calls me his beloved," I say. "It's super nice."

"What the fuck about us?"

I frown. I hadn't expected this reaction. Sure, Evert and I have always flirted, but they all made it clear that I couldn't be more to them, and I made it clear that this cupid needs some love and sex of her own.

"Last I heard, you guys needed to find a genfin mate to fix your powers and your covey bond. I promised you that I'd use my cupid mojo to help with your mate, and I stand by that promise."

Even though the thought of that leaves a bitter taste in my mouth. They all share a look that doesn't communicate anything to me. "So I won't leave," I repeat. Not that I *can* leave, but they don't need to know that. "Is that still what you want?" I ask quietly. "To find a genfin mate?"

Please say no. Please say you want me instead.

Ronak nods tersely. "Yes."

Evert shoots him a scathing look. "I said I'm done with that. Fuck the magic. We have enough."

Ronak sighs, and Sylred mumbles something I don't catch.

"But—"

"Scratch," Evert interrupts. "Enough. We'll talk about it later. But you said you're not leaving us, which means you don't need a fucking mate. So get rid of him."

I narrow my eyes. "So you all can go get a mate, but I can't? That's not how this works, you selfish ass. You should be happy for me. *He* wants me."

"And what if I said I want you?" he snaps.

Well. I didn't expect that.

My mouth opens and shuts a few times before my brain can catch up. "You want me? As what?" I challenge, growing angry. "A quick screw? Maybe I offered that in the beginning, but I want more than that now. And you aren't offering me more. That decision is a covey thing. Not just an Evert thing. And the covey already voted against me."

How dare he act as if this is my fault? Like I'm the one who rejected them, when we all know it was the other way around.

"We already established you're not breaking the covey up. So unless you, as a covey, are offering me something more, this matter is closed."

"Un*fucking*believable," Evert says, throwing his arms in

the air. "Syl. Take over. I can't talk to her when she does the thing where she disagrees with me."

I let out a big breath. "Look, I don't want to fight. Please. I just wanted to see you. I'm worried about you guys."

"We'll be fine, Emelle," Sylred assures me.

I so badly want to fall against his chest so he can wrap me up and hold me.

"Can't you just use your super strength powers and break out of here?" I ask Ronak.

He shakes his head and raps a knuckle against the cell bar. "Iron and magic-infused cells. No one's powers work inside these."

Well, that sucks.

Okot cuts in before anything else can be said. "We don't have much longer."

The thought of having to leave them again so soon kills me.

Okot's eyes soften at my pained expression. "I will try to get you back to see them again."

"You will?" I ask, crying again.

Ugh. How do I cry so fast? I must have tears with super-speed.

"Of course. These are the genfins that have my mate's heart. I will do anything to make my mate happy."

Okot's words impact the guys immediately. The three of them stiffen, and I feel their assessing stares burning into me. I guess they didn't expect to hear how much I care about them from a stranger.

I clear my throat awkwardly and change the subject. "Yeah, umm, so anyway…I really missed you guys ,and I also really needed to see you, and…"

"You still didn't answer my question," Ronak says, cutting me off with a tug on my sleeve. "You're missing your arm. Just like you were when you got back from Arachno's island. Tell us why."

Evert's and Sylred's gazes lock onto the spot of fabric that Ronak's still gripping.

"Oh, this old thing?" I shrug with a fake laugh. "This... umm...happens sometimes."

I can't tell them the truth, especially not right now when they have plenty else to worry about. They need their heads on straight for the culling tomorrow.

Plus, I already promised myself that I wouldn't guilt them into choosing to stay with me. They might not want me to leave, but that obviously doesn't mean they want to take me for their mate. I refuse to guilt them into that.

Instead of admitting what's going on, I quickly reach my other—still tangible—arm through the bars. "I just need you all to touch me. Please."

Ronak holds the others at bay with an outstretched hand and then turns back to me. "Tell us why."

"Do you always have to be so difficult?"

"Do you always have to be so stubborn?"

"You haven't told them?" Okot asks with surprise.

When the genfins start glaring at me again, I look over my shoulder and glare at Okot.

Are we about to have our first couple fight? Wait. That actually sounds kind of fun. Domestic stuff excites me. After we fight, we could have hot angry sex. Or frenzied makeup sex. That sounds super fun. I'll take one with a side of the other, please.

Except...oh, who am I kidding? I can't have sex while my genfins are in prison. I need them safe first. Safe and alive, and then I'll get the sex. All the sex. Sex for days.

Under my glare, Okot's expression falls. "What?" he asks, all innocent-like.

I make a face at him for spilling my secrets. "Just...play it cool."

He frowns. "I don't know what this *playing cool* means. It is nearly summer. It's hot out."

I grin, barely holding back the impulse to squeeze his big cheeks. "I just can't stay mad at you when you say adorable stuff like that."

He grins back at me, but the moment is interrupted when Evert claps his hands. "Hey! Break it up." He points at me. "Scratch, tell us what the fuck is going on already, where the hell your arm is, and why you need us to touch you. And then get your ass over here and kiss me, because I fucking missed you."

He practically growls that last part, but it doesn't matter because *Ohmygodshewantstokissme.* I barely suppress the urge to squeal.

Before I can reply, we hear the prison door open and the guard yells over to us. "Time's up!"

Using this momentary distraction, I quickly jam my hand against Evert's arm, then Sylred's chest, and then slap Ronak's hand, making him let go of my dress in surprise.

Immediately, the pain in my stomach disappears and my missing arm pops back into view. I breathe out a sigh of relief and move it around.

"Whew. That's better. Thank gods for that."

Evert stares wide-eyed at my reappeared limb. "What the fuck?"

"Let's go!" the guard shouts.

"I'm sorry, we have to leave, my beloved," Okot says, taking my hand.

"Wait!" I press my cheeks against the bars, smashing my face in as far as I can so I can peck a kiss on Evert's lips, then Sylred's, and I even get Ronak's cheek.

"Be careful tomorrow. Don't you dare get hurt or die. Understand?"

Okot pulls me away, but I feel like I'm leaving three pieces of my heart behind.

"You have to win, okay? Protect each other!" I say over my shoulder as Okot continues to lead me further away.

"Don't worry about us, Emelle," Sylred calls back. "Just take care of yourself."

"And you'd better fucking take care of her, too, lamassu. Anything happens to her, and I'll do more than just punch you in the throat," Evert adds.

A half-laugh, half-sob escapes me, but before I can say anything back, I'm led through the door, and the guard shuts and bolts it behind us. Okot passes him something and nods his head in thanks before leading me out of the amphitheater.

I walk, numb, all the way back to our cabin.

When we get back inside, Okot sets me on the small couch before going over to the little kitchenette. He places a steaming cup of tea in my shaking hands. "Drink."

I do as he says, but I don't taste it. My throat burns as I swallow but not nearly as much as my tear-filled eyes.

Okot sits next to me and puts his huge arm around my back, pulling me close. He doesn't talk, doesn't press me for anything at all, even though there were plenty of discussion-worthy moments back at the cells.

He's content to simply be here for me, giving me quiet comfort. I appreciate it more than he can possibly know. We may not know each other very well yet, but this—this moment right here—tells me more than a thousand words ever will.

When I've finished my tea and my tears have dried, Okot picks me up and settles me in the small bed against the wall. He tucks me in and kisses me on the forehead, breathing me in slightly.

"Sleep now, my beloved," he tells me.

So I do.

CHAPTER 12

*A*pparently, when you're pretending to be a lesser-noble high fae attending the royal culling games, you get a goodie bag.

"Ohmygods," I squeal, digging through the velvet pouch on my chair. "Okot, feel this," I say, shoving the silk eye mask in his face to rub it on his cheek. "It's so soft."

Okot, being the good-natured bull boy he is, lets me fangirl about the swag as much as I want, because really, he knows I need whatever distractions I can get today.

"Oh, what's this?" I ask, pulling out a glass funnel-looking thingamajig.

"A monocular."

I turn it around in my hand and then bring the smaller end to my eye.

I gasp. "Holy super sight! I can see everything down there," I exclaim, pointing the device toward the ground floor of the arena.

I slide the lens across, trying to find something—anything that will give away what the first culling game will be, but there's nothing down there except hard-packed dirt.

Putting my monocular away, I dig through the bag some

more. There's a single-serving bottle of fairy wine, a small pillow to sit on so my butt doesn't get sore on the wooden seat, and a bag of candied nuts that I inhale in about two-point-five seconds.

By the time I sit back beside Okot, I'm nearly bouncing in my seat in nervousness. Dressed in casual clothing rather than his guard armor, Okot looks good in a black shirt studded with golden buttons, his long mohawk flopped over on the right side of his head.

We're sitting at the end of our row, about halfway up in the amphitheater. There must be at least five thousand fae here. I use my monocular to scan the royal seating box. It's in the very center of the arena, a swathe of gold and white tapestry hanging from it. Thrones sit at the front, although they're still empty.

"Have you ever been to a culling before?" I ask Okot.

"Once. About fifteen or twenty years ago."

I nudge him. "And..."

I can tell he doesn't want to divulge, and that alone makes me bite my bottom lip with worry. "How bad is it?"

He sighs slightly. "It's not good. It's never good. They are designed to break, maim, and kill the competitors in the name of faked mercy. It'll be brutal. You must prepare yourself."

I take a deep breath and nod. "I'm glad you're here with me."

His huge hand engulfs mine. "You are my mate, but you are also put under my protection by the princess. I go where you go."

"I'm a fan of the buddy system."

A huge gong rings out, silencing the gathered crowd. I pull out my monocular and whip my head toward the royal box. King Beluar Silverlash is now sitting on the center throne, and his son, Prince Elphar, is standing next to him. I can see Princess Soora sitting on the smaller throne beside the prince's empty seat.

Prince Elphar raises his blue-tinged hand to further quiet the fae gathered in the stadium. I can see the glint of reflections off thousands of monoculars, all pointed at him.

He sweeps his hand to his throat, and I see a tinge of sparkling magic surround his throat. His voice booms out to the crowd, enhanced enough so everyone can hear him speak.

"Welcome to the royal trials of the culling. Five years have passed since twenty-five noble fae have been banished for their treacherous deeds. But we are a fair and just monarchy. So today, we give those nobles a second chance. A chance to fight to regain their respected positions, repledge their loyalty to the crown, and prove that they deserve to rejoin society."

Everyone watches him in rapture. The fae girls beside me positively titter when he smiles. Yet that charming smile of his turns sinister when he adds, "However, for those who fail in the culling, their death will be vindication from the gods for betraying their sovereigns. So, let us cull the unworthy from our midst in a tradition that has spanned centuries. Let the culling begin!"

The gong sounds again and the crowd goes wild. Fae are on their feet, stomping, screaming, clapping. Celebrating a glorified death ring. I feel like I'm going to puke.

Suddenly, the empty dirt in the center of the amphitheater transforms. Four strips of vastly different terrain suddenly appear, one after the other. Lush, green grass first, speckled with trees, bushes, man-sized flowers.

After that is a hundred yards of nothing but polished, black ground that looks like onyx. Then a perfectly cut-in road of calm, crystal-clear water. Lastly, a wall of unmoving fire. The flames look paused as if they're waiting for something.

The gong goes off again, setting my teeth on edge, and then a portal appears. One after the other, the contestants step through. They all vary in size, shape, sex, and type of fae. My three guys are the very last to step through.

I keep my monocular trained on them. Ronak is one of the largest fae down there and by far the strongest-looking. Even with the last week of them not eating nearly enough, he looks formidable and capable. Evert and Sylred flank him, looking just as fierce.

"The rules for the first competition are simple," King Beluar's voice rings out. "All contestants must pass through each of the four elements. Contestants are forbidden from harming another contestant. If you cannot successfully pass through each of the elements and make it to the end, then you are disqualified from being reinstated into society and will thus be killed. You may begin at the sound of the gong."

The king sits down again, and all eyes swivel back to the contestants. My hand shakes on my monocular as I grip it. When the gong goes off again, all of the contestants take off running.

I watch as the first group makes it to the green patch of land that represents earth. The moment their feet touch the grass, huge arms of earth shoot out from the ground, crashing into a group of contestants and sending them flying across the stadium with a crash.

Two of them don't get back up again.

Another group of contestants step onto the earth next, including my guys. The earth instantly rocks and rolls under their feet, knocking everyone to the ground.

Ronak is barely down for a single second before he's springing to his feet again, pulling up Sylred with him. Evert is up a second later, and the three of them barrel past. More contestants are also running through now, and the earth takes swipes at them left and right.

Tree branches come smacking down, trying to hit anyone

that gets too close. Vines seem to shoot out from nowhere, wrapping around others and asphyxiating them right before my eyes.

One fae disappears entirely when the earth just abruptly opens up and swallows him whole. Somehow, my guys make it through, along with a good number of others, to the second part of the competition—air.

This section is so unlike the first. All that's there is black stone on the ground, so shiny I can see the fae's reflections in it. Nothing happens when the contestants step onto it. It's not until the very last fae makes it out of earth element and onto the stone that it happens.

Powerful, violent air blasts against the contestants, knocking each and every one of them down. My guys were nearly to the halfway point, but the air is pushing at them, sending them flying right back to the beginning.

That's when I realize that the stone ground isn't for show. It's there because of how slippery it is. No one can get any traction on it with the air pushing at them so violently.

Hair is whipping around, clothes are getting torn from their bodies, even the skin on their faces is being blown back. No one can stay on their feet. The second they try, the relentless air knocks them over again.

Ronak is in front, Sylred and Evert behind him, each of them flat on their bellies, digging in their heels and fingers, trying to stop from blowing further away from the end.

"Come on, come on. Do something," I murmur.

I see Sylred reach for Evert, grabbing hold of his forearm. He pulls Evert closer, muscles bulging. When Evert's face is right beside Sylred's, I see the blond-haired genfin shouting something into Evert's ear. Evert nods and looks back at the other contestants, while Sylred grabs hold of Ronak's foot to relay the same message.

I watch as Evert reaches for another contestant and shouts something to him. Systematically, one after the other,

Sylred's message is passed on, until all of the contestants are linked together, joined by the grip on arms and legs, feet and hands.

Using the link, the fae at the very back starts to climb up each body like a ladder of limbs. When he gets to where Ronak is, he settles himself in front, and Ronak grabs hold of his leg.

I watch in complete awe as this fae chain works slowly but surely to inch forward. Every time the fae from the back climbs over the bodies and makes it to the front, the next person does the same thing, until they all finally reach the end.

And maybe some of these fae did heinous things. Maybe some of them deserved to be banished. But even when the first ones make it past the air section, not one of them moves on until every single contestant is pulled out of that treacherous air and onto solid ground again.

"They helped each other," I say in wonder.

"They did. They acted with honor."

I shoot a glance toward the royal box. "Prince Elphar doesn't seem too pleased about it."

Okot follows my gaze. "He wouldn't. He is threatened by each and every one of those contestants. He wrongfully imprisons and banishes fae all the time, knowing that he can get away with it. It seems your genfins outsmarted him this time by acting in a way completely foreign to his way of thinking."

"What do you mean?"

"They banded together. He would have stayed stuck in that section until the end of time. Helping others and working together never would have crossed his mind."

Giving Sylred a mental kiss, I turn my attention back to the arena. The once still, calm pool of water is now a churning, swirling, angry mass. It's like the most treacherous of seas in a tiny rectangular strip.

It crashes down on fae, trying to drown them, spinning them in whirlpools and spitting them back to the beginning. But whatever transpired between the contestants in the air section seems to have carried over to this element, too.

I watch as everyone once again works together to make it out of the water. Like he weighs nothing, Ronak picks up Evert and hurls him out of the water. Sylred is next, nearly crashing on top of him.

Ronak, much to my surprise, picks up another three fae and tosses them onto land before getting sucked into a vicious whirlpool.

Just as it pulls him under, another fae who's boasting gills and webbed feet, dives back in the water after him.

I hold my breath, counting the seconds that I don't see Ronak's head reappear.

My chest starts to burn. I still don't breathe.

Where is he?

The water is an angry, violent entity that crashes against the ground and sends sprays of water into the stands. My lungs want air, but I deny them. Not until he gets it, too.

Dammit, Ronak, if you die...

I won't take a breath until he does.

Resurface, dammit!

Just as black dots appear before my eyes, I see the fishy fae reappear, and then Ronak finally comes coughing and spluttering to the surface a second after.

I breathe in a huge sigh of relief.

The fae on the sidelines reach in and haul them out of the water. Ronak turns and yaks up about a gallon of water.

When he's on his feet again, he stands in a line with the rest of the fae, all of them staring at the fourth and final part of the competition.

The giant wall of fire.

"Fuck."

CHAPTER 13

*H*ow the hell are they supposed to get past a motherfucking wall of fire?

My hands grip the armrests so hard that my knuckles turn white.

Okot notices and pats me on the back. "Breathe, my beloved. They will get through this."

I try to listen to him, I do. But my body has definitely forgotten how to breathe correctly. Instead, it's making fast hyperventilating gasps instead.

One of the fae contestants, a female with dreadlocks down to her ankles, goes forward and tries to make some slashing movement at the fire. The preternaturally still flames suddenly roar to life, incinerating her in a second. She didn't even have time to scream.

My throat makes a little squeaking noise and terror crawls up my spine. Now, the flames are no longer immobile. Instead, they rage and roar like a great inferno, and the contestants stagger backwards from it as tendrils lick out toward them.

My guys are looking around, as if they're trying to find

some way, some trick around this. None of the other contestants seem eager to try to pass through the flames.

I don't blame them.

Still, another fae takes a tentative step forward and raises his hand in front of him. I'm not sure what type of fae he is, but then I see jets of water spraying from his palm, trying to douse the flames. He's some sort of water fae, then.

Good idea sending him forward, except nothing happens. The fire doesn't even spit or sputter. It's completely unaffected by his stream.

He drops his hand, at a loss, and I can see some of the other contestants grouping together, talking animatedly to each other, trying to figure this out.

A pixie releases her wings and shoots to the sky, deciding to try to fly over the wall instead. I think maybe she's solved it until she reaches the top. As soon as she begins her way over it, a flame shoots out like a frog's tongue and catches her like a fly.

She's just ember and ashes by the time her form falls to the ground.

"Oh, gods," I groan, barely stopping myself from covering my eyes.

I'm sweating all over, my heart is racing, and I still can't breathe right. How in the hell is anyone supposed to make it through this?

Oh, right. They're not.

A pixie male falls to his knees over her pile of ashes in an anguished sob. He lifts some of it up, clenching it in his hands, and screams. He looks up at the royal box and sends out a vicious, agonized roar that echoes through the massive arena. The prince smirks cruelly.

"This is horrible," I whisper.

Okot reaches over and takes my hand, and he doesn't complain at all when my nails dig in and I squeeze him way too tightly.

When the sounds of the pixie's screams turn into sobs that we can no longer hear, he suddenly staggers to his feet.

"Oh gods, he's gonna—"

One, two, three contestants try to stop him, but it's no use. His grief is too strong, his goal too determined. He slips and shoves past them all.

Without a second of hesitation, he takes off and leaps into the flames. He's incinerated immediately.

He ran to his death. Wanted it. Needed to follow the pixie girl straight to it. I feel sick.

I squint at the fire and then raise an arm to point at it, just as so many others in the stand start doing the same thing. "Look." I watch, wide-eyed, as the fire changes.

It pulls back like a stage curtain, separating right where the pixie sacrificed himself. Now, a narrow path is etched in its wake, and the fire is once again still.

The contestants don't hesitate. They start sprinting forward, single-file, racing through the passage that the fire wall made for them.

"I don't understand."

"It was a message," Okot says.

"What message?"

"Sacrifice before mercy. Death before life. That they only live if he allows it, and he only allows it after a heavy price."

When my three guys make it to the end, the breath I didn't know I was holding releases out of me.

"So someone had to go willingly into the fire, knowing they'd die?"

"Yes."

I swing my eyes to the royal box when Prince Elphar's voice rings out again. "This marks the end of the first part of the royal culling trials. Twenty-five contestants entered, and sixteen came out. Tonight, there will be a celebratory bonfire. Tomorrow, our contestants will be allowed a day of rest. The second part of the culling begins the following day."

When everyone starts emptying out of the amphitheater, I keep my eyes glued on the ground. My guys are dirty, wet, and tired. But they're alive.

I stay until a high fae creates a portal, and the contestants are forced back through it by the palace guards, one by one.

I'm on my feet, leaning over the balcony when all three of my genfins turn and look up at me at the same time, as if they knew exactly where I've been this whole time.

I lift my hand and give them a pitiful wave, even though there's no way they can see very well from that far away. Then they're shoved roughly ahead by the guards, disappearing through the portal.

"What's that guard's name?" I ask through clenched teeth. There was no need for him to manhandle my guys.

Okot lifts his monocular. "That's the prince's right hand. Gammon."

"Well, I hate him."

Okot tucks my hand in the crook of his arm. "Come. The bonfire will start soon."

I put my other hand on my belly. "I still feel sick with nerves. I don't know if I can eat."

"Would you like to go lie down for a while?"

I shake my head as he starts leading me down the first of many flights of stairs to get out of this place. "If I sit and stew by myself, I'll just feel worse. Do you think you can take me to see them again?"

"For you, I will try."

I stand up on my tiptoes and pull him down far enough so that I can give him a peck on the cheek. "You are the sweetest."

"Lamassus are not sweet," he says gruffly. "Lamassus are a proud, fierce race that protects and adores our mates with unending loyalty."

"Yeah, and that's about the sweetest thing I've ever heard."

He grunts out a chuckle and shakes his head at me, pulling me down more stairs. I start panting, naturally.

I also trip. Repeatedly.

He catches me every time.

When my heel turns and my ankle rolls on one of the steps, Okot stops in front of me and lifts me up for a piggyback ride. I hold my arms around his neck as he grabs me under my thighs.

"This is better. I hate stairs. And heels. And walking."

"You are not very good at any of them, either."

"Now you just sound like Ronak," I say with a smile on my face.

My smile droops when I'm instantly reminded of the terrible things they faced today and what is still to come.

As if he can sense my distress, Okot squeezes my thighs slightly. "Your Ronak is a warrior."

"Yeah. I mean, I think so? His power is strength, and he's a super good fighter. They all are."

"That will help them win," he reminds me.

"Yeah, but the game is tipped. It isn't fair. The prince purposely weakens them by bringing them a week early, making them live off scraps and terrible conditions before throwing them into his deathtrap."

"Even so. They showed no weakness today."

Yeah, let's just hope it stays that way.

I try to shake off the direness of the situation, because that's not going to help my guys, anyway. I also don't want Okot to feel burdened with being mated to a Debbie Downer.

By the way, poor Debbie. She's seriously typecasted. I'm sure there are super fun Debbie's out there.

At the bottom of the stairs, Okot keeps hold of me, and I relax against his back. Lots of fae give us weird looks, but I don't care at all. They're just jealous they don't have a bull boy to walk for them.

"Can you just carry me everywhere? This is so much better."

I feel more than hear Okot's rumbled laughter against my chest. "It would be my pleasure, my beloved."

I sigh in pleasure. "Okay. Let's go to this bonfire, stuff our faces until we wanna puke, and drink fairy wine until we pass out."

"Sounds like a plan."

CHAPTER 14

"*Y*ou are *sooooo* pretty," Mossie, my favorite earth sprite croons.

I lean forward to pet her vine hair, but I miss and hit her in the eye instead. Aside from her eye getting red and teary, she doesn't seem to really notice. "Stop it. *You* are pretty. You have flowers growing from your head. I freaking *love* flowers."

"Me too!" Mossie says, taking another drink. "What's your favorite flower?"

"Pink," I answer without hesitation.

She nods solemnly and passes me the bottle so I can take another swig.

Fairy wine is so much better than that fermented mead crap that the guys made back on the island. Like, way, way better.

"I want to drink this forever. We should make a fairy wine pool and just float in it with a straw."

I look over at the huge bonfire that's glowing in the middle of the field. I have no idea what's fueling the thing, since nothing is technically burning. But the colors keep

101

changing, so no matter what kind of magic it is, it earns pretty points.

There are wooden benches and tables set up all around the field, but it's late now. The bonfire celebration started hours ago, so fae are mostly dancing and screwing by now. This population sure isn't suffering from losing me as their resident cupid.

Mossie picks up the bottle of wine and starts pouring it over her head to water her flowers with it.

They start swaying, which sends me into a fit of laughter. A burp erupts from my mouth, cutting it short. "Your flowers are drunk."

She tilts her head back to try to look at them, but of course that doesn't work and only makes me laugh harder.

"I have buzzed blooms," she supplies.

I purse my lips in thought. "Plastered plants."

"Sloshed shoots."

"Say that ten times fast," I challenge.

Mossie taps her nose in *challenge accepted*. "Sloshed shoots, shloshed shootsh, slosheds shootses...shit."

I cackle delightedly.

Several fae get up from the wooden benches beside us and move away.

I stick my tongue out at their retreating backs. "Party poopers."

"They should've had more wine," Mossie says, leaning fully into my side to stay propped up.

"You took their bottle," I remind her.

"Oh, yeah."

The bonfire is still in full effect, but none of the royals ever made an appearance. "Fricking royals," I slur.

"You said it," she says with a nod. "Wait. What about the royals?"

Gods, my head feels spinny. "Have you ever counted your blinks? I think we must blink, like, a bazillion times."

Mossie starts blinking excessively, making her whole face wrinkle up as she does it. "I can't stop thinking about blinking now. Am I blinking weird?"

I stare at her as she blinks with the force of a full facial spasm. "Yeah, tone it down a notch or twenty."

She starts fluttering her eyes instead, like a bug just got trapped in her cornea.

I nod. "Way better."

"Phew. Blinking is tricky."

I catch a glimpse of a particular water sprite across the way and quickly sit up. "Hey, isn't that your guard sprite super crush from the prison tower?" I ask, pointing across the bonfire.

Or at least, I try to point at him. My aim is off by a few feet. "You looooove him," I singsong.

Mossie pushes off me with a squeal, making me topple off the bench and fall onto the ground.

"Hey, bitch," I snap. "That was not cool. Anti-cool. Uncool."

"Shh!" she hisses, slapping her green hand over my mouth. "He'll hear us!"

I lick her hand until she squeals and rips it away. Planting my hands on the bench, I try to pull myself up. It takes me three tries.

"Go pinch his butt," I giggle.

She blushes dark green. "No!"

I frown. "Why not? Does he have a gross butt?"

Mossie frowns, tossing a hair-vine over her shoulder. "I don't know. I didn't look. Should I have looked?"

"Umm, duh. What if he has a bad one?"

She claps a hand over her mouth, horrified. "I never even thought of that!"

"Mm-hmm. I know. That's why you have me."

"You are *so* smart."

I try to take another drink of wine, but when I tip it all

the way back, I discover that the bottle is empty. I look down into the neck of it just to make sure, then I start swinging it around like it's a monocular. Wine drips into my eye, and I drop it to the ground with a yelp.

"The bottle pretended to be empty," I grumble, wiping my eye. "Lying liar fairy wine. It tried to blind me."

Mossie isn't listening. She's too busy trying to stand. She falls and stumbles several times before she gets it. "Okay," she pants, wiping the dirt from her dress. "I'm gonna do it."

"Okay, good," I nod. "Do what?"

"His butt. Gonna pinch it."

"Whose butt?"

Instead of answering, she reaches in her dress and props up her boobs so they sit higher up in her dress. She runs a hand through her flowers, too, just for good measure.

A thought pops into my head, and I point at her crotch. "Hey! Do you have flowers down in your lady garden, too?"

She quickly covers her crotch with her hands like I can suddenly see through her clothes. "That is a private garden," she says haughtily.

"Oh my gods, you do! You have vagina vines! Or, I guess it would be vulva vines? Or labia lilies? Whatever. Can I see?"

She sends me a scathing look. "No, you can't see," she retorts snootily. "Now. How do I look?"

I lift my hands to give her two thumbs up, but they kind of flop back down before I can get my fingers to cooperate. Oh well. I'm sure she gets it.

"I'm gonna pinch his butt so good," she says with a smile.

"Yeah you are! Get it, girl."

"I am. I'm gonna pinch his butt and then invite him to tend to my private lady garden." She waggles her brows.

"That's the spirit. Fingers crossed he's a good plougher. Or sower. Or whatever other garden term that also fits as a sexual innuendo."

She smiles and stumbles off, disappearing around the

bonfire and away from my view. I'm envious of her butt pinching. I wish I could pinch some fine genfin butts right about now.

I realize when I face forward that I can see the sky. When did I lie down? Or maybe someone tricked me and put up some sort of sky-star wall in front of my face? Dicks.

"Who's a dick?"

I pop my eyes open to see an upside down Okot standing over me. "You have two nose rings. And noses. And heads."

He grins. "And you have double vision."

I wrinkle my nose. "Uh-uh. That's not one of my cupid powers. Have you even been paying attention? You're supposed to be getting to know me," I whine.

His grin just grows, and then I feel my body rise off the ground. "Ohmygods, I'm flying!"

"I'm carrying you."

"Oh. Good. Cuz I'm supposed to be hiding my wings. Besides, flying is *hard*. Drinking fairy wine is so much easier. I'm good at drinking wine. I could be a professional wine drinker. I like it. A lot."

I frown at the sound of that word in my mouth. "A lot. Alot, alotta, alots lot lot lot lot." I scrunch up my nose in dislike. "That word is weird. It's like it doesn't even mean anything anymore. Anyway, the point is, I like fairy wine."

He chuckles in a low, sexy sound. "I noticed."

"Nuh-uh. No, you didn't. You've been gone for hours," I say, flopping a hand around.

"Do you think I'd let my mate drink herself into a stupor and not be nearby to watch over her?"

I stare at him. He has pretty red-rimmed eyes. They're all...red and black and stuff. Wait, did he ask me a question? I can't remember. I wanna tug on his nose ring. Would that hurt?

"Yes," he says.

I gasp. "You can read minds?"

"No. You said that out loud."

"Oh, well then that's not nearly as impressive."

That rumbly laugh of his comes back, making me shiver against him. "Are you cold?"

I squeeze my eyes closed tight so I can think. "No, I don't think so. I wanna sing. I bet I'm awesome at singing."

"You did sing. Many songs that no one recognized. Although your sprite friend tried to sing along with you, anyway. Then you danced. Or at least, I think it was dancing. There was a lot of jumping involved. You had quite the audience."

Did I? Now that he's mentioned it, I can remember some spinning and leaping. I think I might've even done the chicken dance. Classic.

"Yeah, everyone thought I was awesome."

When I open my eyes again, I see that we're already back at the cabin. He sets me on the bed, takes off my shoes, and starts rubbing my sore feet. I plant my face into the pillow. "Ommgomdonsop."

He pauses and leans down to my face to better hear me. "What?"

I turn my head to the side so that I'm not speaking into the pillow. "I said, 'Oh my gods, don't stop.'"

He grins and starts moving his magical bull hands to massage my very aching feet again.

"You're, like, such a good mate," I slur.

His red-rimmed eyes light up in amusement. "I'm glad you think so."

After a few minutes of the awesomely epic foot rub that I'm definitely going to tell Evert about because I want to guilt him into one, Okot stops and tucks me into bed. He gently extracts the empty wine bottle that I'm still somehow clutching in my hand.

"I wanna buy more of that stuff. Like cases of it. Does the fae realm sell it in cases?" I ask with a frown. "I don't know your measuring system. Bushels? Bales? Baker's dozen? They don't teach fae math in cupid school. Actually, there *is* no cupid school. I probably would've failed if there had been. Stupid cupid."

I lower my voice to a very loud whisper. "Don't tell my superiors, but I'm a terrible cupid. Well...I wasn't in the beginning. At first, I was awesome. I'm awesome at a lot of stuff, you know."

I think I hear a laugh, but I can't open my eyes to check because they're too heavy. "Like singing and dancing?"

"Exactly," I mumble. "Anyway, I was an awesome cupid in the human realm. For like the first two decades."

I stop and think. "Okay, maybe just the first decade? Fine, the first seven years at the very least. Anyway, it got tough, you know? Spreading all that love around, watching people get all their romance and sexy times. I got too jealous. I was lonely. Couldn't be heard or felt or seen. Then I got sent to this realm, and I was gonna try to be a good cupid again, but then the stupid prince with his stupid black heart ruined all my plans for royal married bliss. He's stupid."

I feel Okot brush some of the hair off my face as I snuggle deeper into the pillow. "Let your wings out to breathe, my beloved."

He's somehow loosened my dress enough for me to do so without ripping anything, because he thinks of everything. The second they're free, the relief is almost instant.

I flex them out, letting my feathers ruffle before settling back. "You are so smart." He breathes a laugh out, and I realize that there's a huge chasm inside of me brought on by talking about my invisible years spent utterly alone.

"Okot?" I say quietly.

"Yes?"

"Would you lie with me? I don't want to be alone."

I hear some rustling, then the covers are pulled back, and

Okot settles in next to me. Careful of my wings, he draws me close to his body, pulling me right up against him.

I'm immediately engulfed in his warmth. The feel of him like this, holding me like I'm cherished, is enough to bridge the dark chasm of my soul. I snuggle closer to him, using his arm as a pillow as I press my face into the crook of his shoulder.

"I don't want to disappear again," I whisper.

"If you do, I'll find you."

I feel his lips on my forehead just as sleep comes for me, lulling me under like rocking waves.

CHAPTER 15

"*I*'m dying," I mumble into the mattress.

I'm pretty sure someone cut the top of my skull off and poured knives inside it. It hurts like a bitch.

I try to regain some spit inside my dry mouth while trying not to gag from the awful taste stuck on my tongue. It's like I chewed on stalks of wheat after they'd been stuck under sweaty man armpits all day.

"Can you sit up and drink this?"

I open one eye to look up at Okot, but as soon as I do, the light filtering through the small window sends a blade jabbing right through my throbbing brain. I hiss in pain and close my eye again.

"Turn the window down," I snap.

Okot chuckles and I can feel the bed dip as he sits down beside me. After a few minutes, I manage to open both eyes and look up at him. "Never drinking fairy wine again. Head. Hurts."

"If you drink this, it will help."

Sitting up sounds terrible. I want to go back to sleep because not moving sounds way better. But I realize I have to pee. Like, really bad. Plus, the whole wheat-sweat-mouth situation needs tending to.

I lazily lift one arm. "Help."

He grabs my arm and hauls me into a sitting position. "Dizzy, dizzy, dizzy!"

"Do you still think fairy wine is awesome?" he teases.

I glare at him, but it's more of a grimace since my head is pounding. He hands me a cup and tilts it to my lips, making me drink the whole thing.

When I'm done, I wipe my mouth with my arm. "That was gross."

"Yes."

"Do I want to know what was in it?"

He looks at me levelly. "No."

"Hmm." I perk up a bit when I feel the drink hit my system. "Hey, it helped my head already."

He nods with a smile. "Good."

"Okay, I gotta pee."

I hop out of bed and quickly fix my dress before heading for the door.

"Your wings, my beloved."

I look over my shoulder and smile. "Oh, yeah. That'd be a bit obvious, huh?"

With a quick and nearly painless *pull*, I make my wings go back inside my body before heading outside to the row of temporary outhouses. I'm pretty sure I pee the equivalent of eight wine bottles. With my head and bladder situation taken care of, I feel much better.

When I get back, Okot gives me a plate of food that I inhale. "What time is it, anyway? And where is everyone? I didn't see many people up and about."

"There's a fete down at the amphitheater since the contestants aren't competing today. And it's nearly six o'clock."

I pause, the piece of bread halfway in my mouth. "Six o'clock? You woke me up at six in the morning after I drank most of the night away? You're supposed to let drunk people sleep in. Everyone knows that."

Okot crosses his arms as he settles back in the chair, his smile widening. "I did not wake you. You woke yourself. And it's six o'clock in the evening."

I drop the bread. "What? You let me sleep the entire day away?"

He chuckles at my change of heart. "You needed it, my beloved. Besides, you would've just worried and fretted over your genfins all day."

Well, he has me there. "Hmm. I guess you're forgiven then."

He tilts his head and runs a hand through his thick red mohawk. Studying me, he says, "You are different from what I thought my mate would be like."

I feel myself get immediately defensive. "How? What did you think your mate would be like?"

"Soft spoken. Demure."

I blink. "Oh. Well...I'm sure I could talk softer or something. You mean, like, you want me to whisper? I'm sure I could be super good at whispering," I whisper.

Okot breaks into laughter, and I'm not entirely sure if I should be offended or not.

"What? You don't think I can be quieter? I totally could."

He laughs even harder, his red eyes sparkling. "No, no. You misunderstand me," he says, trying to stop his laughter. He sucks at it because it keeps leaking out. "I don't want you to be quieter. I like you the way you are, my beloved."

I straighten up in my chair. "Oh?"

He nods, his eyes smoldering. "Yes. You are unexpected, but I happen to like it. Don't change."

I grin. "You're trying to get lucky, huh?"

His laughter cuts off immediately, and he blanches. "I'm not...that wasn't...do you..."

I get to my feet and walk over to sit on him. His arms go

111

around me immediately. I look down at my seat that is his lap. "Gods, if you were an airplane seat, you'd be private jet plane status for sure. Not coach. Not business class. Not even first class. Straight to private jet."

He frowns. "I have no idea what any of that means."

I wave a hand. "Human realm stuff. The point is you're comfy and spacious."

"Ah."

"Anyway, I am totally gonna have sexy times with you. We can like, sniff and sex at the same time. It'll be epic," I promise him.

I grin when he blushes. I, Emelle, the cupid, am making this fierce-looking bull guy blush. I take a breath, unsure of how he'll react to this next part. I don't want him to get his feelings hurt or become jealous.

"But... I sort of need to wait until my genfins get out of this. Is that okay?"

The big teddy bull rests his forehead on mine. "Don't worry. I understand."

"You're not mad?"

"You are my mate," he says, as if that explains everything.

I bite my lip in thought. "I know you said that, but are you sure? What if I just smell super good? Maybe it's the dye?" I say, looking down at my pink arms with a frown.

"It's not the dye."

"Maybe it's a whole Veil smell thing, since I'm not supposed to be here."

"You're supposed to be here. Of that, I have no doubt. Fate brought you to this realm."

"But—"

"No more worries about this. Lamassus can sense their mates immediately, and I sensed you. Many of my kind are never blessed enough to find their mates. It matters not what you are. You are mine."

I smile. "Okay."

He pecks me on the top of my head and then lifts me up so we can both stand. "Now, Duru has arranged a private bath for you to re-dye your skin today. The tub should be here soon."

"Okay, that's probably good. It's fading a bit."

"I can go talk to my guard acquaintance to see if we can get you into the cells again, or I can stand watch outside while you bathe, if it would make you feel safer."

"No, go ahead. I'd love to see the guys again, if I can."

A knock sounds on the door, and Okot goes to answer it. Two servant boys bring in a wooden tub, and another half a dozen follow behind them with buckets of steaming water. I feel bad that they had to carry it all this way. It was probably heavy.

Okot gives the boys some coins and then closes the door. He mixes in the bottle of dye for me before kissing me on the top of my head again. He seems to like that spot. "I shall be back soon. Do not open the door to anyone but Duru or myself, and do not go outside without me."

"I'll be careful," I promise, eyeing the steaming bath. It looks heavenly.

When Okot leaves, I bolt the door after him and then strip out of my clothes. When I step into the bath, I dunk my head under for as long as I can and let the dye soak into my skin and hair.

The hot water feels amazing. I wash and soak for a while, until my skin is a deep fuchsia color. When I get out, I air dry to let the dye soak in, and then go to work on the tangles in my hair. When I'm dressed and pacing around the cabin like a crazy person, Okot finally comes back.

The expression on his face is all I need. "We can't go to see them," I say dejectedly.

He shakes his head. "I am sorry. The guard I know was not there tonight, and I don't want to risk it. Too many eyes for the prince, and I am already not a favorite since I am a personal guard for Princess Soora."

I'm totally disappointed, but I'm thankful he tried.

"Well, what should we do for the rest of the night? I'm too wired to sleep anytime soon."

"I was thinking I could take you somewhere to let you stretch your wings."

My brows raise and a smile spreads across my face. "Really? Are you sure it's safe?"

"I found a private place. And everyone is at the fete. Once we get in the air, no one will see us in the night sky."

Excitement takes over. "Oh my gods, you'll actually fly with me?"

"I hoped I could. If you are agreeable."

"Are you kidding? That sounds super fun! Let's go."

I grab his arm and yank him toward the door. Really, he's just being generous by moving, because we both know that I'm not strong enough to move him.

Before we get to the door, I stop short and Okot nearly stumbles into my back.

"What's wrong?"

I look down at myself and frown. "My outfit. If I push my wings out in this, it'll rip the dress, and I only have two. Duru will probably beat me with a scouring brush if I ruin this one."

"Hmm." Okot looks me up and down in thought and then digs out one of his shirts from his bag. "This should work. When we get there, you can change into this."

"Perfect. Let's go."

Outside, we pass by the many rows of cabins. Some of them are bigger and nicer than others, denoting higher social status. The cabins farthest away are much smaller. Nothing more than shacks, really. I guess those are where the servants are staying.

Once we make it past the cabins, there are no longer

lanterns to light our way. Still, Okot pulls me onward without hesitation, up a hill and then down to the other side. I stumble to a stop to rip my heels off.

"I hate these things," I say, clutching the shoes in one hand while Okot retakes my other. It helps to walk barefoot, but I still can't help but trip.

After I stumble for the seventh time, I huff out a breath. "I know I'm a slouch in the balance department, but how in the heck are you not stumbling, too? It's pitch black out here."

"I can see in the dark."

I whip my head in the direction of his shadow. Huh. That explains it.

Between the hills, he leads us to a small field. The grass is so high that it reaches my waist. "Here," he says, handing me his shirt. "Put this on backwards and let your wings out."

I do as he says, knowing that we're plenty far away from the amphitheater. No one should be able to see me.

Okot, being the gentleman he is, turns around while I strip out of my dress and pull on his shirt. Hearing me finish, he covers my fumbling hands at the open back as I push out my wings.

He deftly ties it up, securing it between my wings, and steps back. "There. How does it feel?"

I turn and hop around a bit, then flex my wings for good measure. "Feels good."

He nods once. "Ready?"

"Yeah, but just be warned, I'm not a very good flier. I get tired quick."

"That's alright. Stop whenever you want."

I nod. "You gonna cow out now?"

I can't see his expression, but his gravelly chuckle makes me smile. "Yes."

One second, I'm staring up at his bulky form, and the next, he's transformed into his huge winged bull body. I rub

115

my hand against his nose and then step back and turn around.

Looking over my shoulder, I shoot him a smirk. "Try and catch me if you can." I launch myself into the air, my red-feathered wings extending all the way out. They carry me up and up and up, and then I'm not just under the dark night sky, I'm in it. I go higher than I've ever gone before, and Okot is hot on my heels. I can hear his amused snorts as he flies behind me, so close I can feel his hot breath against my ankles.

Just as he tries to overtake me, I feint right and then shoot upward again, right through the center of a cloud.

When I make it through the other side, cool mist envelops my body, and joyful laughter escapes me. Okot's nose nuzzles my feet, and I let out an excited shriek, heading for yet another cloud.

When I make it above that one, too, dewdrops cover my hair and face, and Okot catches up to me, his huge, wet snout nuzzling my leg as he huffs a breath against my skin.

"Okay, okay. You win," I laugh over at him. I know he probably let me stay ahead of him the whole time, but regardless, the chase was invigorating and exactly what I needed.

Up this high and with the moon hidden behind more clouds, the stars steal the show. They're everywhere. Thousands of them. Twinkling against the dark canvas like crystals.

I can't help but be in awe of them. As I fly side by side with Okot, I beam at him, because I've never felt so alive. The wind at my face, the air under my wings, all while under the most perfect backdrop, is enough to feed my soul after decades of hunger.

As much as I'm enjoying myself, I'm still a novice, and my back and wings get sore quickly. Even though Okot can't

116

speak, he must sense this somehow, because the next thing I know, his huge body is beneath mine.

I extend my legs on either side of his back, slipping in front of his wings, and then wrap my hands around his neck. I bury my head into his crook, burrowing into his warmth. Straddling him like this, I can feel just how strong he is.

I pull my wings back in my body to let them rest, and Okot lets me ride on him as he takes me higher still. The stars look close enough to grab.

By the time he touches back down to the ground, my eyes are heavy with sleep. He shifts back into his regular form, and after picking up my discarded dress and shoes, Okot swings me up into his arms, as if he never gets tired of holding me.

"I don't," I hear him say, my ear pressed against his chest.

Did I say that out loud? Geez, I'm always doing that. A yawn takes over my mouth.

"Rest, my beloved. I've got you."

I listen to his heart beating. "I know you do."

My body drifts off, lulled by his steady steps and his strong arms wrapped around me. "Thank you for flying in the stars," I say on a quiet breath.

I feel a kiss pressed against the top of my head. "For you, I'd pluck them from the sky."

All those years I hoped and wished and prayed to know what falling in love felt like?

Yeah. I think I know now.

It feels like this.

CHAPTER 16

*T*urns out, the second day of the culling sucks just as bad as the first day did.

We're in our seats again, sans goodie bags, and I've bitten my nails down to stubs. Okot grabs hold of the fingers currently at the mercy of my teeth and tugs them away.

I try to chew on my left-hand fingers instead, but he grabs that hand, too.

"Okot," I snap.

He shrugs, not at all sorry for interfering in my nervous gnawing.

He keeps both my hands beneath his, resting on his forearm as he calmly strokes me. "They have not even been brought out yet, my beloved."

"I know," I groan, tapping my feet on the floor nervously. "The waiting is awful. Almost as awful as watching."

"They will make it through."

"They better, or I'll go back into the Veil, drag them back to this realm, and force those assholes to become cupids."

Okot chuckles. "The frowning one would not be a good cupid at all."

I smile at the image of Ronak breathing some Lust into

118

people's faces while scowling. "Oh my gods, can you just see him with my pink hair?" Even under current stressful circumstances, I can't help but laugh. "He'd probably be called to the superiors and terminated after a week for trying to kill people with Love Arrows."

"Perhaps the other two would fare better."

"Nah, only Sylred."

My nice distraction is cut off at the sound of the gong. The pile of threads in my stomach instantly tangles into knots of unease again as I raise my monocular to look at the royals.

Prince Elphar stands, just as regal and composed as ever. His dark-blue hair is slicked back, his skin matching the pale blue of the sky. He raises a hand over the crowd, demanding silence in the amphitheater.

So because I'm super mature, I clear my throat. Loudly. Then I do it again, because fuck him. It's not like he can hear my small rebellious act of noise, but it makes me feel better, so I do it again until the fae behind us shush me.

Okot turns and glares at them. They stop their shushing and look away pretty fast.

"Today marks the second day of the culling trials. Sixteen contestants will enter. Two groups will be formed. The winning group lives. Let the culling begin!"

The gong sounds, and just like last time, a portal is opened by a high fae. Sixteen contestants march out, one after another, looking even worse for wear than the last time. Whatever the prince said about having time to "rest" between competitions was clearly a lie.

I hiss through my teeth when I see the state of my guys, and my hand flies to my mouth. "What the fuck happened to them?"

Sylred's shirt is ripped and spotted with blood, and he's limping badly. Evert has no shoes, and he's wearing a makeshift sling over his left arm. Ronak is missing a shirt altogether, and I realize that's what Evert's sling is made out of. Ronak's face is bruised and battered, one eye swollen shut.

Who knows how long they were beaten and by how many. The fact that Evert can't use his powers to stitch up their cuts and scrapes because of the magic iron cell makes it even worse. The rest of the contestants don't look much better, so I guess it was an equal opportunity beating.

A grim look crosses Okot's face. "Looks like the prince showed his appreciation for the contestants working together at the last competition."

My eyes glance to the prince, watching his smug expression as he looks down at the beaten and bruised contestants. My hands curl into furious fists. "Oh, I'm going to ki—"

Okot cuts me off by taking hold of my chin and forcing me to look at him. His red eyes glance left and right, reminding me of who's around and listening.

I force myself to take a steadying breath. Right. Can't threaten to kill the prince of the realm in front of his loyal subjects. Especially when said subjects are fae, and fae like nothing more than to stir shit up.

Yeah, they'd hand me over in a second.

"Thanks," I grumble.

Okot nods and releases me just as the gong goes off.

The bottom of the arena shimmers slightly, and then the contestants disappear, only to reappear again, eight on one side and eight on the other. The magic arena has turned into a battlefield.

The two teams have been dressed in opposing colors. One side has black armor, the other shining gold. My guys are in black.

I can tell that something's wrong by the reaction that all the contestants are having to the blue-glowing swords that are now in their hands.

Some of them are shaking their arms, some are trying to

120

pry the swords out of their grips, and some are just staring down at them in horror. My guys are looking at them with a sort of grim acceptance.

"What's happening? What is it?"

"It's the king's power. The swords are Beluar Blades."

"What does that mean?"

Okot doesn't take his eyes off the contestants. "It means the metal has a will of its own. The contestants are mere bearers."

I gulp. "So you're saying…"

"That they have no choice but to fight each other to the death."

My eyes widen in horror as I stare down at them. "They did this because the contestants helped each other last time."

"It would seem so, yes."

I look up at the royal box. Prince Elphar and King Beluar look way too pleased with themselves. I realize that this isn't just meant to be a spectacle to the masses. This punishment is personal.

"Okot, these contestants…why were they banished?"

He leans in close to my ear so he won't be overheard. "From what I've heard, most of them don't deserve it, with the exception being only two or three."

I wonder if he counts Ronak attacking the prince as "deserving." I don't ask.

Okot goes on. "The prince counts disloyalty as anything from a fae not giving up his wife so the prince can sleep with her to not bestowing the crown with the land or money he wants."

"And so he banishes them, forces them from their homes, resources, and their families for years, and then tosses them into his death games?"

"Yes."

I watch as the contestants face their opposing team, and a huge wooden scoreboard magically appears on the side of the arena, like this is nothing more than a trivial sport. The blue glow of the swords hovers around the metal like an eerie aura.

Then the gong sounds. There is no warming up. No tentative swings or deflects. The swords do indeed have minds of their own—and they are vicious little fuckers.

There is only one female fae left, and it's clear that the long sword is too heavy for her. It nearly drags on the dirt ground as it pulls her forward. She's crying. I can see the tears falling from her eyes as she tries to fight the sword's hold and get it out of her hand.

With both hands on the sword, it drags her forward, and even though she digs her heels in to try to stop her progress, she keeps going, leaving drag marks in the dirt behind her. The sword will not be deterred.

Her opponent is trying to get rid of his sword, too, but the second she's within striking range, it jerks up, lifting his arm, and swings down at her.

It's strange to watch. It looks more like puppets being pulled on by strings. A macabre spectacle to show everyone exactly who is in charge. Spoiler alert: it's not the fae holding the swords.

One powerful swing is all it takes for the female fae to lose her head. Her body crashes to the ground in a puddle of blood, her head rolling away, and a point goes up for the gold team on the scoreboard.

The crowd cheers.

I want to shriek, cry, or cover my eyes, but I can't, because there are seven other fights going on, too. Some of the contestants seem to work with the swords better than others. Ronak is one of them.

Even though I know the sword is the one with the blood-lust, Ronak handles it with refined skill. It seems like the less the contestants fight against the will of the blade, the more it acts as an extension of their arms, rather than a puppet master.

Ronak's opponent is smaller than him, but he obviously has some skill with a sword, because they're somewhat evenly matched. Ronak's muscles flex, shining with sweat, but I wince when his bare chest gets sliced with a tip of a blade, and blood trails down his skin.

When the crowd gasps, my eyes swing to find the reason for it, and my heart leaps in my throat at the scene.

Evert is on his back, dazed and struggling to catch his breath on the ground.

I'm standing before realizing it, my fingers gripping the railing as I lean over. "Get up, get up, get up."

But he's hurt. His already injured arm hinders him from getting back to his feet, and his other hand still clutches the sword.

There's a deep gash in his right thigh, and blood is puddling under him. For him to have lost that much blood that quickly, I know the blade had to have hit an artery.

His opponent pauses, not wanting to hit Evert while he's down, but the sword has other ideas and lifts his arm up anyway, swinging it down in a killing blow.

"No!"

I watch the sword arc down, straight for Evert's heart.

Time slows.

My entire body tenses with unimaginable grief and helplessness. Evert watches the blade coming for him, knowing he can't do a thing to stop it, and closes his eyes to accept his fate.

The sword comes down.

And jolts against the blade of another. The sound of metal clashing reverberates in my eardrums. I stare, wide-eyed, at Ronak.

He's bleeding, he's fierce, and he's completely feral. The genfin animal has come out to fight. His slitted golden eyes, his poised tail, and his animalistic roar that erupts from his throat stalls the entire crowd.

With his preternatural power of strength, he slaps the opposing blade away from Evert. He grabs the arm of the contestant and, like he weighs nothing, sends him soaring across the arena.

The man slams into the wooden wall, his body exploding in a pile of blood, bones, and splintered wood.

Dead on impact.

The gold team rears back from their own fighting to watch, and then, as one, their swords all pull the unwilling contestants toward Ronak.

It seems their new objective is to end him.

But feral Ronak isn't deterred. Even as six male fae come barreling toward him, he shows no fear. His animal side knows no fear.

When they surround him, I clutch the railing even harder, splinters cutting into my palms.

He's strong and he's a good fighter, but against six? And when those six all carry murderous blades intent on killing him? How can he possibly get through this?

I can see in the six male faces that they are no longer hesitant to fight. They've accepted the drive of their blades. Their will to survive is stronger than their hesitation to kill.

The moment the first wave of three fae are upon him, he leaps and twists midair. Swinging his sword, he cuts down all three of them in a single swipe.

Holy shit.

The last three stop running to watch the bodies fall to the ground. Doubt and fear flicker across their faces.

A fight that they ran toward, one that they thought was in the bag, suddenly doesn't look like such a sure win.

And Ronak? He looks more animalistic than ever. His spine is curved, his nails have elongated into terribly sharp claws, and I can see sharp canines have punched through his gums.

Whoa. I've never seen him go *that* animal before.

He stalks them all like prey. He toys with them as he circles around, his eyes and tail flicking simultaneously.

I can see the wariness of his team hanging back, helping the injured teammates back to their feet. Sylred is kneeling beside Evert as he attempts to heal himself.

Then one of the contestants on the gold team makes the mistake of turning his head to look at Evert still lying on the ground, and Ronak totally snaps.

A great roar rips through the air, vibrating the very oxygen I breathe and causing the little hairs on the back of my neck to rise up.

Ronak runs at him, not even using the sword anymore, and rips the fae's head right off his body.

The last two gold contestants try to run away, but I see their mistake as soon as they do—without thinking, they run toward Evert and Sylred's direction.

I cringe.

Ronak leaps between them, protecting his covey in animalistic possessiveness. He stabs one of them through the chest and plows through the other, knocking him flat on his back before shoving the blade through him as well.

In what feels like hours but could really be no more than a couple of minutes, he's ended them all. When he's done, panting in the middle of bodies and covered in their blood, I can't help but stare down at him in horror.

The scoreboard dings six times.

The gong sounds.

The crowd's cheering grows to uncomfortably loud proportions. The amphitheater vibrates with stomping feet and clapping hands. The second day of culling is over. So are the lives of ten contestants. Eight golds and two blacks. Eight of those at the hand of Ronak.

I don't know whether to feel relieved that my guys made it through or horrified at how.

When the portal is opened and the surviving six are led away, it takes both Sylred and Evert to calm Ronak enough to get him to go through. Even the guards give him a wide berth.

I desperately want to fly down there—to get his animal side to recede—but I can't. Instead, I have to watch him growling, spitting, gnashing his teeth as Evert and Sylred pull him through.

"I have to see him."

Okot takes hold of my arm, forcing my eyes away from all the dead bodies that litter the arena floor. "We cannot. At least not yet."

"I have to," I say desperately. "He's feral, Okot. I can help. I need to pull him out of it, I need to—"

Okot bends down so we're looking eye-to-eye and holds my chin, forcing me to meet his eye. "There's nothing you can do right now. He has his covey. They'll take care of him."

"But he's going to regret it," I say through a choked sob that wants to escape. "When he switches back and realizes what he's done, it'll hurt him. I know he acts like an asshole, but he's honorable. He'll hate what he's done."

Okot pulls me against his chest and rubs my back, and I don't care about the departing fae that cast us curious looks. They can go jump off the balcony for all I care.

Some of them are collecting money from bets, some of them are laughing, going about their days as if we didn't just watch ten fae get killed and one genfin totally lose it because a member of his covey was threatened.

"I hate this," I say, pulling back from him. "I hate pretending."

"I know. Unfortunately, we're not done pretending today."

"What do you mean?"

"It's tradition that on the eve of the final part of the culling, the royals hold a ball. Everyone is required to attend."

"Okay, so we have to go to a ball. That's not so bad."

Okot grimaces. "Everyone is required to attend," he says again. "Including the contestants."

I gape up at him. Me, the guys, and the prince, all in one place.

Well, fuck a fae. We're so screwed.

CHAPTER 17

"*I*'m so nervous I'm gonna pee my pants."

Okot strides next to me, my arm looped through his. He eyes my dress up and down. "You're not wearing pants," he points out.

"Fine, my ball gown, then. I'm gonna pee in my ball gown, Okot."

"That would be a shame, as it's a very nice ball gown," he says, looking at me appreciatively.

"It is, isn't it?" I reply, looking down at the gossamer material.

It's pale blue, and even though I should look like a ridiculous swirl of cotton candy, the dress against my skin and hair somehow looks elegant.

Okot hums in approval. "You look stunning, my beloved."

I smile over at him. His usual floppy red mohawk is slicked back, giving off a polished yet still kick-ass vibe. His nose ring helps with that, too. As this is a royal event, he's wearing his full armor and cloak, which doesn't look at all comfortable but is sexy as hell. I don't know what it is about breastplates. They just do it for me.

"You look pretty scrumptious yourself, bull boy."

Like hundreds of other noble fae, we're making our way up the hill under the night sky. There are torches lit along the path to guide the way. As if we'd somehow miss the freaking *castle* up ahead.

Once we get through the main gates, I see that the party has spilled out from the main hall and into the courtyard. It seems that the little temporary castle can't fit everyone.

Still, the courtyard isn't exactly the kids' table. There are ice sculptures, musicians, acrobats, fountains spewing fairy wine, and food everywhere. Okot leads me past the courtyard and into the main hall where the rest of the nobles are.

As soon as we're inside the opulent space of crystal, flowering vines, and shining marble, I grimace. "It looked more fun outside."

Okot glances around at the noble fae, all dressed to the nines, mingling politely and dancing like they all have sticks up their butts. Seriously, how do their backs even stay up that straight?

I should totally start an orgy right now. At least it would make me feel better.

The grand hall is set up with a dining area, a dance floor, and a platform with entertainment. Music fills the air, and if I weren't so on edge, I might even enjoy listening to it.

I try my best to look calm and collected as we pass through the archway toward the dining area, but my head is swiveling in all directions. "I don't see the guys."

"They'll be here. The royals have not yet arrived, either."

That doesn't surprise me. Prince Elphar likes to make an entrance. As if on cue, an announcer calls for a halt in the music. Everyone stops moving and talking as King Beluar, Prince Elphar, and Princess Soora walk down from the grand staircase and head to the royal table.

They take their places on the raised dais, and the king wastes no time calling for everyone to find a table and sit. Okot guides me to a table in the middle of the room, where we have a good view of the royals but not too close that they'll pay us any attention.

Princess Soora plays her part as usual, always the graceful and composed fae to sit alongside her pig of a husband. When her husband isn't looking, her eyes dart to me and she gives a nearly indiscernible nod before turning to pay attention to the all-important nobles chosen to dine at their table.

When all the fae inside have found their seats, Prince Elphar stands. "We are here to celebrate the coming conclusion of the culling trials," he announces to the room. He's dressed all in his regal opulence, including a golden crown that looks so heavy I'm surprised his neck doesn't buckle under the weight.

"As is custom, the contestants will now enter to observe the feast."

Observe the feast? Well, I don't like the sound of that.

With a signal of his hand, a fae comes forward and steps to the side of the raised dais where a space has been left empty of any tables. With a slap of realization across my face, my eyes widen in recognition of the green-colored high fae who is now working to create a portal.

"Chaucel."

Okot bends his head closer to me. "What?"

I gulp. "That fae opening the portal. That's Chaucel."

Okot follows my gaze. "Yes. He is the prince's personal assistant."

"He was there that day. When I...he saw me when the prince's magic turned me physical. Then later, when I was on the banishment island with the guys, he came there searching for me. I hid from him."

In a pile of shit, I almost add, but I manage to stop myself. Wouldn't want to spoil supper.

"You think he will recognize you, even as you are now?"

I look down at my fuchsia-dyed skin. "I don't know. My skin is pink, my hair is darker, and my wings are hidden. "It's possible he won't. He didn't have that long to look at me. But it's fair to assume he knows what I look like, since he's been the one searching, and it's also fair to assume that he can see through some of my changes." Maybe I should have asked Duru to dye me blue instead.

Okot reaches under the table to squeeze my hand. "I won't let anything happen to you."

The thought of being caught does not give me the warm and fuzzies. I look over at Okot, worrying my lip. "I need a sniff."

With a quirk of his lips, he bends closer to me. I lean my nose into his neck and take a nice, long inhale. The warmth of his smell immediately comforts me. A little contented sigh escapes my lips.

When I lean back again, my eyes slowly open, and Okot rubs the nape of my neck with his thumb. "Better?"

I nod. "Totally."

I don't know what it is about this mate smell stuff, but it's the best anxiety remedy ever.

Chaucel, finished with making the portal, steps back and with a nod from the prince, the portal suddenly expands. A light emits from it, so bright that everyone inside the room exclaims in surprise and covers their eyes, including me.

When the light fades and I'm able to blink enough to regain my spotted eyesight, I see that the portal has disappeared, and in its place is a cage.

A. Fucking. Cage.

Inside are all six contestants, including my guys. They're wearing the same black armor as they were during the culling, and it's clear that none of them have been given any water to clean with or had their injuries tended to.

Most of them are still streaked with blood, though none as much as Ronak. Their dirty and beaten appearance is much more noticeable now that they're only a couple hundred feet away and surrounded by the castle's showy lavishness.

I don't even realize I'm on my feet before I feel Okot tugging me back down to my seat. It takes everything in me to stay where I am and not go to them.

I crane my neck to get a better look, but when I do, I realize that all three of them are staring, not at me, but at the royal table. When I follow their gazes, I home in on one female fae in particular.

Unlike the rest of the pastel-colored high fae at the table, this female has sun-bronzed skin and dark eyes. Her wings are different, too. Instead of butterfly-like wings, hers are covered in fur that matches her hair color, and they're folded up in heavy creases behind her back.

I sit up a little straighter. My wings are totally better than hers.

Still, I can't deny how beautiful she is. Except there's an unkind smirk on her face that immediately sets me on edge. I realize that she's looking right back at my guys now, so that cruel little smirk is directed at them.

Looking back and forth, my brow furrows. "Gods, if it weren't for those hairy wings sticking out of her back, I'd say she looked—"

"Genfin," Okot says with a nod. "She's a genfin."

I whip my head around to look at him. "What? But she has wings."

"Yes. Once genfins form their mate bond, their wings emerge."

I can't help but gape. I was not informed of this very important fact. I look back at the fae woman, and suddenly I know who it is that they're glaring daggers at.

Delsheen. The female they were originally going to mate with.

Except Ronak caught her having sex with the prince before the final ceremony could happen. Caught up in the

132

betrayal of the worst kind, Ronak attacked them, and, well…
that's what led to them being banished in the first place.

She's the whole reason that they're here now, in a cage,
fighting for their lives in the culling, and now she's parading
herself in front of them while sitting next to the prince.

Yeah, I hate her so hard.

If she has wings, then maybe she ended up mating with a
different covey. That probably irks the guys even more. I try
to gauge Ronak's expression. Is that pure hate on his face? Or
is there a shade of lust there, too? I can't help but bristle.

"Delsheen. Why?" I don't hear him say it, but the words
are easy to read on Ronak's lips.

My eyes ping pong between them. I was wrong before.
It's not just hate or lust that I'm seeing on his face. It's hurt.
That's what I'm also seeing. Some part of Ronak still cares
about her, and she's using it against him in the most humili-
ating of ways.

To answer him, Delsheen lifts a shoulder in a bored
shrug. The prince leans down to say something in her ear,
raking his lips over her neck, and Delsheen tips her head
back and laughs throatily.

Oh, this bitch. I'm gonna end up in an embarrassing
catfight for sure.

As the two of them flaunt this display of familiarity in
perfect view of the cage, I know that this move was
completely purposeful. Prince Elphar brought her here to
throw the guys off their game.

He wants them distracted, but more than that, he wants
them to turn on each other again by bringing them face-to-
face with Delsheen's betrayal by flaunting her in their faces.
It's a brilliant move, actually.

"He's good. I'll give him that," I mutter to myself.

I suppose the royals are pleased with the spectacle,
because King Beluar calls for the feast to begin. While all the
fae in the hall point at and talk about the contestants like

circus animals, servants start walking in and piling food on the tables.

Soon, the entire room is filled with mouth-watering smells and the sounds of silverware against dishes, but my appetite is gone. Not one single piece of food or cup of drink is passed to the contestants. Platter after platter of lavish food is set out, more food than any of us could possibly eat, and the contestants are forced to watch this garish display of overindulgence while they sit behind their bars, dirty, beaten, starving, and thirsty.

I'm pissed.

No, not just pissed. I'm fucking livid. I want to leap onto the prince and bludgeon him to death with my dinner plate.

"This is bullshit."

Okot's grim expression matches my own. "Yes. But not here. Not now," he says quietly but firmly.

He indicates the other fae sitting at our table, and like my glance is some open invitation, the fae male to my left smiles at me. "Is the food not to your liking?" he asks, indicating my empty plate.

"I've lost my appetite," I say flatly.

When he sees me glance away, he follows my gaze to the cage. "Ah, yes," he says primly. "Ghastly view. I'm sure the sight of the traitors in their present condition would turn many a stomach, but it is tradition. It's good for them to be forced to observe as outsiders, since they wronged the realm. Best to ignore them, my sweet. They probably won't live past tomorrow, anyway. I've bet a pallet of gold that they'll all be killed, so let's hope I'm right! Right now, they're worthless in the sight of the court."

I tense, staring at this idiot high fae who, for some reason, doesn't think I'll stab him in the eye with the bread knife I'm currently clutching in my fist. Maybe it's the pink hair that's throwing him an *I'm harmless* vibe.

I prop my elbow up on the table, holding up the knife in

my grasp. He uneasily eyes the blade that's now pointing at his face. "What's your name?" I ask.

His eyes flick from the knife to me. "Quorred."

"Ever have a knife stabbed into your pupil, Quorred?"

He blinks, his mouth parting in shock. "I beg your pardon?" he sputters.

I feel Okot's fingers close around my jaw, probably trying to staunch the crazy that's leaking out. He very deliberately turns my face away from Quorred while simultaneously peeling my fingers apart to take the knife away.

When my face meets his, he leans forward and presses a kiss to my cheek. "As much as I love watching you threaten to stab a man in the eye, now is not the time," he murmurs into my ear.

"It was just gonna be a little stab." He gives me a pointed look, and I sigh. "Fine."

He distracts me enough that I miss most of the conversation as it continues on around our table until I catch the tail end of it when a female high fae says, "...and no wings, either! Look at them. They're positively filthy. They probably never bathed during their entire banishment. But then, they're genfins. I wouldn't expect much more from their kind anyway," the female jokes, making the others laugh.

Rage washes over me.

I can't stand it anymore. I can't stand to be a part of whatever this is. I won't sit by while these fae openly ridicule the occupants of that cage, flaunting their food in front of them like it's some big joke.

Leaning forward, I grab an entire loaf of untouched bread and toss it onto my plate with a clang. Then I reach across the table and slap a female fae's hand away when she tries to reach for the meat. She gasps at me, all indignant-like, cupping her hand like I just burned her. The look on her face makes me snort.

I snatch the huge hunk of perfectly cooked meat before

she or anyone else can get their greedy hands on it. The entire table is now quiet and gawking at my admittedly terrible table manners as I stack the meat on top of the bread.

I give the members of my table a fake smile before standing and snatching up a pitcher of fizzing blue liquid. Before Okot can stop me, I'm on my feet, pitcher in one hand, the plate of bread and meat balanced in the other.

I feel eyes on me as I stride straight for the cage. I don't give a shit. I'm done.

Noise in the hall dulls with every step I take. By the time I make it to the cage, you could hear a pin drop in this place.

Reaching through the bars, I hand the pitcher over to the contestant to my left, and then pass along the bread and meat to the two others. I don't dare hand anything to my guys.

The contestants take the offering, staring at me with surprised yet wary eyes. When I chance a look to my right, I see my genfins staring at me like they want to wrap their hands around my throat and strangle me.

Even Sylred. He doesn't look so nice right about now. Oh, well.

I refuse to stuff my face while they starve. I refuse to take part in this ruthless display of public humiliation.

"What the fuck do you think you're doing?" Evert hisses.

I quirk an eyebrow at him and then turn on my heel. Chin raised, shoulders back, I give the haughtiest fuck-off look imaginable to the rest of the dining room.

"What?" I snap. "They were distracting me with their drool."

With that, I stride back across the dining room and sit down at my table next to Okot as if nothing is amiss. Hushed voices and pointed looks lock onto me, but I pretend not to care or notice.

Knowing all eyes are still on me, I start serving myself portions of food, sans bread and meat, obviously. Only when I skewer a piece of fruit with my fork and take a bite do the voices go back up to normal levels, and movement seems to resume.

Okot leans over to me. "That was a very brash move, my beloved."

"I know," I whisper, keeping my eyes on my plate.

I can tell he wants to say more, but he doesn't. Okot lets it drop, not once lecturing me or making me feel like an idiot. I'm immensely grateful. And surprised as hell that I got away with it. I don't dare look back at the cage.

"Did they all get some to eat?"

Okot looks over at the cage from the corner of his eye. After watching for a few moments, he nods his head. "Yes."

I breathe out my relief. My heart is still beating way too quickly. "Good." Knowing that my guys have something in their stomachs, even if it's not nearly enough, makes me feel a little better.

That good feeling is quickly stripped away from me when I feel a tap on my shoulder.

I turn around and come face-to-face with Chaucel staring down at me.

Well, sex on a horse. This reverse cowgirl's ride is about to get bumpy.

CHAPTER 18

"**G**ood evening," Chaucel says with a slight tilt of his head.

I plaster on a fake smile. "Good evening."

"His Royal Highness, Prince Elphar, is requesting your presence at the royal table."

Sizzling shit on a stick.

He offers me his hand. "If you'd like to come with me?"

Nope. I totally would *not* like to. "It'd be my pleasure." I smile.

Giving Okot a glance, I let Chaucel help me to my feet. He tucks my hand in his arm and leads me toward the table where the royals are. My heart is about to dive right out of my chest.

I feel Chaucel looking over at me. "I'll admit to knowing everyone in this room, apart from you."

"Oh, yeah? That's a lot of people to keep straight in your head."

He narrows his eyes at my evasive answer. "Indeed."

I really need to get him to stop studying me. Time to turn the tables. "Being in such an important position means everyone knows who you are. You're very well respected here."

My ego stroking immediately has the desired effect. Chaucel puffs out his chest and faces forward again. "Yes, well, the prince has always respected loyalty. I have earned my position and esteem."

"Oh, yeah. You definitely have," I croon.

We reach the raised dais, and Chaucel turns, releasing my arm. "Here you are. Enjoy your dinner," he says before walking away.

I'm left standing before the royal table like a sheep waiting for slaughter. I curtsy as best I can but, yeah, I soon learn that I suck at curtsying. I also kind of teeter unsteadily because of my heels.

If my cheeks weren't already dyed bright pink, my blush would do the trick.

Prince Elphar looks at me over the rim of his cup. His posture is relaxed, with one arm resting on his chair and the other holding his golden goblet. He's ridiculously handsome in a formal kind of way, his face perfectly symmetrical. He has his navy blue hair brushed back and clasped at his neck, and his icy blue skin is flawless.

He gestures with his hand to an empty chair across from him. "Sit."

I take the seat between two other high fae nobles. Across from me sits Delsheen.

Don't look at her. Don't look at her. Don't look at—

Dammit. I looked.

She's even more beautiful up close. No wonder the guys wanted to mate with her.

Except her wings, I remind myself. Her wings suck.

Prince Elphar's bright blue eyes study me. I guess I'm about to see if Duru's disguise is good enough to fool the prince. My palms start sweating, and the longer he stares at me, the more effort it takes to not visibly squirm.

Finally, he says, "What's your name?"

"Emelle, Your Highness." Thank gods my voice doesn't shake.

His too-perceptive eyes look me up and down. I hide my arm under the table, just in case he notices the ML cupid tattoo on the inside of my wrist. I flick my gaze over to the king, but he's ignoring us completely. He's too busy with the two fae females perched on his lap and feeding him.

Princess Soora is to the left, eating in delicate bites and in the middle of conversing with some important noble who has her ear. Her eyes meet mine briefly. I can tell by the thinning of her lips that she isn't happy with me for drawing attention to myself.

Yeah. Not my best spy moment.

"Emelle," Prince Elphar says, drawing my attention back to him. "You appear to be high fae."

I don't know if he's trying to trap me with that statement or not, so I just wait.

"You appear to be high fae," he repeats. "But you are not completely high fae. For one, your eyes are too small. Plus, your height is too short. And you also lack a high fae's certain…" He pauses, twirling his hand around for dramatic effect. "Grace."

Delsheen laughs shrilly.

Well, isn't she sweet.

I look down at my fingernails. Damn. They're all short and blunt. Note to my stupid cupid self: Grow those suckers out and sharpen them to a point so I can claw her face next time. I guess it takes a lot of planning to have a proper catfight.

He cocks his head. "What are you?"

Although he's keeping the bored tone of voice and posture, his eyes tell a different story. He's staring at me like he's trying to read my mind.

"I'm half high fae, Your Highness."

This makes him sit up straighter. The fae on either side of me look over. "Half? And what's the other half?"

Gods, I hope this lie works. "Human."

Prince Elphar is taken aback. His head swivels to Chaucel, who sits a few seats down, and then returns to me. "You're a halfling?"

Uhhh... "Yes, Your Highness."

"Impossible."

Dammit. Is it? I don't freaking know!

Princess Soora speaks. "Rare, but not impossible, husband," she says politely.

He doesn't even spare her a glance. "Halflings nearly never survive their first year of birth," he says. "How did you survive?"

Well, shit. It's not like I sat around and invented a whole fake backstory on the off chance that I'd be an idiot and draw attention to myself from the one freaking person I was trying to hide *from*.

I guess I'll just open my mouth and hope it comes up with something good. "I'm not sure how I survived, but here I am." I laugh nervously.

Yep. Brilliant as always.

His eyes narrow on me, and because they're so large, the effect is pretty freaky. "Who are your parents?"

"Dead. They're dead." Nice, Emelle. Really smooth. I clear my throat. "I'm not sure who they are, to be honest."

Ha! That's actually the first honest thing I've said.

"I'm assuming your mother was high fae? She took a portal to Earth, mated with a human, and returned here?"

Wow, that's actually a pretty good story. I'll stick with that.

"Yes, Your Highness."

"If she died, who raised you?"

Gods, it's like he's trying to catch me out in a lie. Oh, right. He is.

I say the first thing that pops into my head. "Hearth hobs."

This seems to surprise him, too. "Hearth hobs?"

"Mm-hmm. Yep, hearth hobs. You can't imagine the amount of tidying that went on in my childhood. They really take the 'clean your room' rule to a whole new level. I'll admit, I'm a complete slob now. Just the thought of sweeping the floor sends me over the edge."

I'm getting so good at this lying stuff. I'm gonna be such a good spy.

Prince Elphar cocks an amused brow, but Delsheen sneers at me. "You're actually bragging about living like a pig? You really are half human," she snickers.

"At least I don't have wings that look like hairy flapjacks."

She bristles. "At least I'm not bare-back and useless," she fires back. "Only the lowliest of fae have no wings."

"You didn't always have wings," I remind her. "Who agreed to shack up with you for life, anyway? I'd like to offer my condolences."

Furious, she tosses her napkin down on her plate. "Why, you little—"

"Ladies, ladies," Prince Elphar interjects. "Play nice."

I snatch the cup in front of me and down the entire contents in one gulp. The fairy wine immediately travels to my head. I really shouldn't have done that, but fuck it. I need alcohol to deal with these two.

I badly want to steal a look at the guys, but I can't. I don't dare let the prince see me. Besides, I probably don't want to see the look on their faces as they watch me sit here being interrogated by the prince. Evert is probably losing his mind right now.

Prince Elphar takes a sip from his own cup before setting it down in front of him. A servant immediately comes to fill it, and my eyes widen when I realize that it's Mossie. She's giving me a *what-the-fuck-are-you-doing-dressed-like-a-noble-and-sitting-at-the-royal-table* look.

I shake my head in tiny little spurts, hoping she'll catch the hint, and luckily, she turns and walks away without a word.

"So," Prince Elphar says, bringing my attention back to him again. He seems irritated that I keep looking away. "You are a halfling who was raised by hearth hobs, and now you are here with one of my wife's personal guards," he says, tilting his head in Okot's direction.

"Yes, Your Highness."

He chews on a piece of fruit and takes another swig of wine, all while eyeing me. "Curious company."

"I'm his mate."

It seems I'm not done surprising him. He turns to Princess Soora for the first time. "Is this true?"

I don't know if Okot has even talked to her about it, but either he has or Duru told her, because she says, "It is true, husband. They only just met, and I was informed of their bond."

"I have never heard of a lamassu having a mate outside of their own kind."

Princess Soora nods. "It is rare, to be sure."

Prince Elphar taps the arm of his chair. "That makes two rare occurrences in Emelle's life. Three, if you count her being taken in by hearth hobs. They aren't naturally inclined toward outsiders."

"I'm just super likable," I joke.

His face stays expressionless. "Is that so." It isn't a question. He lifts his goblet to take another drink. "So then, perhaps it is your orphan status, along with having been raised as an outsider that has fueled your misconstrued sense to sympathize with outcasts. Is that the reason why you felt the need to embarrass yourself and give food to the contestants? Food, might I add, that is not yours to give away?"

His reprimand is as clear as the crystal goblet in front of

me. This is what all the small talk has led up to. And this guy has been known to kill people for much, much less.

I have two choices. Stand up for the guys and myself and most definitely be punished for it, or buckle and maybe get out of this punishment-free.

Well, cinch me tight and call me a belt, because buckle it is.

I let my eyes fill with moisture. Yeah, I'm that good of a crier that I can do it on demand. Let the supplication begin.

"I'm so sorry, Your Highness," I say with a sniffle. "I don't know what came over me. I'm totally embarrassed by my behavior." Sniffle, sniffle.

I have the perfect pretty-cry going on right now. Prince Elphar wouldn't be impressed with real, ugly crying. I'd lose my head for sure.

"I know that the contestants only live by your mercy, and I am ashamed to have overstepped. Please forgive me." Tear, sniffle, sniffle.

Would it be too much to cover my face with my hands? Or to fling myself at his feet? Personally, I think it'd be a nice touch. Real theater material.

I steal a look at him through my lashes to gauge his reaction. He looks adequately mollified. Good, because these forced sniffles are really drying out my nostrils.

Prince Elphar looks like he's still debating whether or not he wants to publicly punish me, so I use the other thing in my arsenal. Well, two things to be exact.

I lean forward on the table and prop my boobs up, giving him a nice little peep show of my cleavage. Delsheen looks like she wants to stab me in the throat, so I know my girls must look pretty good.

Prince Elphar's eyes flick down and linger. It makes my skin crawl, but it beats getting beheaded. I sit back when I can't stand it any longer by using the excuse of wiping my eyes on a napkin.

He sits back too, ready to give me his ruling. "See that your misguided notions do not displease me again."

Phew.

I smile sweetly. "Thank you, Your Highness."

He motions to someone behind me, and I hear the musicians begin to play. "Come, Lady Delsheen," he says, getting to his feet. "I believe the contestants are growing restless. We should entertain them with a dance."

Delsheen shoots me a victorious sneer as she gets to her feet. She hangs off the prince's arm as he guides her to the dance floor.

Of course, they purposely dance right in front of the cage. Another show of the prince getting back at Ronak and the others. I'm learning what a master game player the prince is. He's all about the power plays.

Now that the prince is no longer at the table talking to me, I'm completely shunned by the high fae around me. That's fine with me. I shoot Princess Soora an apologetic look and then carefully make my way back to Okot.

When I get there, his hand clamps down on my thigh as if he wants to make sure I can't go anywhere else. He's talking to the fae beside him, but I can tell that his attention is completely on me.

When it's polite for him to leave the conversation, he turns to me and leans in close to my ear. "Are you alright?"

Nope. I'm freaking out, and I kinda want to puke. "Yeah, I'm fine."

He sees right through my spoken words. In the sweetest gesture ever, he tucks a strand of my hair behind my ear. "We will leave as soon as it's appropriate to do so."

I nod. My nerves are completely frazzled. The last thing I want to do is hang out some more, but Okot is right. If the prince saw me bail right now, he'd be suspicious.

I finally allow myself to look over at the cage. Just seeing the iron bars fortified with magic makes me want to ugly cry. I swallow the lump in my throat.

Ronak is standing with his arms crossed, glaring at the crowd. Evert is lying down on his back with his hands propped underneath his head and his eyes closed like he doesn't give a shit about the prince's little game. And Sylred is busy talking to the other three fae in the cage. Always so friendly, that one. They're careful not to look at me, and I know it's smart, and it's deliberate, but I still can't help but wish they'd spare me a glance anyway.

"Let's dance, my beloved. It will help to pass the time."

"I don't know how."

He tucks my hand in his arm and helps me to my feet. "I've got you."

He leads us to the back of the dance floor where we won't have so many observers. Fae glide around us with regal movements reminiscent of ballroom dancing.

Okot clasps my hand and my waist. He starts to move, guiding me as best he can, but I keep faltering and stepping on his feet.

When I hear snickering from other dancers, my cheeks burn with embarrassment and tears prick my eyes.

Okot brings a finger to my chin and lifts my face up. "Ignore them. They don't matter."

My chin wobbles, but I nod, trying like hell not to cry. This whole evening sucks big sweaty man balls.

I fumble the steps some more, and I'm about ready to scream when the bitch next to us laughs out loud at me.

I try to wrench away from Okot, but he grabs my waist, lifts me up, and sets me down again so that my feet rest on top of his. He starts to dance again, and all I have to do is hold on and let his feet move me. His grip on my waist and hand is sure and steady, and now my eyes are prickling with tears for a very different reason.

"First you flew me to the stars, and now you're holding me through a dance. I don't deserve you, Okot."

He looks down at me with the softest expression on his face and kisses the top of my head before tucking it beneath his chin. "It isn't that you do not deserve me. It is that you do not yet see your own worth. I see it. Those genfins of yours see it, too, even if they have not yet admitted it."

I think my heart just crawled out of my chest to go cuddle with him.

CHAPTER 19

This is it. The third and final part of the culling. Only six contestants left, and half of them are mine. Ish.

Okot keeps hold of my hand in the crook of his arm as we wait in line to enter the amphitheater.

When we get to the front of the line and veer off to our normal seats, Chaucel appears in front of us. If his haughty expression and general proximity weren't enough to set me on edge, his next words sure would be.

"Prince Elphar has invited you to sit in the royal box today."

Fuckity fuck fuck.

I plaster on an automatic smile. "How exciting."

Chaucel turns on his heel, not even checking to make sure that we follow. Okot and I share a look before we grudgingly trail after him.

I wring my hands together as we walk, nervous as hell. I'm really regretting that whole feeding-the-contestants thing right about now.

Getting a personal invitation to sit with the prince? Yeah, that's not good.

Who knows what his intentions are. He plays with everyone, and I have no desire to be on his game board.

Chaucel leads us up another three levels of stairs. Rather than our usual mid-level, conservative seats, we go to the top floor, right at the center. Prince Elphar and Princess Soora are already here, as is King Beluar, but he's snoring in his throne.

As usual, he's wearing his long nightdress-looking thing, and I can see his knobby knees poking out from under the fabric. Princess Soora barely spares me a glance, but she nods to Okot as befitting of her personal guard. The prince is in the back of the royal box, standing around the drink table with his posse.

When he notices us enter, he motions a goblet-clad hand in our direction. "Ah, thank you, Chaucel."

Chaucel bows his head and retreats but not before casting an assessing eye over me. How long before he or the prince realizes I'm the one they've been searching for? My disguise suddenly feels flimsy at best.

It's only Okot's hand at the small of my back that keeps me moving forward. He drops into a bow at the waist, and I stumble yet again with my curtsy. I see one of the servants actually cringe at my very awkward movement.

There are half a dozen high fae men surrounding the prince, and they all eye me curiously. "This is the halfling?" an orange fae male asks.

"Mmm," the prince hums, watching me. "Come, drink and celebrate," he says to us.

I walk forward, totally aware that I'm in the lion's den. His crown halos his head like a mane, and his predatory blue eyes watch my every movement. At least I have a bull at my back.

Okot takes two of the offered cups of wine from the servant and passes one to me. "Thank you for the invitation into your box," he says.

Prince Elphar nods his head and claps Okot on the back. "My wife tells me you once served under Hule's regiment?"

"I did," Okot replies. "He was a good commander."

"Indeed. Allow me to introduce you to his son," Prince Elphar says, pulling Okot away. "I'm sure the two of you will enjoy speaking."

With us successfully split apart, Prince Elphar comes back to my side and motions for me to sit beside him. I shoot a nervous glance at Okot, but he's distracted with conversation.

When the prince sits next to me, he raises his cup to mine with a clink.

"What are we celebrating?" I ask.

"The final part of the culling, of course. Are you not excited?"

Not even a little. "Yes, Your Highness."

He smiles, revealing his perfect line of teeth. His large, icy eyes look me up and down, and even though he's not touching me, I feel completely skeeved out. "Come now, we both know you'll be rooting for the underdog, as much as you may try to hide it."

I try to play off my nervousness with a shrug and a sip. He watches my mouth when I lick the residual wine left on my lips. "Doesn't everyone like to root for the dark horse?"

He leans leisurely against the arm of his throne. "I prefer betting on the sure winner."

"And which of them is the sure winner?"

His lips turn up into an arrogant smirk. "Who said any of the contestants win?"

I wipe my sweaty palm on my lap. "What do you mean?"

Is he saying that he's made sure none of them will survive this? My stomach churns with anxiety, but he doesn't answer me. Instead, he takes a sip of his drink, glancing down at the arena full of spectators. I shoot a look over my shoulder to check on Okot, but he's nowhere in sight.

Dread ties itself to the bottom of my stomach. Where did he go?

The prince hands off his cup to a servant and gets to his feet. Passing a hand over his throat, I can see magic crackle out of his palm. When his voice rings out, the entire amphitheater easily hears him. "Welcome," he says, lifting a hand to the crowd to quiet them. "We have six contestants left. For all the fae who have failed thus far, the gods have passed their judgment and found them lacking. After today, we shall see whom the gods have deemed worthy of returning to our great society. Let the culling trials begin."

The gong sounds, making me jump in my seat. I'm pretty sure I peed a little. The portal opens and the contestants walk out onto the empty dirt floor of the arena.

When all six are gathered and the portal disappears, nothing happens. The contestants look around warily, waiting for the competition to start. The fae in the stands begin to whisper and crane their necks, the excitement of anticipation building higher and higher.

I feel my heart beating inside my head, because I know. I just *know* that something is going on. The great, terrible something. The something that I've been holding my breath for, ever since the prince blasted me into my physical body.

When I turn my head to look at the prince, he's already staring right back at me. He digs his manicured hand into his pocket and pulls out some playing dice.

He plucks one from his palm and holds it out, ignoring the growing tension in the waiting arena. "Take it," he says.

I look down at the die in his palm. I don't want to take it. I'd rather pick up a piece of burning coal. But I do anyway, because it's not like I really have a choice. It's made of beautiful white polished wood. Perfectly cubed, smoothed, and balanced. I turn it around in my fingers, feeling the edges as I study the sides. My heart continues to pound in my head.

"I have always been quite fond of games," Prince Elphar says conversationally. "How about you?"

I watch as he brings his hand to my arm and with one finger, starts stroking it slowly. Calculatingly.

I clear my throat. "I've never played one."

He cocks his head. "A truth, I think. One of the first you've spoken to me."

I feel the blood drain from my face.

I don't say anything. I can't. His finger keeps caressing my arm.

He nods at my hand. "It's a poetic game piece, don't you think? Two or more are called dice. But just one, and it's a die."

I keep twisting it around in my fingers, feeling the engravings like the blind feel braille. I look around at the fae spectating, seeing their confused faces and raised monoculars, half of them staring at the stalled contestants while the other half watch the prince.

"I don't understand."

"You said you haven't played a game, so you'll play one now. Roll the die."

I don't want to. I know I don't want to. "Where's Okot?"

"He's safe. For now."

I recognize the threat for what it is. "What do these symbols mean?"

"You'll find out when you roll the die."

He always looks so perfect and handsome, but up this close, I can see the feral hate burning in his eyes. Mixed with his glittering excitement, the combination is terrifying.

"Which contestant are you here for?" he asks.

My heart pounds behind my eyes so hard that my vision blurs a little. I feel my head shaking. "I—I'm not…"

He tsks and leans in closer, his touch on my arm like a snake wrapping around my limb. "A lie. Another one to add to the stack. I'll ask again. Which. One."

I swallow my fear down, refusing to give in. "None, Your Highness."

His touch on my arm goes from a stroke to a sharp pinch as his fingers dig into my skin. It's the snake squeezing me into submission. "Hmm. A loyal liar. What an enigma you are. But no matter. I don't want this to be easy. Like I said, I enjoy the game," he whispers into my ear like a hiss. "And so I will find out your secrets the fun way."

My fear leaks out of my eye, leaving a damning trail of moisture down my cheek. He smiles and closes my fingers around the game piece in my sweaty palm.

"The game has begun. The pawns and the spectators are waiting for the first move. *Your* move. Because, with that die, you are the one culpable for whatever it is the contestants will face. The roll is yours to cast, Emelle. So unless you want me to kill them all right now and end the game prematurely, which would be no fun at all, cast it now."

Behind him, I can see Princess Soora's purple face has paled. Even the rest of the noble fae in the box have backed away, cautiously watching the exchange. The king is still sleeping.

With my eyes closed, I tip my hand and let the die fall.

CHAPTER 20

The die drops to the floor and bounces on the wooden planks.

It rolls and rolls and rolls.

It feels like it's going to roll forever. That I'm going to be stuck in this awful in-between of dread and terror where I don't know exactly what's happening except that it's about to get so much worse.

The quiet sound of it rolling on the floor is somehow so loud that it jars my teeth. The die comes to a stop, and so does everything else.

The prince glances down at the die at his feet, and whatever he sees makes a smirk appear on his face. He picks it up and holds it out for me to see. A symbol that resembles two overlapping circles is displayed.

"What does it mean?" I ask breathlessly.

His smirk widens into a grin.

I try to snatch my arm away from his grip, but he only tightens his hold. "You think I did not recognize you? You think that by hiding your wings and dyeing your skin, that I could not see?" He pulls me close until his lips touch my ear. "The moment I saw you walk up to that cage, I knew you. No one plays me. *No one*. You say you have never played a game? Wrong. You've been playing mine."

He backs up, leaving me swaying in fear, and makes some sort of signal to one of his men. In the next instant, the ground of the arena begins to shimmer and rumble. Everyone gasps when the huge monster appears.

It's a grotesque giant, with a single eye held high on its skull that swivels around like an owl's head. Gray-scaled skin covers him, and a wicked-looking axe is clutched in his grip. Fifteen feet high with arms and legs like tree trunks, he homes in on his prey. He sprints at the contestants from across the arena, making them scatter. But he only follows one.

Sylred.

Sylred dodges it left and right, doing all he can to shake it off, but the giant keeps after him. Even when another contestant gets in its way, the giant completely ignores him. It even goes so far as to run around him.

His single-mindedness is clear. This is Sylred's monster and no one else's.

The giant corners Sylred and, raising his massive arm, swings his axe. I flinch as the weapon comes down, but Sylred somehow rolls on the ground and dodges it.

Meanwhile, Ronak, Evert, and two of the other contestants have decided to go on the offensive and run at it from behind to attack it with nothing but their limbs.

Evert runs right at its heels, sliding in the dirt, and then stops suddenly, crouching down. In a perfectly orchestrated move, Ronak sprints forward and leaps onto Evert's back.

With seamless timing, Evert blasts upward at the same time that Ronak squats down, and with their shared momentum, he then launches into the air and latches onto the giant's head.

I don't know how he still has any of his strength power, considering he's been locked up in an iron cell for days and is half-starved, but Ronak somehow manages to snap the giant's neck in one brutal move.

It takes everything in me to try to not react. The prince is watching me too closely for me to do anything but let out a tiny breath of relief.

I've barely blinked when the prince already holds two more dice out for me. "Roll. Two, this time."

I look at the offending game pieces. "The symbols. Each one represents a monster?"

"Very good, Emelle. And each die belongs to a contestant. You determine who gets what. Now roll them."

I shake my head and lean away. "No."

He laughs at my pathetic resistance and takes hold of my hand, shoving the dice inside. He curls my fingers over them and then flips my hand over. I clutch the dice in my palm until my nails cut into my palm.

I don't want to cast the dice. I don't want to be responsible for who will have a monster unleashed on them. "Please. Please don't do this. I'm not a threat to you. I wasn't attacking you that day, not really. And I wasn't spying!" Not the way he thinks I was, anyway.

But the prince just grips my wrist and squeezes hard enough to make tears spring to my eyes and my fingers automatically pop open.

The dice fall.

He picks them up and signals to his fae again. Two more monsters appear. One resembles a giant serpent, the other a figure made of fire. The fire female sets her sights on one of the contestants I don't know—the fae that I'd given the bread to.

The serpent sets his yellow eyes on Evert. Ronak and he try to take it down, but it's viciously fast and has wicked sharp fangs. It's at least twenty feet long, and when it spits, a steaming spray of venomous acid shoots from its mouth.

I flinch at a strike that Evert barely evades, but the prince

156

is crushing three more dice into my hand, his cruel grip hurting my fingers. I swivel my head to look at him in horror. "Three more."

I shake my head defiantly, even as my lip trembles. "No, please. That many at one time, and they'll all die!"

He looks at me with fake pity. "Emelle. Haven't you realized? That's the whole purpose of all this," he says, gesturing around the amphitheater. "It's just one elaborate game to show them how easily I can end them. It's nothing but a form of amusement for me and my court. You think I want them to survive? You think any of us really care about them?" He laughs, and the sound makes me want to claw his face.

He shakes his head at me. "I *want* them to suffer. To be humiliated. To have their honor stripped away from them. I want them to see me watching and realize that they are nothing but pawns here to entertain me. And every single spectator in here wants to watch it happen, too, because they're secretly grateful that it isn't them down there."

"And what about me?" I challenge, trying not to wince under his punishing grip.

"*You* will roll three more dice."

With a squeeze on my wrist, he forces me to drop them again. Three more monsters come into the arena to join the other two. A massive hound with red eyes and a frothing mouth. Then there's a rolling, slick and faceless blob with iron spikes jutting out all over it. Lastly, what is perhaps the most terrifying monster of all. A little fae girl.

She looks young. Innocent. Completely angelic. Until blades split out of her limbs and her skull splits in half to reveal rows of spiked iron teeth.

The prince releases my wrist only to roughly grab hold of my face. "You spied on me. Attacked me with strange magic. Tried to hide in my own realm. And then you had the audacity to show up at my ball, stand in my castle, and feed my contestants," he spits out. "Now tell me—which one of them was the food really for? Was it because you are working together to undermine me? Or simply because you care for him?"

I grind my teeth, refusing to answer.

His blue eyes glitter. "Still defiant? Hmm. What fun you are." He releases my aching jaw with a cruel smirk. "I love it when things don't come too easily. I shall take great joy in beating you in this game."

He snaps his fingers, and four guards appear suddenly, taking me roughly by the arms. "Wait!" I struggle against them, but it's no use. "Wait, it's not over! Let me watch! I need to see who lives!"

He just watches the guards drag me away. "No. That's part of the game. You don't get to know."

The guards manhandle me out of the box. I barely register Princess Soora's blank face before I'm dragged out. I hear the cries and shouts of the crowd grow quieter as I'm taken downstairs and into the cells below the amphitheater.

In my panic, my wings burst out of my body. I try to use their sudden appearance to my advantage and throw the guards off me, but they barely pause before dragging me forward again.

"I've never seen wings like that," one of them says.

They take me down the dark corridors and then throw me into a cell with solid iron walls. The force of them tossing me inside makes my body scrape across the wooden floor, skinning my shins and palms in the process until I smack against the wall and come to a stop.

Someone hauls me up before I can even shake off the pain. The guard wrenches my arms behind my back, crushing them against my wings painfully.

Chaucel saunters through the door with another guard in tow. I see his green eyes widen at the sight of my wings before a smile crosses his face. "Ah. There she is in all her glory. The traitor who attacked the prince."

I fake some courage and bitchiness, because the last thing I want is to appear weak. Somehow, I manage to roll my eyes at him. "Don't be so dramatic. I attacked him with love."

Well, Love Arrows. About fifty of them. But it's not like they would've been fatal. I don't think.

"Who sent you to spy on the prince?" Chaucel asks.

"Your mother," I sneer.

He looks over at the guard beside him. "Help her be more cooperative, won't you, Gammon?"

Oh, yeah. It's the dick guard who roughed up my guys. And by the way he's stalking toward me, I'm guessing he's about to rough me up, too.

Bam!

The punch to my gut sends me keeling over and heaving violently. I cough up bile, tears filling my eyes as I try to breathe through the pain. The guard holding me straightens me up before I can recover.

"Let's try this again, shall we?" Chaucel asks pleasantly, as if he were discussing the weather. "Tell me who sent you and why you were spying on the prince."

"No one. I wasn't," I say imploringly.

This time, Gammon backhands me across my left cheek. My neck snaps violently to the side, and I see stars and taste blood.

Gods, this guy is like a professional hitter.

"Who sent you and why?" Chaucel repeats.

"No one! I swear."

Another hit, this time right at my eye. I cry out in pain, but I can't even raise my arms defensively because of the other guard holding them back.

"What kind of magic did you attack the prince with?"

I'm sobbing now. I don't want to. The last thing I want is to give them the satisfaction of my desperate tears, but I can't help it. I've only had a physical body for a few weeks, and I'm certainly not strong enough to withstand torture.

"I told you! Love magic."

I don't expect it when Gammon goes for my wing.

He takes the right one in his hand and bends the top ridge back until there's a loud snap.

I scream.

Agony makes me bend over and vomit all over the floor. Chaucel is speaking again, but he has to repeat himself several times before I can clear my head enough to hear it.

"Who runs the rebellion?" Chaucel asks.

"I don't know," I cry.

"Who?" Chaucel yells.

"I don't know!"

I'm panting in both pain and adrenaline, but Chaucel just shakes his head at me and sighs. "I feared this would happen. That you would make things difficult for yourself. A pity, really. You are very beautiful. I'd hate to see you ruin your pretty face permanently," he says, pulling up my chin to look me in the eye. "And those magnificent wings. What a shame we'll have to cut them off if you continue to lie."

Horror washes over me. He catches the look on my face and smiles again. "Ah. I see I have your attention. I think we'll leave you with one last parting gift before we let you think about what is to happen if you should continue to disappoint us and not give the prince the answers that he seeks."

Chaucel nods to Gammon. This time, he doesn't stop at one hit. He goes for my face, my arms, my stomach, my back, and my wings.

I lose count at his brutal punishment. Then I'm in a heap on the floor, black dots swimming in my vision, and they're leaving, slamming my cell door shut with their promise of a swift return. Probably with a saw to cut off my wings.

Tears, snot, saliva, and blood drip from my face and soak into the wooden floor as I lie sobbing. My guys are up there, maybe being ripped to shreds by monsters, while I'm down here being ripped apart by different kinds of monsters.

I don't know if they're okay. I hate that the prince took that from me. The not knowing is as debilitating as my current injuries are.

Then I remember Okot. I try to crawl to the door so I can call Okot's name in case he's locked up here, too, but I can't move more than a few inches before the pain becomes too much.

A giant swell of applause vibrates through the arena all the way down to the floor of my cell, and my gut churns. Their applause could mean anything. The fae have cheered for the contestants both evading death and meeting it.

I'm not sure how long I lie here, but I'm jolted into full consciousness for a soul-deep intuitive reason.

I *feel* it.

Like a rubber band being pulled too tight, my body suddenly snaps.

And then I disappear.

CHAPTER 21

I'm too shocked to move.

I just stare at my incorporeal body.

And stare.

And stare.

And stare some more.

I'm back in the Veil. I lost my physical body. Which means I lost hold of my anchors. Which means they are either gone or...*gone*.

But they were in the arena. They weren't far away from me. Which means...

Nope. I can't. I can't finish that thought.

I'm not sure how long I float, frozen in shock in the cell, but I hear footsteps and my door suddenly swings open. The guard stares inside, slack-jawed, before cursing and running back out.

"Escaped prisoner!"

Oh, yeah. He means me.

And duh, I'm not trapped in this cell anymore. That's one thing I have going for me in this intangible body, at least. That, and the fact that I can no longer feel my injuries. That's a giant relief because those hurt like a bitch.

Yet when I take stock of myself, I can still see the proof of my injuries. Bruised skin, crooked wing, bloodied lip, swollen eye. My body is still the way they left it, I just can't feel it anymore.

When I look over my shoulder to check out my wing, I'm surprised to see that I've acquired a new quiver full of Love Arrows and my trusty cupid bow. That's certainly a perk. Too bad I didn't get a Veil reset on my beaten body, but having my bow and arrow back is a win.

I float through the walls, down the empty corridor, and to the entry room. The guard who saw my empty cell is now arguing with two others.

"Go inform the prince at once."

"I'm not fucking telling him! She didn't go missing on my watch."

"Well, I'm not telling him, either!"

"Are you *sure* she wasn't in there?"

The fae glares at him. "Yes, I'm sure. It's not like she could hide in an empty cell! Besides, they beat her real good. She couldn't have gotten out on her own."

He must've been the one who held my arms back while I was getting beaten. I hope he's the one that has to tell the prince that I'm gone. I'm pretty sure Prince Elphar is the type of monarch to shoot the messenger.

A girl can hope.

"She shouldn't have been able to get out at all!" the other one screams back.

I leave them to it and fly up to the upper floors of the amphitheater. Fae are streaming out in droves. I fly up the stairs, passing right through them, and go all the way to the royal box.

When I get there, the only fae inside are two servant girls cleaning up. "Dammit."

I need to find the prince or even the princess. One of them will surely talk about me? Then I can figure out what happened. I peer down at the ground of the arena, half-expecting to find bodies. Luckily, I don't. But the dirt is littered with blood splatters, burnt craters, and deep gouges. If I were physical, I'm sure I'd already be crying.

I take a deep breath.

Well, kinda. I make the motion of breathing, anyway.

"Okay, Emelle. Get it together. Think."

I fly over the walls of the amphitheater, watching the droves of people already standing in line at portals to be taken back to wherever they came from. I don't spot any of the royals, but that doesn't surprise me. I don't spot the guards who were arguing about my empty cell, either. I do a couple of loops around the lines, but when I still don't see anyone I recognize, I decide to fly to the castle.

As soon as I'm inside, it's clear by the bustling servants clearing the place out that the royals have already left. I go to the lower levels, all the way to the castle's dank bowel to check and see if there are any dungeons.

They took Okot. I need to find him to make sure he's okay. But either the dungeons are really well hidden or they don't exist, because I don't find any. Maybe this temporary castle just doesn't have any? I hope so, because otherwise I run the risk of leaving Okot behind to rot where no one will find him.

I float through the bottom level of the floors, just in case, but all that's there is stone and dirt. When I get back outside of the castle, I look around at all of the floating islands on the horizon. I don't recognize any of them.

"Great. Just freaking great."

I have no idea where I am. I have no idea which direction I need to fly back to get to the kingdom's island. It's not like I can take a portal in my current condition. I try anyway.

It doesn't work. I pass right through. "Dammit!" I glare at all the fae beside me as they pass into the portals, easy as can be. I eavesdrop, too, hoping, yet dreading, to hear how the culling ended, but nobody is going into any specifics, and many of them have already moved on to other topics. Apparently, watching fae die brutally isn't high enough on their list of importance.

My guys could be...*dead*. And here I am, stuck in the Veil, unable to do anything. Broken and invisible, I have the most powerful fae in the realm as a mortal enemy, and all I have in my arsenal is some love and desire.

I'm a freaking cupid. I'm not equipped to deal with this crap.

Maybe if I were smart, I'd leave right now. Fly as far away as I can and just go back to doing my job. Keep my head down, stay in the Veil where I'm safe, and be a cupid again.

There's only one problem. Well, four to be exact. I can't leave them. I also can't go back to what I was before. Not now that I know. That I've *felt*.

I float up high in the sky, leaving the culling island behind. I don't realize that I'm flying in the same exact airspace where Okot flew with me until I look down again.

Grief stabs my heart. Okot was dragged into this because of me. He did nothing wrong, but he's probably being imprisoned, tortured, or killed because of me. The panic inside of me pushes me to hurry, to go, go, go.

I don't care if he is the prince of the realm, I will make Elphar pay for taking my guys away from me.

I look around at the countless floating islands in the distance. The number alone is staggering. But I have to start somewhere, so I pick north. Doesn't everyone? It seems like the right direction to go when you're searching for something.

Except as soon as I start that way, a horde of high fae fly right through me. Jolting in surprise, I wheel around. They're heading west, and they're all wearing familiar uniforms.

Royal servants.

I fly after them, sticking in close to the middle. This

group either isn't permitted to use the portal or they simply want to fly. Flying probably gives them a nice break from all their work.

There are a dozen of them, male and female, and they laugh and do tricks in the air as they zoom around. If I were in my physical form, there'd be no way I could keep up with them.

We fly for a couple of hours at least. Then finally, I see the impressive kingdom island in the distance. A giant river flows right off the side of it, the water landing somewhere far below. The sparkling city spans out against lush gardens and forest. And there, at the edge, lies the huge palace that calls me forward like a beacon.

"Thanks for the directions," I say to the flock of servants.

They're flying considerably slower now, as if they don't quite want to get back. I don't blame them. I was a servant for, like, three days, and I'm still exhausted.

I head down to the island, through the city's town square, over the castle walls, past the stables and courtyard, and right through the front doors of the palace. I go straight to Princess Soora's room.

When I see the familiar purple-colored noble sitting in front of her vanity, I fly right up to her. Two of her hand-maidens are busy lacing her in her evening gown and fixing her hair.

"At least I found you," I tell her.

She looks straight ahead at the mirror, but I can see that her mind is elsewhere. Her face is impassive as usual. One thing I've noticed about her is that she doesn't ever fidget, even when she's really upset or anxious. She's too practiced for that. She probably spent her whole life making sure that none of her thoughts or emotions ever showed through unless she wanted them to. But after all the time I've spent watching her as her cupid, when she was alone and at her most vulnerable, I've learned her tell. I might be the only one who knows it.

It's small. Barely noticeable. But if you watch closely enough, you can see it, and I'm seeing it now. She sucks in the inside of her cheeks—a tiny part—between her teeth. And she bites. *Hard.*

She does it so subtly, though. If anyone were to glance at her, it simply looks like her cheeks are slightly more hollowed out than usual. But the real kicker is that she spaces it out. Draw in. Bite. Release. Then she waits sixty, a hundred, maybe two hundred seconds before she does it again.

And again.

And again.

By brutalizing her own cheeks, in spots no one can see, she works out her frustrations. She'll wash the blood out later. I have no idea how she manages to eat or drink wine after, but she never winces. Her mouth must hurt like hell.

I perch myself on the arm of her chair just like I used to do. "Gods, I wish you could hear me. I wish you could tell me what happened. I'm freaking out here."

A knock sounds on the door, and then one of her personal guards appears. The violet insignia on his armor makes my chest hurt. All I see is Okot dressed in that same armor, seeing me for the first time and looking at me like I was the bee's knees. I miss him smelling me.

"Are you ready, Highness?"

Princess Soora stands and walks to the door. "I'm ready."

"Ready for what?" I ask. Of course, no one answers me.

When we get to the bottom of the stairs, she doesn't go to the dining room like I thought she would. Instead, she goes past the great hall and into the ballroom, which is in full swing of a grand party.

Of course. Another party. The prince lives for them. He doesn't know how to sit still or be alone. He's constantly surrounding himself with fae pawns to play with. The place is packed. There are pixies dancing from platforms hanging off the ceiling, moving to the music in see-through gossamer clothing. High fae, gnomes, bogles, sprites, hearth hobs, you name it, all types of fae are here for the celebration.

Instead of dining tables, this party is set up with chaises and pillowed floors where fae are lounging behind panels of sheer drapery. Rather than hide anything, it just highlights their silhouettes doing all sorts of debauched things.

"My cupid senses are tingling," I murmur.

I'm practically getting high off the lust in here. There's also a distinct haziness in the air from whatever is in those pipes that everyone's smoking. Of course they'd break out the fae drugs when I don't have a body to try it.

She cuts across the room, making her way to the gold-and cream-colored dais where her husband is already sitting with a pixie perched on each thigh.

Princess Soora doesn't even acknowledge them. "Husband."

"Wife."

The greeting is colder than my first bath.

With that, she leaves to take up her own chaise and is immediately swarmed by fae who want her attention. I stay to watch the prince. He looks perfectly relaxed as he strokes his blue hands up and down the pixies' bodies, but I can see the clenched jaw and the hard eyes behind the mask.

"Bet you're pretty pissed I escaped, huh?" I say smugly. Disappearing does have some advantages.

He cuts his eyes to the entrance, and I see a group of fae walk in. Prince Elphar stands, making both pixies fall to the floor with surprised yelps. He ignores them, never taking his eyes off the approaching group.

I try to see over the crowd, but I can't get a good look at them until they get to the bottom steps of the dais and stop, waiting on the prince. My mouth drops open, and I stagger forward. I leap into Evert's arms.

And yeah, I go right through him and fall to the floor. My feet go through the floor a little before I can stop, but who cares? I'm *so* fucking relieved. I want to cry, scream, kiss them stupid, and punch them in the faces for making me so worried.

I touch all three of them, just in case some magic-anchor-mojo happens and they can somehow pull me back into their dimension, but it doesn't work. "Of freaking course not."

I come around to face them again, my eyes taking in their faces with intense scrutiny. "You all look really different. You bathed. And shaved. And got haircuts."

They look like totally different genfins. If it weren't for their tails and eyes, I might not have recognized them. Their five-year banishment beards were really wild and scruffy but now, Evert and Sylred are clean-shaven.

It's weird. Also superhot. But pretty weird.

Ronak opted to just trim his beard shorter. I like it. The hair on their heads is way shorter, too. Ronak's brown hair is shortest of all. He barely has anything left up there, so I'm glad he kept some on his face, at least.

Sylred's blond hair is a bit longer, styled in messy spikes. Evert has left his black hair the longest. He has it sexily flopped to the side, like he's been running his hands through it.

"You three clean up good," I say through a choked voice. I notice that they've finally been healed, too.

Thank the gods that they're not dead. They must've been transported through a portal, leaving the island immediately after they won the culling. That's why I suddenly got thrown into the Veil again. My anchors were too far away from me. The chains snapped, and I drifted away.

They didn't die. They're okay. Those truths go on replay in my brain.

I may have lost my anchor to the physical world, but I didn't lose *them*. And even if I can never talk to or touch them again, I'm grateful for that.

"I love you assholes," I whisper.

They don't hear me, and I hate that.

"Kneel."

I whip my head around at the prince, sending him a glare.

My guys get to their knees, as does another fae male. He must've been the only other contestant to survive the culling. He's cleaned up, too, probably dressed up by one of the palace handmaidens before being forced to stand before the prince.

The music and revelry has stopped, and everyone is watching the spectacle.

"Congratulations on your victory in the culling trials," Prince Elphar says. He doesn't sound congratulatory at all. "Twenty-five contestants entered. Four survived."

The prince watches them as if he'd like to turn into a lion and rip out their throats. The four of them keep their heads down, knees against the marble floor. "You are right where you belong. On your knees. Before your prince. Ready to beg forgiveness for your transgressions and swear fealty to the crown," he says in a quieter voice, his tone filled with evil amusement. I see Ronak's fists clench. "The king is indisposed, so you may make your declarations to me."

As one, they all speak. "By all the fae before whom this declaration is witnessed, I swear fealty to the crown. Through the laws of the royal culling, I have been castigated and tested. The gods of the realm have seen to absolve my offenses. The crown has thus seen to forgive in their righteous mercy. I swear now to submit myself to the will of the crown and the gods. Long live the king. Long live the prince. Long live the princess of the realm."

They all say it perfectly in harmony, which is no simple feat. "You guys totally practiced that."

The prince lets them sweat it out for a few more moments on their knees, in the deafening silence. He finally moves his hand and says, "Rise."

When they do, he looks each of them in the eye. "It seems the gods have allowed you to prove yourselves worthy of this realm again. You will not get another chance. Displease the crown again, and you shall be executed, no matter your noble status."

"I'd like to see you try," I snap.

"Go. Celebrate your victory and your return to society."

They bow before him and then turn away. I follow the guys like a lost puppy hoping for a scrap. The moment they step away from the dais, fae nobles swarm them. They're congratulating them, talking about bets won and lost on their behalf like it's not incredibly insulting to have someone bet on your life. Then there are the suicidal fae twits who start flirting with them, some even having the audacity to put their hands on my genfins.

Yeah, *my* genfins. There's no doubt about that anymore, and I can't lie to myself or to them about helping them find another mate after this. There's no way I can do that. I'm going to have to break my word as a cupid, but eff it. I'm terrible at my job, anyway.

"I'm memorizing all of your faces right now," I say, narrowing my eyes at the stupid females with their stupid tangible bodies. Luckily for the hussies, my genfins have the good sense to politely break away from their fair-weather fans.

You'd never guess that just the night before, these were the same dirty, beaten genfins locked in a cage that everyone scorned and ridiculed. You'd never guess that these same fae now fawning over them were the same ones that mocked and sneered at them last night.

These fae change loyalty like a stripper changes lingerie. Different for every audience but still just as put-on.

CHAPTER 22

The guys continue to field endless fake niceties and praises for the next half hour. It's clear by the set of Ronak's chin and Evert's clipped tone that they're getting impatient. Sylred stays polite and nice, of course, but even he looks restless.

They deny (many times) the requests to dance, too, which I can't help but be smug at.

"I bet you'd dance with me," I say.

They totally would. I'm pretty sure. I could probably get a twirl out of them at least.

The guys do okay with the crowd right up until some dumbass tells Evert he bet against him on the second day and lost a ton of money, and could Evert please reimburse him for the loss?

Evert's glare turns positively murderous. "You want me to pay you for living?"

Ronak tugs him away before he can snap off the high fae's pompous head from his slender neck. Personally, I'm a bit disappointed at the interruption, but you know, high society decorum tends to frown upon ballroom beheadings. Ronak breaks them away from the gathered crowd, veering the covey toward the drink table. They fill their cups and toss them back, then refill for a second.

"Umm, hello? What about me? Can you stop mingling and getting drunk for five seconds and talk about me? I'm starting to feel overlooked."

They finish their second drinks before going for thirds. Every time a fae comes up to speak to them, they glare until the fae awkwardly walks away. I don't blame them. Before, they looked wild and brutal. Now that they're cleaned up, they look...just as brutal. Just because they're in sexy formal wear doesn't mean their muscles and scowls are hidden.

Sylred breaks the silence. "This tastes a hell of a lot better than that damn stuff we brewed on the banishment island."

The guys smirk. "I agree wholeheartedly," I tell him. I look down at my see-through chest. "Well, you know what I mean."

"Incoming," Ronak says.

The three of them stiffen, and I whirl around to see Delsheen heading right for them.

"What does that bitch want?" Evert and I both say at the same time.

I grin at him and pat him on the shoulder. My hand goes through it, but I think it still counts.

Delsheen is wearing a dress made entirely of shiny white fur. It hugs her curves in soft draping. The front of it shoves her boobs up practically to her chin. I look down at my smaller ones and scowl. "Hello, boys," she purrs as she reaches them.

Her furry wings are on display again, and her brown hair is gathered on top of her head with a huge claw. I wonder if her hair accessory is from the same animal as her dress.

"Delsheen," Ronak says in a clipped tone.

She reaches out a finger and trails it down his chest.

"I will bite that off," I threaten her.

"Do you like my dress? It's the best fur that money can buy," she says, drawing their attention to her shapely form.

Evert looks her up and down and then shrugs, unimpressed. "Someone else wore worse fur and looked better."

I beam.

She huffs but otherwise ignores him. "It's been so long, Ronak. Did you miss me?"

Ronak captures her hand, stopping its descent before she can reach the waistband of his pants.

She pouts. "Come now, you can't be mad? That little incident was ages ago, and now everything is over and done with. Your little outburst has been paid for, and everything is set for us to move forward with our mating ceremony."

"What the fuck?" Evert and I exclaim at the same time.

Sylred looks at her incredulously. "Delsheen, you can't be serious. That wasn't a 'little incident.' We were banished for *five years* because of what happened. And you were just openly flaunting yourself last night with the prince."

She turns to him, crossing her arms in front of her chest. I'm sure it's a move just to push her boobs up more. "As if I could deny playing the part the prince wanted me to play. Last night was for show, I promise."

Evert scoffs. "As if your promises mean anything."

"So what?" she snaps. "My wings emerged. Our mating ceremony was cut short, but the fact that mine came out shows just how close we were to completing the bond. We need to finish it. It's your duty to me as a genfin female."

"If you think we're still bonding with you after you fucked the prince on the eve of our last mating ritual, you are as delusional as you are bitchy," Evert growls.

She scoffs. "Oh, grow up, Evert. It was just a fuck. And he's the prince. What was I supposed to do? Say no?"

Evert rolls his eyes. "Please. I'm sure you offered yourself up on a shiny fucking platter. The prince was just another step to climb on your society ladder. You've always been a sycophantic cunt."

The last of Delsheen's coy expression dissolves from her face. She stares him down with fury and then turns to Sylred. "Are you going to stand there and let him talk to me like that?" she demands.

Pleading to the nice one of the group is a smart strategy, I'll give her that. But Sylred just shrugs. "He's right, Delsheen."

She turns about three shades of red. "Well, it doesn't matter what you two think," she snaps. "You're not the alpha in this covey. You didn't grow up in noble houses. You have no idea the pressure Ronak and I are under. I may be a sycophant, but at least I didn't come from the proverbial gutters back at home. You were nothing. Nothing until Ronak bonded with you. You should be kissing my feet that I would even consider mating with you."

Gods, this bitch. I'm gonna make her fall in love with the ugliest, stinkiest, poorest fae I can find. Or a troll with their steaming sex juices. Either way.

I can feel the fury rolling off Evert. Even Sylred has a hard glint in his eye.

"So I suggest you fall in," Delsheen tells them with phony sweetness. "Because we are going to finish this mate bond as soon as we return home. Everything is already arranged. Let's go, Ronak."

All four of us look at him. He studies Delsheen like he's seeing her for the first time. He looks her square in the face, cold mask in place, and finally says, "No."

She blanches. "What do you mean, *no*?"

"No, Delsheen. We won't be bonding with you."

She laughs in his face. "A united front, is that it? Well, you can't say no to me, remember? You're the alpha. That means that, for you, it's your animal side that chooses the mate. And your animal chose me a long time ago," she says in a victoriously sultry voice, pressing up against him. "So you have no choice but to go through with it, unless you want your animal to rage and fight against you for all eternity. He'll reject any other female because he already chose me. You have to finish the mating ceremony. Your animal won't accept anything less. Besides, since we already started, you won't get your magic or your wings unless it's me. So be a good alpha and control your covey, yes?"

She reaches around and grabs hold of Ronak's tail while her own starts wrapping around his leg. Evert curses under his breath. By the look on the guys' faces, it's obvious that this tail-touching thing is a super big deal. For a moment, Ronak looks defeated.

Until his animal side comes roaring out.

And I mean that literally.

He roars. In the middle of the ballroom.

People scream dramatically and run away. Even Delsheen jumps. It's awesome.

Ronak's eyes are no longer his own. Now his animal is in control. His neck cricks to the side in an animalistic way, and his golden eyes flash at where her hand still has hold of his tail.

Like a feral beast's, his lips lift into a snarl, baring his teeth. His growl is deep and loud and super scary, especially considering what everyone saw his animal do in the culling.

Delsheen pales and her own eyes flash gold. She immediately whimpers and drops her hold on his tail like it burns, while her own tail unravels from his leg. She bows her head and cowers submissively. When he growls and snaps his teeth, she takes the hint and starts backing away.

Once she's twenty feet away, she turns and races from the room. I pump my fist in the air. "Yeah! You better run!"

Ronak continues to snarl and gnash his teeth. His whole body is tense, like he's ready to spring for attack.

"What are you looking at?" Evert snaps at all the staring

fae gathered around. "Go dance and shit. Mind your own business."

When Ronak growls at the spectators, Sylred moves to stand in front of him and blocks his view. Ronak growls at him, too.

Sylred raises his hands. "Easy. Ronak, come back out."

"Yeah, you can cut the alpha shit, genfin. You scared the shit out of her. Did you see how far her tail was tucked up her ass? She's not coming back," Evert says with a chuckle.

"Ronak," Sylred coaxes again.

Finally, the gold bleeds out of his eyes, and his posture shudders. When he blinks, his dark eyes look back at his covey.

He looks equal parts shocked and confused. "Did my animal just publicly reject Delsheen as a mate?"

Evert grins. "Sure as fuck did. It was awesome."

"I've never heard of alphas rejecting a mate they previously chose," Sylred says.

"She must have really pissed your animal off," Evert adds gleefully. "Good. Glad that shit's over. If your stupid-ass animal still wanted to keep her, I was going to be pissed."

Ronak just blinks, like he can't believe that just happened.

Evert refills their cups and passes them around. "A toast to the poor assholes that end up mated with that crazy bitch."

They clink their glasses together and drink.

CHAPTER 23

"*A*lright," Evert says, tossing another drink back. *Seriously, how are they not even tipsy?* "We need to figure out what the hell happened to Scratch. We should've seen her by now, or she would've passed on a message. Maybe we should try tracking down that lamassu asshole. If he even is her mate. Fucker's probably faking it."

"Really?" I roll my eyes.

Sylred frowns. "I doubt it. Lamassus are very reverent toward their mate match. He would find it a grave disrespect to lie about it. And anyway, why would he?"

Evert tosses him an incredulous look. "Because she's hot. Obviously."

"Can we get back on topic?" Ronak interjects.

"What? She is." Evert shrugs, making me smile.

He thinks I'm *hot*. The feeling is totally mutual.

"I agree that something isn't right. No way she wouldn't have been here to see us by now," Sylred says.

Evert's face grows stony. "Fucking lamassu. If he did something…"

"We'll find her," Ronak replies, all confidence.

"I'm right here!" I say desperately.

If only there were some way to get through to them. To let them know I'm here.

"What was with her disappearing arm trick?" Evert asks.

The other two shake their heads. "Now that I think about it, I can't feel her. I usually have some sense of her," Sylred admits.

Ronak frowns. "So did I. Now that you mention it, I haven't felt her since…"

"Since the end of the culling."

"Yeah. I wonder what that means."

"Nothing fucking good," Evert replies.

I groan. "Ugh, I should've told you guys what happens when I get too far away from you."

"Do you think the prince recognized her?" Sylred asks.

I nod. "Yes, yes!"

"No way of knowing," Ronak says, cutting his gaze to the prince where he sits. "It's not like we can ask him."

"If he recognized her, and she told him about us…" Sylred trails off.

"She wouldn't," Evert replies.

"No," Ronak agrees. "Besides, if the prince knew we hid her from him, we wouldn't be standing here right now."

"But if they *do* have her, they will try to force information out of her," Sylred says.

The idea that I could be imprisoned and tortured seeps into their horrified expressions.

Evert curses. "Fuck. If he hurts her…"

"The prince is watching. Like he's waiting for something. We can't give anything away."

I wish there was some way I could communicate with them. But how can I do that when my only ways to pervade the physical realm is to…

I gasp and snap my fingers. Well, you know, not really.

"That's it!"

I get close to them, waiting for someone to ask another question. I don't have to wait long.

"Do you think she's back on the culling island still and that's why we can't feel her?" Sylred asks.

I fly up to him and trail a Flirt-Touch down his face. He cocks his head in confusion but doesn't say anything.

"Could be," Ronak replies.

"Or maybe she's here and we just can't sense her," Evert says. "She could've made it back."

I fly over to him and blow a big puff of Lust-Breath in his face. His blue eyes grow sharp with sexual hunger, and he shifts his legs. "What the fuck..." he mutters.

"She'd like this party," Sylred muses, unaware of Evert's sudden change. "Think she'd be over at the food table stuffing her face right about now?"

I blow a Lust-Breath into his face next. Now it's his turn to be taken aback and look all hot and bothered.

When they both keep fixing the front of their pants and shifting, Ronak frowns at them. "What are you two doing?"

"I'm fucking harder than a rock right now," Evert says, throwing me into a fit of giggles.

Ronak's nose wrinkles in disgust. "Too much info."

"No, he's right. I mean, I'm feeling...strange, too," Sylred says, blushing slightly.

"You're adorable when you blush," I tell him.

"Strange how?"

I blow a Lust-Breath into his face next. His head rears back in surprise, and his chest starts heaving. Now I have three very hot, very horny genfins in front of me, and I'm invisible. What a waste.

Sylred takes in his expression. "You feel it, too?"

"Like if Scratch were here, you'd bend her over the drink table and fuck her 'til she can't walk?" Evert supplies.

Sylred groans and fixes his pants again. Ronak just nods, although it looks painful.

"Aww, you're all lusting after *me*?" I ask, ecstatic. "I knew it! You totally like me. Now be clever genfins and figure this out."

"Wait a second…" Sylred begins.

"Lust-Breath," Ronak adds with a nod. He would know.

Evert looks around. "She's here. She's right fucking here, isn't she?"

I blow a big fat yes of Lust into Evert's face. He groans and bends over slightly. "Fucking Scratch. It *is* you. You're killing me here."

"Let's, uhh, go somewhere a bit more private," Sylred suggests.

They walk, somewhat stiffly, out of the ballroom until they find a quiet alcove.

"Okay, Emelle is here, but for some reason, she's in the Veil again, and we have to assume she can't get out. Is that right?" Sylred asks a little uncertainly, like he's embarrassed that he might just be talking to air.

I blow more Lust at him. Maybe I should've made the Flirt-Touches designated for yes… Oh well.

"Okay. So Lust is a yes, then," he strains to say.

"What's a no?" Evert asks.

I trail a Flirt-Touch finger across his shoulder. He frowns.

"Well?" Sylred prompts.

He lifts his hands, at a loss. "I don't fucking know."

Sylred turns to Ronak. "What was her other power again?"

Ronak shakes his head. "I don't remember. All I remember was the hard-on she left me with for four hours."

I chuckle.

"Well?" Sylred asks Evert again.

"I don't fucking know! It just felt…different."

"Like what?" he persists.

"The Lust one makes me want to fuck her. The other thing she just did makes me think of stupid shit. Like writing

181

her poems or getting her flowers or some pansy-ass shit like that."

"You really need some improvement in the romance department," I tell him.

"Flirtation," Sylred says, snapping his fingers. "That's it."

"Very good," I tell him.

"Okay, so only yes or no questions, then."

"If she answers yes many more times, I'm gonna blow a load in my pants," Evert admits.

"That was graphic," I tell him.

"Well, we need to figure out what the hell happened to her."

"Okay, this is what we're going to do," Ronak cuts in. "We're going to go back to the party and be seen for a little bit longer to appease appearances. Then we get somewhere where we won't be overheard, and we can communicate with her without embarrassing ourselves, okay?"

Sylred and Evert nod reluctantly. "That work for you, Scratch?"

I blow a kiss of Lust at him. He covers his face with his hands. "*Fuck.* Sorry I asked," he rasps out.

I dissolve into giggles. This is just way too much fun.

"Ready?" Ronak asks.

"I need a fucking minute," Evert replies, looking pained. "Or a jump in a frozen lake."

Sylred narrows a thoughtful look at him. "Prince Elphar. Delsheen. The snake monster from the culling. Your mother. *My* mother. That gnome with the oozing nose—"

Evert glares at him. "What the fuck?"

He shrugs. "Did it help?"

Evert tilts his head. "Yeah, a bit."

Sylred turns and starts walking away. "You're welcome. Now come on, Stiff."

"It's Stitch," Evert bites back.

His growl doesn't cover up the laughter that follows him.

CHAPTER 24

"**C**an we fucking leave now?" Evert says way too loudly.

It's been at least two hours, and it's clear that Evert is at his play-nice-with-others limit. Sylred gives him the side-eye and then smiles at the noble who's been talking their ear off about some boring crop growth or something. Or maybe he's still talking about the rise of the fish population? I don't know. I spaced out after about thirty seconds of the drawling fae opening his mouth.

You'd think this party would be more exciting, what with the pipe smoking and the moaning going on behind the drapery. But no. We're here, stuck with crop talk.

When the noble fae gapes at Evert's rude interruption, Sylred just pats the fae on the back. "Long week with the culling. I'm sure you understand."

The fae attempts to look unbothered as he strokes his muddy mustache. Like, *literal* mud. I don't know what kind of fae he is, but he looks like he just strolled out of a swamp. "Yes. Yes, of course. Your covey must be looking forward to returning to your island."

Sylred nods. "Definitely. If you'll excuse us."

The guys try to make their getaway. I get slightly distracted at the very interesting orgy taking place on the pillowed floor beside the dance floor.

I tilt my head. "Huh. Interesting positions." I make sure to memorize the scene. For science.

I hurry to float back to the guys, and I catch up to them just as Princess Soora heads them off. The three of them stop and bow. She smiles kindly at them, and as usual, she still looks beautiful and poised. Her lavender hair is impeccable, even after all the dancing she's been subjected to.

She ignores the sounds of the orgy going on in full swing behind her. Seriously, it's loud. Even Sylred's eyes keep darting over.

"Your Highness," Ronak greets her.

She runs her bright purple eyes over the three of them as if she's sizing them up. She has a gaggle of high fae followers behind her who I'm pretty sure are trying to undress my guys with their eyes.

I stand in front of them protectively. It's not like I'm actually blocking their view, but I feel like it's the thought that counts in these situations.

"Congratulations on making it through the culling," she says.

"Thank you."

"I am glad that your entire covey made it out."

"That's very kind," Sylred replies, smiling with his eye crinkles. Gah. Those damn eye crinkles get me every time.

She glances out the nearby window. "Lovely night, wouldn't you agree? The moon is positively vivid."

Evert looks like he doesn't give a single fuck about what the moon looks like, but somehow manages to stop from rolling his eyes. He's respectful like that.

Ronak nods. "Yes, Your Highness, it is."

"I often like to take walks in my private courtyard in order to enjoy it all the more. I find that midnight is often the most illuminating time. Wouldn't you agree?" she asks, looking at them pointedly.

The guys share a look.

"*Oooh.* You're speaking spy right now, aren't you?" I say excitedly.

"I do," Ronak answers carefully.

Princess Soora nods. "Excuse me, I see someone I must speak with. Congratulations again. I had a handmaiden who did so root for you to be victorious."

"Me! She's talking about me."

The three of them bow to her as she walks away, and she's trailed by her fluttering followers. One of the hussies passes Evert a slip of paper, asking to meet her in the broom closet later. I frown.

He stops a water sprite walking by and passes it to him instead. "Here you go, mate. Have at it."

The water sprite takes the paper, dripping water drops onto it from his drizzling hair. "Thanks!" he gives Evert a boyish grin and saunters off.

"Good boy," I tell Evert, patting him on the shoulder.

"You got what the princess was saying, right?" I ask them. "That was code-speak for she knows me, so you'd better get your tailed asses out to her courtyard at midnight."

Sylred glances around to make sure no one is near enough to hear before he says, "Think the princess knows something about Emelle?"

"She fucking better," Evert growls.

Ronak rolls his eyes. "Can you not speak like that about the princess when we're in the middle of the palace?"

Evert shrugs and picks up another drink to guzzle back.

"Aww," I smile. "You miss me so much you're turning into a grumpy alcoholic."

"I don't trust her," he says.

"We don't trust anyone outside the covey," Ronak nods.

"But she knows something, that much is obvious," Sylred

points out. "And why would she risk meeting with us unless she wants to help in some way?"

"You never know with these royals," Ronak bites out.

"How about her comment about her handmaiden? Was she talking about Scratch?"

I blow Lust into his face mid-drink as my yes. He chokes on it and coughs, alcohol dribbling down his chin. He shoots a glare into a spot that I am currently not floating as he wipes his chin. "Dammit, Scratch. Give a guy some warning."

"Well, I guess that's a yes," Ronak says with a slight tilt of his lips.

"Fuck off."

"So that settles it. We'll go meet with her and see what she has to say. But we don't give away anything unless we all agree," Sylred replies.

I find myself staring at his luscious lips as he talks. "I never realized what nice lips you had before. Your beard totally did them a disservice."

"How long until midnight?" Sylred asks.

"About a half hour."

"Good. Let's make our way out there right now."

It takes them twenty minutes to make it the last twenty feet out of the ballroom. You'd think fae wouldn't keep stopping them with the way Evert glares at them so openly, but it's like they just can't help themselves.

When they finally make it outdoors, they head for the courtyard. It's made of the same stone as the palace walls and sits smack in the middle of a lush garden. They take up spots near the fountain to wait.

"I'll do some recon," I inform them, because I'm a super awesome spy like that.

I fly around the vicinity to check for any fae lingering nearby, but I don't see anyone. After making my second swoop, I return to the guys in time to see Princess Soora approaching. She's successfully ditched her followers.

"Princess," Sylred greets her.

"This way," she says without stopping, her dress swishing with every step.

She leads them past the fountain and into the entrance of the rose maze. "Man, I wish I could smell these," I say, looking longingly at all the blooming roses that we pass. "I love smelling flowers. And fruit. And fresh bread. And pretty much all food."

The princess doesn't stop until she reaches a part of the maze that is completely closed off on all sides except for the small opening they came in through. Behind us, the rose bushes sit against a wall, so there's no way anyone can be hiding back there.

"Thank you for meeting me," she says, turning around to face them.

"How can we help, Your Highness?" Ronak asks warily.

"I'll be blunt," she says. "I recognized Emelle when I saw her in the city loitering near the castle walls."

The three of them don't reply or let their expressions give anything away, and she sighs.

"I realize your hesitancy to trust me, but I assure you, I am on your side. Unfortunately, we don't have the luxury of time right now to establish that trust. This may be the only time we can speak, so let us do it frankly," she says sternly.

Ronak crosses his arms and makes an intimidating stance. The princess doesn't back down an inch but meets his glare with an arched brow. "You say you recognized Emelle. If you know her, tell me what she looks like and what she is."

She doesn't miss a beat. "Pale skin, red-feathered wings that don't exist in this realm, pink hair, short stature—"

"I'm not that short."

"—and has a silver tattoo with the letters ML on the inside of her wrist. She is a cupid from the Veil. She's a bit clumsy on her feet and tends to ramble." The guys exchange a look.

"Yeah, that's her." I'm not sure if I should be offended or not.

Princess Soora nods. "I snuck Emelle into the palace and disguised her as my personal handmaiden while she awaited the culling. She told me she was unable to be far apart from you. I helped ensure she was able to attend the culling and pose as a noble. I gave her one of my own personal guards to look after her."

"Why?" Ronak challenges. "Why go to all of that trouble for her?"

"She looked out for me while she was a cupid in the palace," Princess Soora says with a shrug. "But I won't lie. I saw her for the opportunities she presented. She was invisible, obviously passed through your island's barriers untouched, and fae magic did not seem to affect her."

"And you wanted her for…"

She gives them all an assessing look before answering. "I know your histories, Covey Fircrown. And I know you have no love for the prince."

"To say so would be treason," Ronak points out.

"It would," she agrees. "But the fact remains."

"Yeah, we hate the fucker," Evert says.

When the guys give him an exasperated look, he shrugs. "What? We do."

Sylred sighs. "Tact, Evert."

"And maybe some restraint," Ronak adds with a frustrated shake of his head.

"We can stand around all night, or we can cut to the fucking chase. I'd rather get the fuck out of this palace. No offense," Evert adds to the princess as an afterthought.

"Sorry about him," Ronak tells the princess. "He doesn't know when to shut up."

"It's quite alright. I find his honesty refreshing," she admits. "You don't get open honesty in the fae court. But let me cut to the chase, as you said. I asked Emelle to spy for me.

To help my attempts in the rebellion. I'm hoping you will join that cause as well."

The genfins weren't expecting that. Sylred's brown eyes widen, Ronak's jaw clenches and Evert scoffs. "Wait a minute, you want Emelle as a spy?" he laughs. "She's not spy material."

"Hey!"

"He's right," Ronak agrees.

"Congratulations," I snap. "You're known as the asshole again. And you," I say, pointing at Evert. "Watch it."

"My agreement with Emelle has no standing on this conversation," Princess Soora replies sternly.

I sidle up next to her. "Yeah, that's right. Chicks before dicks. We stick together."

"Aside from hoping you'll join my cause, I am also here to inform you that the prince recognized her. At last night's gathering."

"Fuck," Evert curses, running a hand through his hair. "She should never have tried to fucking feed us. She stands out even with the disguise."

"What happened?" Sylred asks worriedly.

Princess Soora's expression turns unhappy. "He invited her and my lamassu guard, Okot, to the royal box to watch the third part of the culling. He hadn't let on to anyone that he recognized her, save perhaps Chaucel."

"And?"

"I'm not sure exactly, but he arrested her in the middle of it. She wasn't sure whether you lived or died. They dragged her away to the cells, where I'm told she was questioned. I don't know what, if anything, they learned from her. But I do know that when they went back to her cell, she'd disappeared."

"Yeah, she's in the Veil again," Sylred says, rubbing his brows.

She nods. "I assumed as much. As you were her anchors,

189

she was unable to hold her physical form when you all went through the portal at the end of the culling."

The guys all stiffen.

Eek. Cat's outta the bag.

Their expressions shift to varying degrees of pissed the hell off. I wish I could bite my nails right now. Or scratch my arm. Or do anything physical to dispel this nervous tension in my stomach. I try to pace around, but that doesn't really help when you can't feel the gravity of your steps.

"What the fuck are you talking about?" Evert asks incredulously.

"Okay, cool it, Mount Vesuvius. Maybe don't erupt at the *princess* of the freaking realm," I hiss. "Be a bit more respectful."

For all her grace, Princess Soora doesn't even look perturbed by his outburst, even though she could totally have him beheaded for being a dick.

She tilts her head. "She never told you?"

"Explain. Please," Ronak grits through his teeth.

"Well, that's why she had to stay so close to you all. Apparently, when the prince hit her with his raw magic to turn her physical, the effects would have worn off if not for the three of you touching her and anchoring her to the physical world.

"If she was too far apart from you or went too long without your presence, she'd start to fade. She started fading while she stayed here. It was one of the reasons I assigned Okot to her—so he could keep an eye on the progress of her disappearance. It made her ill, too, although she tried to hide it. When you went through the portal, I assumed the distance was too great and she vanished back into the Veil."

Evert looks up at the sky, shaking his head. I can't read Ronak's expression because he looks stony as usual. Does he hate me? Gods, I hope not. Me wanting to stay with them was not just about me needing my anchors.

"No, she didn't tell us," Sylred says quietly.

"Fucking hell, Scratch," Evert snaps.

"Sorry," I say, feeling chastised.

"She was using us," Ronak says.

I shake my head adamantly and try to grab onto his arms, forgetting myself. "No, I swear."

Evert points at his face. "That's not what she was doing. Stop always trying to see the worst in her."

Sylred looks thoughtful. "If she'd only wanted to stay with us to use us as her anchors, then it would've made more sense for her to tell us that," he points out to Ronak.

Ronak scoffs. "Yeah? Then what's her reasoning behind *not* telling us?"

I wish I had some Anti-Lust to blow into his stupid face right about now.

Surprisingly, it's Princess Soora who answers. "I don't believe she withheld that information in order to take advantage of you. That's not the impression I got from her at all. In fact, I believe she didn't tell you because she wanted you to know that she only wished to stay with you for the right reasons. For all her lightheartedness, she's actually quite thoughtful."

Ronak grunts but doesn't say anything more.

I lift my chin haughtily. "That's right. I'm *thoughtful*, you butthead."

"Regardless of motives," Princess Soora goes on, "I think I may have found someone who might be able to help bring her back again."

I whirl around to face her. "Really?"

"Who?" Evert demands.

"Most call him the Horned Hook."

The guys look at her incredulously. "He's a thief," Sylred points out.

She doesn't deny it. "He is. But he's notorious in the realm for a reason. He has ways of getting you whatever you need.

In this case, I believe he may be able to find the magic needed to restore her. If it was done once, it begs the argument that it can be done again. Since it's quite obvious we cannot ask the prince to use his magic, we must find someone who has similar magic that would be willing."

"I heard he was banished again."

"The Horned Hook has been banished and imprisoned many times. He always escapes," she points out.

"You're putting yourself at great risk by associating with Emelle, even if you do want her as a spy," Ronak says.

She lifts a shoulder. "I am at risk every day. I am also a very good judge of character. I see fierce honesty and loyalty in her, which is exactly what I need for members of the rebellion."

I grin. We're totally besties.

Sylred blows out a puff of air. "No one even knows where to find the thief."

"No, but it's well-known in the realm how to ask for an audience."

"Yeah, bring a stolen object of great worth to the elder grove."

"Indeed."

Evert rolls his eyes. "He's a showy asshole."

"That may be, but he also may be your only chance at getting her back. But you'll need to ensure she's around somehow, although I have no idea how you'll manage that."

Evert smirks. "Don't worry, she already found us."

Princess Soora looks around. "What, she's here?"

"Yep."

"How do you know?"

Sylred grimaces. "You don't want the details, trust me. Just leave it at her cupid wiles making us aware of her presence."

"Very fucking aware," Evert mumbles.

"...Alright." Princess Soora looks around. "Then there's

the matter of my guard, Okot." She looks at them carefully. "They formed a close relationship in a short amount of time."

"Yeah, mates. We heard," Evert says dryly.

"Yes. He was taken also, but I have no idea where he's being held or if he is indeed still alive. All my careful inquiries have come up empty."

A wave of pain washes over me. "Oh no, Okot," I whisper. This is all my fault.

"I'll try to find out more, but for now, I'm at a dead end," she says. "I need to go. I've been gone far too long already. Oh, I almost forgot." She pauses. "I hate a stuffy bedroom, don't you?"

They look at her like she's crazy. And I do, too, because: hello, random.

She goes on, undeterred. "I hate it so much, in fact, that I left my bedroom window open this evening. Not many guards patrolling this side of the palace, either," she says conversationally. She points up the palace walls, past a grove of trees near where we're standing. "That's my window, there. Did you know, I'm certain I accidentally left out some *objects of great worth* on my dressing table tonight?"

Evert frowns, bewildered. "Uh, okay…"

Ronak rolls his eyes at him and mumbles, "Idiot," under his breath.

"She's helping us to 'steal' something to bring to the thief," Sylred says.

Realization dawns on Evert's face. "Oh."

I pat him on his cheek. "That's okay. You're pretty. You don't have to be smart."

The princess starts walking away. "Gain an audience with the Horned Hook. I'll keep in contact when I can by sending my personal handmaiden, Duru, to speak with you. There will be no other means of communication, is that clear?"

They all nod. "I wish you good luck, then. And Emelle?"

she says, addressing the night air. "Don't lose hope. We'll see you soon."

Determination settles into me. Her words are like a promise, and for the first time since turning invisible again, I feel like there's a real chance that I can come back.

One thing is for sure—I'm going to find Okot and save him if it's the last thing I do.

CHAPTER 25

$\mathcal{I}$n the human realm, I heard a lot of fancy sayings like, "absence makes the heart grow fonder," and "you don't know what you got 'til it's gone," and "I wanna really really really wanna zig-a-zig-ah."

Like I said. Fancy.

But if there's one thing I learned being an invisible cupid, it's that people say fancy words all the time that they don't actually mean. Like the man exchanging sacred marriage vows, only to break said vows during an employee mixer on top of his work desk the very next week.

But some words actually *are* genuine, and it's those ones that seem to sink into your skin and stay with you—because you know they really meant something.

That's how I feel when I think of every word Okot ever spoke to me. It's totally true that we haven't known each other for long. He just sort of bumped into my life. But I liked the bump. I want my bump back.

When he spoke to me, every fancy word he said was true. I could just tell. When he said I was his mate, he was being sincere. When he called me his beloved, he meant it.

I didn't get enough of his fancy words. I meant it when I said I was going to keep him. So I have to get him back.

"Right," Evert says, staring up at Princess Soora's open window. She's already gone, so it's just the guys standing around the private courtyard now. "Guess I'll just go and steal some of her shit," he says, starting to stride toward the palace wall.

Ronak and Sylred wait, watching as Evert climbs a tree near the wall with effortless precision, and then he leaps to the princess's balcony.

He disappears inside and comes out a short minute later. Forgoing the tree, he climbs on top of the balcony railing and then jumps.

"Holy hotcakes."

But he lands on all fours in a crouch, his tail upright behind him. Right. Part feline.

When he comes strutting back, he shows the sparkling necklace he has fisted in his hand. "Let's go."

We leave the palace grounds, walking out of the gate and into the city of Highvale. This late at night, most of the shops and eateries are closed, but the nightlife scene is in full swing. The nocturnal fae are out and about, sipping drinks in night cafes and dancing in nightclubs.

I float behind the guys, their steps clacking against the cobblestones. The guys are quiet as they make their way up the street, and they end up walking into *Hellfire &* *Hounds Inn*.

"Really? I would've gone with the *Snug & Dandy Inn* down the street, but whatever razzles your berries."

The innkeeper practically trips over himself to welcome the infamous genfins who made it out of the culling. After a lot of blubbering, he gives them his best room.

When we get upstairs, I wrinkle my nose. "*This* is his best room? It looks like there was *actual* hellfire up in here," I say, looking at the scorch marks and soot stains.

"Huh," I say, studying a burned outline on the wall. It clearly shows someone's silhouette in a compromising position. There's also a second pair of hands above the head. I smirk. "Someone totally had hot fire sex against this wall."

Aside from the walls that only a demon would love, the space isn't too bad. The most important part is that there are three fairly cleanish-looking beds.

I can see that the exhaustion has settled over the guys now that they're away from watching eyes. They managed to keep their masks on all this time, but now they've come off.

They might've had their physical wounds healed, some haircuts, and a bath, but the weariness of the culling competition is still there. The guys kick off their boots and start undressing.

"Oh. Right. I guess I should turn around?"

I keep watching. Because, yeah. I've been totally imagining them naked since I first saw them. Invisibility has its perks. I perch my voyeur ass on one of the beds and watch the show.

Evert is the first to lose his formal jacket and then his shirt. His pale skin is even paler in the moonlight coming through the window, but he has sculpted abs and pecs, as well as a small happy trail of black hair that leads right to the promised land.

I totally want to go to the promised land.

Leaning up, I wait for him to lose his pants. To my great disappointment, he doesn't. "Tease."

Sylred and Ronak have their shirts off, too. Sylred is leaner, while Ronak is all sculpted granite and bulging muscles. If I had saliva, it'd be dripping down my chin.

"My, my, my. Post-banishment looks good on you."

Much to my disappointment, they don't take off their pants, either. I only pout a little.

"Enjoy the peep show, Scratch?"

I jump. "What? No. Totally wasn't watching you guys

strip or anything," I say in a rush, forgetting that they can't actually see or hear me. Evert chuckles like he knows he caught me, anyway. "You're such a jerk face."

"I keep forgetting she's hanging around," Ronak mumbles before flopping onto one of the beds.

"Me too. Unless…maybe she didn't follow us," Sylred says.

Evert snorts. "Course she followed us. Didn't you, Scratch?"

Well, since he asked.

"Fuck! Stop doing that! It was rhetorical. I know you're fucking here," he says, scowling at his erection.

Sylred and I chuckle. I'm pretty sure Ronak's lip twitches, too.

Evert and Sylred settle onto the other two beds, and soon, their breathing evens out nice and slow. I lie down in the bed next to Evert. If I position myself just so, the outline of my ghostly body almost looks like we're touching. He shifts in his sleep, flinging an arm over where my waist is.

I close my eyes, just imagining how it would feel to be held by him like this. Then I remember when Okot did.

I lie next to Evert for the rest of the night, pretending I can feel and pretending Evert can feel me, too. What? I'm freaking lonely. Also bored. I miss sleeping. Watching people sleep isn't nearly as entertaining as that Edward vampire dude made it out to be.

Ronak is the first to wake up in the morning. Not that it surprises me. As soon as he sits up, there must be some freaky covey alarm clock that goes off, because the other two wake up, too.

The guys quickly dress in the same fancy clothes as last night. They move nearly in sync, always aware of each other in the small space, moving aside for one to get his boots, leaning away as another puts his arms through his sleeves.

When they plod downstairs and out onto the street, the sun is barely coming closer from its spot high in the sky. Soft yellow and blues are forming around it in a ring, pushing the dark away like a pupil grows inside an iris.

"Where are we going, anyway?" I hate that they can't hear me.

They walk out of the city of Highvale altogether. They're still walking when the sun is no longer a pinprick but a grapefruit in the sky. More fae are awake by now, so the guys get plenty of looks as they make their way into the forest that borders the city.

Almost as soon as we step under the first row of trees, there's this ominous *quiet* that closes in on us. The trees are ancient-looking, too, with gnarled roots and rough gray bark. To make matters worse, the bark has these black circles knotted into them that look like eyes are watching us.

"Okay, so super creepy eye-trees. That's comforting, yeah?" The guys just keep stomping onward. "Gods, why are you all so quiet? Seriously, you haven't spoken a single freaking word since you woke up."

I don't think that's natural. Can't be. It's probably bad for their voice boxes. Or their tongues. The tongue is a muscle, right? It needs to be worked out. I bet my tongue is totally ripped. I mean, as far as muscles go, I totally win that one for sure.

I guess the guys know exactly where they're going, because their steps never hesitate or falter. If I'd had to walk all this way, I would've been panting by now. And probably gotten leg cramps. Also feet cramps. And stomach cramps. Probably all the cramps. I don't care what anyone says, walking is super hard.

We reach a small clearing in the forest, and there in the center is what can only be classified as the Elder Tree. I know this because it's larger than all the other trees around, and it looks like an old man. That…and there's literally a sign next to it that says, "Elder Tree." So there's that.

"Oh. I guess we're looking for this Horned Hook thief, huh?"

The guys look at the grotesque face carved into the center of the Elder Tree. It has those black knots for eyes. The leaves really give me the heebie-jeebies. If they can even be classified as leaves, which I seriously doubt. Instead of green leaves like the rest of the grove, the Elder Tree has long silvery-white strings growing off its gnarled branches, resembling gray hair.

"Okay, do the thing, hang the object, request the meet, and let's blow this balloon stand, because this place is spooky," I whisper. Realizing my idiocy, I snort. "Stupid cupid. Whispering when no one can freaking hear you anyway."

I see a ghost meandering around the grove. "Well, except that guy. Hey, ghost!"

He ignores me. Figures.

Evert reaches into his pocket and approaches the Elder Tree. He hangs up Princess Soora's 'stolen' necklace on a branch. When that's done, the three genfins stand in a row, their arms crossed and scowls in place.

We wait forever.

Or, like, probably twenty minutes.

If the forest hadn't been so silent and still, I might not have picked up on the slight movement above. One second, nothing. The next, a gray hand reaches down and snags the hanging necklace from the branch.

CHAPTER 26

"*H*ey! Get back here!" Evert exclaims. "Go steal your own shit!"

He's gearing up to pounce on the tree and make a climb for it, but Ronak puts an arm out to stop him. "Wait."

Well, that's all fine and dandy, but *I* don't have to wait. So I decide to do some recon because I'm badass like that.

Wait, is it recon if I'm chasing after someone? I shake my head at myself as I float up the tree. I actually don't know what stipulates a strict "recon" mission, if I'm being honest. I just get pumped up when the guys are around doing important sneaky things and I throw around mission words like "recon" in my head because it seems appropriate. I clearly need to study some spy terms.

Maybe I should have spied on more military humans when I had the chance. Although, I did do a stint in a boot camp once. There weren't a lot of romance embers to stoke to life over there, but I liked watching all the drills and the yelling. It was very titillating. But only because I wasn't the one doing the drills and stuff. That would've sucked.

When I reach the top of the tree, I catch up to the fae who stole our necklace. She's perched precariously on the highest branch, crouched with her knees pressed against her chest. She has straight, silvery hair that looks exactly like the tree's, and skin to match the color of the bark. It's uncanny how much she blends in with it.

She cups her hands around her mouth and makes some strange whistling and clicking noises, the gold chain of the necklace still entwined in her fingers.

She waits with her head cocked, and then flicks her tongue out at the air, and I shriek a little in surprise. "Whoa, that thing could take out an eye." It's super long and bumpy and is coated with a green slime. Yuck.

After a moment, we both hear the replied whistles off in the distance. Seemingly satisfied, the fae stands, and like a spider monkey, she starts swinging down the branches until she lands in a crouch at the bottom of the Elder Tree, facing the guys.

I realize then that she's totally naked. Like, I can see *everything*. Her nipples look like tree bark. And the carpet definitely matches the silver stringy drapes.

I turn and point at the genfins. "If any of you check her out, so help me, I will Lust you to death in your sleep."

Aside from some widened eyes of surprise at her appearance, the guys keep their gazes steadily above her neck. It's like they know I'm thinking of murdering them with their own erections.

"Your token is accepted," she tells them, her voice much deeper and raspier than I expected.

I notice that her bare feet and legs are shimmering slightly, and then they're no longer gray, but brown and green to match the forest floor. The top of her is still gray though, so it looks really weird.

"You're a chameleen," Sylred says with a bit of awe in his tone.

The fae nods and pulls off three pieces of braided tree-hair that had been twined around her biceps. "Put these on over your eyes."

The guys exchange a look and then dutifully tie the hairy blindfold thingies around their heads. Satisfied, she whistles, and two more chameleen females appear out of nowhere. They're also naked.

"Can't you guys make some camouflage clothing, or something? This is unprofessional."

The three chameleens each take hold of my genfins' hands and start pulling them forward. A bout of irrational anger washes over me. The intense jealousy takes me a bit by surprise, if I'm being honest, but—*Is Ronak checking out her ass?*

I fly around and get right in his face, and it's like he knows. His eyes immediately snap up. A bit of a growl escapes me when I continue to glare at him.

Damn. I'm getting salty in my invisible new age.

"That's your only warning, Not-First." I point in his face. He walks right through me. I would be so much more intimidating if I were corporeal. "We'll talk about this later!" I eye Sylred and Evert as they pass. "I'm watching you two."

The chameleens lead us to a circle of mini elder trees. The leader drops Evert's hand and strolls forward to a tree. She places her palm against one of the knots, and with some magic forest juju, the ground suddenly opens to reveal a stairwell made of hard-packed dirt.

"The Horned Hook will see you now," she says, her skin changing to accommodate her surroundings as she moves.

"Thank you," Sylred tells her as the three of them strut toward the stairs. The second we start climbing down, the ground above us closes back up.

"That's comforting," I mumble.

The guys don't look the least bit concerned that we're practically buried underground. Shocker.

It should be pitch black down here, but the Elder tree roots poking out are giving off a soft phosphorescent blue glow. At the bottom of the stairs, a narrow passage awaits. The guys have to duck their heads to walk down it. At the end is a door. Ronak balls his fist, pounds on it once, and then lets himself in without waiting for any kind of reply. Sylred sighs in exasperation.

The room inside is weird.

There are all kinds of different-sized hooks hanging from the ceiling and walls, and they're holding all sorts of what I'm guessing are stolen objects. Most of it is jewelry, but there's also clothing and weapons.

Standing in the center, lit up blue by the glowing roots, is a man wearing a silver mask. It has four horns on either side, starting from the top and curving around to the chin. The mask even covers his lips and eyes, leaving only small slits for him to see and speak through. Looking at him standing in the midst of his hanging treasures, I totally get his nickname.

"Welcome," he says. Ronak crosses his arms as Evert and Sylred flank him. "Ah, genfins. Can't say I've ever had the pleasure of doing business with your kind before."

"Genfins are not ones to deal with thieves," Ronak replies.

Sylred puffs out another exasperated sigh, but the Horned Hook just laughs. "Indeed. Yet here you are, and thieves yourself," he says, nodding his head toward the necklace clutched in Evert's hand.

Evert holds his fingers open, but before he can hand it over, the Horned Hook makes a flicking motion with his hand and the necklace zooms right to him.

"Whoa," I breathe. "Guys. He can move stuff without touching it. What's that called again? Tele-something. Telephone, telemarketing, telegraph, telescope, telepathic…I know I'm close."

"You are telekinetic," Ronak says.

"That's it!"

The Horned Hook tosses the necklace back and forth between his hands. He ignores Ronak's statement and makes the necklace float in front of his face to better study it in the blue light. "This is worth quite a lot. It also has the crest of the royal jeweler on the back. Very valuable indeed."

He flicks his hand again, and the necklace goes flying up to hang on an empty hook above us. "Very well, you've earned my services. But first, do you know the reason that I require not just a precious item, but that it also be stolen?"

Sylred is the one who answers. "Because you trade in secrets."

The fae nods. "Exactly. Any good thief who's worth their weight can find things and be paid in jewels," he says, gesturing to the many items on display. "But a great thief knows that the most valuable things to take are secrets. When I require a stolen item in exchange for my services, it's not just to be paid, it is also to ensure that I have a secret over you, just as you will have one over me. You stole from the royals. That is my advantage over you."

The guys watch him carefully, and I have to say, I'm a little impressed. Okay, a lot impressed.

"So tell me your secret," he continues. "How did you steal this necklace?"

"During the culling commencement ball at the palace," Evert explains smoothly. "While everyone was busy, we went outside, and I climbed onto the princess's balcony and slipped inside her open window. That was on her dressing table."

The fae cocks his head, and even though I can't see it, I'm pretty sure he's smiling. "You stole the princess's necklace right out from under their noses? You three must want something very badly. Very well. I'm listening."

The guys exchange a look, and my nerves amp up several notches. If he can't help us...

Sylred clears his throat. He's always the one to talk during

205

delicate matters since he's the best at it. Ronak goes into his scary caveman speech too often, and Evert just says *fuck* a lot.

"Someone we know is trapped in the Veil. We want to get her out."

The fae rears back in surprise. "In the Veil?" He shakes his head. "Impossible."

"It's not," Sylred says evenly. "She was brought out once before by a fae with incredible raw power. The magic caused her to anchor to other physical entities, keeping her here. Unfortunately, her ties to those anchors were broken when the distance between them was too great, and she got forced back into the Veil. We need you to find someone who can bring her back and anchor her more securely."

The Horned Hook starts rubbing his chin in thought from underneath the mask. He says nothing as he starts walking around the small room, lost in thought.

His body is leaner than all of my genfins, and he's shorter, too, but still taller than me. Based on his body and his voice, he seems around the genfins' age, but the fae age weird, so who really knows?

"The fae who did this in the first place—I am guessing it's not an option to simply ask him or her to do it again?" he finally asks.

Ronak says a stern, "No."

"I need to think on this," the fae replies.

"We need this to be done now."

The Horned Hook sighs, not at all cowed by Ronak's growing temper. "Yes, yes, everyone who wants something wants it *now*. The problem is, there is not a single fae in the realm that I know who has this level of raw magic."

Evert curses, Sylred looks around like he's trying to spot me, and Ronak's fists clench. "If you're wasting our time—" he begins, taking a menacing step forward.

The fae holds up his hands. "Calm yourself. I said there is not a *single* fae. I do, however, know of a pair of fae with the ability to combine their magic. They may be able to do what you need. But they do not see outsiders much. It'll take some convincing."

"Then fucking convince them," Evert snaps.

"My, my. You three do want this fae out of the Veil. A female, was it?"

None of them answer, but I can hear the mirth in his voice. "It's always a female." He swings back around to Ronak. "Alright, I'll secure a meeting for you. Deal?"

Ronak and Evert begin to nod, but Sylred cuts them off and steps forward. "Not quite." The other guys share a confused look.

"Oh?" the Horned Hook drawls. "You have someone else trapped in an impossible location, too? Perhaps a water sprite in the underworld?"

"This isn't a fucking joke," Evert growls.

I can practically hear the fae roll his eyes. The fact that he's not intimidated by the three genfins is actually kind of impressive. "My sincerest apologies," he says, amusement evident in his tone as he puts a hand over his heart. "Please continue," he tells Sylred.

"Since you don't have to actually do much for this first job except set up a conversation, we also require a second job from you. And based on the priceless token we brought, this request should be more than fair."

The Horned Hook doesn't answer for a few beats, and it makes me a bit freaked out. I mean, what if Sylred pissed him off, and now he's going to refuse to help us? But the guys stare back at him, cool as a cart of freaking cucumbers on ice, and he finally relents.

"Very well. What is this *second* job?" He doesn't sound pleased.

Sylred totally shocks me by saying, "The princess's personal guard was taken prisoner. We need to know where he is."

Oh my gods. If I could kiss him right now, I would. He didn't forget about Okot. Even though he's nothing to the genfins, Sylred knows he's something to *me*. "I like you so hard right now."

The Horned Hook laughs humorlessly. "The royals do love to fill their dungeons. I'll tell you what, I will do this second job for you. Mostly because I like to piss off the prince whenever I can," he admits as he rolls back on his heels.

The idea of committing treason against the prince really put a pep in his step. "Where and when was he taken, and what is his name?"

"Okot. He's a lamassu," Sylred replies. "One of the princess's personal guards."

"And he was taken from the spectator box during the third day of the culling," Ronak finishes.

The Horned Hook snaps his fingers and smiles. "You're the infamous genfins who survived the culling! I should have known. Five-year banishment, was it? I was banished once... or twelve times."

I gape at him. Twelve times? He wasn't kidding about liking to piss off the royals.

He looks excited about doing it again. "Done. I will set up a meeting to get your Veiled female back and find this lamassu for you. You're lucky I'm in such a giving mood."

He holds out his hand, and Sylred shakes on it. "Go now. I'll be in touch. Oh, and this meeting never happened, blah, blah, and all that," he tells the guys with a dismissive wave of his hand. The genfins turn and head back up the dirt stairwell.

The ceiling opens before they reach the top, and then we're in the creepy forest again.

"What do you think?" Evert asks quietly. Ronak moves his eyes around the forest.

"Not here. Too many eyes and ears."

"Too many nude-ass chameleens, you mean," Evert drawls.

I punch a fist of Flirt-Touch right through his chest. He shivers. "Scratch, don't do that flirty shit on me. Wanting to pick wildflowers and sing songs to you is not my thing."

Sylred smirks. "Which is why she hit you with it."

"What the hell did I do?"

Sylred looks at him like he's an idiot. "Talked about naked chameleens."

Evert throws his hands up. "They were naked! Hard not to notice."

"Wrong thing to say," Sylred mumbles.

I punch Evert again. Twice. He does this whole-body shake thing and tries to run away like he's a cat that got stuck in the rain. "Knock it off!"

I stick my tongue out at him, because I'm super mature like that.

CHAPTER 27

The Horned Hook doesn't get back to us for three days. And maybe that doesn't seem like a long time, but when you're stuck in the Veil and can't be heard or seen or felt...not to mention no eating or drinking or sleeping or *anything*, yeah, it feels freaking long. Every night while the guys sleep, I fly to the palace and scour the prison towers. Every night, I come away without finding Okot.

By the third day of waiting around, even the guys have become restless. Which I can understand, seeing as how they've been banished for five years on an empty island and haven't been able to go home. Now I'm sort of keeping them from their home for even longer, which I feel bad about.

But finally, the Horned Hook guy sends word by...letter. Yeah. Total letdown on the exciting department. Talk about lackluster. I guess he saves his dramatics for the whole Elder-Tree-naked-chameleen-secret-stairwell-masked-thief spiel. Anyway, the note just gave a location. It didn't say which of the jobs it referred to. So we could be going to the fae who might possibly bring me back or the place where Okot is being held. Both fill me with a sense of excitement and dread.

"The location is here on the kingdom island," Sylred says with a hint of surprise.

"Where?" Ronak asks.

Sylred's blond brows draw together. "The Finitsal Ruins."

"The ruins?" Ronak echoes.

Sylred shrugs. "That's what it says."

"Then let's go," Evert says, pulling on his boots.

The way to the ruins is apparently longer than the guys want to walk, because they hire a carriage in town. The driver looks surprised at their request to go to the ruins, but he reluctantly agrees.

Sylred and Evert sit on one side, while Ronak takes up the other bench. The space is cramped with all three of them, as evident by the way Ronak has to scrunch down so his head doesn't hit the ceiling and how their knees keep knocking together.

"Think this is where the fae is who can fix Emelle?" Sylred asks no one in particular.

Ronak shrugs and makes a noise under his breath.

Evert narrows his eyes on him. "What's with you?"

Ronak whips his head around to face him. "What do you mean?"

Evert points in his face. "That. That tone. What the fuck is that?"

"I don't have a tone."

"Yeah, I think you do."

"Guys…" Sylred sighs.

"No, I want to know what has his balls twisted up."

"Can we not do this right now?"

Evert crosses his arms. "Spit it out, Alpha. Whatever you've been wanting to say for the past few days, just fucking come out with it already."

"Fine," Ronak grits out. "What are we doing here, Evert?"

"I think it should be obvious even to you that we're riding in a fucking carriage."

"I mean with the cupid."

Evert scoffs. "*The cupid?* You can't even say her name all of a sudden?"

"You know what I mean."

"Yeah, I do. But apparently you didn't know what I meant when I said I was serious about being fucking done. I am not going back home to chase some genfin females around. I choose her."

Holy mother of marinara sauce. My poor little invisible heart just fainted.

"She's not a genfin!" Ronak roars.

Evert leans forward to get in his face. "So the fuck what? You want her, too. I know you do. And I bet your animal side does, too. I bet that he chose her already, and you're just ignoring the signs. Your animal reacts to her. Hell, he attacked a pack of beasts to protect her. But you're being a jackass and not letting him out to see for yourself if he'll claim her. What the fuck is the problem?"

Ronak throws his arms up, smacking the back of his hands against the carriage walls. "We won't get our wings, and we won't get our covey magic. Not without a genfin mate. We're supposed to help lead our people when we get back. How will any of them respect us if we abandon one of our core foundations by rejecting a genfin mate? We have so little genfin children as it is. They'll reject us for it, Evert."

Evert just shrugs like he couldn't care less. "I'm not living my life for a bunch of Delsheen assholes. If that's what you care about—politics and power—then have at it. I'm sure you and Syl can find some genfin female to your liking, but I'm gonna stay with Scratch."

The fury rippling off Ronak makes the whole carriage shake. "She already has a mate!"

"The fucking lamassu. I know," Evert replies dryly. "I don't care. I saw her first. The fucking lamassu can get in line."

"You're saying you're willing to abandon us and form a covey with *them*?" Ronak asks incredulously.

"I'm saying that the choice is yours," Evert counters. "Either choose power or choose Scratch. Simple as that. I've already made my choice. I've been up front about this from the start."

"Gods," I groan. "How many times do I have to tell you idiots that you're not breaking up!"

Evert wants to be with me. He *chooses* me. And there's a huge part of me inside that's jumping around and squealing with joy. But there's another part that is despairing about coming between them. I can't let that happen.

"What about her threat?" Sylred asks. "She said she'd never speak to any of us again if our covey dissolved."

Evert's face turns arrogant, and he shrugs. "She might stop talking to me. For a day. She won't be able to resist after that. I'll make sure of it."

"Cocky asshole," I grumble. "You're wrong." He's totally right.

"And what about you?" Ronak challenges, swinging his black eyes to Sylred.

Sylred looks decidedly uncomfortable under the sudden scrutiny. "I think we shouldn't be having this conversation without Emelle," he says smoothly.

"Aww, thanks." It's always nice to be included.

Evert ignores him. "Is that really your only hold-up?" he asks Ronak. "I want to know. Is it really just the political shit and the powers?"

At first, I don't think Ronak is going to answer. He's clenching his teeth hard enough to break at least a molar or two. "Yes," he finally growls.

"Huh." That surprises me. I thought maybe...

"So you don't still 'hate' her or hold a grudge?" Evert persists.

"No."

I scoot a bit closer to him. "That's the sweetest thing you've ever said about me."

"I don't think that's just it," Evert counters. "I think you actually *like* her. That's what the real problem is."

My face scrunches in confusion. "I don't get it."

"What are you talking about?" Ronak snaps.

"After what Delsheen did, you don't want to trust another female. You were determined to find a mate that would be good for political reasons and that's it. You were going to make sure you didn't actually have feelings for her. But you like Scratch. And *that's* why you've been such an asshole this whole time. You don't want her to have that sort of power over you. You resent that your animal likes her, too."

My head swivels to Ronak. "Is that true?"

His jaw tightens.

Evert's voice lowers. "Fuck it all, Ronak. Let's do what we want *with* who we want. You know you want her. We all do. It doesn't matter if she's a cupid or a fucking demon. She fell ass-first onto our island for a reason."

"I didn't fall ass-first—"

"Fuck the politics. Fuck outside opinions, and screw the powers. We're strong enough without them. I don't want to leave this covey, and you don't really want to mate with a genfin female you don't even like," he declares. "Let's go all in. For once in your life, do something because you want to do it. Not because you're supposed to."

Ronak stares at him, as if he's slowly churning over Evert's words.

"How about you, Tune?" Evert asks, looking over at Sylred.

Sylred clears his throat. "We are a covey. We need to stick together. And Emelle...it feels like she's a part of us already."

Ronak runs a hand over his short hair and sighs. All the fight has seeped out of him. "She won't want me." He says it so quietly that I almost don't hear him.

"Maybe you should ask her," Sylred suggests.

I don't even hesitate. I perch myself onto his lap—which is hard to do without sinking right through, but I manage because I'm awesome—and I blow a huge burst of Lust into his face. His whole body clenches.

Evert and Sylred start laughing. "It's funny when she's not doing it to me," Evert says.

"Hilarious," Ronak says dryly, while simultaneously covering his crotch with his hands.

"So. We're doing this?"

"My animal needs to decide," Ronak replies.

Evert waves him off. "Yeah, yeah. I'm not worried about that. Are we doing this or what?"

Ronak shifts in his seat and looks between them. Then he nods. He freaking *nods*! "Okay."

Evert smirks. "Okay."

They both look at Sylred. "Okay," he mimics.

The guys just decided to take me as a mate by okay-ing. I'm okay with it.

My head swims with emotion, and I feel like my whole body is about to burst. These damn genfins are choosing me. Thank the gods. And it's about damn time.

If I really had to go through with helping them find a mate, I probably would've shanked someone with a Love Arrow. I'm gonna be a way better mate, anyway.

Evert leans his head back on the carriage wall and closes his eyes. "You hear that, Scratch? We're keeping you. I knew these assholes would agree. It was just a matter of time."

Sylred and Ronak have settled back as if they're going to go to sleep, too.

I scowl at them. "You can't just drop a bomb like that and then go to sleep. You don't get to just okay yourselves into my super awesome cupid covey." I mean, they can, but that's beside the point.

I take in a huge breath and then blow out every last

particle of Lust-Breath I have in me until pink tendrils fill the inside of the carriage like smoke. All three sets of genfin eyes snap open.

"Fucking *hell*, Scratch."

Sylred shifts uncomfortably while Ronak covers his junk with his hands. "Too much," he wheezes out.

"Serves you right," I say primly, leaning up to try to peek at their packages standing up in formation. "And yes. I'll accept you into my covey. But there will be requirements. We'll discuss it at a later date. When you can see me. And hear me. And give me orgasms."

"Does this mean she's happy or irritated?" Sylred asks.

Evert smirks and leans back again, fixing the front of his pants. "Knowing her? Probably both."

"My dick can't take this kind of punishment," Ronak grumbles.

"Get used to it," Evert says dryly. "We just chose a cupid for a mate. I have a feeling our dicks aren't getting off easy."

With that, all three genfins burst into laughter.

"Hilarious," I drawl. "You're freaking hilarious."

But I can't help the smile that creeps out onto my face. Because I just got exactly what I've been desperately wanting since I came to this realm and saw these three sexy genfin tail guys. It just took me going invisible again to show them what they're missing. Me.

CHAPTER 28

The Finitsal Ruins is a place at the very edge of the island, with absolutely nothing around it for miles. At one time, the structures here were probably impressive with their huge columns and crumbling statues, but now it just looks depressing. What once was a huge stately building is now a collapsed pile of rubble.

The carriage driver dropped us off and refused to stay and wait, no matter how much money Ronak offered him. He murmured something about the place being haunted before taking off like he was trying to outrun the shit stuck to his shoe.

Technically, the place *is* haunted. But no more than usual. I can see a few ghosts milling around aimlessly, mumbling incoherent thoughts. As the only other entities in the Veil with me, I've had plenty of ghostly encounters.

Too bad they're terrible conversationalists and have no idea about anything going on around them. I'm used to ignoring them by now, but I can see a couple of female fae ghosts circling around a statue, and a few more male fae over by the collapsed building.

Besides the ghosts, the place does have an unnaturally cold feeling to it—like the weather isn't quite right here.

"Good place to stash a prisoner you don't want anyone to find," Sylred says grimly.

Ronak grunts in agreement. "Split up."

Ronak heads toward the largest of the collapsed buildings, Evert heads to the statues, and Sylred circles around back to the fence containing an overgrown garden.

I float around slowly, looking for any sign that Okot might be here, but the place looks untouched and forgotten. It doesn't seem like anyone has been here for years.

"Over here!"

I whirl around and zoom past the columns, toward the direction of Sylred's voice. He's crouched down on the garden floor, wiping dirt away from a spot nearby a toppled pillar. At first, I can't see what he's doing, until he swipes again and I notice the trap door.

Ronak and Evert come into the garden from different directions at nearly the same time and stride over to him. Sylred attempts to shove the pillar off, but the thing must weigh a ton, because it doesn't budge.

"Ronak?" Sylred says, moving aside.

Ronak moves toward it and with one hand, pushes it easily aside without any effort. When he moves to pull the lever on the trap door, Sylred stops him. "Remember what happened the last time?"

Evert snorts. "And the time before that."

"And probably a few other times, too," Sylred adds amicably.

Ronak grunts. "Not my fault handles are always so fragile."

"You snap them right off, every time. Then we have to spend that much longer trying to wedge the damn doors open. Let us handle this part."

Ronak moves aside, and with a forceful heave, Sylred

manages to wrench open the trap door. "There's a drop straight down. Maybe about ten feet."

"I'll go first," Ronak says. He squats down and then leaps down into the dark space. After a moment, he calls for the others to follow.

I float on ahead of them, although the space is pitch black. "How are you guys seeing anything?" I look back to see three sets of glowing genfin cat-eyes. "Of course you can see in the dark."

The dirt tunnel is cramped and short, but after a while, it opens up to a larger space. In the ceiling, there's an ancient piece of warped and cracked glass that's allowing a few weak beams of sunlight to filter in, and the sight stops me cold.

"Oh my gods!"

I rush forward to the wall where Okot sits chained. He's slumped over and breathing erratically, his face and arms covered in bruises.

I settle in front of him, running my hands over his face and hating that they go right through him. "Okot," I whisper on a choked sob.

His head snaps up. "Emelle?"

I rear back in surprise. "Okot?"

For a moment, he looks right at me. Then his red-rimmed irises shift away, landing on the guys. "She's here. I can feel her. Where is she?" he croaks. "Is she hurt? Is she safe?"

"She's...back in the Veil," Sylred says.

I'm not sure the answer registers, because Okot mumbles something unintelligible and then slumps his head back down against his chest. Ronak strides forward and yanks the chains off him.

"Let's get you out of here."

Okot lifts his head and struggles to stand on his own two feet as Ronak steadies him.

"He can't walk out of here on his own," Sylred murmurs

to Evert. "I'll run back and find a horse or a carriage to hire if I can."

Evert nods grimly. "Get some food and water, too. We'll have to find a healer once we get back into the city." Sylred nods and sprints away.

With Ronak's help, Okot is helped down the passage and hoisted up to the surface. In the sunlight, I can see what terrible shape he's really in. Besides being covered in bruises, he's deathly pale and has cracked, bleeding lips.

Ronak sets him down against the crumbling building. Okot has his eyes closed and his breathing is labored.

"He's in bad shape," Ronak mutters.

Evert's lips are in a thin line. "He's obviously been down there all this time without food or water. And lamassus pull most of their strength from the sunlight. He barely had enough to survive on. Too much iron contact, too."

They watch him, grim-faced, as I hover at his side. I pretend I can smell him as I put my face in the crook of his neck. My sweet, gentle bull fae has been punished like this, left to die in a terrible way, all because of me.

We wait for two agonizing hours until Sylred comes back with horses pulling an empty cart. Ronak picks up Okot as if he weighs nothing, even though he's bulkier and arguably heavier. He carefully sets Okot down in the back of the cart, and Sylred jumps back up to drive.

Evert props him up and pours some water down his throat. Most of it drips back down his chin, but I see his throat moving a tiny bit, taking in a few precious gulps.

"Don't you dare die," I tell him sternly.

If I demand it, maybe he'll listen.

CHAPTER 29

The ride back to the inn is brutally long.

Once we get back, the guys rent an extra room and sneak Okot up the back stairs. A healer comes and does some tricky glowing magic mumbo jumbo, and now all we can do is wait.

I don't move from the spot on the bed next to Okot. I'm perched right between his legs, making sure he's breathing (he is), making sure his color looks better (it does), and wishing he would wake up (he hasn't).

He somehow seemed to sense that I was there with him in the tunnel, which is in*freaking*sane. Unless he was just delirious. I'm mostly sure that's what it was. About ninety percent sure. Like, sure, but with a minus of "what-if." No one has ever sensed me in the Veil before. That would be awesome if it were true.

The moment he starts to wake up the next day, I'm right there, up close and personal. Still perched between his legs, I lean in, probably looking like a crazy stalker, but I don't care because he can't see me, anyway.

His eyes peel open like it takes considerable effort on his part, and he looks around, trying to catch his bearings.

"Thank gods," I breathe.

He tries to sit up, only to fall back on the bed again. "Wait right here."

I fly straight at the wall separating his room and the genfins' room. They're eating lunch, talking about other genfins I've never heard of, when I come zooming in.

"Hey, genfins! He's awake. Chop, chop, go tend to my mate."

They keep on eating. I blast them with Lust-Breath and punch some Flirt-Touches into their bodies just for good measure. "Come on! You can stuff your faces later!"

Three sexually frustrated groans are my reply.

Wait for it...

"Fucking *hell*, Scratch!"

There it is.

"What the hell was that for?" Ronak demands, cradling his package. And it's, like, a large package. Like, if he went to a post office on the human realm, he'd have to pay extra to ship that thing. Not that they'd ship a penis. I don't think.

Right, focus.

Sylred has a grimace on his face and a nice flush to his cheeks. "Maybe she's trying to tell us something."

"You think?" Evert snaps, pushing his plate of food away.

"The lamassu is probably awake. Let's go check."

"We have to go check on her fucking *mate* with a trio of hard-ons," Evert gripes. "That's not awkward at all."

"Come on," Sylred says, opening the door.

They follow him out and knock on Okot's door before letting themselves in. He's managed to sit up by now at least. He starts to stand, but Sylred stops him. "Don't get up on our account."

Okot nods and looks between the three of them and then frowns. "Is she okay? Where is she? She's nearby, I can sense her."

My mouth falls open. So he *wasn't* delusional. This mate

match must be some strong stuff. We haven't even confirmed it yet. I don't know if it's just a lamassu power or if it's just an Okot thing, but it gives me the warm and fuzzies.

I fly over to him and sit down before attempting to put my hand on his thigh. He looks down and frowns.

My eyes widen. "Whoa. You can feel that?"

The guys watch him curiously. "What can you sense?" Sylred asks.

Okot shakes his head as if he's trying to think of the right words. "I'm not sure, but I feel her near. I feel her...here," he says, putting his hand over mine.

I smile and lay my head against his shoulder, not caring when some of me goes through him. "We are so confirming our bond," I tell him. "I'm gonna confirm the hell out of it when I turn solid again."

The guys stare at his hand on his thigh, and they look like...like they wish they could feel me, too.

Okot clears his throat and addresses the genfins again. "I failed her."

I pick my head up to look at him. "You did not!"

Ronak shakes his head. "No, you were arrested by the prince's men. There was nothing you could have done."

Okot clenches his fists and looks down at his lap with a dejected expression.

"Can you tell us everything that happened?" Sylred asks.

Okot answers without looking up. "Something was in my drink. It made me feel strange. The next thing I knew, they were leading me out of the royal box, and then there was a bag over my head. I tried to fight, and I should've easily been able to overpower them, but whatever was in that drink incapacitated me. I could not even shift into my lamassu animal form. When I next woke, I was in the place that you found me."

"Yeah, then that's not your fault," Evert says. I look over at him in surprise. He's the last person I expected to try to make Okot feel better. "Nothing you could've done."

"What did they do to her?"

Ronak clenches his jaw. "We don't know. But we're working on meeting with someone to get her back."

Okot stands and bows his head to them. "You saved my life, and you have looked after my mate when I could not. I am in your debt."

Evert puts his hands in his pockets and smirks. "*Our*."

Okot frowns. "What?"

"She's *our* mate. All four of us. You okay with that?" His tone is challenging.

I try to bite my nails in nervousness as I await Okot's answer. But he just nods. "Like I told her, she has my heart. If you have hers, then I will respect that."

Evert claps him on the back. "Good. But be warned—she likes to Lust-Breathe the fuck out of us when she wants to talk or get us to do something or just because she can. Welcome to the fucking party. Your dick will never get a break."

Okot just grins. "I can live with that."

Evert chuckles darkly. "Good. Then let's get our girl back."

CHAPTER 30

e get the second letter from the Horned Hook a day later.

"We'll have to go by portal," Sylred says. "Since we can't fly."

"But then Scratch will get left behind," Evert points out.

"I can fly," Okot says. "I'll follow you there, and she can go with me."

"You should stay behind. You can't be seen," Sylred points out, but Okot shakes his head.

"No. I'm going. I won't be caught."

Sylred looks like he wants to argue, but Ronak gives him a small shake of his head, so he drops it.

"I don't like being separated. What if something happens to her?" Evert asks with a scowl.

"Like what? She can't get hurt or caught in the Veil," Ronak points out.

"Trouble follows her," Evert replies. "What if she gets all cupidy or some shit? Gets distracted, starts blowing Lust all over the place, and shoots Love Arrows up some fae asses? You know how easily distracted she is. Her cupidity shit might sidetrack her, and then she'll lose track of us."

I stop playing with the Love Arrow in my hands and frown.

Sylred blinks. "Is that a thing?"

I huff. "No! Well...yes. But right now, no. I'm not gonna get caught up in my own stupid cupidity. I'm not a goldfish. I *do* have an attention span." I continue to twirl the arrow through my fingers like it's a baton. "And I resent you thinking—Oh, look!" I exclaim excitedly, zooming toward the window. "That fae down there is riding a unicorn!"

Okay. I see his point.

"We need to go," Ronak says behind me. "We're wasting time."

"Fine," Evert says. He snaps his fingers in the air and looks around for me. "Scratch. You'd better be here listening to us right now. But if you're on some flirty tangent or whatever the shit you cupids do, then I'll leave a map on the bed, too, just in case. If you *are* here, which you'd better be, follow your fucking lamassu. Tell Okot how to get there, Syl."

"We need to get to Icidel," Sylred explains. "You know it?"

Okot tips his head. "I have heard of it."

"It's not far from here. All you'll have to do is fly directly up from this island. You're going to pass about five or six islands above until you find one that's covered in ice and snow. It'll be a bit north. There are a lot of mountains on it, and the island should stand out from the rest. We'll meet you at the base of the tallest mountain."

"I understand."

"And Emelle?" Sylred says, looking around awkwardly at the empty space in the room. "Send one of us a Lust-Breath when you get there so we know you're with us. I know that Okot can sense you, but we want to be sure. We can't do whatever is going to happen without you there."

I force myself to turn away from the window and salute him. "Aye, aye, captain."

The genfins waste no time leaving the room and heading

out to the city to find a portal. Only high fae have the ability to open portals, and even then it's a rare power. I follow them to the portal shop in the center of town, and man, is this place fancy.

The inside has marble floors and gilded walls, there's a musician playing softly in the corner, and a table has little finger-foods and bottles of fairy wine set up on it.

At the back of the room, there's a high fae reading a book and looking utterly bored and too good for everything in the entire realm. He doesn't even look up from reading when the genfins walk in.

Ronak, Evert, and Sylred stand like a wall in front of him. When the fae continues ignoring them, Sylred takes the lead. "Good day. We're here for a portal."

The fae sighs and turns a page. "Obviously. Gold first, then talk."

Ronak looks like he's about to punch him, but Sylred quickly tosses a pouch of money at his head. The fae catches it with much more dexterity than I expected. He still hasn't looked up from his book.

He tosses the pouch back and forth in his hands, as if he can deduce it's worth simply by holding it. Looking around his gold-gilded storefront, I realize that he probably can.

"Fine. How many and where to?" he says, finally standing up and putting his book down. He holds his place with a golden coin. Now that's an expensive bookmark.

"Three of us. We need a portal to Icidel and back."

"Fine," he says again, as if it's a huge inconvenience and not, you know, his *job*. "I'll keep it open for one hour."

With a flick of his wrists, some swirling blue and white appears in his hand, and with a flourish, he spreads it until it stretches from floor to ceiling. He takes his seat again and picks up his book to resume reading as the guys step through and disappear.

As soon as they're gone, I float to the alleyway behind the

building where Okot is waiting. When I get near him, he snorts in my direction and jerks his head.

"Yep, I'm with you, big boy," I confirm, petting him on the head.

At my touch, he launches into the air, and I follow easily beside him. We go up, up, up until the city of Highvale is far below us. I count the islands as we go by, but I don't really need to do that, because I can see Icidel far off in the distance. Unlike the other floating islands with rock and soil on the bottom, this one is pure ice.

When we make it to the top, I see incredibly tall mountains and a landscape covered in snow. We easily spot the tallest mountain and make our way to the base of it. I spot my genfins immediately. Granted, it's not hard since they stand out against the snow.

Okot and I land beside them. While he's busy shifting back into his man form, I blow some Lust into Ronak's face. He clears his throat and flushes slightly.

Evert cocks a brow. "I take it she's here?"

"Yep."

Evert chuckles darkly. "Let's go."

I now notice the small cabin that's situated at the bottom of the mountain. When they reach the door, Ronak knocks. Well, he more like punches the poor door, making an audible splintering noise as the wood slightly buckles.

When the guys look over at him, he just shrugs. "Whoops."

Evert rolls his eyes. "Rein the strength power in, yeah?"

Before he can answer, the door flies open and there stand two fae to greet us.

I blink at the sight. "They're...they're stuck together at their butts. They're butt-stuck. At the butt cheeks. They're naked. Penises. I can see their penises. They're identical." For some reason, I feel like this all needs to be said.

I'm having a hard time looking away with them just

hanging out in the open like this. "I just...do you think they both poop and pee at the same time? Or does one of them take over for that? What about sex? Or sitting? What happens when one of them wants to sit and the other doesn't?"

Yeah, I know. I'm rambling again.

"Genfins," they both say at the same time. It's weird. "We are Plik—and Plak. Come in. We've been expecting you." Their gazes fall on Okot. "We did not expect you."

Okot just stares at them all bull-man-y until they shrug and let him go inside, too.

"Umm, should I be concerned that these are the fae that hold my physical fate in their hands?" I ask no one.

I'm practically inside of Ronak as he walks indoors, because the fae penises are looking at me. When in doubt, just stick with the guy with the strength power to protect you from rogue penises. I should put that on a T-shirt.

Aside from being conjoined at the butt cheeks, the fae brothers have deer-ears that swivel on the tops of their heads, and they have noses that resemble pig snouts. The brother on the left has one wing, and the brother on the right has another. Flying must be a bitch.

I snap my eyes toward their wooden table when I notice movement. Sitting there with his feet propped up on the table and his hands behind his masked head, is the Horned Hook. The guys notice him, too.

"What the fuck are you doing here?" Evert asks.

He puts his hands and feet down at the same time and sits up straight. "Well, if it isn't my favorite genfins. I see you found your lamassu," he says, tilting his head in Okot's direction. "You're welcome."

Evert is about to pop off something when Sylred smacks his shoulder to silence him. "Thank you. But what are you doing here?"

The Horned Hook stands with a flourish. "I am a trader of secrets and a collector of priceless things. You have a female stuck in the Veil. I have never, in all my years, heard of that particular secret, and believe me, I have heard thousands. Count my presence today as the second half of your payment."

"That wasn't part of the deal," Ronak growls angrily as the other guys close in.

"Don't get your tails tangled," the Horned Hook says cheerfully. "I won't tell. This secret is purely for my own curiosity."

The guys look like they're considering pummeling him and throwing him off the snowy island, but he just laughs. "Yes, yes, you could try and beat me to a bloody pulp. Four against one and all that. *Or...* He waves his hand, making the chairs and table flip over and act as a barrier between them. It's a good visual of what his telekinesis power is capable of. "I might just beat you four while ruining some perfectly adequate furniture in the process, which would mean Plik and Plak here would become angry and most likely refuse to help your female."

The guys exchange a glance. Ronak looks like he still wants to take those odds. The Horned Hook interrupts their silent covey-speak and says, "The third option is to simply let Plik and Plak do what I've asked them to do, and then we'll all go on our happy way. Seems the less destructive and violent choice, don't you think?" he asks, waving his hands around and making all the furniture return to its rightful place.

Okot is the one to answer. "You will not tell anyone about her." It's not a question.

The Horned Hook tilts his head. "You have my word."

Evert gets up in his personal space. "If you break our trust, I will hunt you down and kill you."

I can't see behind the mask, but I'm pretty sure he rolls his eyes. "Yes, yes. Maim, torture, death. I know the stakes."

"Fine," Ronak snaps. "Let's get on with it."

CHAPTER 31

*T*urning our attention back to Plik and Plak, we see them busy in the kitchen, pulling out random objects and setting everything on the table.

The way they move their joined bodies is fascinating. Not once do they get twisted up, even with four arms and four legs. Plus, you know, the swinging penises. Can't forget those.

The butt-conjoined twins take turns speaking every other word while they carry on a constant stream of chatter. It's disorienting but totally entertaining.

"Get the—white one, yes. And then—oh, will be perfect. But what if—yes, yes, we must account for that. I'm certain we can find—oh, that will be suitable."

Looking back and forth between their dislocated speech is making me dizzy.

The guys share a look. "Do you know what you're doing?" Ronak asks.

Plik and Plak stop moving and turn their necks at exactly the same time to look at him. "Of course—we know. Why do —you think—we're preparing? The great magic—that you require—comes from the combination—of our good magic.

Raw magic—that can touch—the Veil. This is not—simple magic. This is not even—fae magic. This is magic strong enough—to reach past this realm. Through it. We do not often—help outsiders—but when the Horned Hook asks— one must listen. Too many secrets—floating around—in his horned head—to ignore him. Now be—quiet—and let us work—so we can—try to get your—female out of the Veil— and get back to our—peaceful lives."

They mix a bunch of the stuff they pulled out and make a gross-looking cocktail. They surprise me when they each take a cup and drain the contents. One of the twins drinks something black and smoking, while the other drinks a cup filled with what looks like white light.

"What are they doing?" Sylred asks.

Plik—or Plak, I'm not really sure which is which— answers. "I am drinking death."

I gape at him and his smoking cup. "I'm pretty sure no one should drink freaking *death*!"

Just as I say the word, Plik (or Plak) slumps over. Not breathing, the upper half of his body comes to rest against the top of the table. We all stare at him bent over at his conjoined butt, but he doesn't move.

"What just happened?" Evert asks.

Plak (or Plik? Gods, this is confusing,) continues drinking his drink cheerfully. "Plik just died, of course."

"*What?*"

Plak drains the last drop of white light from the cup and sighs. He has a soft glow about him now. He looks over at his dead twin and scratches his half of their butts.

"Can you explain to me why he just fucking killed himself?"

Plak rolls his eyes. "Don't be dramatic. He didn't kill himself to die. He drank death because it's the only way for us to reach the Veil and find your female. The living are not permitted inside."

Oh. That actually makes sense.

"Okay...but won't your brother stay dead?" Sylred puts in.

Plak blinks at him.

The Horned Hook laughs, startling us enough to turn around and look at him. "You should see your faces right now," he gasps out.

"Never fear," Plak answers. "We are connected."

"Yeah, we can fucking see that," Evert drawls.

Plak looks down at their conjoined butts and then back again. "Yes. But no. I meant that we are the only fae who have connected life forces. He has died many times, as have I. As long as the other one of us lives, we pull the other back to life. He will be walking in Death's Hollow soon. Once he finds your female, he will perform some magic, which I will feed to him from the living realm, and he will bring her back." He taps his chin in thought. "Or...this will fail, and he won't. Either way."

Okay then.

I suddenly see a shadow poking out of poor dead Plik. No, not a shadow. His invisible ghostly form. He floats up out of his body and stands beside his brother, strangely whole. No half butt for him in the afterlife, so that's something.

He shakes his arms out and looks around, his eyes immediately landing on me. "Ah. The female, I presume?"

"Umm, yeah. Yes. That's me. I'm the female."

"Hmm." He studies me from head to toe, his eyes lingering on my wings. "You're not a ghost, nor angel, nor demon. What are you?"

"I'm...really ready to have a body again."

He waits for me to say more, but I keep my mouth closed, and he finally gives up. "Fine. Come on, then."

I float up beside him, and he puts his hands on my chest. We don't touch exactly, but I can feel *something*, a sort of tingling sensation where his hands rest against me.

"What—"

"Shh!" Plik snaps.

I clamp my mouth shut and see that both he and his brother have their eyes closed tight in concentration.

Suddenly, his brother's glowing light starts steaming off him like he's a cup of coffee. In turn, the steam sinks into dead Plik's body. Then it appears around ghostly Plik's body, too. I watch as the tendrils start travelling from him to the spot where he's touching me.

"This may hurt a bit," he mumbles.

The warning is barely spoken before excruciating pain slams into me. Blackness floods my vision, and I can hear screaming.

Oh, wait. That's me.

It feels like I'm burning alive.

Just as suddenly as it came on, the burning pain is gone.

I fall. Yep. My knees actually *hit* the floor. The pain I feel from it is the most welcome thing in the world, because it means one thing.

"She's back!"

I'm not sure who says it, but suddenly I'm being lifted up off the floor and pressed against a hard, warm chest. Before I can get my bearings, I'm pulled out of one set of arms and into another, while yet another body presses up against my back, jostling against my quiver and bow.

Then I'm yanked away again and different arms encircle around me, holding me like he's afraid I'll disappear again. I feel his nose against my neck as he slowly inhales.

Okot.

"My beloved."

I turn my face slightly so that I can have a sniff, too. Yep. He still smells *amazing*. I just wanna bottle this stuff and spritz it into my face.

When he finally lets me go, I take a step back so I can see

all my guys. But I watch as four faces go from ecstatic to furious.

I blanch and take an involuntary step backwards away from them. "What..."

Evert is suddenly in my face, his blue eyes flashing dangerously. "Who. The. Fuck. Did. This."

I blink. "Did what?" Then I register all the pain. My face. My arms. My stomach. My wing. "Oh. That."

"Yeah, fucking *that*."

Okot presses in closer to my left, Sylred to my right, and Ronak at my back. It's like I'm barricaded in by four big hunky man beasts. It's intimidating to suddenly be at the center of such intense attention after being invisible. A small shudder passes through me as I struggle to meet their eyes.

"What happened, Emelle?" Sylred asks quietly, touching my arm.

"Who hurt you?" Okot asks, his tone furious. I've never seen him angry before. The red circles in his irises are pulsing.

"It doesn't matter," I hedge. "I'll heal. Besides, I have my bow and arrow again. That's pretty exciting, am I right?"

"Nope. It matters," Ronak says, ignoring my attempt at distracting them.

"He's right. Tell us, Scratch."

"Well, when the prince arrested me and put me in the cells, he sent Chaucel and his guard to...question me."

"Beat you. He sent him to beat you."

"Eh. Semantics." I start scratching my arm at the spot where my old itch used to be. Thank gods I didn't get stuck with another itch this time around.

Okot cocks his head. "Do you have fleas?"

That makes Evert bark out a laugh. I level a glare on him. "No," I answer Okot primly. "I just like scratching. A girl can never be too careful. You should always scratch right when you feel an itch crop up. Trust me."

"Your skin is turning red," Ronak observes with a frown.

I look down at all the red scratch marks marring my arm. "Yep."

His hand reaches around and clamps around my wrists, preventing my movements. I pout up at him.

"Stop stalling and tell us."

I blow a piece of hair out of my face. "Fine. Yes. I took a few hits. They wanted to rough me up a bit, make me hurt and scared. You know, Torture 101."

"Who did it?" Okot asks again.

I hesitate but decide it's best to just be honest. "It was Gammon. Chaucel would ask a question, I would answer, and then Gammon would beat me. It didn't last long. I'm fine."

"He will be punished," Okot vows.

"I'll fucking help," Evert puts in.

"I think we should all pay him a visit," Ronak adds.

"Look, that's sweet that you guys are getting all murdery, but can we not right now? I don't want any of you going off on a dangerous mission to exact vengeance just yet. I just got back, and I'm hungry. Feed me."

Sylred chuckles and kisses the top of my head. "There's our girl."

When they shift aside, I can see Plik's ghost-form soaking back into his body. Simultaneously, Plak loses the last of his glowing light. A shudder passes from Plak into Plik, and then his prone form suddenly bolts upright again. The twins look at each other with matching grins. "Well done, brother," they both say at the same time.

"Thank you," I tell them. "I don't know how you did that, but thank you."

"Is she still anchored to us?" Ronak asks.

"Oh yes—can't undo her anchor. Tried. But she no longer —depends on your—proximity. Only your lives. Should all of you die—she will, too. Much like we depend—on each other," they say, motioning to one another.

"Well, that's good news," I smirk. "Nice to know I can get away from these jerks once in a while."

"You're not going anywhere," Evert says sternly.

I'd forgotten about the Horned Hook until he pushes his way through my guys and stands in front of me. I stare at his silver-horned mask. "Thank you, too," I say. "You saved Okot and me."

Instead of answering, he just keeps staring.

I shift on my feet awkwardly. "Umm…"

After another weird lull, he reaches to the back of his head and shocks everyone when he removes his mask.

Holy moist macaroons.

CHAPTER 32

Flinging his mask to the table, the Horned Hook keeps his eyes locked on me. I feel my mouth drop open in surprise.

"You," I breathe.

My guys look from me to him and then back again. "What's going on? You know each other?" Evert asks.

"How is that possible?" Sylred adds.

I wrack my brain, trying to remember his name. He looks so different now that he's put on some weight. He's filled out, no longer looking gaunt and sickly. When I first saw him, he'd been on death's doorstep. But I was right. He is handsome when he's not covered in filth and looking like a skeleton.

His silver skin looks much healthier, his white hair is cleaner, and his silver eyes are brighter. But it's the gray curved horns coming out of his head and curling below his ears that I remember the most.

"Belren?"

A smile spreads across his face, and he nods. "I almost didn't recognize you with the red wings and the pinker skin and hair," he admits. "But even under all of that and the bruises, I can see that it's you."

"Okay, one of you needs to tell us how the fuck you know each other."

"He was on Arachno's island," I explain. "He helped me escape."

"Technically, we helped each other," Belren interjects. "I used your dagger to cut myself out of the web."

"Right."

He tilts his head, assessing me. "You told me you were half high fae, but you aren't, are you?"

I shake my head. "No."

His expression becomes intense. "You weren't trapped in the Veil. You belong there, don't you? What are you?"

I open my mouth to answer, but Ronak cuts in. "That's enough of our secrets for one day."

Belren's face smooths out, and he smirks. "Fair enough."

"I'm glad you escaped," I tell him.

"I always do," he says with a wink. "Well, I'm off. Things to do, fae to extort, and all that. Enjoy your Veiled female," he says as he heads for the door. He pushes his long silver wings out of his back through the perfectly sewn-in slits of his blue shirt. "I'll be in touch, Emelle."

Evert rolls his eyes at his departure.

"What?" I ask.

"Nothing. You. Stop making friends."

I laugh. "What? Why?"

"Because. Now let's go." He grabs hold of my hand and starts tugging me out the door.

I twist around to wave at Plik and Plak, but Evert covers my eyes. "What are you doing?"

"They're naked. Don't look."

I laugh again. "Umm, I was here the whole time. I saw everything already."

"Stop picturing their penises, Scratch."

"I'm not!"

"You're doing it right now, aren't you?"

Dammit.

I huff. "It's not something you can just ignore."

Evert snorts. "You mean like the naked chameleens?"

A frown settles on my face. "No. Definitely not. That was totally different," I defend haughtily. "Wait, are you picturing them?"

He just laughs.

He tugs me outside, and I can hear Sylred and Okot saying thank you to the twins before we're all back at the portal. "Should we take her through it?" Evert asks.

Ronak shakes his head. "Too dangerous. She and Okot can't be seen. Flying will be safer."

"Agreed," Sylred says. "But they should wait until nightfall. Too many sentries in the sky at this time."

"I'm not leaving her," Evert insists.

"Fine," Ronak relents. "Sylred and I will go now, and you and Okot can stay here with her. We'll reopen the portal tonight for you, Evert, while Emelle and Okot fly back when it's dark."

"Sounds good."

"Will you be okay until tonight?" Sylred asks me, his eyes running over my injuries.

"Mm-hmm. Yep. Of course. Totally fine." I try not to grimace.

"I'll heal what I can," Evert offers.

"Okay. We'll see you tonight," Sylred says.

He and Ronak give me a nod before walking through the portal and disappearing.

Left alone with Evert and Okot, I look between them expectantly. "I wasn't kidding about being hungry."

Okot chuckles and then shares a look with Evert. They seem to have a silent conversation without me, which is weird because they just met, but whatever.

After a moment, Okot looks back at me and says, "You

two catch up. There's something I must do. I'll come back as soon as I can, and I will bring food, my beloved."

He kisses me on the top of my head and walks away before I can ask where he's going.

Evert shrugs out of his jacket and puts it around me. I snuggle inside of it. "Mmm. Warm."

He scoops me up in his arms. I yelp a little, partly from the pain and partly from surprise. I look around at all the snow and ice and shiver. "Where are we going to go?"

"Someplace where I can get you warm."

"You don't want to ask Plik and Plak if we can hang out in their house for a bit?"

He snorts. "No."

Evert somehow finds a small rock shelf on the side of a mountain, with just enough space for us to sit beneath and be sheltered from the snow and ice. As soon as he sets me down, he starts running his hands over me with his healing touch. All of my scratches, cuts, and splits start stitching back together.

"Thank you."

"Don't thank me. If I was a proper healer, I could fix your broken wing and your internal injuries, too."

Is that self-deprecation I sense? It's so unlike Evert that it makes my heart squeeze. "You heal me in more ways than you can see, Stitch."

His blue eyes settle on my face. "Come here," he says huskily.

He picks me up and deposits me onto his lap so that I'm straddling him with our faces only inches apart.

"Hi," I say a little breathlessly.

He smirks at me, letting his dimples show. "Hi."

"Did you miss me?" I whisper.

"You have no fucking idea."

"I didn't like being invisible again."

I think he can see the anxiety in my expression, because

241

his grip tightens around me. "Stop. The Veil doesn't have you. I fucking do."

Then he kisses me. Or I kiss him. I'm not really sure who initiated it, but our lips connect, and I'm falling so hard inside of him that he's all I remember.

He doesn't wait for me to open, and he doesn't ask permission. His tongue just spears inside my mouth like a demand and takes control of my mouth.

His hands grip my ass, and I shamelessly grind against him, trying to appease the building pressure at my core. He groans against me. I can feel the vibration all the way from my head to my toes.

I want more. I want to be reminded that I really am here and that my body is my own. I want to feel *everything*.

"Please," I beg.

"You're hurt," he reminds me.

"I don't care," I say earnestly. "*Please*, Evert."

I don't know what exactly I'm asking him to do, but he seems to. He moves one of his hands between us and drags it under my skirt. His hot palm trails up my bare leg.

Slowly. Brutally.

He roughly palms my thigh, making it prickle with exquisite pain.

"Please," I beg again.

He chuckles darkly against my mouth. "You want my fingers on your pussy, Scratch?"

My breath hitches at his words. "Yeah."

He moves his hand from my thigh, only to tease around the spot that's panting for his attention. I bite his lip hard.

He hisses and then chuckles. "Rabid fucking cupid. You're gonna pay for that."

"No teasing," I whine.

He scrapes his scratchy five o'clock shadow against my neck, making me shiver. "I'll fucking tease you as much as I like. I'll get you so worked up that you'll be panting on your knees, begging me. But I'll only give you what you want if you're a good girl," he says, his fingers still barely flitting over my clit. The *almost* contact is torture.

Reaching up, I thread my fingers through his black hair and yank forcefully. In response, he slaps my ass hard enough to make it sting. I groan.

"Naughty little thing," he admonishes. He takes hold of my hands and forces them down. "But you like getting punished, don't you? I can feel how wet you are. Now push your dress down. I want to see those pretty tits."

I start to object, so he pulls his fingers away from my clit completely, making a half-sob, half-growl come out of me. "Evert!"

He quirks a brow and pinches my ass, making me jump. "I told you. Be good, and I'll give you what you need. Don't get shy on me now, love. Let me see them."

Pissed that his fingers aren't doing their job and way too worked up to do anything else, I hastily undo the ties at my bodice and then yank my dress down. When my breasts bounce out, Evert wastes no time grabbing them and running his thumbs over my nipples. They harden immediately and send a zing down my belly.

I close my eyes and let my head fall back, loving the jolts of pleasure that his touch brings. "Mmm. These perfect tits shouldn't have hidden away from me for this long."

I arch into his palms.

He reaches up with one hand and grips my chin, bringing my head back down. "Look at me. This is just me and you, Scratch. I want you to watch me touch you. I want you to see who's fingering your cunt and making you so wet."

I swallow, mesmerized by his dirty talk, and do as he says. With a satisfied smirk, he continues playing with my breasts with one hand, while the other starts its descent back to my clit.

Fucking yes.

Finally, his finger presses against my clit and, ohmygods, I'm going to combust.

The more he strokes me, the more I grind against him, relishing in the feel of his hard erection against my ass. "That's right. Fuck yourself on my hand like a good little cupid," he says against my ear.

"Evert," I moan.

He nibbles my lip. "What? Tell me what you want. Beg me for it."

He's turned me into a hot, tangled mess of need, and he knows it. "More. I want more," I pant.

"Say it," he growls.

"Fucking asshole," I snap, earning a painful pinch on my nipple this time. "Fine! I want your fingers inside me. Fuck me with them, please!"

"Good girl." Just like that, his finger plunges inside of me, instantly slick. He growls in satisfaction. "So fucking wet for me."

I moan as his finger thrusts in and out of me while his thumb continues to play with my clit.

"Oh my gods…"

"That's it. So ready, aren't you?"

All I can do is whimper and writhe.

"Your pussy is drenched and begging for more." He adds another finger, curling and pumping them both inside of me, and I'm so, so close.

And it feels *so* fucking good.

He moves his other hand up to my hair and fists it. When I open my mouth to either curse him or moan, he starts pumping into me even faster.

"You love me fucking you with my fingers, don't you?"

I grab his shoulders, my nails digging into his back. "Yes!"

"Good. Now come for me, Scratch. Let me feel you come all over my hand."

And I do. Gods, I do.

As I cry out his name, my body arches into his hand while I explode with pleasure. Toes curled, eyes shut, head thrown back, my whole body spasms with delicious delight.

For my whole stupid cupid life, I've waited for this. To feel this moment of intense bliss. All the years of pent-up loneliness and want barrels out of me, fleeing with Evert's touch.

To be honest, I worried that it wouldn't be everything I thought. I worried that I'd built it up too much in my head. But no. It's everything I thought it would be and much, much more.

By the time I come back into my body, I'm curled against his chest, and his hands are wrapped around me, careful to not hurt any of my injuries. His fingers are lazily rubbing my back, but it's the sound coming from his chest that makes me shiver. I can feel the sound he's emitting all the way into my bones.

I pop my eyes open in surprise. "Are you...purring?"

The sound only pauses for a second before picking back up again. I grin and lean back so I can look at his face. "Oh my gods, you *are*! You're totally purring! That's adorable."

He pushes the back of my head down so that I'm forced to rest against his chest again. "It's not adorable."

I trace my fingers over his collarbone. "It kinda is."

"No, it's not. A genfin purr is badass. We only do it for our mate."

"Adorable," I giggle.

"If you call it that again, I'm going to stop."

"No! Don't stop. It makes me feel...I don't know. Safe. Happy. I can feel it inside me. It's the best sound ever. I don't ever want you to stop," I say, snuggling in closer to him.

I feel his smug grin. "Genfin mate perks."

"I knew you'd be good for something."

He chuckles. "You mean more than orgasms?"

I hum. "You are pretty good at that. Even if you are a domineering asshole about it."

He grins cockily. "You like it. Besides, that was only the beginning. Once you're healed, the real fun begins." He wags his eyebrows.

I turn my face up to look at him. "You're smug about giving me my first orgasm, aren't you?"

"Are you kidding? Of course I am. I'm going to rub it in all those fuckers' faces."

I shake my head and laugh against his chest. "Well, your arrogance aside, I'm glad it was you," I admit quietly.

And I am. Evert was the first one in my corner. I felt a connection with him as soon as I landed on his island and flirted with his dimpled face.

He kisses the crown of my head as his purr kicks up a notch. "Me too, Scratch. Me too."

CHAPTER 33

Okot doesn't come back for hours. It's well after dark when he saunters back to our mini-cave with some watery soup and a loaf of bread in tow.

"Where did you go?" I ask, sitting up from where I'd been dozing on Evert next to the fire he built.

After setting down the food, Okot comes over to me. "Here, my beloved," he says, handing me something wrapped in cloth.

I put it in my lap and start to unwrap the cloth coiled around it to find out what this mystery item is. When I uncover it, all I can do is stare.

And stare.

And stare some more.

When I blink and it's still there, I look up at him. "Ummm. It's a hand. A severed hand. There's still blood on it. And the bone is poking out. The cuticles look terrible," I ramble. "You gave me a severed hand... Why?"

He points at it proudly. "The guard named Gammon. He struck you with that hand. Now that hand is yours."

Realization settles in, and I gasp. "Aww, you cut off his hand for me?" I croon.

He grins. "I did, my beloved. No one is allowed to hurt you."

I jump up, forgetting the severed hand was still in my lap. We watch as it rolls across the floor. Huh. That went farther than I thought it would.

I throw my arms around Okot's neck. "Thank you!"

I kiss him square on the mouth. Okot doesn't even hesitate before cradling my neck in his massive hand and deepening the kiss.

"What the fuck?" I hear Evert mutter. "*That's* how you react when he cuts off some guy's hand and brings it to you like it's a fucking daisy?"

I pull away from Okot, my lips pink and swollen from his very thorough attention. "So sweet, right?" I beam.

Evert shakes his head and walks away, but I'm pretty sure I hear the words "crazy fucking cupid" as he leaves.

"He's obviously never had someone sever a hand for him," I say wisely.

Okot nods. "Obviously."

A thought crosses my mind, and I frown. "That was dangerous, Okot. You could've gotten caught."

"He never saw me."

"You managed to cut off his hand, and he never even saw you?"

He nods. "Correct."

Huh. I don't know whether to be impressed or leery.

To my surprise, Okot and Evert get along without a hitch, and conversation comes easily as we wait out our time in our little cave.

Still, I'm having a hard time not feeling a little bit guilty about my time with Evert. Would Okot be upset if he knew?

I don't know what's appropriate to do with one in front of the other, either. If I touch Evert's hand, will Okot get jealous? If I nuzzle Okot's neck, will Evert get pissed? I don't know, and it's killing me. This is new territory for me, and I don't want anyone to get hurt.

When Evert goes outside to look for wood, leaving Okot and me alone, I set myself beside him and lean against his shoulder. He pets my hair and breathes me in while I bask in the fire's glow.

I can't look him in the eye as I broach the subject, so I continue to look at the flames. "Okot...are you really okay with all of this? I won't be mad if you aren't. I'll understand. You deserve a perfect mate. I don't want you to have to share if you don't want to."

He stops playing with my hair for a moment before resuming. "You *are* my perfect mate. Lamassus may not normally have shared mates, but it is not unheard of for fae. Many breeds share mates."

I pick at my nails. "So you really aren't bothered? I just don't want you to be resentful or upset. I don't want to mess this up or be selfish. I care about you, and I want you to be happy. It's not just about me here. You have a say. I don't want you pressured into anything."

He kisses the top of my head. "You are a caring mate, and I am lucky to have found you. If I were bothered by the genfins, I would tell you. But I'm not. You have nothing to worry about. The five of us are a team now."

"We're a covey," Evert corrects, not bothering to hide the fact that he was eavesdropping as he walks back in with some more firewood to throw on the flames.

"A covey," Okot agrees. "You are ours, and we are yours. You don't have to be shy in your affections of us."

I look up beneath my lashes at them. "Really?"

Okot nods. "Really."

"You better not hold back, Scratch," Evert scolds me. "The five of us are a covey now. You hear me? There's no room for being shy. We're way past that. Besides, aren't you the one who blatantly admitted to wanting sex the very first day we met?"

I shrug, unconcerned. "It was my first day with a real body. You'd have done the same. I want lots of orgasms."

He laughs, showcasing both dimples. "Fucking demanding little thing, aren't you?"

It's my turn to smile, but I look between them one more time. "So this is really okay?"

"Yes, Scratch," Evert says, sitting down so that I'm sandwiched between them. "Now stop worrying so much and just enjoy our covey."

"Emelle's Covey. Covey Lust-and-Love. Cupid Covey. Covey Cupid," I ramble off. "Hmm. I'll work on our team name."

Evert shrugs. "Don't care what the fuck you call us as long as you remember that in the end, *I* won first place. I was the one that got to be your first kiss that you always fucking talked about back on the banishment island. And now I got your first orgasm. So fucking there."

"You did end up winning first place. Even though you sort of tricked me into my first kiss."

He smirks cockily and leans back, putting his hands behind his head. "Yep."

Instead of getting jealous, Okot just brushes my hair to the side and leans in. "He may have stolen your first kiss and earned first place for it back on the banishment island, but once we confirm our mate match, I will be the first one to be inside of you. That is one title I am looking forward to earning."

Liquid heat pools in the pit of my stomach, and I clear my throat loudly. These guys are going to be the death of me. Can someone die from too much arousal? I feel like I should know this.

Evert just rolls his eyes. "Fucking lamassu."

CHAPTER 34

*R*onak returns on a portal to get Evert, while I ride on the back of Okot's bull form to the kingdom island. We make it under the cover of night without anyone spotting us, and sneak into the inn through the back door that Sylred has propped open for us. When we're safe inside our rooms, everyone lets out a relieved breath.

Okot helps to slip the bow and quiver off my back as I sit down on the edge of the bed. I grimace at the pain in my wing when I jostle it too much.

"I'll get her a healer," Sylred offers.

"No. The healer will see her wings and recognize her. We can't risk it," Ronak argues. "There are notices posted every-where on the island about her."

This is news to me. Worry knots in my already aching stomach.

"Look at her," Sylred says, pointing at me with a flash of anger. "Her wing is broken, and she probably has some internal injuries. She might keep saying she's 'fine,' but I know all of us have noticed the winces she keeps trying to hide. She needs a healer. Evert could only do so much."

Sylred's right, I *do* need a healer. My wing hurts, my face feels puffier than a marshmallow, and my stomach is aching from Gammon's punches. But Ronak is right, too. I don't want to risk anything happening and us all being separated again, and I definitely do *not* want the prince to get me.

"I'll be able to muddle the healer enough," Sylred promises.

Ronak considers him. "You don't have any of your instruments. Are you positive? Because if not…"

"I'm sure."

Ronak finally nods, and as soon as he does, Sylred slips out of the room.

"Umm, what?"

"Sylred's power," Evert explains.

"Oh, the sound stuff?"

"If by 'stuff,' you mean that he's a Sound Soother, then yes."

I remember the way he warded off the banshee cries. "He can make it so that the healer won't remember me?"

"Not quite. It's more like he'll be able to make the healer feel such strong emotions that he won't be able to focus on your presence, except just enough to heal you. He's not as strong without instruments, but he'll protect you. Don't worry."

Ronak pulls out a clean handkerchief and starts ripping it into pieces. "Here." He hands two pieces to me and two to Okot. "Sylred's power will work on you, too. Put these in your ears. It won't block it completely, but it will help."

"What about you guys?"

He shakes his head. "His power doesn't negatively affect us since we share a covey bond. His magic is a part of us already. It will be a part of you, too, once we complete the mating ceremony."

I scrunch up the small pieces of fabric and stuff them into my ears while Okot does the same. I can still hear, but everything is muffled.

When Sylred gets back, it's with a different healer than the one who saw to Okot's injuries. The fae is graying and slightly wrinkled, but he has a kind face that doesn't really go with the set of demon-like horns coming out of his forehead.

The guys move aside for the healer, but my eyes are on Sylred. The moment he came inside the room, he started to hum. The only reason I know this is because although his lips are closed, I can see his throat moving.

I can't hear what kind of tune he's humming, but I can see the healer's eyes go from *very* interested in my wings to being slightly glazed over.

The healer mumbles something before his hands are on my swollen face, then my ribs and stomach, then my arms and legs. I feel a heavy, powerful force of magic sweeping through me. Some of it is ice cold, some of it is hot as flames. When he gets to my wing, I feel the bone snapping back into place and let out a weak cry as tears fall onto my cheeks.

When I look up at the healer again, his eyes have a faraway look like he's unable to focus properly. He keeps blinking and shaking his head, but Sylred is whistling now, loudly enough for even me to hear it. And...wow.

Pretty music.

Whistling is awesome. How did I not know this before? In fact, I love it. I don't ever want him to stop. I try to purse my lips together and join in, but I actually don't know how to whistle, so I just blow out a big breath of air and a little spit flies out and lands on the healer.

Whoops.

It's fine. The music is so nice that everything is just fine. I smile and pat the healer's cheek.

When the healer's magic ebbs away and he stands again, he stumbles slightly. A giggle bubbles out of me.

Sylred ushers him out of the room while I try to whistle again. Nope. Still can't.

The moment the door closes, someone plucks the cloth from my ears.

"Okay, Scratch?"

I loll my head to the side to look at Evert, and a goofy smile spreads over my face. "Mm-hmm. So good. So, so good."

He chuckles and looks over at Okot, who is also swaying slightly on his feet and frowning at the door like he can't remember what's on the other side.

"What were we talking about?" I ask with confusion. "My lips feel funny. And I'm hungry again. Also, I think I'm drunk. Am I drunk? Can you be drunk without drinking? I can't remember."

Ronak smirks. "I'll order some food. Be right back."

I look down at my body and over my shoulder at my wing. "Hey! I'm healed! When did that happen?"

Evert just laughs, so I smack him in the chest. "Stop laughing at me. What's funny, anyway?"

He traps my hand and keeps it against his chest. "Nothing. Nothing at all. Once you eat some more, then you can sleep."

Food and sleep. Two of my favorite things.

CHAPTER 35

"*T*his bread is, like, the *best*," I say, stuffing another piece of the warm loaf into my mouth.

It practically melts on my tongue. I wash it down with something called nectarale and then devour the piece of purple fruit on my plate next. "This fruit is the best," I moan.

"You said that about the bread already," Sylred points out, his brown eyes crinkling at the sides.

"She also said that about the meat she practically inhaled," Evert adds.

"She's a big fan of fairy wine, too," Okot says.

Ronak looks at him, amused. "She got drunk, didn't she?"

Okot laughs but quickly smothers it when I shoot him a glare. I try to remind him not to tell my secrets, but my mouth is so full that I pretty much just mumble incoherently.

Evert is leaning back against the wall, sitting across from where I'm perched on the floor as I enjoy the last of my meal. "You keep eating and drinking that fast, and you're going to make yourself sick."

He looks around at my plethora of empty plates on the floor and sees gluttony. I see success.

I open my mouth so I can retort something dazzlingly

witty, but my stomach clenches, and my throat heaves with a forceful noise. It's so sudden that it startles me, and just as my first ever hiccup erupts from my mouth, I pop into the Veil.

I stare in shock at the four guys who are gaping open-mouthed at the space I was just visible in.

After a moment of silent shock, Sylred says, "Did she just…"

"Hiccup herself invisible? Yep." Evert says as he picks up one of my plates and starts helping himself to my leftovers.

I glare at him. "You ass(hiccup)hole. Stop (hiccup) eating (hiccup) my food." Oh my gods. I already had to deal with an itch that lasted over half a century. If I have to deal with hiccups for even a whole day, I will literally go on a cupid tangent.

"Umm, should we be concerned?" Sylred ventures.

Evert just keeps eating *my* food. Asshole.

"Emelle?" Ronak says. "Try to pop yourself back in."

I scoff. "Oh, yeah, I'll just (hiccup) snap my fingers and (hiccup) pop myself right back into the physical (hiccup) realm like it's no big (hiccup) freaking deal!" I pretend to snap my fingers for added drama.

I blink when my fingers don't go through themselves. "Oh."

The genfins smirk at me in all my physical glory. My hiccups are gone, too, thank gods.

I look over my body, but my eye catches on my wing. "What the hell?" I yelp.

On the edge of my right wing, growing right between all my red feathers, is a single black feather.

Evert reaches forward to touch it. "Huh. That's weird."

"Her eyes," Sylred says suddenly. "Look at her eyes."

"What's wrong with my eyes?" I ask shrilly.

They all lean in for a closer look. "They're not blue anymore."

"What? What color are they?" I ask, poking at my eye as if that's going to help answer the question.

"They're sort of...all the colors?"

I blanch. "What do you mean *all* the freaking colors, Sylred?"

He passes me a small mirror from the bedside table, and I snatch it up, holding it in front of my face. My eyes are indeed all the colors. They look like prisms, constantly reflecting light and facets of it shining back like a rainbow. "What. The. Hell."

"So, she accidentally pops into the Veil and then comes back with a black feather and different eyes," Ronak summarizes. "That's weird."

Okot comes over and kneels in front of me. "Do you feel alright, my beloved?"

I put the mirror down and assess myself. "Yeah, I think so."

I look around him to glare at the genfins. "For the record, you guys really suck at being my almost-mates. Okot is *much* nicer than you," I tell them.

I point a finger at Sylred. "You. You're supposed to be the nice one. I expected better from you. You're not supposed to laugh when I hiccup myself invisible. I'm gonna table this whole feather and eye color thing for now, because I can't handle any more crazy, but as of this moment, you're all in trouble. So there."

I put myself in Okot's lap and smirk in victory when the genfins narrow their eyes at my current show of favoritism.

"Not me. I'm not in trouble," Evert argues.

"Yes. Even you. I turned invisible, and you just sat there and ate my food."

He snorts. "Please. You can't stay mad at me. I fucking own this mate shit."

Sylred clears his throat. "Speaking of mates..."

"We should return to our home island and begin the mating ceremony," Ronak inserts.

I sigh in fake boredom. "Hmm, I don't know…I'm gonna need a little wooing."

Three sets of eyes blink at me. "Wooing? What the fuck is wooing?"

"You know, romance. Love. Flirting. *Nice* stuff," I emphasize.

"Oh, here the fuck we go," Evert mumbles. He points at Okot. "You. This is your fault. Stop being so gentlemanly. You're making us look bad."

At first, I think this will offend Okot, but then I feel his rumbling chuckle against my arm. "All I heard was that *I'm* not in trouble," he says with a smug shrug.

I turn to grin at him. "That's right. And we need to confirm our bond."

The red rings around his black eyes flare to life, pulsing in color and size. "You…are ready to confirm our bond?"

Oh. Should I have said that in private? And am I making things weird for the others? Crap, I don't know how to do this covey mate stuff.

I quickly scramble to my feet, and all four of the guys rise to stand with me. "Okay, so I know Okot and Evert talked to me about this stuff, but I think all of us should talk. Or, I mean, at least discuss a bit about…you know. Because this can't get weird. If this gets weird, I'll just die. I mean, not literally, but you get what I'm saying, right? So we should talk it out. Make sure we're all on the same page. We are on the same page, right? That's what Evert and Okot said, but I want to make sure. You're all gonna be my mates and stuff, but I don't want anyone to get mad, or jealous, or resent me, or—"

Ronak takes pity on me and cuts me off. "Emelle. Stop. Breathe."

I take in a huge inhale. My rambling really has repercussions sometimes. Like lack of oxygen.

My wide eyes focus on Ronak for further command. Guy should be in charge of an army or something. I totally get the alpha vibe from him. He has that title on lockdown. I look him up and down, envisioning him in uniform. Hell yeah. Guy should *totally* be in charge of an army. I'd let him shout orders at me all day long. And all night long, too.

"Emelle."

Right. Focus.

"Hmm?"

"The four of us know what we're agreeing to," he says calmly. "We accept each other as your mates, and we give you our word that there will be no hostility in this covey."

I look between them all. "Really? Just like that? You really don't mind…sharing me? Because I gotta say, I've been floating around the human realm for the last sixty years, and this wasn't a thing there."

Sylred shrugs. "The three of us were always going to share, so it's natural for us. And we are fae, not human."

"And you're *really* okay with not getting your genfin super powers or whatever?" I eye Ronak. "I need you to be positive about this, Not-First."

He's the only one out of all of them that I'm not really sure about. He's harder to read than a Dostoyevsky book.

"I'm positive," he says simply, his dark eyes locked on mine. "And can you stop calling me Not-First? That stupid first kiss competition has been over for a long time."

"No, I can't. It's a pet name. Anyway, are you all *positive* that you want to have me for a mate when it's pretty much a death sentence? The prince hates me. If he finds out you're my mates…"

"Like I said, we know what we're agreeing to."

I blow out a breath. "Okay. So…we're really doing this?"

Evert groans. "How many times do we have to say it? We're really fucking doing this. Get used to it."

CHAPTER 36

"So how does this work? What's the plan?"

"Well, you need to mate with us in a genfin ritual," Sylred explains.

"And you'll need to confirm your bond with me separately," Okot says.

I'm envisioning a lot of naked bodies pressed up against me and...yeah. It makes my blood pump a bit faster. Since Evert gave me my first ever orgasm, I'm totally ready for more.

"We will travel to our home island tomorrow if everyone is agreeable," Ronak says, looking around. Everyone nods. "We should complete our ceremony as soon as possible since we can better protect you once you are our mate."

Evert sighs. "Yeah. So go mate with the fucking lamassu. He can protect you better when your bond is confirmed, too. Then first thing tomorrow, we're going home to our island to perform our mating ceremony. No way is the fucking lamassu getting you all to himself for very long," he says, shooting a shit-eating grin at Okot. My bull guy just chuckles.

"Sounds good to me," I say.

"We'll go make arrangements for our departure tomorrow," Ronak says. In a move that totally shocks me, he steps up to me and grips my chin with his fingers. The sudden contact makes heat flare inside of me. "See you soon," he says, his voice low and growly and filled with hunger. *Whoa, Nelly.* He went from being unreadable to being a wide-open bodice-ripper book in the middle of a steamy scene.

Before I can even attempt to form a response, he steps away and walks out of the room. Good gods, Ronak has been totally holding out on me. Figures. It's always the assholes.

Sylred comes up next, pulling me in for a hug and setting a kiss on the top of my head. "Have fun," he says with a wink before he strides out of the room to join Ronak.

Evert invades my space next. Unlike Ronak and Sylred, Evert doesn't hold back. He grabs me by the back of my head, threads his fingers through my hair and pulls it back hard enough to make my face angle up to him. My breath catches in my throat at the pure want I see in his blue eyes.

Just when I think he's going to kiss me, he leans in and presses his lips against my ear instead. "I had my hands on you and *in* you first. Just remember that, Scratch," he says in a low, sexy murmur. I gulp and find that breathing just got really difficult. "I might share you, but you're still *mine*. You knew that the moment you landed on my island."

With a nip on my ear, he pulls back, a cocky smirk in place when he sees whatever expression is on my face. "Lamassu. Take care of our girl," he tells Okot before walking out, letting the door shut behind him.

I let out a shaky breath. Gods. Those three are intense.

I feel Okot come up behind me and place his hands on my shoulders to spin me around. He holds my face in his huge hands. "Are you sure? We don't have to do this now if you don't want to."

I nod. "I'm sure. I want to. I knew as soon as I went invisible. Maybe I haven't known you for long, but I do know you.

261

I know what's important. I'm lucky to have you as a mate, Okot. You're loyal and kind and strong. And hot," I add. "We can't forget the hot part."

He rumbles out a low laugh. "You are perfect."

"So…" I say, looking around at the small bed, feeling suddenly nervous. I've gone decades wishing, wanting, and craving what's about to happen, but now that I have it within reach, I'm panicking a bit. Oh gods, what if I'm *bad* at it?

"You could never be bad at it," Okot says, still cupping my cheeks.

"I said that out loud?"

"Yes."

I sigh and shake my head. "My mouth is so annoying."

He grins. "I beg to differ."

As if to show me, his mouth lands on mine for a slow, sensual kiss. He tilts my head, and I part my lips for him, relishing the feel of his tongue as he sweeps in and chases my nerves away.

When we pull apart, I start heading to the bed, but he stops me. "I will not confirm our mating bond in a back-alley inn, on a bed much too small for us. I have waited too long for you, and you are too precious for this room," he says. "Put your wings away and follow me."

"But someone might see us."

"No one will see us," he promises.

I quickly pull my wings in before following him out of the inn. It's dark out on the streets of the city, but the moon gives off just enough light so that I don't trip over my feet. I relish in the feel of the cool air sweeping around us and Okot's warm fingers threaded through mine. There are plenty of other fae on the streets, but no one pays us any mind, and we're careful to stick to the shadows.

Pulling me into a dark alleyway, he shifts into his bull form without warning. When he jerks his head to the side, I smile. "You want me to ride you?"

He nods and snorts through his nose. He kneels down so I can climb on, and when I have a hold of his thick, bright red mane, he launches us into the sky. He flies higher and higher before veering west. We fly into the night, with me just enjoying the air and the stars, and him steadily flapping his strong wings.

After a while, he starts to slow, and I look around. It's difficult to see at night, but as he brings us closer, I see that it's an island full of flowers. Hundreds of thousands of white flowers practically glow under the moonlight. The entire island is covered with them. In the middle of the beautiful island curves a lazy spring of gurgling water.

Okot lands right beside it, kneeling on the grassy ground so I can slip off. The second my feet hit the ground, the sweet perfume of the blossoms surrounds me. I run my hands over the soft petals and breathe in deeply. I look over at Okot with my heart in my throat. First he gave me the stars, and now he's giving me an island of flowers.

"This is…"

He's back in his regular form and eyeing me carefully, running a hand through his mohawk. I realize that he's nervous, and I melt a little bit more.

"Do you like it? Is this okay?"

I step into him and press my cheek against his chest. "This is perfect."

"No, I told you. *You* are perfect, my beloved." He brings his thick arms around me, and I swear, I've never felt safer. He pushes my hair over my shoulder and fits his face against my neck as he breathes me in. "You smell sweeter than all the flowers in the realm."

A shiver goes through me when he starts kissing his way down my neck, and my eyes flutter closed. With one hand, he starts kneading my shoulders, making my muscles melt under his touch.

With deft fingers, he loosens the ties of my dress until he

can slowly pull the fabric down from my shoulders. He's unhurried, like he's allowing me to stop him if I want to. I don't.

In his signature move, his other hand circles my neck, and his thumb gently caresses the base of my throat. It's a hold that should make me feel vulnerable. With any amount of force, he could crush my windpipe. But the way he gently rubs his thumb over the spot while his palm cradles my neck makes me feel safe and grounded.

When he moves to kiss along my collarbone and over the swell of my breasts, I cling to him, my arms wrapping around his neck. He pushes my dress off my body in one smooth movement, letting it pool to the ground. He lowers me down against the flowers, and my back hits the soft grass. I pull him to me, no longer willing to wait for his mouth to reconnect with mine. He obliges immediately, making a pleased sound low in his throat.

Keeping one hand around my neck, he moves the other down my chest. My nipples pebble from the attention and the night air, and he fondles each breast, making me whimper and arch against him. I can feel his erection straining against his pants, and I bring my leg up to press into it. A gravelly groan escapes him.

When his hand slips down from my breasts to the apex between my thighs, I shudder. He pulls my panties down, and I lift my legs to kick them off the rest of the way. Now that I'm completely bare, he pulls back and eyes every inch of my naked body in the moonlight.

He looks me up and down, and his red-ringed pupils flare. "Beautiful. So beautiful, my beloved."

He is, too, in a masculine, super-hot way. His bulky, strong body, his bright red mohawk, his intense eyes, and his pierced nose. But I want to see more of him. I want to touch him everywhere.

"Now you."

He reaches behind his back, pulls his shirt over his head, and flings it away. He stands to unlace his pants next, and I sit up on my elbows, watching him hungrily. His chest is wide and muscled, with a few pale scars marring his otherwise perfect flesh. He kicks off his boots and drops his pants, kicking the fabric away in one fluid motion.

Then he's bared before me as much as I am to him. I stare up at him, blinking at the sight burned into my retinas. And suddenly, my body comes to a screeching, squealing halt as my eyes lock onto the python between his legs.

My vagina closes the curtains and pretends not to be at home. "Umm… No. That's not gonna work," I say, shaking my head while my thighs automatically close. "That's your dick?" I ask, as if I need to make sure first. I shake my head at myself. "I mean, I know it's your dick. I can see that it's attached to you, but…"

But nope. So much nope.

CHAPTER 37

With a frown, Okot looks down between his legs and then back at me. I know that I just ruined all of his carefully created romance, and I feel bad about that, but…

He looks confused, the poor guy. "Have you not seen one before?" he asks me.

I tilt my head, still staring at it. "Yes. No. I mean, yes I've seen one. Thousands. Maybe even millions. You remember my job. I watched a lot of sex. If you want to get technical, this is the first one that I've seen in my real body that's been for me. But…"

"But?" He's looking at me like he's not sure what's happening.

"I've seen a lot. Big ones, small ones, dark ones, light ones. Narrow, girthy, wrinkly, smooth, hard, soft. You get the picture."

He cringes like he's suddenly imagining all of those at once. "Unfortunately."

I still can't take my eyes off the appendage hanging from his crotch. I point at it, but it points right back. "But I have never seen one quite like that."

He looks like he's at a loss. When he scratches the back of his neck, I realize that I'm also making him self-conscious. I quickly leap to my feet and grab hold of his biceps.

"Sorry. I'm screwing this up. I know, I'm an idiot. It's just, I knew you'd be big, because duh, you turn into a freaking *gigantic bull*, but you're not just big. You're, like, too big. Way too big for me. And I'm not just saying that to make you feel better. Believe me, I've spied plenty of ladies doing the whole ego-boosting spiel when the guy was nothing better than a hot dog. But I'm for reals here."

He just stares at me.

"Look, that thing is gonna rip something important, I'm sure of it," I say, putting my hands in front of my crotch protectively. "Best we just learn to have a hands-only rule right out of the gate. And don't even get me started on the piercings. Don't think I've overlooked those," I say, pointing at the four metal studs glinting from the head of his cock.

"How did you even...you know what? Never mind. You clearly are a terrible judge of pain if you managed to get both your nose *and* your penis pierced. And someone without a proper pain gauge probably shouldn't be spearing into my feminine hollows."

No longer self-conscious, Okot smiles at me like he thinks I'm hilarious. I frown. "This is not a joke, Okot. This is a code-vagina red alert."

I've been looking forward to sex *forever*. But this is way more intimidating than I thought it would be. Even if he were normal-sized, which he's not, it would be a bit daunting. Why did I decide to try to do the hanky-panky with the flying bull fae first? What a rookie mistake.

Okot brings his hands to my cheeks, forcing my gaze to unglue from the eighth wonder of the world between his legs. The thing is staring at me, its metal piercings winking coyly.

When I meet his pulsing red eyes, he smiles softly. "I would never hurt you."

"Well, not on purpose, but—"

"Just relax, my beloved. Let me take care of you. I will go slowly."

I quirk a brow at him. "Ripping. Like tissue paper. It's like one of those shape puzzles. Can't fit a big circle into the little circle, Okot. It just doesn't go in."

He cocks his neck to the side and invites me in to nuzzle my face against him so that I can get a nice big whiff. I do. I close my eyes and take a huge breath, letting his warming scent engulf me. Blazing fire. Summertime. Spices. Gods, he smells divine.

As soon as his scent hits my system, I feel calmer. The breath travels down my throat, into my chest, and then infiltrates all my limbs and even my mind.

When I pull back, he pets my hair. "Better?"

I gaze at him dazedly. "Mm-hmm."

"Good," he says quietly. "Are you ready?"

"You sure it'll fit? Like really?" I ask dubiously.

He smiles softly. "Yes, it'll fit. But I'll stop whenever you need me to."

I nod slowly. "Okay then. Sorry for the minor freak out."

"Don't be. We don't have to do this."

"I know," I say, running my palms up his chest. "But I want to. Just…go slow."

He kisses me on the top of my head. "Close your eyes and lie back down."

I do what he says, and his naked body comes down on top of mine. He holds his weight off me so that I'm not crushed. He's mindful to keep his neck bared to me so that I can breathe in his scent as much as I want.

I keep breathing in and out, relishing in his mate scent that soothes me so well. He starts to caress me again, making goose bumps erupt over my skin. His hand, despite its large size and calluses, is incredibly gentle. His touch grazes up to my bare arms, my chest, my belly, my collarbone, and then his fingers knead through my scalp, and...yep, I've melted. My nervousness is forgotten. Playing with my hair must be my reset button.

Automatically, my hands run up his back. I try to touch everywhere I can reach while he kisses me. His kiss is possessive and makes me want more. He slides his hand to my breasts and runs his thumb over my nipple, sending sparks shooting down my body.

"Yes," I murmur.

He exchanges his hand with his mouth. As soon as his tongue flicks over my nipple, I moan loudly.

"You like that?"

I can't answer. I just writhe beneath him, and he rewards me by taking my nipple into his mouth and sucking. At the same time, he grinds his hips into my groin, creating amazing pressure against my core.

"Mmm..."

His mouth continues to make love to my breasts, and then he moves his hand down my flat belly to the spot between my thighs. I clench with anticipation.

Going, going, going...*there.*

"*Yes.* Right there."

He circles my clit, putting just the right amount of pressure on it. He works me up so much that I can feel wetness start to spread. My hips jut forward greedily.

His hand continues to work me until I'm arching back, my mouth open in a silent plea, and then the orgasm hits me. My toes curl and my wings pop out. A guttural moan escapes my throat, and I see stars behind my closed lids.

Before the fluttering ends, Okot lines himself up with my opening and slowly starts to enter me. My orgasm ripples out, and then all I can feel is his length filling me up. I bite my lip and watch his handsome face as he struggles to go slow. He's careful with me, and it's a good thing, because he really is big.

He pulls out slightly and then pushes back in a few more inches than before. I feel him stretching my limits, and I tense.

"Relax," he soothes in my ear.

He starts licking and nibbling down my neck, making me shudder as he pulls back out a little and back in again.

So full. I'm so full and I don't know if I can take more. It hurts, but there's also this building throb that craves more. With another thrust, he pushes in all the way to the hilt. The noise I make is half-pleasure, half-pain. He pauses, giving my body time to adjust.

"Hey. I've got you," he says, forcing me to look into his eyes.

He keeps one hand around my neck, as if he knows I need to feel grounded by him, and his other hand he places between us, stirring desire at my clit again. At first, it feels like too much too quickly, but then he starts to move inside of me, and my nerve endings ignite.

When his cock hits a sweet spot inside of me, my head falls back against the ground. "*Oh.* That's…" The piercings. Yep. I just decided that the piercings are awesome. He can have as many penis piercings as he wants.

I'm no longer just feeling full and stretched. Now, the heat he's stirring with his hand is also being stoked to life on the inside of me with every single thrust he makes. Every time his pierced cock hits that spot deep within me, the heat grows. He pulls almost all the way out and then thrusts in again, harder, making me arch my back and cry out.

It feels… Gods, it *feels*. So much sensation that I can barely take it. Tears prick my eyes, and I feel Okot kissing them away, somehow knowing that I'm not crying from pain or fear.

The heat that he's sparked to life inside of me molds

together with the fire he's created on my clit, and it feels like I'm about to burst open. A pleased groan comes from him when my hips jut up to meet his, and my fingers dig into his back.

"Faster."

He doesn't need to be told twice. He starts plunging into me. Over and over again, his pierced cock hits that deliciously perfect spot, and I never want it to end, and yet I'm desperate to reach the pinnacle.

Just when I'm at that perfect peak, he buries his nose against the crook of my neck, and my head automatically turns so I can be surrounded by his scent, too. His smell is suddenly everywhere, headier than ever before. The unique warmth of his scent is feeding the warmth that he's created inside of me. I can taste it, feel it, hear it. It's become its own entity, and it pulsates and makes my pleasure skyrocket.

His thrusts grow harder and more frenzied. "Gods, you feel so good," he groans.

When he slams me into the ground and pinches my clit at the same time, I unravel with a divine orgasm that makes me see stars. "Yes!"

I feel him stiffen and release inside of me as the waves of my own pleasure crash into me again and again. My whole body shudders and sighs.

Gods, that was…more than I ever imagined. I want to do this forever. I want to sign up for a sex rotation so that I can maximize the number of orgasms I can get every week. My cupid covey was an awesome idea. Having my own personal harem is super efficient.

When I'm able to open my eyes again, I see Okot peppering me with soft kisses on my cheeks, neck, breasts, and lips.

I lazily thread my fingers through his hair while my other hand strokes up and down his bare back. When he pulls out of me, I feel a twinge, but nothing more painful than a pinch.

It's surprising, really. My narrow feminine hollow is awe-somely accommodating, if I do say so myself.

Okot stands and scoops me into his arms. He walks us into the stream to wash. His huge hands touch every part of me as he drips water over my skin with loving caresses. I don't feel shy at all, and it's clear that he doesn't, either. He stands shin-deep in the water, proud and tall, as he should. His body is a feast for the eyes.

With both of us standing in the stream, my front pressed against his, he wraps his arms around me in a protective circle.

"Did you feel it?" he asks huskily.

I don't have to ask to know he means the mate scent. "Yeah. That was intense."

"I have heard about confirming mate bonds my whole life," he says, his voice sounding faraway. "Yet even I was not prepared. It was so much more than I've heard."

"I can sense you now," I admit, pointing to a spot on my chest. "Is that normal?"

He kisses the top of my head. "Yes. It is the confirmation of our mate match. My sense of you has grown stronger, too."

"That was intense. And I have a wholly new appreciation for penis piercings."

His chuckle rumbles against my body, making me smile. I feel him stretch to rub his neck, and then his body stiffens.

"What's wrong?" I ask, pulling away.

He takes my hand and lifts it to his neck, and I look up to follow the movement. "You marked me."

I blink up at him in confusion, watching the spot that he covers with my palm. When I lift my hand from his skin, my eyes widen. Right at the crook of his neck—my favorite place to sniff him—is my cupid marking. The exact cupid number that's marked on the inside of my right arm, right below my wrist, now marks his skin. "ML" in silvery white Roman numerals raised up like a brand.

"Oh my gods." I look up at him to try to gauge his reaction, but he doesn't seem weirded out. "I'm sorry. I don't know why that happened. Are you mad?"

He frowns. "Mad? My mate marked me as her own. Why would I be mad?"

I lightly trace the mark on his neck. "I don't know. Because everyone will be able to see it. Because it's not normal."

He captures my hand and kisses my fingers. "I am proud to wear your mark. And nothing about you is normal. I wouldn't want it any other way."

I smile and shake my head at him. "Who knew under the pierced bad boy exterior, you'd be such a romantic?"

"Only with you, my beloved."

"Are you trying to get lucky again?"

He chuckles and smooths my damp hair down. "I wish I could, but I must take you back to the genfins now. I have something I need to do."

The smile immediately falls from my face. "What do you have to do?"

"I must go and meet with Princess Soora. I report to her, and she is in more danger every day that she works with the rebellion. She will need to know that I am alive and how she can find us, and I must get my new orders from her."

I worry my lip between my teeth. "I don't want you to go. Someone will see you. You're huge. And your hair is bright red. You don't blend in."

"No one will see me," he assures me. "I have been doing this for a very long time."

"I don't like it."

"I will be back before you know it."

I sigh in defeat. "Promise?"

He places a kiss on the crown of my head. "I promise. Now let's get you back."

He leads me out of the stream, and we quickly air dry before getting dressed again. When he shifts into his animal form, I climb on top of his back and hold on tight.

The flight is over quickly, and he drops me off at the back of the inn where the guys are already waiting. Without shifting back, Okot nuzzles his nose against my arm in goodbye.

"What the fuck's that?"

I look to where Evert is staring at Okot. In his animal form, my whitish cupid marking is even more noticeable on Okot's neck.

"Oh, I sort of marked him when we confirmed our mate match."

The guys stare at me. "You *marked* him?"

"Yeah. My cupid number just popped up on him after we...you know." They continue to stare at me, so I cross my arms defensively. "What? It's not like I knew that was going to happen. If you're having second thoughts..."

"We're not having second thoughts," Evert cuts me off.

"Look, I know it's weird..." I say, feeling embarrassed. "Lots of things are weird about me. My eyes changed color, I have this black feather now, I hiccuped myself into invisibility...I'm a freak, I totally get that, and—"

"Scratch."

"What?"

"Shut up."

I look at him with confusion. Sylred takes pity on me. "We're jealous as hell."

"You—what? No. Really?"

"Just get your cute ass inside," Evert drawls. "And try not to mark anyone else on the way up."

My nervousness dissipates immediately. At Okot's grunt, I turn back to him and pet his head. "Be careful."

274

He snorts and paws the ground. Leaping into the air again, his wings lift him up into the sky. I watch until I can no longer see his shadowy silhouette.

I realize I'm crying when Sylred wraps his arms around me from behind. "He'll be alright." I sniff through my nod and then let him lead me inside.

We go up through the back staircase, once again not being seen. Inside the room, there's already more food waiting for me. This time, it's a collection of desserts.

"What's all this?"

Ronak shakes out a blanket and spreads it on the floor in front of the plates. "You haven't had any proper desserts yet. Our honeyed fruit back on the banishment island didn't really count."

All three of them sit down on the blanket and look up at me expectantly. My genfins are being...sweet? I narrow my eyes and look at them suspiciously.

"Don't look at us like that," Sylred laughs.

"No, she's right not to trust us," Evert admits, leaning back on his hands. "We haven't gotten her back for all the Lust-Breaths."

I lift my chin. "I don't know what you mean. How else was I supposed to communicate?"

He shakes his head. "Don't play innocent. It won't work on me."

I shrug. It was worth a try.

"So is this a bribe, or are you just trying to distract me?"

Sylred reaches up, surprising me when he pulls me down into his lap. I relax against him instantly. "Think of it more like a reward."

I raise a brow. "A reward for what?"

"For agreeing to take us on as mates. This is us wooing you."

"Hmm." I look around at the embarrassing number of plates. "I approve."

Sylred runs his hands up my arms. "Good. Now which one do you want to try first?"

I focus on the different choices, but my eyes instantly zero in on a particular tray. "Is that..."

"Chocolate cake. Chocolate-covered strawberries, chocolate tarts, chocolate fondant, and chocolate mousse," Evert lists off. "It's all the chocolate desserts we could find in our limited time."

I'm practically drooling before he can get through the list. I wonder how much I can eat...

"You always talked about how good chocolate looked while you watched the humans," Ronak explains. "We figured it's time you tried it for yourself. We didn't know which one you'd like best, so we got all of it."

I look over at the guys incredulously. "This is...really nice."

Evert smirks and takes a bite of chocolate-covered strawberry. He looks over at Sylred. "Told you we'd get out of trouble."

"I didn't say that."

"The drool on your chin does."

I smack him half-heartedly, but he just wags his eyebrows. "Go on, stuff your face to your heart's content."

I flick my eyes back to the chocolate again and ignore their smug smirks. I had my first ever orgasm with Evert. Then I had sex for the first time with Okot. Now they're showering me with chocolate. I am one stupidly happy cupid.

CHAPTER 38

"*S*top squirming or I'm going to screw up the mating rituals before they can begin," Evert hisses into my ear.

I immediately stop wriggling against Evert's body. "Sorry. I can't sleep."

I've been lying in bed with Evert for nearly three hours, my mind too wired to even think about sleeping.

"We gave her too much sugar," Ronak says in the darkness.

"I think it was that last tart. How many did she have?" Sylred replies.

"Three," Evert answers.

"No, I think it was four," Ronak argues.

Evert considers this. "Huh. Yeah, maybe."

I elbow him, making an "oof" sound escape. "Stop talking about me."

"Then go to sleep."

I huff, wriggling against him again. "I can't," I whine. "I'm worried about Okot."

Evert uses his thighs to trap my fidgety legs between his.

He wraps his arms tighter around me so that my arms can't move, either. "The fucking lamassu will be fine."

"His name isn't 'fucking lamassu,' you know. You can just say his name."

I feel Evert shrug. "I like my way better."

For the hundredth time, I close my eyes and try to fall asleep. Exhaustion hangs over my eyes like a mask, but I can't give in to it. I want to roll over, but Evert has me essentially trapped, so I move my hips instead. I hear him groan and then I'm suddenly being propelled up from the bed, making a surprised yelp come out of me.

"I fucking can't handle it anymore." I feel him carrying me across the room in three long strides. "You try sleeping with her writhing all up next to you. It's fucking torture." He drops me, and I land with a bounce in someone else's bed.

"Hey!"

My head lands on a solid arm of muscle, and another one moves to circle my waist.

I stiffen.

Ronak.

He feels my reaction and pauses. The two of us freeze because he's never held me intimately. Other than when he grabbed my chin, he's never really touched me at all.

He clears his throat, a sound way too loud in the quiet room. "Would you prefer to lie with Sylred?"

I hear Evert's retreating steps falter, and then Sylred shifts in his own bed as they witness this awkward exchange.

"No, I just…"

How can I explain that part of me wants to jump away from him while another wants to burrow closer?

Held hostage in the uncomfortable moment, Evert throws a pillow at Sylred. "Come on, asshole. I'm thirsty."

Sylred groans but makes no other complaint as he gets up from bed and trudges out of the room with Evert. When they close the door after them, Ronak and I are left alone. I've never been alone with him before. There seems to be so much between us that I don't know what to say. I hate that my reaction to his touch was to panic. I wish I could turn the clock back and fix it.

I blow a piece of hair away from my face. "I made it weird."

My honest confession makes him bark out a laugh, but he also moves his arm away from my waist and sets it on his chest. The only part where we're still touching is my head using his other arm as a pillow. I hate that I'm forcing more distance between us.

"No, it's my fault for being an ass to you from the start. I can't expect you to just move on from that."

I bite my nail nervously. "I guess I'm still...I don't know. I'm not sure you really want me." My voice sounds tiny and vulnerable even to my own ears.

He sighs, but not in anger or frustration. We lie next to each other in silence. It sucks. It's heavy and constricting, and all I want to do is make this awkwardness between us go away. But then again, we can't continue to ignore it. If we're going to really do this mate thing, we need to clear the air.

"I was twelve when I first met Sylred and Evert," he says, his voice making me relax slightly. "They were younger than me. I'd been at the island for two years already, waiting to find the covey-brothers I would bond with. It was considered a long time to wait. Most coveys form within a few months. They're formed organically upon introductions. It's something that snaps into place as soon as you meet. For two years, I'd been meeting different kids, but none of them were for my covey. So I waited. I trained. I was homesick as hell. I kept feeling like I'd failed before I'd even begun. I couldn't do the one thing that was supposed to come easily. The other kids were ruthless about it. I was the alpha without a covey. A joke."

He snorts bitterly, and I can picture him, just a boy, hating his failure. "You must have been upset. Lonely."

"I was," he admits. "But then Sylred came along and Evert not long after. They were good genfins to form a covey with. Not of noble blood, but noble in other ways that counted. I had a feeling I'd be alpha, but I didn't expect the crushing expectations that came with it. Our covey raised in ranks quickly. We were naturally talented fighters together, and our covey magic came easily to us. Other young coveys that formed years before us didn't share the same harmony that ours did. I was proud. I felt that our success was because of me. Because I'd willed it."

Entranced by his words, I turn to face him, tucking my hands under my head so I can look at his dark silhouette.

"And then we graduated from our training. It was time to submit our request to our elders to find a mate. Delsheen was my only choice."

Just hearing her name makes my nose wrinkle in aversion. "Why? I know genfin females are rare, but there had to have been others that were nicer. She's awful."

He shrugs a shoulder. "She was noble. Came from a great genfin house. Rich. Beautiful. And yes, I chose her for her title. I knew that I could catapult our already illustrious covey into even higher status by mating with her. I overlooked her many faults. She was cruel, greedy, and disloyal, among other things, but I didn't let myself see it. I didn't listen to Evert when he tried to warn me. I convinced myself that she was the best. I fooled myself into loving her when she never loved anyone other than herself. And it was because I was still trying to make up for being the joke alpha without a covey when I was a kid."

His voice is hoarse, but he continues staring straight up at the ceiling, and even in the dark, I can see his jaw flex.

"When I found her with the prince on the eve of our final mating ceremony, I lost it. I was suddenly ten years old again, without a covey, totally alone. I was the alpha kid who couldn't form a bond. This time, a mate bond. For all the pride that I tried to hold onto, it had failed me. Blinded me. Add that with the betrayal I felt...and that's why I snapped.

"I attacked the prince of the realm and my would-be mate, and I didn't care. I wanted to kill them. I would have if the prince hadn't stopped me with his magic. When they banished us, I knew I had broken my covey. I knew Evert hated me, that Sylred was disappointed in me. But it was nothing to how I felt about myself."

"It wasn't your fault she was a backstabbing bitch."

He shakes his head. "I was a prideful bastard. I knew I didn't deserve my covey's forgiveness, so I didn't ask for it. I withdrew. I wanted Evert to hate me. I wanted to keep disappointing Sylred. Because I deserved it."

That admission makes me want to cry. I know that nothing I say will get through to him, though. Only actions. With only a little bit of hesitation, I move my head to lie on his chest instead and wrap my arm around his middle. I feel him stiffen slightly, but then his arm comes up to rest on my back.

"It was a long five years of self-loathing. Evert barely spoke to me. Sylred was always stuck in the middle when we blew up at each other. Our once strong covey was broken. And then a little red-winged demon landed on our island."

I smile against his chest. "You shot me with an arrow."

I hear his own smile crack through. "Always with the arrow."

"It's important to correctly depict history."

"I'm still not convinced you're not a demon."

I laugh and pinch him, but his skin is so taut against his muscular chest that I barely get a grip.

"You were like this wild wind that threatened to toss me on my ass. I didn't know what your angle was. I was so hardened by that point I couldn't even see you."

I swallow the thick lump in my throat. "And now?"

"And now I see that you're not Delsheen, and I'm not the same genfin I was," he admits. "I don't have to keep proving myself or my covey. It took a crazy-ass demon to make me see that."

I pick my head up and balance my chin on his chest. He turns his face to look at me, and we study each other in the darkness.

"I'm still an asshole, but I'm yours if you'll have me. And if you won't, then...I'll leave my covey in your capable hands."

My mouth opens in shock. I never expected Ronak to talk to me like this, and I never in a million years imagined that he'd willingly step aside if I told him I didn't want him. I can tell by the frantic pace of his heart how nervous he is, even if he'd never otherwise show it. His power is strength, after all. He doesn't like to show weakness.

I lightly trace the exposed part of his collarbone that is visible above his shirt. "Thank you for telling me." His skin jumps under my touch. "I don't want us to start over, but I want us to move on. As mates. Okay?"

He nods slowly, a small smile playing at the corner of his lips. "Okay."

Since he bared so much of himself to me, I want to repay the favor. "I know I joke around a lot, but I want you to know that I am completely serious when it comes to how I feel about you all," I tell him. "When I came to this realm for the first time, you were the first fae I saw. And when I saw you...I don't know, it was like I was drawn to you or something. Like it was always going to be you I saw first. I just knew that you would protect me. That if I could just get to you somehow, it would be okay," I tell him. Then I smile mischievously. "Then you shot me with an arrow and turned out to be a total asshole. So I guess I was wrong on that front."

His hand that has been on my back suddenly moves, and

his fingers start digging into my side, tickling me relentlessly. I squeal and kick, trying to get him away, but of course, it doesn't work because he's freaking strong.

He continues his assault against me, no matter how much I try to get away. My laughter is so loud that Evert and Sylred come running back in, only to find me hysterical, half on the bed and half hanging off. Ronak shows me mercy and stops, and I flop to the floor, still trying to contain my laughter.

"You. Freaking. Bastard," I pant.

"I take it you two have kissed and made up?" Evert asks.

Sylred lights the lantern so that we're no longer bathed in darkness, and I relax on the floor, propping my back up against the bed. "There was no kissing, but that's part of Not-First's punishment for the arrow incident."

"Don't make me tickle you again."

I launch to my feet and dart around Sylred, hiding behind him. Ronak lifts a sardonic brow. "Really? You think he'll protect you from me?"

Evert tuts. "Bad choice, Scratch. If anything, Syl will just step aside so that you two can 'work it out.' Believe me, I know. Asshole thinks he's the great and mighty peacekeeper."

"Shut up," Sylred says, rolling his eyes at Evert.

"Wait," I say, remembering their conversation in the carriage. "There's still a chance your alpha animal guy will reject me, and then this will all be for nothing, right?"

They exchange a look. "Well…"

"Then let's do this." I clap my hands and rub them together, hopping from one foot to the other. "Bring him out, Ronak. I got this. I'm gonna charm the hell out of your animal. Your animal is gonna think I'm kick-ass. He'll be like, 'Delsheen who?'"

Ronak laughs and rolls his eyes, but even I can see that he's nervous. Worried. Because there's a chance his animal side will reject me. Which would…really suck.

"Come on," I urge. "Do it! Do I need to, like, hit you or something?"

Ronak frowns. "What? Why would you need to hit me?"

"Like threaten your life? Is that how it works to make you flip your switch? Is it a Dr. Jekyll, Mr. Hyde thing? Or are there some magic words to make him come out and play?"

Ronak rubs a hand down his face. "No. Don't do any of that. I'll just call him to come out."

I drop my arms. "Well, that's anticlimactic. I would've rather had to hit you."

He sighs and closes his eyes, but when he blinks them open again, they're pure gold and shining. They move around the room, taking in the scene. His back is hunched slightly as if he's suddenly poised to pounce.

"Hey, kitty cat, remember me?" I croon. "It's your friendly neighborhood cupid," I say as I take a step closer to him.

He zeroes in on me and growls. I freeze in my tracks. Welp. This isn't going as planned. The genfin starts to circle around me, sniffing the air.

Speaking through unmoving lips, I say, "What do I do?"

"Just keep talking to him," Sylred suggests.

"Right. Keep talking. I can do that. I'm super good at that," I say. "So. Umm, alpha genfin beast guy? I'm Emelle. Nice to meet you. I don't think we met properly before. I really like what you did with the beasts trying to eat me alive. It was some of your best work. It was very alpha-ish and impressive. Lots of...blood and breaking bones. Really, top-notch animal stuff."

His animal stops behind me, so close that I can feel the heat coming off of his chest.

"And the whole growly thing you did at Delsheen? Classic. I'd love an encore of that. She looked like she was about to pee her pants. Or her gown. Whatever."

He leans in close to my neck and growls low against my

ear. Flashing my eyes up, I see that Evert and Sylred look worried. Shit.

"Umm...so yeah, anyway...I was thinking, maybe you could choose me as a mate instead? I'm, like, super fun. Way more fun than Delsheen. And my wings are better, am I right?" I ask with a nervous laugh.

"Plus, I'm sure I'm good at sex. At least, I think I am. Probably. Maybe I should have Okot take a survey? He seemed to enjoy it, but maybe he was faking? Wait, do guys fake it? I thought that was just a female thing, but I could be totally wrong. Which would be embarrassing given my profession. Anyway, point is, I'm sure we'll have lots of awesome cupid covey sex."

His animal circles around to my front and stares down at me. A low grumbling sound in his chest makes my heart race in fear.

"Guys!" I hiss. "What do I do? Nothing's working. I think he's about to eat me!"

"Ronak. Come back out," Sylred says firmly.

"Wait," Evert says. "Look."

Suddenly, I feel something wrapping around me. I don't dare move, even as it slithers around my waist and pulls me toward him. I look down. His tail. It's his tail. The tail he wouldn't let Delsheen even touch.

He pulls me forward again, and once I'm flush against his chest, he starts to purr. If he weren't holding me up, I'd collapse in relief. His purr suddenly cuts off, his tail falls away, and when I look up at his face, Ronak is back.

I blow out a shaky breath. "See?" I say with forced confidence. "Totally hit it off. Never had any doubt."

Ronak raises an amused brow, but I can see the relief in his face, too.

"Well, fuck me. Had me worried there for a second," Evert confesses.

Sylred whistles low. "Glad that's over."

Ronak nods. "My animal is…aggressive. Sorry if he scared you."

I pretend like my heart isn't trying to beat out of my chest and run away. "Psh. Please. I don't scare easy. Besides, your animal totally digs me."

"He wrapped his tail around you like a boa constrictor," Evert points out. "He definitely digs you."

I perk up at that. "Really? What did he do to Delsheen?"

Ronak frowns as if remembering. "Barely let her hold onto the end. He never initiated touch before."

I practically preen.

Evert groans. "Don't tell her all that. She's all smug and shit now."

Sylred ignores him. "Emelle, do you want to try to get some sleep?"

I shake my head. "Are you kidding? I can't sleep now. Ronak's alpha animal just totally boa-constrictored me."

Evert makes a face. "Don't ever say that again."

I shrug.

"I guess we might as well get ready to leave now. It's not like any of us are getting any sleep tonight."

A sudden knock on our door jolts all of us. Our heads whip toward the offending sound, and panic grips me. We were too loud. Someone heard. Someone saw. The guards have come for me.

I hear Evert curse under his breath. "Fuck."

My thoughts exactly.

"should've heard someone approach," Ronak hisses. "I was too distracted."

I realize that I'm digging my nails into Sylred's arm when he starts peeling my fingers off his skin and threads his hand through mine reassuringly. Evert steps in front of me in a protective move while Ronak goes to the door. With a look at the others, he opens it an inch while I peer out from behind Evert.

When there isn't an immediate sound of a fight breaking out, I relax slightly.

"Well? Are you going to stand there all night flicking your tail, or are you going to move aside before the whole inn comes to the hall and sees me standing here?"

I quickly move around Evert. "Duru?"

She pushes past Ronak, and he shuts the door behind her. The guys look at the short hearth hob woman with distrust. "This is Duru, Princess Soora's handmaiden. She kept me hidden in the palace," I explain. "We're besties."

Duru rolls her eyes. "We are not."

"Eh. We are, though."

Duru's attention is already off me. She's now staring with

distress at the dirty dishes strewn around the room. She starts tidying up immediately.

"What's up, Duru? What's with the pre-dawn house call?"

She's piling all of the uneaten food on a tray while she starts stacking the dirty dishes and silverware in neat piles. "The princess sent me, of course."

"What did she say?"

"Your lamassu mate told her you'd returned. She wanted to warn you. Come morning, there will be an active search of the city. There is a planned sneak-search at dawn. Every building in town will be raided, portal shops closed, and the skies will be watched. You need to leave immediately."

She says this all in a matter-of-fact tone as she pulls out an empty sackcloth from her apron pocket and starts dumping all the uneaten food in it. Once she's done with that, she pulls out a cleaning rag and starts shining the cleared plates. All the four of us can do is stare. She's practically buzzing with cleaning power. Her frizzy hair even crackles a bit.

"Okay. Thanks for the heads-up."

"Hmph."

"You can stop cleaning now."

She doesn't even spare me a glance. "Don't just stand around. Get moving. Dawn is only a few hours away."

The genfins, clearly chastised, spur into action. I'm impressed with her ability to boss them around. "Nice. I always have to blow Lust in their faces if I want to get their attention."

She ignores me as she starts making the beds.

"Can you tell the princess something for me?"

She fluffs a pillow. "What's that?"

I move close to her. "I don't know if Okot mentioned it, but I think I might be able to turn invisible voluntarily now. I'll start practicing so I know for sure, but if I can, I'll be able to help her with that *thing* she wanted help with," I try to say quietly, but of course the genfins hear.

"What thing?" Ronak frowns.

I straighten up from Duru and pretend to help her by yanking on the corner of the blanket. She slaps the back of my hand and fixes it again. "Oh, nothing much. She just wants me to help her. Remember? Spy stuff?"

"With what?" Evert persists.

I cough and speak as quickly as I can. "Shewantsmetosneakontothesupersecretweaponislandtoseewhattheprinceishiding."

"I'm sorry? What was that?" Sylred asks.

I sigh. "She wants me to sneak onto the super-secret weapon island to see what the prince is hiding," I repeat. "Then we can know what he's up to."

The genfins glower at me.

"Absolutely not."

I roll my eyes at Ronak. "I'll be invisible. It'll be fine."

He crosses his arms. "*If* you can even do that again. And what if you can't turn back? Or what if you turn back while you're still there and someone spots you? You're not exactly trained for this. Spying takes finesse and training."

"I'm totally finessed."

Evert snorts.

"I'm gonna be an awesome super spy. Like, the best. She's gonna give me spy awards when I'm done."

Ronak draws a hand over his face.

"It's dangerous, Emelle," Sylred says gently.

"I know that. But she saved me and hid me from the prince when she didn't have to. This was the deal, guys. She helps me, I help her. She's more than kept up her side of the deal. I gave her my word that I'd help her with the rebellion."

"Shh! Not so loud," Duru snaps from her spot at the window where she's currently dusting.

"Sorry," I whisper-yell. I turn back to the genfins. "I'll be careful. Believe me, I don't want to get caught. The prince is a total tool. But I can't go back on my word. Besides, I want to help."

"We need to discuss this as a covey," Ronak says. "That is how we make decisions. Together."

"Yeah, and we'll do that *after* our mating ceremony," Evert interjects.

"We should leave. Get to our island now. Emelle isn't safe here," Sylred says.

Duru, looking around for anything else she can clean, straightens up. "Yes. Hurry and leave. I will visit you at your genfin island to check in."

Stacking the dishes in her arms, she turns and waits for someone to open the door for her.

"You could leave those here," I say. She looks at me like I'm an idiot.

"Leave them—No. No." She shakes her head adamantly, as if the very thought abhors her. "You're the ones that should be leaving. The last thing we need is for you to be imprisoned again and able to be questioned. Besides, the genfins' continued presence on the kingdom island has not gone unnoticed by the prince. Stay much longer, and he will grow even more suspicious. You need to return to your island."

Before she can leave, I stop her. "Wait, what about Okot? Where is he?"

"Her majesty had an errand for him."

"What errand?"

She looks at me with irritation clear on her face. "I don't presume to question my princess. She sent him to do something, and he left to do it. That is all I know. Now stop being idiots and leave before all of you are captured and I have to tell my princess you couldn't follow simple instructions."

Sylred opens the door for her, and she sweeps out without another word. After she leaves, the four of us exchange glances. Initially, our plan was to wait for Okot to return so I could fly on him. We were going to meet the genfins later on their island since neither of us can be seen in town and take a portal. But now, that's obviously not going to work since we don't know when Okot will be back and the raid is set for dawn.

"She can't fly on her own all that way. It will take days as it is, and she's not the strongest flier," Sylred says.

"She's not flying alone. Way too dangerous," Evert insists.

"Can you try and turn invisible just while we go into town? Then we can hire a portal first thing, and you can turn back for that part," Ronak says.

"I don't know. Let me practice." I blow out a breath and scrunch my eyes closed, concentrating. I whisper under my breath. "I'm invisible, I'm invisible, I'm invisible..."

Peeling open one eye, I look at the genfins. They stare back at my still-solid body. "Dammit."

"You thought you could just repeat 'I'm invisible' and that would work?" Evert asks with a grin on his face.

"It's called speaking something into reality, Evert," I snap.

"Mm-hmm. And how's that normally work out for you?"

"Well, this was my first time trying it, but I'm pretty sure it's gonna work."

He barely holds in his laughter. "Then by all means." He waves his hand out. "Please continue."

I scrunch my eyes closed again and visualize myself popping back into the Veil. "I'm like the wind. I'm invisible!"

When I check my body again, I'm still solid. "Godsdammit!"

"Should we order you some more food? See if we can induce you into invisibility with some more hiccups?" Evert teases.

"Ha ha," I say dryly.

"I think we've determined what you're doing is not going to work," Evert drawls.

I puff out a frustrated breath. "Well, I don't know how to

do it," I snap. "Why don't you try turning invisible and see how easy it is?"

With his shit-eating grin still in place, he does a terrible impression of my voice as he calls out, "I'm invisible like the wind!"

I glare at him. "I don't sound like that."

He lifts a shoulder. "I think it was a good impersonation."

"Do that again, and I'll be impersonating kicking my foot into your ass."

He just laughs. I need to work on my threats.

Ronak flicks his gaze to Evert and then suddenly comes forward. He takes hold of my arms and forces me to look at him. He blocks out everyone else, probably so I don't throat punch Evert.

"Focus, little demon," he says quietly.

"I am," I retort.

Surprisingly, he doesn't call me out for acting like a five-year-old. "Close your eyes," he says soothingly. "Good. Now picture your body slowly fading," he says, his tone steady and soft. "First you feel it in your feet as they start to go. Then it spreads up your legs, your stomach, your chest, your shoulders."

His voice calms me completely and pulls me into an almost trancelike state. "Your head is last, and now every-thing is light and insubstantial. Your whole body is invisible. Your body knows exactly how to fade into the Veil. Trust it."

I feel weightless. For a moment, I'm positive it worked, but before I can open my eyes to confirm, I hear Ronak curse under his breath. I barely hear him whisper Evert's name, and then...

Lightning-quick, someone snatches me from behind and yells, "BOO!"

"Ah!" I jump about three feet in the air from Evert scaring the absolute crap out of me. I also think I peed a little? But when I land...I don't *land*.

I whirl around to see a cocky looking Evert. He's looking at the spot I disappeared from. "Well, that worked." Ronak scratches the back of his head. "I guess she has to be startled into it."

"You assholes!"

I blow Lust into both of their stupid faces and enjoy the matching growls that follow. It's half-lust crazed and half-irritated.

"We helped you," Ronak feels the need to point out.

"Come on, let's go now before she sneezes herself back into visibility," Sylred says cheerfully, opening the door.

"Sneezing doesn't happen in the Veil, thank you very much."

I float after them as they hurry downstairs. The sky outside is already lightening, the horizon like a dark bruise.

"You're sure that high fae female will be there?" Sylred asks.

"She'd fucking better be. I paid her triple what a portal is worth," Evert says.

"We're paying for her discretion. Not just for her to open a portal," Ronak tells him.

"Yeah, yeah."

We pass by all the closed shops on the quiet street. The guys keep their eyes peeled. According to Duru, the palace soldiers should be making their way into the town soon.

We make our way to the end of the main road, and then the guys divert into an alley. They stop in front of a tiny two-story house made of stone that has bright white shutters. Ronak knocks on the door. Even though the place is completely dark, the door swings open immediately. Not creepy at all.

CHAPTER 40

"*C*ome in, come in," a hurried voice whispers.

She shuts the door before I can float all the way inside, so I'm forced to fly through the wood to make it inside. The high fae woman pulls all the curtains closed, and only after she's done with that does she light a single candle.

Her house is small but tidy, and the three big genfins look totally out of place in her sitting room filled with floral prints and short ceilings. She's older with yellow skin and puce-colored hair.

She holds her hand out. "An extra gold will do for coming early."

Evert starts to argue, but Ronak silences him and hands her another coin.

She snatches it up and buries it into the front of her dress between her breasts.

I wrinkle my nose. "I don't think that's sanitary."

"Right," she says, patting her gold-laden breasts. "Where am I taking you?"

"We paid you very, very well for your discretion," Ronak reminds her.

She rolls her yellow eyes. "Yes, yes. You were never here, I never saw you, and I definitely *don't* open portals since doing so would be breaking the law, as I have no permit. This isn't my first time. I know the song and dance. Now tell me where you want to go so I can get you overgrown brutes out of my house and forget you ever existed."

She's super friendly.

Seemingly satisfied, Ronak tells her where, and she quickly works her magic to open a portal to their home island. Before any of them step through, Ronak hands her another gold piece. "Another gold piece for you to close your eyes and not open them again until I say."

She rolls her eyes again but snatches up the coin and stuffs it down her bodice. "If you're planning on trying to sneak your snake under my skirts, just know that I'm not interested," she says haughtily.

"Our snakes want nothing to do with your fucking skirts," Evert says dryly. "Now turn around and close your eyes."

She does as he says with her hands on her hips. "Hurry up, will you? My tea is getting cold."

The genfins look around the room as if they're trying to find something. "Oh. Right. Me."

"What if she can't…" Sylred murmurs.

"She will," Ronak says decisively. "She has to."

Well, alright then. No pressure.

I focus with all my might on turning visible again. This time, instead of focusing on my body, I focus on the pull I feel from my anchors. Because of whatever magic Plik and Plak used on me, popping into my physical body seems to be easier than forcing myself to return to the Veil. Which is ironic, really, when my problem has always been that I couldn't *leave* the Veil.

I feel for those invisible strings that tether me to the guys. I grab hold of them in my mind and tug. Just like that, I'm back. Sylred gives me a relieved wink.

I look over at my right wing to see if I've sprouted

another black feather, but I haven't. There's still just the one on the edge of my wing. Phew.

Then Evert points to my left wing. I turn my head and scowl when I notice the black feather that's sprouted there, in perfect mirrored placement as the one on the right side.

I open my mouth to say something, but Evert shakes his head. Without a word, he grabs my hand and pulls me through the portal. It's only my second time going through one, so I'm still not used to it. I immediately feel like I've walked under a waterfall, and yet no moisture touches me.

Then there's the sensation of falling, as vertigo hits me. Luckily, Evert still has hold of me, because in the next instant, gravity hits me again and I'm slamming into his body.

He breaks my fall, somehow managing to stay upright. I blink at our new surroundings and watch as first Sylred and then Ronak walk through the portal behind us. After another second, the strange whirlpool disappears.

I stand upright and look around. It's nearly dawn but still too dark out to see much of anything except that we're in the middle of a forest. "Where are we?"

"The Winged Wood," Ronak answers. "We're a few hours walk from our capital city, Rochbrook. I didn't want to bring us too close in case that high fae could not be trusted."

"Oh," I say casually, scratching at my arm. "So we're just gonna walk? For a few hours? All the way through the forest to the capital? That's...yeah, that sounds fine," I say unconvincingly. "Walking is like, refreshing and stuff, right? People swear by it. Not me, but, you know...people. I'm sure walking for hours is gonna be great. My feet aren't even gonna get sore. Nope. Definitely not. I'll probably take up walking as a fun hobby after this."

The guys exchange a look. "Are you done?" Evert asks.

"Yeah."

He turns and kneels down in front of me so that his back is facing me. "Hop on."

I don't hesitate. I jump on his back and curl my arms around his neck. He grabs hold of my thighs and hoists me up.

I sigh contentedly. "You just get me."

"I just don't want to hear you complaining about it all morning."

"I don't complain…" I retort. "That much."

"Sure you don't, *Scratch*. You done with that itch, yet?"

I frown down at my hand that's still scratching the non-existent itch on my arm. It just does it on its own now. Call it self-preservation.

"We know you hate walking," Sylred says, drawing my attention to him.

"I mean, I don't *hate* it. I just find it inconvenient. Gravity and limbs and muscles and balance is all hard to get used to when you keep popping in and out of your body," I defend.

"If you keep eating ridiculous amounts of food the way you've been and letting Evert carry you around like this, you're going to grow bigger than your lamassu before you know it," Ronak says behind us.

"I feel like it's worth it, though."

Ronak snorts. "You know I'll be training you again as soon as we get settled, right?"

I groan against Evert's back. "*Nooooo.*"

"Yep," he counters jovially, as if my dread for exercising amuses him. "If you're going to insist on being an 'awesome super spy,' as you put it, then you have to do things like… walk. My training will ensure you can take care of yourself."

"You're just using that as an excuse because you like torturing me. Also so I don't get fat."

I feel him swat me on the ass. "Enjoy your break, little demon."

"Ugh. You're mean."

"So, you have another black feather," Sylred notes, breaking up our griping.

I look over my shoulder. "Yeah. Are my eyes the same?"

Sylred studies them and nods. "Still multihued."

I shake my head in exasperation. "I don't get it."

"Something seems to change every time you return from the Veil," Sylred points out.

"Maybe Plik and Plak did something to me?"

Beside us, Ronak's face darkens. "If they did, I will make them regret the day they were ever born."

My eyes widen at his deadly tone. "Calm down, you crazy alpha. It was just a thought. I don't actually think they did some sneaky evil magic on me. But if they did, I'll be the first to cheer you on while you do your super scary genfin stuff."

He tosses me a look. "When you say things like 'super scary genfin stuff,' it doesn't actually sound scary."

Personally, when I look at his muscles now, I don't think of how he can use them to hurt me anymore. I think of how they might bunch up under my touch. How they strain sexily when he's lifting stuff. How they'll feel without the barrier of clothes between him and my hands...

"What the *fuck*?"

Evert jolts to a stop so violently that I nearly tumble to the ground, but Ronak's strong arms catch me before I can fall.

Ronak sets me down and shoots him a pissed off look. "What the hell was that? You could have hurt her."

Evert whirls around and points at me. "I couldn't help it! She fucking Lusted the hell out of me just now. I could feel that shit under my skin."

I notice that his face is flushed and his pupils are dilated with hungry arousal. I lift my nose in the air, sniffing. Yep. He's super turned on. I'd be able to smell that a mile away. But wait...

"I did not!" I argue.

He gestures to the front of his pants. "Yes, you clearly fucking did!"

I prop my hands on my hips. "I did not," I repeat. "Don't blame me for your dirty thoughts."

He opens his mouth to argue some more, but Sylred stops him, stepping between us. "Wait. Look."

All three genfins stare at me, and I huff out a breath, feeling self-conscious under their scrutiny. "What?" I demand.

"You're...leaking."

I blanch and blush at the same time. *Leaking?* I look down between my legs. I don't know why. It seems weird in hindsight that it would be the first place I'd check for leakage.

I look back up at him. "What are you talking about?"

Sylred snaps and points at my face. "There! Did you see it?"

The other guys nod, still staring.

I run my hands over my chin to see if I'm drooling. I'm not. I check my nose, eyes, and my ears next. No leakage anywhere. Now I'm getting irritated. "Leaking *what*? Stop looking at me like that!"

"Sorry," Sylred says quickly. "You're leaking Lust out."

I blink at him. "Umm...no I'm not."

"You just did it again."

I sigh in frustration, and that's when I see it. Pink tendrils sift out of my mouth. It dissipates quickly, but it was there. "Oh. I am leaking."

"Why would she be leaking Lust without knowing?" Ronak asks.

Sylred frowns, staring at my mouth. "Maybe it has something to do with the black feathers and her eyes changing. It seems like something happens to her every time she gets back from the Veil."

This is just way too freaking weird. I'm leaking Lust? That can't be good. My cupid powers have never, ever gone haywire before. They've always worked exactly as they were meant to. And Sylred's right. It does seem like the only correlation is when I return to my physical body. I pinch my bottom lip in thought.

"Can you...turn it off?" Sylred suggests.

"I'll try."

I close my eyes to see if I can feel my cupid powers at all. They've always just sort of been there. It was never something I needed to focus on. But now that I concentrate, I can feel the Lust-Breath inside me, waiting to be used. I pull it back deep into my chest, envisioning it being stoppered with a plug.

I open my eyes. "Did it work?" I ask, blowing breath out.

"Yeah, I think so."

"I'm malfunctioning," I grumble, looking down at my feet and kicking at the grass.

Sylred lifts my chin with his finger. "Hey. It's okay."

"I'm sprouting black like an emo teenager and leaking Lust out of my mouth. It's definitely *not* okay. I'm broken."

His brown eyes soften and he rubs my jaw lightly. "You're not broken. Just changing. We'll figure it out. But none of these things are causing any real harm."

I guess that's true. No harm except freaking me out and giving Evert unintentional hard-ons.

I raise my arms. "Who's gonna carry me now?"

Evert shakes his head. "Nope. I'm tapping out. If you hit me with another wave of that shit, it'll be an embarrassing walk back into town."

My lips twitch with a smile, which I know was his intention. He always knows just how to lighten the mood.

Ronak lifts me up and swings me over his back like I'm light as a black feather. I wrap my legs around his waist, but his body is so broad that I have a hard time getting a good grip without my hips pinching in protest. "You're too big," I grumble.

I can feel his chuckle against my chest. "You'll appreciate that later."

"You guys are so dirty."

"This coming from the girl who propositioned us almost as soon as she met us."

I shrug. "I was excited to have a real vagina," I deadpan.

Ronak nearly trips.

I win.

CHAPTER 41

*W*e walk—well, they walk and I ride on their backs—for a long time. The sun makes its debut and is shining brightly above us by the time the city of Rochbrook comes into view and the forest starts to thin.

I'm on Sylred's back at this point, and I'm not embarrassed to say that I dozed off against him. I wipe the drool from my chin on the sly as I force myself to wake up.

"Sleep well?" Evert drawls from beside me.

"Mm-hmm. Yep. Thanks for asking."

"Think you can walk to the city on your own? It's about five minutes from here, but we don't want to strain you," Ronak says.

I slide off Sylred's back. "I should be able to handle that," I answer seriously, taking in the distance. When I look back at the three smirking faces of the genfins, I scowl. "Oh. You were mocking me. Ha ha."

"You make it way too easy."

"Keep it up, Ronak, and I won't be *easy* at all," I challenge.

The amusement falls from his face, and he scrubs at his brown beard. "Believe me, once the mating ceremony gets started, you will be."

His words make heat erupt at my core. I shift so that my legs press closer together. He notices the movement and smirks. Asshole.

I turn around and stomp away from them. After a few minutes, I get a good view of the city, and it's awesome in a weird kind of way. Instead of normal stone houses, everything is made of wood.

Every wooden building erected out of the ground is a dome, the wood bending in beautiful tension. The wood is polished so well that the sun glistens off it. The domes aren't very tall at all, so it's obvious that the majority of the living spaces are underground dens. There are a few larger, aboveground domes at the center of the city, as well as one that looks like a giant wooden egg.

"Huh."

"What do you think?" Sylred asks, suddenly flanking me.

"I like how all of the domes look like they're part of the ground. They look like little wooden hills. Some look tiny, but there are really big ones, too," I note.

He smiles, his brown eyes crinkling at the sides of his face. "Genfins often expand their dens, inviting their extended families to live with them, which is why some are so large."

"So, where are we going?"

Sylred points. "See that tree with the white blossoms?"

I squint. "Next to the hill?"

"Yep. The dome built into that hillside is ours."

From my vantage point, the dome looks big but not huge. The spot is beautiful, nestled into the hillside the way it is, and I can see a wooden fence circling around it with a garden. The nearest neighbor is about five hundred yards to the east, and the garden and trees separating them offer plenty of privacy. Evert and Ronak join us, and all three of my genfins twitch their tails in pride.

"Did you guys build that?"

Ronak nods. "When we graduated from training. Genfins must build their dens by hand before we can apply to the council for a mate. Our dens are never lived in until we take a mate home. They are considered a sacred space."

"So you've never even lived there?" I ask, surprised. The grounds look so well kept.

Ronak shakes his head. "No. Genfin males live in communal housing until we gain mates. It's about an hour away from the city. This is the first time we'll be staying here."

Based on the look on their faces, it's something that they've been looking forward to for a long time. They look over at me, and I can see that they're nervous about my reaction.

Ronak rubs the back of his neck. "It's not as big as some, but the land was good and not too close to other dens and—"

"I love it."

They breathe a shared sigh of relief.

Sylred smiles at me again. "Good. We want you to feel at home here. Shall we?"

"You show her around while Evert and I go speak with the elders and get the things we'll need for the ceremony. Put your wings away," Ronak instructs, and I do.

We part ways, me following beside Sylred as we skirt around the town, while Evert and Ronak head straight to the center toward the egg building.

When we reach their property, I round the small hillside and grin. "It's even better up close." I rush to the gate and fling it open. "Look at this garden! You have so many things growing in here."

"Yeah, Ronak hired on a caretaker after we finished building it."

As if on cue, an older genfin male rounds the corner, garden spade in hand. When he sees us, he momentarily stops in his tracks. "My lord Sylred!" he says when recognition settles over him. "I did not expect you for another few days."

Sylred smiles warmly at him. "I apologize that we did not send word ahead of time."

The fae shakes his head, dropping the spade in a bucket next to the fence. "No need for apologies. I can't tell you how pleased everyone is that you have returned to us at last."

"Thank you, Fenian. I'd like to introduce you to Emelle. We've decided to take her as our mate."

I smile. "Hello."

The genfin gapes at me in open-mouthed horror.

My smile falters. Sheesh. What a way to make a girl feel welcome.

He stutters. "You...she...mate? But she is not a genfin."

"No, she's not," Sylred says simply. "But she is our chosen mate all the same and deserves the respect of one," he gently rebukes.

It takes Fenian another moment to recover. "Of course, my lord. Forgive me. I will get out of your hair. Everything in your den is exactly as instructed. The food stores are stocked, and the clothing you requested has been brought. Your garden is doing very well, too."

"I can see that," Sylred says appreciatively. "Thank you, Fenian. The place looks great."

"You're welcome, my lord. I'll be back to tend to the garden in a few days. If you need me, send word."

"I will."

"Good day," he says, nodding. He flicks me a gaze before hurrying away, tail tucked under him.

When he walks through the gate and flees from view, I blow out a breath. "Well, that was awkward."

"Genfins don't ever choose non-genfin mates. It'll take some getting used to, but they'll get over it."

I bite my lip. "And if they don't?"

He shrugs. "Then they don't."

"But these are your people, Sylred. I don't want them to shun you because of me. You're already giving up a lot. Your powers, your wings, political gain…"

Sylred cups my face in his hands to staunch my rising panic. "Emelle. Breathe. Relax." When I do, he continues. "We knew what we might face. We decided this with our eyes open. We chose this. All that matters is our covey. Don't let the opinions of others ruin us before we can even get started. Okay?"

I grudgingly nod. "Okay."

He leans in and places a soft kiss on my lips. It's over before I can deepen it, and his smile proves to me that he purposely left me wanting more. "Wait here a second."

He walks to the end of the house and rounds the corner, leaving me alone in the garden. I look around at all the pretty flowers and dangling fruit, and find a spot with a wooden birdbath sitting beneath the white-blossomed tree that I noticed when he first pointed out the place. There's a bench right below it, and I can just picture spending time here, feeling the sun and wind on my face, smelling the plants, and stuffing my face with all the fruit I'll pick.

When Sylred comes back, his sleeves are rolled up against his tanned forearms and his shirt has drops of water on it. "Lose a fight with a puddle?"

"A water well. And I won," he smiles.

Taking my hand, he pulls me through the garden and toward the front door. We have to take a set of steps down to get to it, and then there's another set of steps on the other side of the door.

When we get to the bottom of the stairs, I walk over the wooden floors and take it all in. The den is warm and inviting, with circular windows high on the walls and a skylight on the ceiling. The whole place smells clean, if only a little musty from disuse. A fireplace sits at the far end of the room, a kitchen to the left, and there's a nice sitting area equipped with plenty of bookshelves.

"The washroom is through that door," Sylred says, pointing. "We have a basement with extra rooms and food storage downstairs, the office is at the door next to the kitchen, and our bedroom is through this door here."

Our bedroom.

Our. Bedroom.

I don't know why that hits me so hard, but it does. I'm going to be mated to three hot genfin males and get to enjoy things like the garden and *our* bedroom. I've never had anything that belonged to me before, aside from my bow and arrows. Now, I have a bedroom to share with my mates and a den house that they built for me. I stand on my tiptoes to kiss him on the cheek.

"What was that for?"

I lift a shoulder, a smile spreading across my face. "Just because."

With a pleased look, he leads me forward and opens the door to our bedroom. Inside is a space almost as big as the sitting room. There's a massive bed at the center with different colored pillows against a feather white blanket. There's another fireplace inside this room, too, as well as beautifully carved shelving and drawers inlaid into the walls. A huge circular skylight overhead bathes the entire room in inviting light.

I fling myself onto the pillowy bed, stretching my arms and legs as far as they can go, and run my hands over the silky covers. "Oh my gods, this is comfortable."

Sylred puts his hands in his pockets and smiles down at me. "I'm glad you approve."

"Look at all these pillows. There's like a hundred."

"A dozen, but who's counting?"

I throw one at him. He catches it before it can hit his face.

"It's so big. I've never seen such a big bed."

"Genfins sleep near their mate. It's part of our protective instinct. We need a large bed to be able to do that."

And to do other things, is what he doesn't add.

I sit up and look around at the curved ceiling. "I can't believe you guys built all this. You were holding out on me on the banishment island."

"We weren't going to build a replica of our mate-den on our banishment island," he says with a frown. "We built only what was necessary to sustain us for five years."

"And a training yard," I add.

"Believe me, that was necessary. If we hadn't had a training yard to work out our frustrations, Evert and Ronak would have killed each other."

"Poor Sylred, always stuck between them."

He sits down and picks up my ankle. Taking off my slippers, he starts kneading my arches. And yeah, I moan a little. It feels that good.

"I don't mind sticking by my covey," he says quietly, just as my eyes flutter shut from the bliss he's wreaking on my foot.

"You should definitely keep being the peacekeeper. The gods know those two assholes need it," I say, moaning when he hits a particularly tight spot on my arch. "You should be a professional foot-rubber," I sigh.

"Can I ask you a question?"

"Mm-hmm," I tell him.

"You have your Love Arrows back, but you didn't use them on us…"

"I wouldn't do that. I just use Lust on you because it's funny."

I hear him smile. "I know. But why not use the arrows? It seems like a lot of other females would have used one on Ronak to get him to come around. All along, you could've used your powers to seduce us. But you didn't. Why?"

I shrug a shoulder as he continues rubbing. "I want everything that you guys feel to come just from you. I don't want to influence anything with my cupid powers. When someone does finally fall in love with me, I want to know, without a doubt, that I didn't force it in any way."

I can feel him smiling, but I'm too focused on the foot rub. "That's very honorable of you."

"Yep," I sigh. "I'm totally honorable. Keep rubbing."

Laughing, he pats my feet and then lets go. "Later. Come on."

I groan and open my eyes. "*No*. Touch the feet. Do the rubs."

"I figured you'd want to get clean. I'll show you the bathroom and bring you the clothes we ordered if you're ready."

I look down at my dirty, torn dress and grimace. It's the same dress that I wore the last day of the culling, including when I was beaten, so there's even some of my blood stained on it, which has not gone unnoticed by the guys.

"Yeah. Clean would be good."

I follow him out of our bedroom and into the washroom. "Whoa."

If I thought the place was great before, it's perfect now. There's a huge bathtub next to an exposed brick wall with a window overlooking the flowers on the other side. There's a toilet in one corner, a pedestal sink and a vanity in the other, and an ornate mirror that stretches above the sink. The marble tile at my feet is gray and impossibly shiny.

"This is super nice."

Sylred looks around like he's seeing it for the first time. "This took us a while to build," he admits. "We got all the materials from other islands. We wanted this room to feel more luxurious. A place our mate could relax."

The bath certainly looks relaxing. When I see the silver spigot poking out of the wall beside the tub, my mouth falls open. "You have indoor plumbing?"

He smiles. "No more outhouses or outdoor baths for us."

"Is the water cold?"

He shakes his head, and I practically beam with excitement. "There's a water basin outside set above a fire pit on the other side of this wall," he explains. "When I told you to wait in the garden, I was filling the basin and lighting the fire for you. It'll heat the water quickly, and then you can fill your bath."

"You genfins are geniuses."

"Always so impressed with baths."

"Well, yeah. Baths are awesome."

Sylred walks over to the vanity and opens some of the drawers. "You should find everything you need in here. Clean towels, soaps, and...lots of other girly crap that I have no idea about."

"I'll figure it out."

"I'll leave you some clean clothes outside the door. Holler if you need anything."

"Thanks."

When he leaves, I quickly strip out of my gross dress and pile it on the floor. Then I go through the vanity drawers, checking the inventory. Hairbrushes, combs, shaving razors, scissors, soap, shampoos, hair oil, lotion, perfumes, and more awaits me.

After choosing my stock, I turn the valve on the spigot and watch as steaming water starts spurting into the tub. Pouring in some soap and perfume, I don't hesitate to step into the bath and melt under the water.

By the time I finish, I'm washed, cleaned, perfumed, smoothed, scrubbed, and shiny. I even pushed my wings out so I could wash them, too, and was very excited to find that the tub was plenty big enough to accommodate them. It could also easily accommodate a genfin or three. Just saying.

After drying off, I lather myself in so much lotion that my skin practically drips with it. Then I carefully brush my hair, which takes way too long because of the amount of tangles in it, but I finally manage to braid it over my shoulder before my arms fall off.

When I grab the clothes Sylred left me, I pull on a nice, comfortable dress. It's not fancy like the stuff I wore at the culling, but it's simple and light linen that fits my curves perfectly and even has accommodations in the back for my wings. These damn genfins thought of everything.

Satisfied, I start to leave the bathroom…and walk right into the wall. "Ouch," I mutter, rubbing my hurt forehead.

Note to my stupid cupid self: I can't just float through the walls when I'm not in the Veil. Geez. Popping in and out of invisibility is confusing. And makes me prone to injuries.

I grab the doorknob, thankful my guys weren't around to see that.

I leave the bathroom to search for Sylred, only to stop short at the sight in the sitting room. I stare at the lounging figure sitting on the chair. My mouth opens and closes several times as the fae watches me with growing amusement.

Finally, my brain manages to make my mouth talk. "Umm…"

Wow, Emelle. After all that time, that's what I come up with?

With his feet propped up on a table and his hands behind his head, he continues to smirk at me.

"What are you doing here?" I finally ask the Horned Hook.

Belren grins. "Hello to you, too."

Should I keep standing here? Or should I sit? I scratch my arm absently as I work through what to do. I should definitely walk further into the room and take a seat across from him, right? Or am I supposed to kick him out? This is considered our love den, right? Gods, I can't handle these social situations.

"Won't you join me?"

I practically sprint forward, grateful for the direction. When I sit down, I start to fidget nervously under his smirking gaze. I can't get my arms to set comfortably on the armrests. Putting both arms up on either side makes me feel like I'm pretending to sit on a throne. But putting them in my lap feels weird, too. Maybe if I put one on the armrest and one in my lap, then—

"You look better than the last time I saw you."

I breathe slowly, attempting to act normal. "Yeah, I can't really pull off the beaten and tortured look," I quip.

He continues to lounge easily as he takes me in, causing me to blush. "Stop it," I snap.

His brows raise. "Stop what?"

"Looking at me like that. You're freaking me out."

Belren laughs. "How should I look at you?"

Irritated, I shoot him a look. "What are you doing here? Where's Sylred?"

"Which genfin is that?"

"The nice one."

"Ah, the blond feline. Don't know. Haven't seen him."

I frown. "Then who let you in?"

He lifts his capable hands. "I did."

"You broke in?"

"I turned a doorknob. That's hardly breaking. Technically, I didn't even touch it," he says, reminding me of his telekinesis magic.

"What are you doing here?" I repeat.

"I came to see how you are."

"Oh. Why?" I ask suspiciously.

He smiles, displaying his perfect white teeth against his gray lips. He looks around the room. "Nice genfin den. I take it you've come here to form your mate bond with them?"

"Umm, yeah."

"Hmm."

Hmm? What the hell does that 'hmm' mean?

I'm about to ask when the front door opens and all three of my genfins walk inside. They stop in their tracks when they notice Belren, and their expressions turn murderous. Great.

CHAPTER 42

"*W*hat the fuck?" Evert asks.

All three of them turn their pissed-off eyes on me. "Hey, don't look at me. I just got out of the bath and found him here," I say, holding my hands up.

Ronak returns his glare to the fae. "You intruded into our den while our mate was bathing?"

Belren picks his feet up from the table and stands. "Calm yourself, alpha feline. You act as if I were peeking through the keyhole while she washed. A tempting visual, but I have my honor. Besides, I prefer to spy through windows."

I have to jump between them to stop my genfins from pummeling him. "You idiot," I hiss over my shoulder at him. "Don't say stuff like that!"

Belren just laughs. "Sorry, I couldn't resist. Besides, you aren't their mate yet."

All three genfins growl.

I roll my eyes. "Oh, gods. Please stop antagonizing them."

"Fine," he says disappointedly, turning to walk around the room.

"Why are you really here?" I ask him, careful to keep the genfins at my back.

"The prince launched his search on the city. His soldiers arrested thirteen fae suspected of housing you."

My stomach drops. "What?"

Belren nods as he picks up a book from the shelf, flips through the pages, and puts it back. "Yes. One of them was the owner of the inn you stayed at, though he knows next to nothing. The innkeeper didn't have much to offer."

I share a look with the guys. "Was he tortured?"

Belren looks over at me. "Do you really want the answer to that question?"

I start to open my mouth to say that yes, I do, but Ronak steps in front of me. "Enough. Don't come in here and upset her."

"She has a right to know. The prince won't stop looking for her. He thinks one of his guards helped to sneak her out of that cell and that the same guard released her lamassu. Ten guards have already been executed."

The breath leaves my chest, and I clutch my throat. "Oh my gods…"

Ten fae. Dead. Because of me. Maybe thirteen more innocent fae will follow.

"Stop it," Sylred snaps at him.

Belren studies my face, his expression softening. "I apologize. I thought you should know. It's important not to get complacent. You cannot trust anyone. Not even other genfins. The prince is suspicious of why you stayed on the kingdom island and didn't immediately return home after the culling. You would be wise to keep her hidden," he tells the guys.

"Don't try to tell us how to protect our mate," Ronak growls. "We will guard her with our lives."

"Down, boy," Belren says. "I came to warn you to stay vigilant. Trust no one."

"Not even you?" I ask. His silver eyes flick back to me.

"I'm a liar and a thief. Especially not me."

A knock on the door interrupts us, and Sylred steps away to answer it. Ronak and Evert move to stand in front of me, blocking me from view. When Sylred comes back in the room, there's an elderly genfin male following behind him. He has a long gray beard and a white spotted tail with furry wings to match.

He holds out a chalice and a pouch to Ronak. "As you requested."

"Thank you, Elder."

"I still counsel against you taking a non-genfin mate. This is a mistake, Ronak."

I slink lower behind my genfins' backs.

Ronak's reply is hard. "I heard your concerns."

"Where is she?"

"Indisposed," he lies.

The elder sighs. "Taking a non-genfin for a mate will change things. Your covey was set to take over as elders one day. The council may vote against it now," he says, making me feel even guiltier. "Our rare females are revered. Genfin children are coveted. For you to go against mating one of your own kind is to go against your genfin nature."

"There aren't enough genfin females for every covey as it is," Ronak points out. "Our taking an outsider as a mate will help another covey to take a genfin female for their own. Maybe it should happen more often."

"We would die off," the elder argues vehemently. "Our numbers lower every year as it is."

"Our decision has been made."

The elder sighs again. "Very well. I cannot forbid you. But this is a mating ceremony you will complete on your own. There will be no open celebration like there would normally be."

"We don't care about festivities."

The elder mutters something else under his breath and

then turns to leave. Before he walks out the door, he says, "For what it's worth, I am glad to have you back. Your covey was greatly missed."

"Thank you, Elder."

The door shuts, and I stare down at my feet, biting my bottom lip. Ronak and Evert turn around to face me again, but I can't look at them.

"I think this might be a mistake," I hear myself say. "I can't let you do this. I wanted you to choose me, but I didn't really get it. I didn't understand what I was asking from you. I'll just stay until Okot comes for me and then...I'll leave."

"Fuck that," Evert snaps. "You're not going anywhere."

"This is not a good idea. This kind of sacrifice...it's going to make you hate me, and I can't deal with that."

Ronak's hand grips my chin, and he forces me to look at him. "Stop."

Irritation swarms into me as I pull out of his grip. "No, *you* should stop. You should've seen how your caretaker looked at me. That's going to happen every time you introduce me. And now, besides missing out on your powers and wings, you're also going to lose your spots as elders. Plus, I can't give you little genfin babies!" I add shrilly. "Oh gods, I'm going to single-handedly cause the genfins to die off. Everyone is going to hate me. I'll be remembered as the cupid who killed off an entire breed of fae!"

Ronak's gaze moves away from me. "Get the box before she starts hyperventilating."

"On it," Sylred chirps helpfully.

"What box? I don't need a box," I snap, waving my arms. "I need to not ruin your lives or be the downfall of all genfins everywhere."

"Scratch. You're overreacting a bit."

"Is she always this dramatic?" Belren asks. I glare at him. I'd forgotten he was still here.

"Pretty much, yeah," Evert answers.

I punch him in the arm and then wince at the pain in my hand. Why are his muscles so hard?

Sylred appears in the next instant with a box of chocolates.

I glare at him. "Chocolate isn't going to help this situation," I snap.

He plucks one out of the box and pops it into my mouth before I can stop him.

"Sylred, this isn't… *Mmm.* That's really good," I say as I chew.

"Give her more," Ronak instructs.

Sylred practically shoves another one into my mouth before I've even finished the first. This one has sprinkles on it. And is that a strawberry center? Yum. Sylred passes me another. Ooh. Double chocolate.

After I've had another three, Sylred puts the box down. "Better?"

I lick the remaining chocolate off my lips with great satisfaction. "Yeah," I admit.

"That was…interesting," Belren says, looking impressed. "Is it just chocolate that works?"

"Nah," Evert says. "Any kind of food, really."

"Huh," he replies thoughtfully, stroking his curled horn.

"Ready to start the mating ceremony?" Ronak asks.

My eyes widen. "*Now?* What about everything the elder just said? Everything I said? And don't forget about my malfunctioning."

"Malfunctioning?" Belren chirps. We ignore him.

"We've been over this. We still choose you," Sylred answers.

I cross my arms angrily, my bottom lip poking out. "Fine."

"Are you seriously pouting because we're *keeping* you?" Evert asks incredulously.

"Shut up. I need another chocolate."

Already waiting, as if he expected this, Sylred pops another one into my mouth. Caramel. Yummy.

"Do you still want us?" Ronak asks point-blank.

"Well, yeah, but—"

"But nothing. That's all we need to know. Are you ready or not?"

I throw my hands up. "Yes, I'm ready! But the second any of you assholes start hating me, I'm going to kick you in the balls and remind you of this moment."

Evert shoves a truffle in his mouth. "Noted. Now let's do this, Scratch. Don't be scared."

"I'm not scared." I totally am.

"You totally are."

I narrow my eyes at him. He just smiles, showing both adorable dimples as he eats another one of my chocolates. "Fine, maybe I'm a little scared," I relent. "But…"

"You don't have to be scared. We wouldn't let anything happen to you. We aren't backing out, and you aren't leaving," Sylred says, making me melt more than the chocolate in my mouth.

I take a deep breath. "Okay."

They all say it back to me. "Aww. It's like in the carriage," I say, grinning. "'Okay' is totally our thing now."

Evert shakes his head. "It's not a thing."

"It's totally a thing."

Ronak turns to Belren. "Since you're here, you might as well make yourself useful."

Belren rubs his hands together, looking perfectly entertained. "I always love a good mating ceremony. Should we move this into the bedroom?" He wags his eyebrows.

"You're not staying for the mating part," Ronak snaps. "Just hold the damn chalice," he says, shoving it into his hand.

Ronak opens the pouch and pulls out a small knife, a vial

319

of clear liquid, a dried herb, and a rolled up parchment. "Now, normally, the mating ceremony would take place over a few days. There would be a dance, a ceremonial opening of the mating den, a feast, and then the final part is the drinking of the chalice. The vows would be read by the elders and be a public event," he explains.

"We're skipping all the bullshit," Evert adds.

Ronak pours the entire vial of liquid into the chalice and then crushes the herbs into it. Taking up the knife, he presses it against his palm to cut himself. He holds his cut over the cup and lets a few drops of his blood drip into it before passing the knife along. The other two do the same.

Sylred takes my hand. "Forget about the opinions of others," he says quietly. "Forget about the powers and the politics and the population. Okay?"

"Okay."

With a nod, he takes the knife and makes a tiny cut on my fingertip. Holding it over the cup, he waits until a few drops of my blood fall into the cup before bringing my finger to his mouth and sucking.

The intimate gesture and the hungry look in his eyes as he flicks his tongue over my cut makes heat pool into my belly. When he releases it, I don't know what's throbbing more, my finger or my lady bits.

"Here, read this, Horny Hooker," Evert says, shoving the parchment toward Belren.

"It's the *Horned Hook*," he says testily.

Evert shrugs. "Whatever."

Belren rolls his eyes but uses his telekinetic magic to unroll the parchment and float it in front of his face.

Ronak takes the chalice from him. "Ready?" he asks again.

The way his dark eyes look at me now reminds me of the first time I saw him on his island. Only now, instead of seeing through me, he's looking at me.

I decide right here and now that I'm going to let all the

other crap go and just enjoy this. All my stupid cupid life, I've waited for the things that I'm getting now, and I'm not going to let anything ruin it. I choose them, and they choose me, and that's all that matters.

A smile spreads across my face. "Ready."

CHAPTER 43

*B*elren starts reading the genfin mating vows, and this moment feels like it's come very suddenly and yet has been a long time coming.

Ronak is the first to drink from the chalice.

"With the cut of your flesh, you now reside in each other," Belren reads.

Ronak passes the cup to Evert.

"Blood to blood, you align your life with your mate's. You willingly give your power, your strength, and your loyalty."

Evert drinks while watching me. The intensity of his gaze makes a blush rise to my cheeks. As soon as he swallows his sip, he passes it over to Sylred.

"By this ceremony, you swear to honor your mate. With this promise, you shall cherish and protect your covey with your life. With this drink and mating, let it be known that you vow to stand together until your final breaths."

Sylred drinks and then passes it over to me. I look down, seeing only a small amount of liquid left, tinged red with our blood.

"May your mate bond be strong. May the gods smile upon your union. With this drink, your bond forms."

Finished reading, Belren looks up just as I tip the cup back. I let every drop pour into my mouth before swallowing it down in one gulp.

Ronak takes the cup from my hand. "It's done," he says, his voice raspy.

As soon as the liquid travels down my throat, a rush goes through my body, and I start to feel...tingly. What the heck was in that drink?

"That's my cue to leave," Belren says cheerily, using his magic to toss the parchment to Sylred. "Emelle, care to walk me out?"

"S-sure," I say, my voice shaky and strange.

I lead the way to the door, stopping at the bottom of the steps. I tuck a stray piece of hair behind my ear.

"I'm glad the last of that dye washed away," he says, watching the movement. "It was too..."

"Pink?"

"Exactly. I much prefer your naturally pink hair."

I shuffle nervously. "Hey, thanks for coming here and telling me everything. Even though I hate what's happening, I should know. I'm responsible, after all."

Belren puts his hands in his pockets. "I didn't tell you to upset you. I told you because I'd want to know."

"Yeah, I know."

There's a growing commotion going on behind us, and we both turn around at the sounds coming from the sitting room. My guys are...yanking pillows from the sofas and piling them into one corner of the room.

Evert, arms full, comes striding out of the bedroom and dumps blankets onto the pile next, while Ronak and Sylred start taking down the drapes that cover the windows.

I frown, stuck in place as I watch them. "Umm... What are they doing?"

The corner of Belren's mouth quirks up. "I believe they're building your heat burrow."

I whirl my head around to look at him. "Say what now?"

"I've heard that the genfin mating drink kickstarts their natural impulses. Your new mates will be ruled by pure instincts for a while. Part of that instinct is driving them to make a safe, comfortable spot to hole up in."

"Oh."

His smirk grows. "Thanks to that drink, you're all about to go into heat together. They'll bring you into the heat burrow once their animal sides deem it worthy of you. Which, by the looks of it, they're taking very seriously."

I look back at the corner that is quickly filling up. It looks like they're stripping the entire house of every single article of fabric and cushion that they can find. I even see piles of their clothes being used. Evert starts scrunching up blankets so that it looks like a huge, fluffy multicolored ball of softness.

"I mean...it *does* look comfy."

Belren chuckles. "I'm glad you think so, because they're about to hold you hostage in it for about a week."

"*What*?" I squeak.

He winks at me and turns to walk away. "Have fun," he says over his shoulder as he walks out the door. Using his magic, it shuts and locks behind him.

I blanch. "Wait, *what*?"

The next thing I know, someone has come up behind me and thrown me over his shoulder. I squeal in surprise, my arms flailing to gain purchase. "What are you doing?"

I don't get an answer. I'm carried across the room, and before I can even look to see who's carrying me, I'm being tossed into the "heat burrow."

Instead of landing on hard wooden floors, I bounce back up from all the piles of pillows and blankets like it's a damn bouncy house. "Oof."

Evert, Ronak, and Sylred climb into the burrow right after me. They've even made walls in a kiddy fort-style by draping curtains over chairs to surround the cushiony center. It gives the burrow a nice enclosed feeling.

I suddenly find myself in a triple-layer genfin sandwich.

The tingling I felt after taking the drink has multiplied a hundred times. Instead of just a subtle tingle, my body feels like electricity now dances over every inch of my skin. It's both hot and cold, and my body feels totally charged up and...*ready*. My core pulses.

"Oh my gods, I think I'm in heat."

The genfins look at me expectantly, and man, are they close. Like, no-personal-space close. I keep seeing their eyes morph into their animalistic genfin golds that shine back at me like cat's eyes. Their tails twitch back and forth in the small space, and three sets of very intense purrs start emanating from their chests.

I clear my throat because, wow, it's intimidating to be stared at like this, like I'm at the mercy of three very strong predators. The purring is nice, though. It relaxes me, attempting to drown out my nervousness.

"Umm...so this heat burrow is super nice. Like, as far as burrows go, I'm sure this is really impressive." I pat my hands on the pile appreciatively. "It's very plush. Lots of squishy... plushness. Did you guys have to take a burrowing class or something? Because this is inspiring stuff. Really. You should be proud. Should I do something? I feel like I should be doing something. My skin is tingly, and I'm hot. Is it hot in here?"

I start fanning my heated face.

They keep looking at me, saying nothing, but now they're petting me, too. Stroking. Sifting through my hair. Then their tails start in. Flicking over my skin, wrapping around my limbs. So much touching. I can't focus and my breathing grows erratic.

My body temperature hikes up even more. I guess they

don't call it going into *heat* for nothing. And still, their intense animal eyes stay latched onto me.

Naturally, I keep babbling.

"You guys would be sprouting wings right about now if I were a genfin, huh? Wings. Growing wings must be crazy. Anything else I should know about you?" I ask, just as my eyes flutter closed from all the nice petting and purring they're doing. "You're not gonna grow feathers on your backs and start to mulch, right? Or lay eggs? Wait. That would be the females."

My eyes fly open.

"Oh, gods, *I'm* not gonna lay an egg, right? I mean, I'm not a genfin, but *you're* genfins," I remind them, because I feel it needs to be said. I try to get their attention, but they just keep petting me, and it's clear their animal sides aren't listening to me anymore.

Their pupils are blown, their breathing is fast, and I can see the hard outlines of their erections straining beneath their pants.

"I want to go on record and say that I'm *not* on board with laying an egg. Or is it more of a cat thing? Am I going to birth a litter?" I ask, panicked. "I'm not on board with laying eggs *or* birthing litters. I'm slender down there. Are you guys listening to me? I have a narrow channel, and I can't be...*oh*."

The petting has turned to soft kisses trailing all over my body. I can't think anymore, let alone speak, because three mouths are on me and six hands are working together to make sure I'm high on sensual stimuli.

Plus, there's the ceaseless purring. It's louder, more intense now. The vibrations travel from their bodies to mine, and it's slowly turning me to mush. My body hums with anticipation and need.

Sylred strokes my left arm and my back, causing goose bumps to sprout all over my electrified skin. Evert kisses the left side of my neck and trails his hand around to fondle my breasts.

Ronak moves behind me and grips my waist with one hand while threading his fingers through my pink hair with his other. He jerks my head back roughly to give Evert more access to my neck.

All that exists in our burrow of blankets is the sensations they're giving me. All thoughts of the outside world have vanished. Even my blabbering mouth has been silenced, which is a feat in itself.

It's the first time I've ever had more than one of them touching me like this, and yeah, it's awesome. I feel like a freaking goddess that they're worshipping with their touch.

Sylred is the first one to kiss me. His mouth is soft as he eases my lips to part open. My hand tangles in the fabric of his shirt. Kissing him while he's purring is...*amazing*. The vibration travels down my throat all the way to my core.

Evert, obviously wanting more than just my neck, grabs my face and turns it away from Sylred so that he can take my mouth instead. His kiss is wholly different. It's demanding and sloppy and hot as hell.

He groans into my mouth. "You're leaking."

Yeah, there's no way I can turn the Lust leak off right now.

I feel the cushions shift, and the next thing I know, clothes are being discarded. I don't even have time to feel nervous when Evert breaks the kiss and someone lifts the dress off my body, because their hands start petting me again instantly.

Feeling their naked skin against mine is incredibly erotic. Ronak leans me back into him, and then Evert's mouth is travelling down from my mouth, past the valley of my breasts, over my belly, and down to the apex of my thighs. Without pause, his tongue licks up my wet slit, and then his mouth latches onto my clit.

I nearly jump right out of the burrow.

Ronak and Sylred are on either side of me, holding me down, and this time it's Ronak's mouth that captures mine while his hand paws at my breast. Sylred takes the other in his mouth, flicking his tongue over my nipple and making me moan.

It's too much. My mouth, my breasts, and all of Evert's attention between my legs makes me explode embarrassingly quickly.

I come in a rush of pleasure, crying out wordlessly.

Ronak growls into my mouth and then pulls back, leaving me still shaking with the aftershocks of my orgasm.

The next thing I know, Evert has moved away, and Ronak is hovering over me, his cock prodding my entrance.

His eyes are completely gold, his pupils dilated, canines punched through his gums. When Evert starts giving attention to my breast while Sylred continues his assault on the other, Ronak pushes inside of me in one hard thrust.

Holy macaroni.

My back arches in both pain and pleasure. He's big, and he stretches me, but my body is also primed and ready for him. His demanding intrusion makes me feel so blissfully full. When he starts rocking into me, his muscles rippling, Sylred's mouth leaves my hardened nipple, and he licks up the side of my neck and nibbles at my ear.

When I feel Evert's and Sylred's cocks pressing against my thighs, my hands automatically reach out for them. Double groans escape from their lips when I curl my fingers around them and squeeze. Evert thrusts inside my hand and bites at the crook of my neck.

Their cocks are thick, velvety soft, and hard as steel. I swipe my thumbs over the beads of pre-cum collected at the tips.

Curious, I lift my hand from Evert's shaft and pop my

thumb into my mouth to taste him. His eyes flash, and a hungry growl reverberates from him.

"*Fuck.*"

He forces my hand back down to hold his cock, and I oblige by stroking him and Sylred both.

Watching me as I please the others, Ronak's thrusts get faster and faster, his gaze even more intense. He hits a spot inside of me that makes me moan and curve upward.

Gripping my thighs, he opens me up even wider as he pounds into me. His touch is so rough that I know I'll have bruises later, but I love it.

I feel myself clench, and with an animalistic roar, Ronak comes inside me.

He's barely had time to pull out before Evert is there to take his place. Wrapping his arm around me, Evert pulls me up.

"Give a girl some time to recuperate," I pant.

With a firm hold on my waist, he brings me down onto his lap and spears me instantly with his cock.

"No."

There's no waiting. No warning. Evert takes what he wants and does what he wants. I love that about him.

Once he's inside me though, he doesn't move, and I grab hold of his arms for leverage. His left bicep has a spiky armband tattoo wrapped around it. It just adds to his hotness.

When he still refuses to move inside of me, I rock my hips impatiently. "Dammit, Evert."

"Tell me," he snarls into my ear.

It doesn't sound like him at all. This is Evert's feral animal side. It doesn't scare me. Instead, I get wetter. His growl sends scorching hot excitement shooting through me.

"Fuck me," I demand, my nails digging into his arms.

Satisfied, his hips suddenly thrust up, making his cock go

even deeper inside of me, and my back arches into someone's chest behind me.

"Yes," I murmur.

Someone cups my ass, helping to pick me up and push me down as I ride Evert's cock. Someone else reaches around to play and pinch at my clit in delicious torture.

I'm lifted up and slammed back down again and again. It's rough, it's dirty, and I freaking love it. I love the way they work together to fuck me.

Their genfin animals growl and snarl and say wicked words into my ear. Lust leaks out of me like a popped balloon. Ronak is already hard again, grinding against my ass, and Sylred is still playing with my clit.

"I'm gonna..."

With a cry, my pussy clenches around him. Evert grips my waist roughly and slams up into me one more time with a lewd snarl.

I feel his hot cum spurting inside of me and starting to run down my thighs. Evert's golden eyes flash in approval, and his animal swipes his tail across it like he's claiming victory.

When I'm lifted off his lap, I turn to find Sylred. I grab his erection in my hand and start stroking him, squeezing slightly as I go. He groans, closing his eyes.

Ronak's tail curls around my arm. "Take him," he orders, rasping into my ear and making me shudder. "Take his cock into your pussy and let him fuck you. Then you'll be ours."

It shouldn't be possible, but Ronak's words send a new rush of heat straight to my core.

Like he can't wait another second to have me, Sylred lies down and pulls me on top of him. Still with my grip on his cock, I guide him inside of me.

I'm slick with a mix of my own arousal as well as the guys' releases, but Sylred doesn't seem to care. You'd think I'd be sore, but I'm too caught up in my own heat to know anything but arousal and pleasure.

Gripping my hips, Sylred watches me ride him. I grind against him, making him roll his eyes in the back of his head.

"Fuuuck."

Ronak reaches over to start playing with my clit again. It's almost too much, too sensitive from having so much attention already. I try to pull his hand away, but his animal growls at me and he bites hard at the spot beneath my ear.

"This pussy is ours," he snarls against my ear, making me shiver. "You don't get to keep it from me."

"It's too much," I pant.

"You'll take it," the alpha orders, and fuck if it doesn't turn me on even more.

Relentless, his finger circles my clit, finding the perfect spot with just the right amount of pressure. "Yes!" I cry.

This time, it's Evert in my ear as he cups my breast and rolls my nipple between his fingers. "You like fucking Sylred while Ronak touches you?"

Hands against Sylred's chest for leverage, I continue to buck on top of him.

"I fucking love watching you," Evert rasps, his teeth scraping over my shoulder while he continues to torment my nipples. "You're sexy as hell. I love all the little noises you make while your mates fuck you. Is this what you always wanted? Is this what you fantasized about? All of us owning your pussy and making you come over and over again?"

"Yes!" I cry out, feeling myself right on the peak again.

"Then be a good girl and come for us again," he growls into my ear. "Milk Sylred's cock until he explodes inside you. I want to see all our cum dripping out of you like the naughty mate you are."

That's it.

The culmination of Ronak's fingers touching my clit,

Sylred's cock ramming into me, and Evert's dirty words makes me erupt.

It's like the mother of all orgasms.

Back arched, mouth open in a scream, I come. My pussy clenches around Sylred's cock until he comes with me.

I collapse against him, sweaty and tired beyond belief. My body is heavy and jellied. I wouldn't be able to move even if I wanted to. My eyes shut in exhaustion, and I barely feel Sylred slip out of me.

Someone picks me up and gently settles me into the center of the burrow. I'm wiped clean with warm wash-cloths, my hair is stroked away from my sweaty face, and then I'm surrounded by genfins wrapping themselves around me.

Nestled in the middle of my three genfin mates, their limbs and tails tangled around me, I fall into the most relaxing sleep I've ever had.

Mating ceremonies are freaking awesome.

CHAPTER 44

*S*even days.

Seven days of sex.

Seven days of so many orgasms that I lost count. Seven days of petting, sleeping in a pile of bodies, and genfin purrs. I've really become a fan of the purring.

They didn't talk much in all that time, because they were mostly stuck on their genfin animal sides, but when they did, it was to growl dirty things into my ear or whisper adoring praises. I'm spoiled like that.

I can tell as soon as I wake up that I feel differently. My heat has passed. I no longer feel charged up or stuck in a haze of sexual hunger that took me over during the entire week. It seems the power of the drink has finally worn off, and our mating bond is complete. I officially have four superhot mates.

Yeah, I'm a little smug.

I'm the last one to wake up, and I find myself alone in the massive bed. It's the first time we've been out of the burrow all week except to relieve ourselves, bathe together, or grab food and drink before returning.

The bed is nice, but I kind of miss being in our heat

burrow. It was like our own little world in there where all that existed was sex. It was awesome. And the guys were awesome, too.

If I were a teacher, I'd grade them all with an "Exceeds Expectations." Just thinking back to their touches and all the things they did to me, all the sounds they made me make... it's enough to make me heat up.

I stretch my body, feeling all sorts of aches and pains from our frenzied sex-fest. I have bite marks and bruises marring my skin, and every time I find one, I blush at the memory of how they got there.

When I get up and grab clothes, I make my way into the washroom. I bathe, washing away the musky scent of the genfins' desire. After I'm clean and dressed, I feel like a new person. A different person. Just like I can feel Okot, I can also feel each of my genfins now. It's like there are four threads inside my chest, allowing me to feel the mating bonds pulse. It's both foreign and familiar. Feeling refreshed, I leave the washroom in search of the guys.

Now that I'm out of the mating haze, worry about Okot's continued absence is at the forefront of my mind. I need answers about where the heck he is.

"I need to find my first mate!" I call out as I round the corner and enter the sitting room.

"Don't call him your first mate," I hear Evert call back from outside the open window.

The front door opens, and he and Sylred make their way down the steps and into the room.

"Why not? He became my mate first. That makes him my first mate."

"First mate makes him sound like he's your favorite. Or a sailor. He's neither," Evert says, coming up to me.

"Maybe he *is* my favorite," I tease.

Evert looks ridiculously sexy today. His wavy black hair

is tousled perfectly, and he has dark stubble shading his jaw that I just want to run my palms over.

He looks at me sardonically. "Really? The fucking lamassu is your favorite?"

I tilt my chin up. "Maybe..."

Evert glances over at Sylred. "Remind me—my animal side is kind of hazy with memories—but what was it that she screamed out last night?"

Sylred tries to stifle his smile, but the corners of his eyes crinkle anyway. "I think it was something like, 'Holy mothballs, you guys are the best at orgasms. I dub you the Orgasm Kings. You're my very favorite fae in all the realms everywhere, forever and ever. And ever,'" he adds helpfully, rolling back on the balls of his feet.

Yeah, okay. I said it.

"Fine," I concede. "If you want honesty, then no one is my favorite, because all of you are my favorite. But stop distracting me. Okot's been gone too long. I'm worried."

"Ronak left first thing this morning to go make some careful inquiries," Sylred says.

I perk up at that. "He did? How?"

"Genfins aren't exactly big fans of the high fae prince, either. There are some of us that are involved in the resistance," Sylred says.

"Really?"

"Yeah, except when we were last here, the 'resistance' was nothing more than a few grumbles and disorganized meetings, where all they did was get together to drink and complain," Evert admits as he sits down on the sofa. "It's gotten a lot more structured since our banishment."

I blink at him. "I think that's the longest speech I've ever heard from you without you cussing."

He reaches over and yanks me down to sit on his lap. I settle my head against his shoulder. "I can talk fancy and shit when I want to," he says, making me laugh.

"Well, your animal side definitely can't. All he did this week was talk dirty and growl."

"Yeah, but be honest. You like that better."

I laugh again and smack him lightly on the arm. Sylred wanders in from the kitchen and starts setting out some food, making me instantly jump out of Evert's lap and start picking up what I want to eat.

"Wow," Evert drawls, sitting up from my sudden departure. "It's obvious in a competition between us and food that we don't stand a bloody chance."

I already have a couple slices of peaches stuffed into my mouth, so when I try to grimace out a look of apology, it doesn't really come through because of the chipmunk cheeks and all. "Sorry," I mumble out. "I'm starving."

"Ignore him," Sylred says. "Eat. You expended a lot of energy this week." He winks. I swallow the bite in my mouth and pick up some cheese and bread to make into a sandwich.

"Speaking of that, when Ronak comes back, can we do it again? I'd like another orgasm. Also, I think I'm ready to graduate to my next sexual experience."

Evert cocks his head, a smile spreading across his face. "Oh, yeah? And what's the next 'experience' you'd like?"

"Well," I begin seriously. "Double penetration, of course. And I mean my lady hollow and my pucker star."

Sylred starts choking on the food in his mouth, while Evert's blue eyes widen. I go on. "I've been doing this sex thing for a week now, so I'm pretty sure I'm ready for back door admittance. We'll just have to get some oil, right?" I ask, looking at them expectantly.

"Ummm..."

"And do we always have to do it together as a covey? Or are we allowed to do it one-on-one, too? I just want to make sure I understand the covey sex rules."

Sylred's still coughing, but Evert's eyes look like he's about to devour me. "You're something else."

I tilt my head. "Does 'something else' mean awesome?"

He shakes his head. "No. It means fucking perfect."

I beam.

"You just can't get enough of us, eh, Scratch?"

"Well, this is why I mated you, isn't it?" I shoot back.

He leans forward, plucking the sandwich from my hand and eating half of it in one bite. I scowl at him. "Maybe," he says around the bite. "Or maybe it's because you just really fucking like us."

My heart starts racing. You'd think after all that we did together during our heat that it wouldn't be possible to feel shy again, but I do. His words are teasing, but he's right. I like them way more than I thought I ever could.

It isn't just about sex or loneliness, either. Through all the craziness, I definitely caught a case of the feels. But I don't want to freak them out by admitting just how much.

Before I can think of what to say, the door bursts open, hitting the wall.

"Emelle!"

I startle at Ronak's bellow, knocking over a plate of food and making it crash to the floor.

"What the fuck?" Evert snaps, jumping to his feet.

When Ronak rounds the corner and comes into the room, we all just stare. And stare. And...

"What...what the actual fuck?" Evert says disbelievingly.

That's my sentiment exactly, because Ronak is suddenly sporting a pair of wings.

Wings.

And they aren't genfin wings, either. No, these wings are bright red and feathered.

He's sprouted *cupid* wings.

I grimace. "Whoops."

CHAPTER 45

"*A*nd they just popped out?" I ask.

Ronak gives me a look. "No, they didn't just *pop* out. The damn things felt like they broke my spine and tore through my shoulder blades. I actually passed out," he says, pissed off. "Passed out! In the middle of the street like some damn weakling."

He's pacing around the room as the three of us stare at the wings protruding from his back. When he passes by one of the tables, his newly emerged wing catches on a vase of flowers, sending it crashing to the floor. He glares down at it.

I push my own wings out and walk over to him. I know he's in shock, so I need to handle this carefully. I take his hand, forcing him to stop pacing. He looks down at me, his frown fierce.

I lift my other hand and slowly begin to trace the edge of his wing. Trailing my finger over the arch, feeling the soft, downy feathers, I stroke slowly, making him shiver.

I continue my touch on his other wing, watching as the tension slowly leaves his body. I know Ronak well enough to realize that he's not really pissed at the wings themselves.

He's pissed about the unexpected. He doesn't like to be taken by surprise. He's an alpha. He likes control.

This caught him off guard, and since the pain of them emerging made him pass out, his reaction is understandable. It's my job as his mate to make him see that this isn't a bad thing.

"They look good on you," I say. And they do. It shouldn't be possible, but he's even sexier with them. "They're a lot bigger than mine," I note, taking in his wingspan.

"They're heavier than I expected," he admits in a grudging voice.

"Yeah, tell me about it," I say. "Do you...hate them because they look like mine? Do you wish you had weird furry genfin wings instead?"

"No. That's not why...I don't even hate them. It's just—"

"Unexpected."

"Yeah."

I smile. "Admit it though, it's pretty awesome."

The corner of his lip twitches.

Now that Ronak isn't so pissed off, the other guys come closer to get a better look. "Did anyone see you?" Sylred asks.

Ronak shakes his head. "I don't think so. I think I only passed out for a few seconds. No one was on the road. When I saw the wings, I rushed off the road and took the back way through the forest to get here."

"So," Evert says, picking up the sandwich again and taking another bite. "She marked the fucking lamassu with her cupid number, and now you have her wings." He looks over at Sylred. "Any weird shit happen to you?"

Sylred shakes his head. "No."

"Huh."

"It's almost like she's imprinting on us," Sylred says. "Gifting parts of herself to mark us with. To show that we're her mates."

Hearing that makes me puff up a little in pride, and my feathers ruffle.

Evert shoots me a smirk. "Possessive little thing, aren't you?"

"Well, you *are* my mates."

His blue eyes smolder as if hearing that makes him want to carry me to the bedroom. "You bet your tight ass we are."

Said ass perks right up because it *is* tight, and it likes being noticed.

"So," I venture, looking back to Ronak. "You have wings. You were the one who wanted them the most," I point out.

He crosses his arms in front of his chest while raising and lowering his wings, testing out their weight. "Maybe."

"And *I* gave them to you."

He snorts. "It's not like you did it on purpose."

"I'm just saying, clearly I'm awesome at this mate stuff if I give you what you want, even if it is unintentional. And I also find it…fitting," I add with a smirk.

He narrows his dark eyes on me. "How so?"

I do my best Ronak impression. Which means I just lower my voice and scrunch my face up into an exaggerated scowl. I also lift my shoulders up to my ears and pretend my biceps are huge and muscled for added dramatic effect. "Oh, I'm Ronak. You landed on my island, and you have red wings. You must be a demon! I better shoot you with an arrow and tie you up and be an asshole," I say mockingly. I beam up at him and return to my natural voice. "Now who's the demon?" I waggle my brows.

He gives me another dirty look, makes an "I'm gonna choke you" gesture, and then turns to walk away.

"Where are you going?"

"I need to learn how to fly these damn things," he says over his shoulder.

My lips curve up. "Remember how hard you were on me

when I was trying to learn? You're about to realize how difficult it is. This is the perfect payback."

He glares at me over his shoulder. His wing runs into a painting on the wall and makes it crash to the ground. He curses colorfully at it.

"Your red feathers are super pretty! They really bring out your scowl," I call to his retreating back.

"Damn red feathers," he grumbles under his breath before the door shuts behind him.

Evert chuckles. "You're probably gonna pay for that later."

I consider what Ronak would count as a punishment. "Are we talking, like, spanking? Because we did that already, and I'm good with it."

He blinks at me and then looks at Sylred. "I never know what's going to come out of her mouth."

"It's part of her charm."

"Tying up is okay, too. Except not with rope. You guys already tied me to a tree with rope, so that kind of ruined it for me."

Evert's lip twitches with amusement. "Understandable."

"Can we get a pet?"

Confusion washes over his face at my sudden change in topic. "What?"

"A pet. Can we get one? Like a little puppy? I've always wanted a pet."

He arches a brow. "*Always*? You've always wanted a pet, or you just now thought of it and decided you want one?"

He knows me too well. "That part's not important. Can I get one?"

He pinches the bridge of his nose and sighs. "No."

"Why not?" I pout.

"Oh, I don't know, maybe because you're wanted for treason and you have three genfins and a fucking lamassu bull for mates. We're all the animals you need, trust me."

"But puppies are cute." I look over to Sylred. Why did I

ask Evert anyway? Note to my stupid cupid self: Always deal with the mate who most likely will say yes to me. "You want me to have a puppy, don't you?" I ask, doing my best to give him a half-sexy, half-pleading look.

Sylred's eyes soften. "Well…"

Evert's hand comes down, covering my entire face and blocking me from view. "Nope. Don't even try taking advantage of the nice one. The answer is no."

I sigh into his palm. "Fine. Party pooper."

We hear Ronak cursing and the sound of a flower pot crashing to the ground outside. I grin.

Sylred smiles back at me. "You're enjoying this, aren't you?"

"Of course I am." I scoop up some berries and head for the door.

"Where are you going?"

"You think I'd miss this? No way. I'm gonna sit and watch him struggle learning to fly. While I'm at it, maybe I'll build him an obstacle course and start yelling at him, too."

Sylred's brows go up and he looks over at Evert. "She's a vengeful little thing, too."

Evert picks up some crackers and follows behind me. "Yep. Now grab some drinks, and let's go watch the alpha squirm."

CHAPTER 46

I thoroughly enjoy myself watching Ronak crash and burn as he learns to fly. I can't even suppress my beaming smile or my gloating when he struggles. It's like karma is smiling down on me.

I enjoy the spectacle…until he masters it in about twenty minutes and gives me a shit-eating grin. And *then* he makes me practice with him. And he actually gives *me* pointers.

Yeah, my victory was short-lived. And now my back is sore.

I plop into the cushy chair in the sitting room, my legs dangling over the arm. "How did you even learn to fly that good so quickly?" I demand.

Ronak just struts around the space like he's the top dog. Or top cat-bird-thing. "I've trained my whole life. Plus, genfins bodies' are meant to have wings. We prepare for their emergence by doing particular exercises during training. Although, these are a bit heavier than genfin wings normally are."

His wings are folded against his back neatly, whereas mine are splayed and crushed behind me. Several of my feathers are bent out of shape from falling outside. I sit up and try to fluff them up to look as tidy as his. Evert catches the movement and smirks.

"Hey, did you find anything out about Okot?"

"Not yet, but I've made inquiries."

I nod. "Hey, do you think—"

Ronak is suddenly in front of me, holding his hand over my mouth. All three of the guys are tense, their bodies facing toward the front door.

Ronak gives me a look before removing his hand from my face. With a silent gesture to the others, he moves to a spot at the bookshelf and pops a secret compartment open. Silently, he passes the hidden weapons to Sylred and Evert, and then surprises me by handing me a bow with a quiver full of arrows.

My heart slamming against my chest, I take it, suck in my wings, and strap it over my back as quietly as I can. Ronak makes some more hand gestures that I'm clueless about, but the guys nod and silently move, heading in different directions. Sylred goes to the hallway and pops open another secret panel where a stepladder comes down from the ceiling. He disappears up the hole in the ceiling and shuts the panel behind him with a soft click.

Evert disappears in the back of the house. Ronak leans in and puts his face right next to my ear. "We're surrounded," he breathes. Tilting his head, he pauses. "At least a dozen are outside. You need to turn invisible now."

I shake my head, the blood drained from my face. "No, I can help," I say, already pulling out an arrow to nock it.

To my surprise, he nods. "Yes, you can," he whispers. "But you need the element of surprise for a long-range weapon. Turn invisible, get behind them, and when they attack, take as many down as you can. You can't hesitate. There will be fae out there who will use magic against you. If you can't take the shot, don't turn visible. Do you understand?"

I swallow. "Yes."

He studies me for a second and then nods. "Good. Do it now, little demon. You can do this."

Terrified out of my mind, I focus on shoving my body back into the Veil. Sweat breaks out over my forehead, and I hear Ronak moving again, keeping his sword gripped in his hand as he prowls toward the window.

Our eyes meet for a second, and then a thunderous crash sounds, sending splintering wood and glass smashing to the floor. I pop into the Veil.

I watch in horror as vines shoot through the broken window and reach for Ronak. He hacks at them before they can touch him, and his animal side comes roaring out.

Fae come bursting in through the door, weapons raised. Eight, ten, twelve of them come running in, all in full armor. But it's the insignia on their armor that makes me freeze. It's the purple color of their cloaks and the violet brand on their breastplates that makes horror wash over me.

"No..."

It can't be Princess Soora's men. It can't be. If she sent them here to arrest us, then that means she was my enemy from the start. How can that be? She helped me. She...I don't understand what the fuck is going on.

The earth sprite controlling the vines launches another attack while a high fae uses magic to whip wind through the room. I can't feel it, but I see it pushing against Ronak, threatening to tear the sword from his grip, sending books and furniture crashing to the floor. Pages from books rip out and blow around wildly.

The vines finally manage to wrap around his leg, and while he tries to hack it away, another creeps up behind him and wraps around his sword arm. The second it does, a soldier comes forward and slices his blade against Ronak's arm to force him to drop his weapon. But it's like Ronak doesn't even feel it.

He roars again, sounding like a ferocious beast, and rips

the vines away with his strength power. They fall to the ground in shreds at the same moment he slices his sword across the throat of the soldier in front of him. The male falls down in red gurgles and wet coughs.

I'm still floating here like a useless idiot when I hear more fighting outside.

Sylred and Evert.

Ronak goes on the offensive and starts slashing at the other soldiers, and even though he's outnumbered, he uses his immense strength to his advantage. With a single punch, he makes one fly across the room and crash through the wall. The male crumples to the ground and doesn't get up again.

The high fae with the wind power is screaming orders, but the other soldiers look nervous now. Even the earth sprite has started to back up. The high fae shoves his way forward with murder in his eyes. He launches an attack against Ronak, using his wind to undermine every movement that Ronak makes.

With him attacking Ronak so ferociously, his men rebound. With one burst of air that pushes Ronak to his knees, the high fae uses the butt of his sword to strike Ronak's skull, leaving him dazed. Four other soldiers close in, grappling him to the ground. I see iron shackles come into the high fae's hands and reach for Ronak. I can't let the bastard put iron on him.

I fly to the kitchen behind them all and take aim. I can't feel the bow and arrow, not yet, but that's okay. All I need to do is line it up. I pay extra attention to the way the wind is blowing, too.

When I have my shot aimed right at the high fae's exposed neck, I pull on my anchor's connections and burst back into my body. The second I can feel the taut bowstring, I let the arrow fly.

I hit my target perfectly. The wind stops abruptly, making papers flutter to the ground just as the high fae falls face-first in a puddle of blood and lost breath. The remaining soldiers whirl around to face me. "Shit."

I grapple for another arrow, but my hands are shaking so badly that it takes me too long to nock it. One of the soldiers runs at me full out and hits me in the chest with his shoulder, sending me sprawling backwards. I land in a flash of pain, the air knocked from my chest.

He straddles me, and the weight of him adds even more panic as he presses a dagger against my throat. I freeze.

"Drop the arrow," he orders.

I hadn't even realized I had it in my hand and was trying to stab him with it. I immediately drop it, letting it clatter to the floor.

"Irons," he barks over his shoulder.

Another soldier comes up and shackles my hands and ankles immediately. Iron won't work to stifle my powers, but they are heavy and cumbersome.

The soldier climbs off me and pulls me to my feet. When Ronak sees me, his golden eyes shimmer, and he lets out a furious snarl, his canines biting into his lip. Even though he's being held down by five soldiers and has vines wrapped around his neck, chest, arms, and legs, seeing the soldiers manhandle me gives him another burst of adrenaline, and he starts throwing them off, trying to get to me.

I internally struggle with what I should do. Do I turn invisible right now? It'll give away my most important secret and means of defense, but if I don't go into the Veil, then I can't help the guys. The soldiers will use me as leverage against them. They'll take us all prisoner and then what? Even if I can get myself out of a cell, I can't free my guys in the same way.

Making up my mind, I look around the room. Noting every weapon and soldier, I take a deep breath. Before I can exhale all the way, I push myself back into the Veil. The iron shackles come with me. Dammit.

I fly through the room until I'm right beside Ronak and turn visible again. It's much easier to switch back and forth now. Before the shouts can register about where I went from my spot in the kitchen, I've already grabbed hold of a soldier's sword, surprising him.

I swing it against the vines holding down Ronak's right arm. The second it slices through, I pass Ronak the sword in his now free hand and go invisible again. And not a second too soon, because the soldier's hand tries to reach for me. Instead, his fingers grasp air.

I fly to the other side of the room, turn visible, and punch another soldier in the face. I startle him more than anything, but he drops his sword to grab his nose. I quickly pick it up, my hand closing around it just as another fae surprises me from behind and slams me into a wall.

Panic swells inside me and then a burning anger overtakes it. That anger burns so sudden and so hot that it's like I can feel it spreading through my veins and trying to erupt out of my hands.

I have to use up this burning energy. I *have* to. Driven on pure instinct, I reach around with an ear-splitting scream and grab hold of the fae's head.

The second my burning hands clutch his skull, there's a pulling sensation, and then I'm yanking something out of him.

It comes out like gray fog. His eyes are open wide, his mouth open in a silent scream. The next second, I've pulled the last of the fog from his body and he's dead. Just like that.

He falls to the ground at my feet. All I can do is stare. My hands no longer burn. The gray fog is gone.

What the hell did I just do?

CHAPTER 47

*W*hen I look up, I see that Ronak has taken the rest of the soldiers out. Breathing hard, I take in his wounds and blood, watching the terrifying feral look on his face. But the reason that my whole body is shaking—that's not because I'm scared of him. It's because I'm scared of *me*.

I hear music before I register it. Turning toward the window, I realize Sylred is using his power to control the soldiers outside into submission. Evert comes charging through the door, sword raised.

When he takes in all the unmoving bodies and sees the two of us, he lowers his weapon. Looking to me, he says, "Okay, Scratch?"

I nod slowly.

Evert watches me warily before looking over at Ronak again. "Ronak, put your animal away and come out. We need help."

It takes him several seconds, but Ronak finally shudders, and the gold leaves his eyes. His muscles roll as he comes back in control of himself. When he focuses on Evert, he flexes his hands and rustles his wings. "How many?"

"Twenty. Took down five around the back. Sylred took out some, too, before we met up. Took him a while to get control, but he has the rest trapped in his sounds now. What do you want to do with them?"

Ronak starts walking, and Evert and I follow behind him. When we get outside, my steps falter. Bodies are strewn around, plants are smashed, grass is kicked up, and blood is smeared all over the place. Our peaceful, pretty garden is ruined.

Ronak immediately takes charge and instructs Sylred what to do. As for me, I'm in a daze as I walk around the trampled flowers. When I see a bed of tulips, I stop. They used to be white. Now they're painted red with blood.

I stare at the bloody petals, unable to look away.

I killed two fae.

I shot one through the neck and made him bleed all over the floor. The sound that he made when he fell is playing in my head over and over again. Gurgling. Gasping. Choking to death on his own blood.

But what really freaks me out is what I did to the other fae. When I touched my burning hands against his head, I drained the life out of him. I...pulled his life force out of him like it was nothing.

I don't know how long I stand there, but I feel a hand touch my shoulder. I startle and swing around, but when I see that it's only Sylred, I stop.

"You can let go now," he says gently.

I look down and notice I'm still holding a sword. I immediately drop it and let it clatter to the ground.

As soon as it's out of my hand, Sylred pulls a key out and unlocks the iron shackles from my wrists and ankles. I hadn't even realized they were still on me. When I start to turn my head so that I can look at the bloodied flowers again, he stops me with a palm to my cheek.

"Eyes on mine."

I meet his brown eyes and words start spilling out of my mouth. "I killed two fae. I pulled one guy's fog spirit out through his face. I stole his soul. I'm a soul thief. A spirit stealer. An essence robber. I—"

"You protected your covey," Sylred says firmly, cutting me off.

"I'm a cupid. I'm supposed to use my arrows to bring love to the world, but instead, I shot one through a guy's throat and killed him. My aim was perfect. Obviously. Cupid," I say, gesturing to myself. I sigh. "There was a lot of blood," I admit.

He just nods, letting me get out all the crazy.

"His blood was really red. Like, super red. I don't think that's normal. You should probably check that out," I tell him, my eyes open *really* wide. I try to tone it down. I blink heavily instead.

"The other guy didn't bleed, though. His spirit just went psshhhh," I say, mimicking some weird noise through my teeth and motioning my hand up like it's fluttering away. "I wonder where his fog-soul went? Do you think it floated to the ceiling? Or out the window?"

I gasp. "Or maybe it got trapped in the chimney? Oh, gods, I clogged our brand new love den chimney with fog soul! I'm a malfunctioning, leaking cupid with black feathers and weird eyes, and now I'm snatching life forces out of people's bodies!"

Sylred puts both hands on my cheeks and lowers himself so that we're eye-to-eye. "Emelle, take a deep breath. You're in shock. You just need to breathe. Listen to my voice. Breathe in and hold it."

I fill my cheeks with air. "Good girl," he goes on. "Breathe out slowly on my count. One, two, three, four…"

I slowly exhale. Some Lust leaks out. He doesn't mention it. He's a gentleman like that.

"Good girl," he says again.

"Good girl," I repeat numbly.

"Now repeat after me: I did what I had to do."

"I did what I had to do."

He nods. "You did good, Emelle. You protected our covey. You protected yourself. Those soldiers would have taken you. You did what was necessary to make sure that didn't happen."

"I don't want to go inside the den," I confess, my eyes blurring.

"You don't have to."

He straightens up, drops his hold from my head, and reaches for my hands, but I jerk away.

"Are you crazy?" I snap, hiding my hands behind my back. "I could suck your soul right out of you!"

Without breaking eye contact, he deliberately reaches behind my back and grabs both of my hands. Once his fingers are threaded through mine, he squeezes hard. "You're not going to hurt me. Trust yourself. I do."

Gods, this guy. I sigh in relief. "Thank you."

"I'm going to carry you now, okay?"

"Where?"

"Away from here," he says simply.

Swallowing hard, I lift my arms and nod. "Away from here sounds good."

CHAPTER 48

$\mathcal{I}$ have no idea when I fell asleep or where I am now, but I can feel my guys nearby, so that keeps me from panicking. It looks like I'm in some kind of shed. Sitting up from the pile of furs I was sleeping on, I realize I can hear voices outside.

I open the door and slip out, immediately finding my guys sitting around a small fire. We're deep in the woods, and night has fallen.

When they notice me, the guys stand up. I make my way over to stand in the middle of them. "Where are we?"

"On Ronak's land. We're still on the island. We don't have a safe way to portal off of it yet," Sylred answers. "How are you feeling?"

"Better."

I sit down in front of the fire, and Ronak passes me a skin of water. "I'm proud of you for what you did," he says, his gaze steady. "Knowing that my mate did not hesitate brings comfort to my animal. You were fierce, little demon. I could not be more pleased."

I know he's partly telling me this because he doesn't want me to feel ashamed for what I did. I squirm a little. "Thanks."

"You were badass," Evert says, sitting beside me. "Don't beat yourself up about it."

"I take it Sylred told you that I'm a soul sucker?"

Evert's lip twitches. Of course he'd think it's funny. "You're just full of surprises. You also have a few new feathers," he adds, tilting his head.

I snap a look over my shoulder and then groan. "*White*? Now I have white feathers sprouting up, too? What the hell?" I shriek. "My wings look like the freaking flag of Yemen! Like a bleeding skunk! Like a—"

"Chocolate."

I screw my face up. "No, not like chocolate. Like—"

Before I can finish, Sylred is there, popping a truffle into my mouth.

It melts on my tongue. "Mmm. What's in that one?"

"Coconut."

"That's yummy," I admit. "What, are you guys just carrying boxes of chocolates in your pockets now?"

"Just me." Sylred winks.

It's not lost on me that he just thwarted another one of my meltdowns. With chocolate. I'm not even embarrassed about it. Chocolate is amazing.

Licking my lips, I manage to speak with a level head now. "So. Elephant in the forest. Those soldiers were wearing the uniform of Princess Soora's personal guards. Like the kind Okot wears. And Okot is still gone." I point out all these facts as if they'll bring more clarity being said aloud.

"Yeah, bloody convenient if you ask me," Evert says.

I frown. "I wasn't insinuating that Okot had anything to do with it."

"Well, I was."

"Hey," I say, getting angry. "He wouldn't do that."

"You've known him for less than a month. You have no idea what he's like," Evert counters.

But I shake my head. He's wrong. I felt Okot's sincerity

354

every time he was with me. I smelled it through his mate scent. He wasn't faking this. There's no way.

"You're wrong. And you shouldn't be so quick to blame him," I rebuke. "Anyway, what I wanted to say is that we don't know what the hell is going on. So I think I should go invisible and spy on the princess."

Evert is already shaking his head before I can even finish that last sentence. "Absolutely fucking not."

"That would be very dangerous, Emelle," Sylred says with a frown. "What if something else changes with you or you can't keep yourself in the Veil? Too much could go wrong, and you'd be too far away from us for us to help. We'd have no idea what was happening."

"I get all that," I say, standing up. "I do. They're all valid worries. But I still have to do this. We have to know what the hell is going on. If Princess Soora betrayed us, I want to know why. Obviously, something much bigger is going on here than we realized. Let me do this. Let me help."

I'm also going to find Okot, but I don't say this part.

Evert scoffs and shakes his head, while Sylred defers to Ronak. I meet the alpha's eyes. He stares at me, calculating, considering everything. I stand before his assessing gaze without backing down.

Finally, he nods. "If you want to do this, I'll support you."

"You can't be fucking serious," Evert growls, leaping to his feet. "You're okay with our mate going right into the lion's den? You're our fucking *alpha*. That's the last thing you should be okay with!"

Ronak levels him with a stern expression. "She's right. She's our best chance at getting information. We have to know where our threats lie. She's the perfect spy. No one will see her."

"Well, I'm *not* okay with this," he fires back. "Not at fucking all."

I grab his bicep and force him to look at me. "I'll be okay.

I can fly really fast in my invisible form. I'll get to the palace, spy on the princess and the prince, figure out what's going on, and come back. No one will see me. I'll probably come back with rainbow feathers, but besides that, I'll be fine." I smile, trying to boost his mood with my terrible joke. It doesn't work.

Evert pulls out of my grip. "This is bullshit, and it's on you," he snaps, pointing a finger at Ronak's face.

He turns on his heel and stalks away, disappearing into the shadowed forest. I watch him go, unable to think of what to say or how to fix this without backing down. I know that I have to do this, despite Evert's feelings. I'm our best shot at getting information, which we desperately need.

I turn back to Ronak and Sylred with a sigh. "Sorry," I mumble.

Sylred comes up to me and pulls me into a hug. "He'll be okay. Just come back as soon as you can."

"I will," I say against his chest. "I'm an awesome super spy, remember?"

He smiles and kisses the top of my head. When Sylred pulls away, Ronak grips my chin and stares down at me with his dark eyes. "Be smart," he says seriously. "Don't trust anyone. Watch, listen, and then come back. Don't reveal yourself, don't confront anyone, and don't lose your advantage. You have three days. Three days and then you come back to this exact spot, whether you have answers or not."

"Okay," I agree.

"If you're not back in three days, we'll assume the worst and we'll come for you and confront the princess ourselves."

"No, you can't—"

His grip on my chin tightens. "Yes, we can. And we will. So come back before your three days are up."

I sigh, knowing that arguing is pointless. "Okay."

He kisses me full on the mouth, biting my lip gently before releasing me.

I consider going to find Evert to say goodbye, but I decide against it. He obviously needs space, although I wish it wasn't space from *me*.

"See you soon," I say with a small smile. Just before turning invisible, I pause. "Wait...which direction is the kingdom island?"

The edge of Ronak's lip curves up, and he raises a hand to point. "Head directly up. When you come to an island that looks like a desert wasteland, go north. It's a straight shot from there."

"Right."

"Good luck, awesome super spy."

With a smile, I turn invisible and then launch myself into the air.

I'm barely past the tree line when I feel it.

An old familiar feeling of being *yanked*.

It's what I imagine those super high roller coasters feel like when you're in the downward plunge.

Before I can blink, the fae realm is gone, and I'm being pulled through space and time.

In the next instant, I'm being spat out in the very last place I want to be.

Cupidville.

And there's only one reason I'd be yanked back here.

Yep. I'm in *big* fucking trouble.

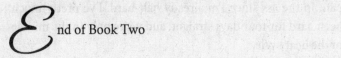

*E*nd of Book Two

BONUS SCENE

RONAK

*B*efore my eyes blink open, the scent of my mate's heat invades me, making my nostrils flare. Cracking open both eyes, I see her curled up in front of me, her ass against my crotch. Her pink hair is fanned out across Evert's chest where she lays her head, and Sylred has a hand curled around her ankle.

I get up, careful not to jostle her, and make my way out of the burrow. My mate will need to eat again soon, but first, I need to take a piss. My animal isn't in full control right now, so I have to take care of business before he takes the reins again. Deep into our heat, all he cares about is fucking her.

Walking into the washroom, I quickly piss, which is a pain in the ass since I'm already half-hard. I've pretty much been hard for four days straight, and we're only in the middle of the heat cycle.

After I'm done in the washroom, I go to the kitchen and gather up some snacks. We made sure to be stocked up with plenty of simple things that we could feed our mate with our fingers during our rut. It also helps that she'll eat anything.

A smile curves over my face just thinking about the way she looks when she tastes something for the first time. Her thick, juicy lips biting around a piece of food, her pink tongue darting out to catch some juice spilling over...and I'm rock fucking hard again.

My intense arousal instantly sends my animal bursting out to the forefront of my mind. My genfin alpha side takes over, and my animalistic instincts take charge. I stalk to the burrow and dump the food beside it. Raising my chin, I breathe in deeply. The scent of our mixed arousal that's saturated into our burrow drives me crazy and sends more blood rushing to my cock.

I groan, my hand coming around to grip my dick when I see my mate's naked body right where I left her.

I settle behind her again, and my cock fits between her ass cheeks. My hand slowly traces up the curve of her waist. My claws are elongated, but my animal is careful not to hurt her. When my fingers pluck at her nipple, she moans in her sleep. My cock jumps between her thighs.

Automatically, she thrusts her ass back to grind into my dick, making me groan. I start pinching her other nipple, needing to feel them both hard and pointing up at attention for me. She has gorgeous tits. Enough to fill my hand, with pretty little pink nipples that I just want to slurp into my mouth and suck on until she writhes underneath me.

When she moans and grinds against me again, I smell the slickness coming from her. She's awake and already wanting my dick again. My animal makes a pleased growling noise against her ear.

When she tries to turn around to touch me, I stop her with a hand against her shoulder blade. "Stay," I ground out.

She whimpers, and the sound nearly makes me blow my load right then.

Biting her ear, I snake one arm around her body. Then I slam my dick into her sweet cunt in one harsh thrust.

Sounds of pleasure escape both of our mouths, and my eyes roll into the back of my head. She's so fucking tight and wet. Her heat makes her body primed and ready for us to take her again and again. She's just as much an animal as the rest of us.

When she tries to wriggle her hips against mine, I smack her ass. "No. Your alpha will tell you if he wants you to move."

"You asshole," she hisses, but I can feel a new wave of wetness flood from her cunt, so I know she likes it. Our little mate likes to be dominated.

I start fucking her hard and slow, making her body jerk against my arm that's holding her. A flush spreads over her cheeks, turning her all pink and sweaty, and I lean down to lick the crook of her shoulder.

"Ronak, please..."

The alpha in me loves it when she begs. Pleased, my tail wraps around her legs and starts flicking against her clit. She moans.

I'm not surprised that her sounds and the smell of her arousal wakes up the other guys. Their cocks are already hard and in-hand as they slowly jerk themselves at the sight of her getting fucked by their alpha.

I can tell that her attention is now on them and their cocks. Her tongue darts out to lick her lips in anticipation.

I pull out of her, and she cries out in protest. "No!"

"Quiet," I growl, giving her ass another smack. "On your knees."

She quickly scrambles up to do as she's told. When she's on her knees, I fist her hair and force her to arch her back as I plunge back inside of her. She screams in pleasure.

"Put that pretty mouth to good use," I order.

She doesn't hesitate. I help her lift her head and she takes Evert's dick into her mouth like a pro. The sound of her sucking on him makes my balls tighten.

Her hand sneaks out for Sylred's dick next, and even though he's thick around, she twists and pumps him enough that it doesn't matter that her hand can't circle all the way around him.

My tail continues to flick against her clit, and I know she's close. I can feel it. I can smell it.

But I'm not done with her yet.

I'll never be fucking done with her.

In a move I haven't seen yet, she pulls back, her lips making a "pop" noise as she releases Evert. His animal growls at the interruption, but she just smirks up at him and then blows Lust directly onto his cock.

Holy fucking shit.

He explodes. Spurts of cum shoot out of his dick and onto her chest. I slam into her from behind again and again, but the little cupid blows on Sylred's dick next, relishing in making him lose control, too.

After Sylred groans and bathes her back with his cum, I curl a hand around her and pull her up against my chest. Moving my tail away, I take its place with my fingers and start grinding against her clit.

"Naughty little cupid," I growl into her ear. "Time for me to make you come now."

Her pussy flutters around my cock and she starts moaning my name over and over, which pleases my animal immensely.

With another rough thrust into her, she comes, screaming. My animal roars as her tight pussy brings me over the peak with her. Her cunt milks me for all I'm worth. When her orgasm ends, she turns into jelly in my arms. Wordlessly, Sylred comes forward and takes her as I slip out. He easily settles her into our burrow again, making sure she has plenty of cushions. Evert helps by grabbing a washcloth and starts to clean her.

When we're all settled again, my animal surprises me when he takes the initiative to feed her. Grunting, he passes her some food to nibble on.

She smiles up at me, and I swear, that damn smile gets to me and makes something in my chest tighten. My animal purrs louder than I've ever heard.

Her multi-colored eyes light up, and she looks at us like she is the luckiest girl in the world. But really, we're the lucky ones.

My tail wraps around her leg possessively. I see Evert and Sylred's brows go up in surprise. The move surprises even me. It's a clear declaration from my animal: She's mine. My alpha animal claimed her for our covey, and he's not ever giving her back.

None of us are.